Other Literary Works by Justin Eggen:

2017 - Outside The Wire: a U.S. Marine's Collection of Combat Poems & Short Stories Vol.1

2018 - Outside The Wire: a U.S. Marine's Collection of Combat Poems & Short Stories Vol.2

2019 - The Art of Warrior Poetry *(2019 Robert A. Gannon Award for Poetry)*

2020 - The Sun Rises in Helmand *(2020 Robert A. Gannon Award for Poetry)*

2020 - From Now, Until Death… I Shall

2020 - War & Select Poems

2021 – The Adahy Series (Part 1-3) *{discontinued}*

2021 - Ten Years Ago, Ten Years Later

2022 - Teufelhunden:1918

2022 – Liberty Subverted

2024 - OTW1 (2nd Edition) - PPPH

2024 – OTW2 (2nd Edition) – PPPH

2025 – Adahy & The King's Bane - PPPH

I0677984

All are being phased into 2nd Edition publications under Pressure Plate Publishing House LLC.

First Edition © 2025 Pressure Plate Publishing House LLC.

Author: Justin T. Eggen/ Justin Eggen/ Justin Thomas Eggen
Editor: Juan Flores Jr. / @jr1711
Publisher: Pressure Plate Publishing House LLC. / @pressureplatepublishinghouse
Cover Design: Justin Eggen / @justinthomaseggen
Cover Art (Skull/Owl/Sea-Service Pistol): Zoro Nano / @mysteriousfour_
Boston Map: Nomad Rule / @nomadrule

@pressureplatepublishinghouse
www.ppph.us
www.justineggen.com

© 2025 All Rights Reserved.

Paperback Edition March 2025
ISBN: 979-8-9897551-1-0
Pressure Plate Publishing House, LLC.

Thank you for reading, and enjoy your journey with Adahy.

—*Pressure Plate Publishing House, LLC.*

Printed in the United States of America

PRESSURE PLATE PUBLISHING
"Uncovering Explosive Storytellers"
West Palm Beach, FL 33405

For Grandpa
Robert Louis Hatcher
09.23.1939 – 01.23.2025

ADAHY & THE KING'S BANE

Justin Eggen

Table of Contents:

In the beginning...
There was nothing but a boundless silence untouched by time
or form.
All was still, and all was nothing. An eruption at the center of
the vast void created two entities from this emptiness. Eternal
opposites yet forever intertwined.
Becoming the foundation for life and creation, they were
neither gods nor mere forces; they were existence itself, the
primordial truths of being.
The first humans attempted to record their names...
Allacritus Lux – the Beacon of Light
&
Nox Tinibrus – the Veil of Shadows.

Together, they form 'Et Omnia' or 'everything and all.'

And so began the Age of Life.

Adahy & The King's Bane

Drowning Virtues

April 1771
Mug Tavern
Brookline, Massachusetts

Picking food from his coffee-stained teeth with the horsehair and iron-wired Wisk and Pick sewn into his navy-blue coat lapel, he pushes the moleskin coin bag across the table with two fingers,

"Are we in agreement, then?"

"Aye, I'll give you the name you're looking for..." the rattled redcoat officer replies as his eyes dart around the busy tavern and leans in,

"*Thomas Young*," he mutters under his breath.

Shifting in his chair, the middle-aged man across from the redcoat is shocked at how easily the name emerged,

"Do you mean city leader Thomas Young?!" He asked in an imitated, cautious tone.

Contrastingly, uneasiness filled the intimate atmosphere amongst the group at the table. The tavern was warm, dimly lit, and full of character. Upbeat stringed music played in the corner, with roars and cheers from every table as conversations melded with the boisterous noise. Its large wooden beams are interconnected into high ceilings, allowing for such elation to echo and double.

"That is what I said. I won't repeat myself… it may have catastrophic consequences," the main British officer says with haste and grabs the coin bag, "Let's go, boys; the ship is departing soon."

The British officers stand up, and their frames tower over the man who has traded coins for a name. As they begin walking out, the salt-and-pepper-haired man drops out his arm, stopping the leading redcoat.

"Let me ask you this…" he says and stands up, eye to eye with the redcoats, "How did you come across this information that you so willingly revealed to me this evening?"

The main redcoat looks to the men to his left and right uneasily… and reluctantly answers,

"Our detail was set to guard the King's shipments. One night, I noticed Boston city leader Thomas Young bribe one of the Massachusetts militiamen for entry to a docked ship… the next morning, a Royal Tax Officer was found murdered, and the shipment was missing. The guards and militiamen claimed only British officers came aboard… but it was not. It was him. I saw him, *WE* saw him…" the main redcoat says anxiously, as the other redcoats shakily nod their heads in agreement.

"Why are you trembling?" He asks softly in a patronizing tone.

"We must be gone with haste; I have said too much," the lead soldier said abruptly and moved quickly out the door with the remaining two soldiers in tow.

As they exit the tavern, a large African American man stands up from a table adjacent to the entrance. His frame towers over all else easily, with his bald head nearly touching the shorter side of the ceiling. His countenance was serious, holding a slight gray stubble. Darting his large brown eyes to the salt and peppered-haired man standing by the table where the redcoats just sat. He stops picking his teeth and nods subtly to the large man. With his large, calloused hand, the massive man exits the tavern.

The gray-haired man then looked around the hall, and he saw her. Through the smoke that was stemming from her white clay pipe, she looked at him. Her white stringy hair was prominent, draped to her shoulders, with her mousy face in between. Even in the large tavern with so many people, she was distinct. Looking at the man with her smokey-gray eyes, she nodded and began stamping out her pipe. She proudly carries a sizeable burn scar on her neck, revealed as she stands. She's petite yet older, but her body is hardened. Leaning over, she tapped her pipe on the hearth and placed it away. She passes the salt and peppered-haired man and exits the tavern.

"Alright, Wilfred! It's been a good night; I will see you next time!" He said to the barkeep as he made his way toward the exit.

"Stay safe, you Devil, too many rancid and vile creatures lurking about," replies Wilfred, with an implied slick smile.

"Do not defecate on my mates like a common whore!" The man replies with a large smile.

"You better leave quickly before I present you with your tab!"

He winces and grabs his chest, imitating a heart attack. The man fake stumbles out of the door with a large smile,

"No! My heart!"

Outside, the rain was loud and making for a melancholic melody. The atmosphere melded perfectly with the half-moon sky. The large African American man and white-haired woman stood under the overhang, waiting for the man to exit the tavern.

"Snap out of it, Shakespeare!" The larger man says to the smiling man as he exits the tavern, steadily growing tired of his antics.

"Oh, Robbie, he's enjoying the banter; you remember what it was like to be carefree, don't you?" The white-haired woman asks fondly in a smooth tone.

"I have never had the luxury of being carefree. I am a negro. My circumstances only allow for a certain way of life," he says in a growling, deep tone.

"Aye, Nyx is right, but you make a fair point, my friend. But lucky for you now, you are no longer enslaved, but a free man, and make a good living torturing the crown... I'd say you're doing well," Shakespeare says blithely.

"Eh, just be quiet."

"Let's follow them. They are headed toward the bay. We take them out quickly and quietly on the road," Nyx adds, hushing their grumbles.

Stepping into the rain, Robbie mounts his large horse and leads it to the road.

"Aye, and I'll see my coinbag returned to me," Shakespeare replies spritely, getting on his horse and leading his steed toward the road. Nyx does the same.

Their stalking of the three redcoats had begun. The rain is thick, and it is hard to see further than a few yards out in front, but the newly placed horse tracks are easy to differentiate on the road, even with the rain. After several minutes, the three were within a hundred yards of the three redcoat officers.

Creeping in silence, the three purposefully muted their gear. It was pinned down for silence, but all sounds drowned in the noise of falling rain. They used extra straps to ensure their packs and bags didn't flap, and their tools were linen-wrapped to ensure they didn't click and clack while they crept on unsuspecting prey.

Robbie, Nyx, and Shakespeare all dismounted their horses and tied them to the nearest tree branch off the path in a clearing. Robbie focused on following the redcoats, not to lose them in the forest,

"Let's move! Be quick, smooth, and quiet," the large, brooding man whispers to Shakespeare and Nyx through the weather.

Robbie makes a one with his index finger, indicating he is taking the first redcoat. With an expert understanding of the coded language they've developed over the years, Nyx raises her two fingers, indicating her selection. The final was left for Shakespeare. Within the falling rain, each of the three silently blended into the surrounding brush, using nature to their advantage. They move skillfully as they stalk the three British officers.

While moving through the wet forest, Nyx removes and preps her bow, readying a sharpened arrow. Under cover of rain, Shakespeare takes out his tomahawk from his waistline and tightens his grip, ready to attack. Robbie is last to ready his weapons and removes a small handheld knife.

Rain muted the approaching noises as the three hunters seized the moment and sprang onto their prey.

Thwipt

Nyx's arrow slices through the falling rain, steady on its fateful path.

"Arrggrrl," the man on the right horse chokes as the deadly arrow enters and exits his neck. Gurgling and choking, he tries to scream through severed vocal cords. Blood mixed with hot breath spray from the hole. Frantically, the man desperately tries to cover it, quickly losing consciousness. His body folds over his horse and lands on the muddy road, with his right foot still attached to the stirrup.

Shakespeare lifts his right arm with the tomahawk in hand; he inhales slowly and exhales. With a fiercely strong throw, the tomahawk folds over itself, making its way through the rain,

"Ahhgg," the British officer winces but is silenced as the sharpened blade enters his spinal column, quieting his life in moments.

Confusion ensues, and the last British officer scrambles to clear his way out of the kill zone where he's found himself. His horse takes off into the wet, rainy night. Robbie begins chasing the third horse into the darkness, close on his heels. The man is sprinting at an incredible pace, but it is not enough to keep up with the horse.

After a few strong gallops, the third and final officer disappears into inclement darkness, avoiding injury and escaping the burly, violent man in pursuit.

"Damn! One has escaped!" Robbie called out to the other two down the road behind him.

"They spoke of the ship departing soon; let's catch him at the docks," Shakespeare shouts back to Robbie, catching his breath, "I'll grab the horses!"

Nyx emerges from the wet shrubbery, putting her bow into her quiver, "Wow, Robbie, you really spoiled that one!" She says playfully, digging at the man who missed his kill.

"Nyx... do not get me started. How many kills have you squandered, misread, or let slip by you for several reasons?" Robbie replies in his deep voice, not fond of the teasing.

"Don't turn this against me; we're not talking about previous times... now is now," she smiles in response.

Knowing he never wins in an argument with her, he stays quiet and keeps his thoughts to himself, "I second Shakespeare's approach; let's catch 'em at the docks," the large man says calmly.

"It is agreed to the docks we go," Shakespeare says, quickly arriving with their horses.

The two others mount their horses in seemingly one motion, and all three hunters make for the docks. Within seconds, they passed the body of the man who was on the receiving end of Nyx's precise arrow. Rain puddles around his body. Next, they pass the fallen officer with a large gash in his spine; his body is face first in the mud. Each set of the horses' hooves impacts the muddy ground with force and carries the three hunters through the wet forest.

The hunters come to a fork in the road through the thick rain. The sign reads: *Left for Docks.*

"There! He's on the docks now," Robbie points out as the other two focus in and see the redcoat officer scrambling to tie his horse's reins and get onto the British transport frigate.

To their surprise, the British frigate was nearly disembarked, as they were a few moments too late.

"Fuck!" Shakespeare spits out aggressively.

"This is not good, Robbie; what are we to do?" Nyx asks eagerly, "We can try to row to it if we hurry!"

"No," Shakespeare says coldly.

"No? This man cannot leave with this name! We cannot allow his departure on that transport!" She shouts with ever-growing impatience.

"Nyx, how many times have we suffered? How much more can we endure? Our path isn't meant for empathy, love, or sympathy. I dare say we have muted these aspects within, have we not?" Shakespeare passionately orates.

"Now, you've done it, Nyx..." Robbie says, rolling his eyes.

"The cache of cannon. There are four atop the old perch; Nemo and I placed them there six months ago. Top plans on selling them to a privateer crew," Shakespeare nods to the perch that sat along the northern route, "who says we cannot use them to maybe... I don't know... sink a frigate?"

"Shakesp—" she tries to speak, but the man continues.

"Are we not but creatures, vultures, and lions, bound to this eternal plane? We've been given devices, words, and actions and enlightened enough to make decisions. I entreat you, my dear lady, are we not then keepers of the sanctity and secrecy of our coterie?"

Robbie exhales and rolls his eyes again.

"And because of that secrecy and sanctity, I am willing to do anything to keep that true, as it has been that way since Top brought me in. But there are women and children, families on that transport frigate… there must be another way," Nyx replies.

"Aye… think about the consequences of letting that information out, Nyx. Think about the cause," Robbie says gravely. His dark brown eyes and her smokey-gray eyes connected with mutual understanding, knowing there was no other way but to sink the ship.

"If we fire on the frigate too soon, we will be sought after by militiamen and civilians; you know this will have heavy repercussions," her words slice through the night air.

"I disagree. Ships merely '*go missing*…' It is a frequent occurrence," Shakespeare argues.

"They do… when sailing around the globe on exploration expeditions, not as common among transports from the colonies to England," she retorts.

The salt and peppered-haired man smacks his teeth, "If Top is revealed, the cause is squandered, and all the work we have been doing, all the information collected, all the lives sacrificed for the opportunity we have before us is voided…" Shakespeare argues, "We will be swift in our actions; only Tory scum will gripe about a missing transport ship."

"Enough! We sink the ship. That's final. It is the low-risk option before us…" Robbie says definitively to the other two, growing tired of debating.

By now, the rain had stopped and left a low-hanging dew that covered the ground while toads croaked and crickets chirped into the clear night sky. The three hunters moved quickly along the ridge north of the main road, steadily keeping watch on the slowly moving frigate departing the bay.

"Just ahead," Shakespeare shouts to the others, nodding his head toward the hilltop.

As they made their way to the perch overlooking the bay, the British transport frigate was in the process of unfurling its sails. Pulling out his telescope, Robbie zooms in on the frigate.

"We only have about 15 minutes or so until they are at full mast and out of range," the large man says calmly.

Shakespeare dismounts and hitches his horse to the nearest low-hanging tree branch and walks over to the hidden cannon under the canvas tarp and broken tree branches. With a strong flick, the tarp removed uncovers four 16-pound cannons, four ramrods, and four triangular piles of 16-pound cannon balls.

"Are ye in the mood to sink a ship?" Shakespeare says to the other two with a devilish smile.

"We need to move," Nyx says, trying to hurry up the process, "and we only need to use one; they are too heavy for us to move all four in time."

"Aye; good point, Nyx," Robbie says as he dismounts his horse. He walks to the closest cannon to the edge and attempts to move it into a good firing location.

Shakespeare gets next to Robbie, and both men exert all of their power to push the cannon toward the ledge. After a few minutes, the men tiredly get the cannon into position, and Nyx rams a charge into the cannon, followed by a 16-pounder ball. She snags up a ramrod and pushes the ball tightly into the cannon.

Robbie angles the cannon barrel in a favorable position, hoping he gauges it properly to hit the frigate.

"Nyx, we need to light some wick; get that lit," Robbie says to the woman as he calculates the perfect angle.

Within seconds, Nyx has her flint and steel out and is sparking into a tinder under the canvas that was once covering the cannon, and after a few slashes, she gets her tinder to burn and sparks her wick.

Shakespeare grabs two more cannonballs and places them next to the weapon. Robbie was ready, and Nyx looked to be it, too.

"Nyx, when you are ready, spark it!" Robbie says to her, and without hesitation, she does.

BOOOOOM! The ground shakes as the noise overpowers the lingering still air. Silence is removed and replaced by a loud ringing in all their ears. As the smoke clears and the three look to the bay…

"It's over!! Reload!" Robbie shouts to the others, and Nyx repeats her process of loading the cannon. Robbie calculates the angle again, this time bringing it down just a hair.

"When you're ready!" He shouts to Nyx, and she drops the sparking wick into the cannon,

BOOOOOM! A second shot erupts from the cannon barrel; the ball rolls through the air with precision, impacting the frigate's top deck. It was a magnificent display of destruction. Shakespeare sees the civilians on the deck scurrying.

"Hit! Again, reload!" Robbie shouts, and the crew repeats the process, "When you're ready!"

BOOOOOM! The third shot hits the lower portion of the hull and pierces the ship, compromising its integrity and safety. Screams of all ages and both genders echo from the bay, eerily sticking to the landscape.

"Look, a fire!" Nyx points out as an orange ball glows through the clearing smoke.

Within seconds, the fire spread, and the frigate was ablaze, the wood catching quickly and the newly unfurled sails. The three on the hilltop watched as the ship attempted to sail but faltered just off the coast. The blaze was intense, and the entire frigate was aflame within several minutes. There were no more screams, just the occasional crack or explosion on the ship when the flames engulfed gunpowder reserves.

In an ominous tone, Shakespeare utters as he watches the orange fire glow, "Hell is empty, and all the devils are here."

"Aye, I'll be tonight's devil," Robbie says combatively as the words carry a darker, more sinister tone, "It needs to sink. Then we will leave."

"Aye; no trace of us, no trace of the redcoat, and no trace of Thomas..." Shakespeare remarks ominously.

"Just another frigate swallowed by the sea..." Nyx adds solemnly, knowing it needs to be done.

The trio stands there, having kept their word; each internalizes their personal views as the glowing blaze eats away at the wooden ship. It took a couple of hours, but the frigate eventually found its way beneath the surface. Each of the three hunters managed to maneuver the cannon back into its discreet, hidden cache to remove any trace of their presence.

Arriving back to the clearing where they left their horses, the trio mounts them. Their thoughts were their own as they made their way down the hilltop and back to Brookline Road. After a few silent minutes along the route, they arrive at the neck, the long stretch of road leading into Boston.

The King's Highway

July 1771

Near Santee River

South Carolina

Pain in Death, he thinks, as Raven's hooves clop along the dirt route known as 'The King's Highway.' The dreary wind rustles the leaves of each passing tree, easing the young man's mind and sending him to a deep meditative state.

Memories ensue. Four full moons have passed since his mother met eternal rest from yellow fever. *She was gone.* Bedridden for weeks, she suffered. Combating the harsh sickness that caused her violent convulsions and black vomit. The useless honey and ginger remedies administered by the tribe Shaman seemed to make it worse. When they returned from their annual winter trading trip, her body began to fail. In her last moments, she weakly grabbed her son's hand, forced a smile,

"It's going to be all right, Adahy. I will be painless," the words released softly, simultaneously letting out a tear from one of her pale eyes.

Adahy could feel her acceptance of death but was not ready to accept it himself. She was tired and understood her role. He could only think of her as a healthy, happy, and warm soul who, on even his hardest days, was there with an uplifting attitude and the right words,

"Get up and dust yourself off. You're strong and capable, Adahy. You need to trust and believe in yourself."

Her words were perfect, always. Adahy refused to leave her side; acceptance had yet to enter his heart or mind. *Death is a path we all are bound to face,* he thought. Yet, he was unwilling to face this reality. Hours pass, and the high sun has settled beyond the horizon, making way for the night.

Upon the highest branch, a snow-colored owl screeches and hoots into the night. The tent flaps abruptly open, and Adahy's uncle comes in.

"Let's go, boy. Time to get up, get out of here, and move on. There is nothing you can do. The time for grieving is over, and your mother needs to be given back to the earth," his uncle says to him, grabs him, stands him up, and forces him out of the tent.

"Wohali, I will not be forced out or pushed to move on so quickly from her death! She is my mother!"

"And she was my sister, Adahy! Now it's time to accept her death and look forward to your path," he says strongly to his nephew.

Adahy stood six feet one inch from the ground and was vigorously built, but he slouched with sadness now. His deerskin-sewn shoes shielded his feet with each step, laced up just above his ankle. Moonlight canvases his face as his eyes swelled with water, but his callous upbringing wouldn't let a tear escape his eyes.

"I'm not sure what to do, uncle," he says, lowering his head.

"You must find your *other* uncle, Adahy," Wohali says calmly, looking at his nephew and tapping the gold talisman hanging around the young man's neck.

Adahy lifts his head, and his green eyes peer up from under the faded black tricorn hat that was once his father's.

"I know," reluctantly, the words flow from his mouth.

Light brown trousers covered his legs as an inner layer from his ankles to his waist. Black outer leggings shielded his inner layer, they are thigh-high and tied off above the knee by handmade black and brown finger-woven garters.

Adahy's square jaw and strong chin rested underneath the high cheekbones and carried a slight stubble, while his countenance was that of perpetual rancor. His eyes held pain, a deep pain, ever darkening the light of his soul.

She wanted me to go, he reminds himself, clutching the talisman.

"I have trained you well. Trust your abilities, and you will succeed in your mission," Wohali says with a breath of reassurance and rests his hands on Adahy's shoulders,

"I have no doubts about that. Death is a part of us all. It is our destiny. We see it, feel it, smell it, and ultimately accept it as our final pathway as we give ourselves back to the earth. Your mother, Aryana, understood this. Your path takes you away from this life, for now, and I believe you will find your other uncle. He is a prominent figure in the Boston city. At least, from all accounts on the King's Highway, Thomas Young is a successful businessman and a respected city leader."

Raven's hooves have stopped, and they are no longer moving. *Now's a good time to stretch my legs,* he thinks to himself as he swings his right leg over the saddle, landing firm on the ground. He takes the reigns and moves Raven off the main route to a shaded grassy patch just off the path.

Blades of grass flow in between his fingers as he squats next to Raven's face. She takes several bites of the high grass. Along her face, his rough hand runs along her strong jaw,

"I love you, girl."

With his blonde hair stringing along the side, softly, he leans his head down and touches hers.

He adjusts his tricorn and stands up. Scanning the route and surrounding area, he spots a plume of chimney smoke stemming from the tops of the trees pretty far down the road.

"That's where we'll aim for tonight. You finish up and let me know when you're ready to go again," he says, sitting on the grassy patch leaning against the old wooden fence.

'It's going to be all right, my son. I will be painless, the words reverberated in Adahy's mind. Adahy tried to carry his pain well in his mind, but it was visible through his lamented green eyes. She was the only person he knew who unconditionally loved him in his life. Her memory captures his thoughts, and her last words weigh on his mind, continuing to plague his daily thoughts.

After several minutes, Raven whines, awakening Adahy from a brief sleep. He stands, puts his left foot in the stirrup, and mounts his horse. Adahy has traveled for a fortnight with his loyal horse, Raven. A rare horse in these parts, gifted by his uncle, Wohali, a member of the tribal war counsel when Adahy turned 16. For the last several years, she has been Adahy's trusted companion. Each of Raven's steps seemed to drown out the silence as they made their way down the King's Highway.

His saddlebags are filled with supplies meant for a journey with no return. Several pistols, ammunition, paper cartridges, extra horns of powder, and a haversack are all stored on right-side saddlebags. Also tightly concealed is a bow and quiver filled with many sharp arrows. In the opposite saddlebags are deer jerky rations, bread, a greatcoat, a tomahawk, and encampment tools. Giving Adahy a proper backrest along the journey, there is a thin wool blanket rolled into a larger one fastened across both saddlebags' tops.

There are three muskets that he carries, each serving its purpose. The blunderbuss with the shorter barrel flared at the tip stayed on his back, fastened securely, and used for close quarters. The second was a British Brown Bess holstered in Raven's leather left side carrier. The French musket passed down from his father sits across his lap, a Charleville model 1728. Adahy was deadly accurate with all three.

The air becomes staler with each step, and the shade from the overhanging trees on the King's Highway is a much-welcomed relief in the late afternoon. Sweating quite a lot, Adahy loosens his chest rig. Welcoming airflow to his chest.

Overtop his long-sleeve shirt, he carries one flintlock dragoon in a custom leather holster and two smaller blades sheathed on his ribs. The weapons are fastened to a leather-weaved chest carrier. The rig covered from shoulder to shoulder and down to his waist. A three-inch-wide waistbelt was woven through the carrier's bottom section and buckled on his left side. Two straps wrapped around his shoulders tightly, keeping the chest rig stable and secured to his body. It was designed so Adahy could modify his pistols and knives for any setup that made him more efficient in combat.

After his mother passed, the tribal war council outfitted him with custom gear. A leather saddle, a fitted leather chest carrier, and a custom leather holster for muskets that rested on the front side of his saddle, among other resourceful tools. Adahy found the chest carrier most valuable, as it was quickly concealable by his greatcoat and could be comfortably worn with everyday clothing.

Adahy's mind returns to those last moments with each of Raven's steps. *'It's going to be all right, my son. I will be painless.'* The words echoed in his mind, trumping the bird whistles coming from the trees. Nightfall soon arrives to claim the day as the birds whistle into dusk. Adahy rides into the darkness before reaching a lodging tavern along the road. He guides

Raven to the hitching post, unsaddles, and ties up the beautiful black horse.

"You are the perfect traveling companion, Raven," he says, petting the side of the horse's long face before ritually placing his forehead on hers. "You never disagree with getting off the road."

He unstraps the greatcoat from the saddlebag and puts it on, buttoning the collar, loosely hiding half his face. Adahy then throws the heavy saddlebags off Raven over his shoulder. He pats Raven's back,

"Good girl," Adahy says as he heads into the lodge with the wooden sign out front reading '*Santee River Tavern.*'

The building was nearly empty, and the atmosphere was quiet. One drunken man is unconscious in the corner, and the barkeep seems to have just woken up to the sound of his arrival. He stands up straight, clearing his throat,

"Good evening, good sir! Welcome to the Santee River Tavern; our motto: *highway travelers deserve warm food and uninterrupted slee*p." The older man shares salutations while pouring his guest a pint of ale before looking up. "Would you be staying the night?"

"Yes, I believe I will," he replies, still scanning the open tavern for any possible threats or entries of leave. Adahy wasn't ignorant of the fact that being a half-native brought its own unique challenges.

"Five pence per night."

"Proper rate barkeep, I will stay three nights and give my horse clean water each morn," he says, placing five shillings on the bar top.

"Excellent, sir. Right away," the barkeep grabs a key off the wall under the number three hook. "Room three is yours until you leave."

Currency never fails to instill excitement and enthusiasm in the colonies.

People have an odd way of acting when they know money is involved; greed motivates evil. It has been almost ten years since King George III imposed his unique taxes on the colonies, and it would seem to have the opposite effect as intended. It wasn't the first time they were taxed, but it was the first time they'd begun seeing the British trying to enforce it. It was all the talk in taverns along Adahy's route.

You don't mess with people's money, he thought to himself.

The old barkeep comes around from the backside of the bar and heads outside to fetch new water for Raven's trough. Adahy opens the left side of his greatcoat, withdrawing a nine-inch clay pipe and a pouch of crisp tobacco. He pulls a generous pinch of tobacco from the bag, firmly packing the pipe bowl with his thumb. Noticing a candle, Adahy grabs it from the candelabra and uses the glowing flame to ignite his freshly packed pipe.

"Shall I take your things to the room, sir?" He asks with an uneasy tone upon reentering the tavern with the empty water pale.

"No, that will not be necessary," Adahy replies and continues, noticing the uneasiness of the barkeep, "doesn't look like you've seen much business as of late."

"Aye, our tavern has met a downturn these last several months. It's a pleasant sight, with fresh faces. We are happy to alleviate the road as a bed and stumps as pillows," his voice is uneasy, unsure of the weary traveler.

Adahy, looking the barkeep in the eyes, sensing the uneasiness, took a long draw from his pipe, paused, and released the smoke and some quick words,

"Many Redcoats travel through these parts?"

The old man takes a short pause as sweat begins beading on his forehead. He looks to the green-eyed Adahy, unsure of his intentions,

"Unfortunately..., yes."

"I assumed. What is your name, barkeep?" Adahy inquires, taking another long draw from the pipe and keeping the ember hot. Smoke dances away from the pipe, melding with the tavern's dry atmosphere. Adahy's tone showcased his disdain for the redcoats, and the barkeep opened up.

"Daniel Mullan. I own this establishment," he states proudly.

Tobacco embers crack and snap as Adahy pulls more smoke through his pipe, "Tell me more, Mr. Mullan."

As he pours himself an ale, he continues speaking, "Please, just call me Daniel. At first, they were infrequent, but with time, they began badgering our patrons after stopping in weekly from Georgetown and Charleston, stealing as they please." He looks around his empty tavern, "As you can see, they are effective in their work."

"That I can see, yes," Adahy says, pulling the final remnants of smoke from the pipe and, again, scanning the empty tavern. "What else?"

"Well, sir… They claim men's wives at will and then burn their properties for disputing their actions." He says, lowering his head, seemingly shameful.

"Typical British foot soldier. Always resorting to destruction when others disagree with the crown's malicious actions they claim are justified. Terrible wretches," Adahy says and continues, "Has an attempt been made to cease their conduct? Or has anyone done anything?" Adahy asks directly as he bangs his pipe against his hand, releasing all the used tobacco, and places the pipe back into his greatcoat pocket.

"No, for they are King's men. A firestorm will erupt if we retaliate with violence. This is not Boston. I've often conjured plans in my mind but never acted on my wishes…" he says anxiously and continues, "What do you suggest we do, stranger?"

"Well... Redcoats won't listen even after a beating," Adahy says plainly. "There is only one solution, old man. That is death, only... not a death that will bring *you* trouble or trouble to this tavern."

Daniel Mullan's face is petrified at Adahy's directness, but the green-eyed traveler appeared to be a man who understood violence with a willingness to act on it. Daniel has thought about this solution once or twice and realized the confrontation is imminent.

"How?" he asks. "If they are killed here, I will be hung in the streets of Georgetown as a traitor."

"Give me the night, Mr. Mullan. I will have your answer in the morn. For now, may I have a refill?"

"Please, it's Daniel. And yes, sir, you may."

Adahy stops Daniel from pouring, "I will require your indefinite discretion, and the Crown's forces will be on high alert after this. We cannot have misunderstandings between us." Adahy says frankly.

"Young sir, the crown and King do not hold my loyalty...the colonies do, the continental cause does. Rest assured, young man, my family and I are no King's men... haven't been for nearly 100 years." He replies confidently before continuing to pour the ale.

The tavern was quiet, all but the peaceful snoring of the man in the corner. Daniel's face has an aura of hope, while Adahy's face sits still, knowing not everyone can be trusted with these sorts of conversations, but Daniel seems trustworthy enough.

"We shall see," Adahy replies before downing the remainder of his ale. He takes his gear and heads upstairs toward room three.

"Excuse me, sir, what do I call you?" Daniel asks the green-eyed traveler before he finishes his ascent up the stairs.

"Adahy."

War Trophies

Santee River Tavern

South Carolina

From the outside, a rolling *tut-tut-tut* chirp was rising and falling from the songbirds in the trees. Slowly, the rhythmic melody enters Adahy's ears. His eyes winced as the sun peaked through the linen curtains of the room window. *Ugh, a few minutes more*, he thinks, rolling over. Moments passed, and finally, he opened his eyes. The privilege of comfort entered his mind, and he quickly got out of bed.

"I have it," he mutters to himself.

The plan, if one could label it, was cut and dry. At least, that's Adahy's hope. He dresses quickly and gets his gear on, putting his greatcoat on last. Opening the room door, he exits but quickly returns for his tricorn, locking the door behind him.

"Aye, proper morning, Adahy!" Daniel Mullan says cheerfully to the empty tavern as Adahy makes his way down the wooden staircase.

"Good morning, good sir. Shall we have some coffee and a conversation?" Adahy asks in good spirits, entering the tavern barroom.

"A fresh batch was brewed not but half the hour ago," he replies, grabbing two mugs and the coffee pot off the coals.

Making his way and sitting down at a larger table, Adahy pulls out his tobacco pouch and pipe. Daniel Mullan sits across from him, pouring the steaming coffee into the mugs for the both of them. Adahy takes the mug and sips the black drink, and it's immediately invigorating,

"Damn, that's some fine coffee."

"It's a batch of beans my trade partners export from the Caribbean, a little town called 'Havana.' They have some of the best coffee beans." Daniel says proudly but quickly shifts topics, "I've been thinking about what you said last night... about the Redcoats." His voice welcomes a more serious tone.

"Aye. I've been thinking about it, too, and I have a plan. It's quite simple..." He says, taking a sip from his coffee mug and then pinching some tobacco into his pipe, "I kill them," he says calmly while lighting the tobacco with a candle.

Daniel stays quiet for a moment.

"I will kill them as if I am a group of natives that are furious with English expansion. I will use only a bow, arrows, blades, and tomahawk. It should be a small element of redcoats, and with surprise, darkness, and shadows, I will eliminate them, hopefully quickly," he says, exhaling a thick cloud of smoke.

"Angry Indians, huh? You think that will work?" Daniel questions.

"Trust me. I am a native, and the disdain and hatred my people have for the British colonizers is vast. Native war parties are always looking for weak spots and moments to wound the British Empire. I believe this moment will be no different."

"Aye, I've never once thought of that angle, but then again, I am no native, nor know nothing about strategy or war.

I know the tavern business and ensuring my guests are comfortable, safe, and well-fed."

"And you do well in that role, Mr. Mullan. This is my role in life; let me put it to use for you and this town." Adahy replies, with a half-smile creasing on his face, knowing violence was a tool to be used, but for him, it was also an outlet for release.

"How do you think the British garrison will react to this act?"

"I'm hoping they put all towns near the garrison on alert for natives, and they stay within their walls for a bit. Giving you and this town some time to figure out a long-term plan of resistance... That's also a very optimistic stance. For all I know, they could come and burn the town down for retribution," he says halfway laughing, "But let's be honest, the British are not the 'go out and attack' type... so I'm sure they won't burn the town down."

"That is not humorous, but I understand your point," Daniel says, not enthused by Adahy's idea of a jest.

"I apologize; I may have taken it a bit too far... but the plan is solid. They will be scared and unaware of the motivations of these 'angry Indians,' as you so aptly put it, so they won't have a clear direction on what to do next." Adahy says confidently.

"How is it you believe this will work?"

"My uncle Wohali has taught me how the British think... or at least, he tried," Adahy smiled, looking at Daniel.

"It appears you have a clear path, and I understand what you need to do. This moves me to trust you, and I pray that no retribution is taken out on our town," Daniel says strongly, "would you like some more coffee?"

"Yes sir, I would appreciate that," Adahy replies, sensing that Mr. Mullan's deep-down attitude toward the whole idea was wavering, "I promise you, Mr. Mullan, I will make sure they are factual in their assessments that angry natives will be to blame for this action."

Daniel trusted the abilities of the young man and the confidence he carried. Daniel also sensed he was a trustworthy soul, recognizing that the moment they started talking on the first day.

"It will work, Mr. Mullan. It has, too," Adahy said, inhaling more tobacco from his pipe.

"I believe you, young man, I do. I have faith it'll happen as discussed." Daniel says to Adahy and stands up, placing his right hand on Adahy's shoulder, "I just hope you are safe in your actions. I will be praying for your safe return. Godspeed."

"Thanks, old man. I will be." Adahy replies slyly as Daniel walks away.

Through the smoke, Adahy looks up to see the glaring morning sun rays leaking in through the glass pane windows. Hymns from the songbirds carry a tune through the day. *Nature is noisy this morning*, he thinks to himself; *that means it'll be a quiet night.* Daniel remembered what the green-eyed traveler said to him during their planning discussion, *"Trust me."*

The two men loaned their trust to each other and would keep it if this operation were successful.

**

Early on the third day, Daniel Mullan received information claiming a squad of the belligerent British regulars had left Georgetown and would be here by midday.

The day started just as any other day along the King's Highway, with unsuspecting travelers, passersby, and civilians roaming into town. Tucked away within a corner of the town, with all the canvas-flapped storefronts selling their wares and handmade goods, stood Adahy. He patiently waits outside the Tavern with a keen eye on the route out front. Walking the road from Georgetown is a vigorous journey, and the twelve British regulars stop at the Santee River Tavern, as expected. But it's a smaller element than anticipated. Adahy watches as all walk into the tavern,

Imagine them trying to chase me, Adahy thinks of the humorous picture. He analyzes each British regular: *Protruding waists, disheveled gear, cartridge boxes are loose, their brown Bess muskets are old and used, not at all like the threatening redcoats I've heard of.*

Daniel Mullan gets to work in the tavern, and within a short time, the redcoats are lively and drunk. As expected, the men are barking insults at the locals, being hostile and combative with the civilian men, and forcing themselves onto the women.

Wild and irregular, these men have no place here, Daniel thinks to himself, watching them men act out.

Hours pass, and their behavior only gets worse as they drunkenly spew anti-patriot language. Two soldiers lay claim to a townsman's wife, promising their return the next day. After harassing Daniel and not paying their tab, they stumble outside under the dark new moon sky.

The air is dank on the King's Highway this late, with frogs loudly croaking in the shadows as if the shadows are speaking. Halfway to the garrison, four furlongs south, the drunken redcoats find themselves chanting their national anthem, happily singing out of tune with their words and steps, blending sounds with the croaking frogs.

> *"God save great George our king,*
> *Long live our noble king,*
> *God save the king.*
> *Send him victorious,*

> *Happy and glorious,*
> *Long to reign over us,*
> *God save the ki-"*

Thwipt

An arrow slices through the neck of the tallest redcoat in the group's rear, releasing a steady outflow of blood, replacing his singing with choking and gurgling. Panic consumes the other men.

Thwipt

A second arrow immediately follows the first, striking another redcoat in the chest. In the stillness of the night, you can hear the arrowhead piercing his air-filled lung. Gasping with their last breaths, the two immediately fell to their knees, quickly bleeding out. The rest of the drunken soldiers begin panicking and aimlessly firing their muskets into the dark wilderness. Flashes erupt from their musket locks, and trees split from the British shots. Another arrow emerges from the shadows and cuts the muggy night air.

Thwipt

A third soldier releases a quick wheeze, dropping on the road. A fierce, precise arrow penetrates between his clavicle bones, snapping his spinal cord on the way out. The remaining nine soldiers huddle around the fallen; two make attempts to treat the wounded. In a drunken stupor, the frantic and overwhelmed redcoats fail to distinguish the origins of the massacre, still firing randomly into the darkness.

The musket firing and smoke blended with the pitch blackness and horrifying screams, making for a hellish sight. Each musket flash showcases another gruesome death. Adahy uses this to his advantage; he knows that confusion is a tool in the battlespace. He moves within shadows, and multiple arrows begin raining misery onto the redcoats from a new position.

Thwipt, Thwipt, Thwipt, Thwipt, Thwipt, Thwipt, Thwipt, Thwipt, Thwipt, Thwipt, Thwipt, Thwipt

Within moments, the firing had stopped, and croaking frogs quickly rejoined the dying men's newly faint gurgles and groans.

From the garrison's outer perimeter, the pair of roving external foot patrols heard the struggling musket fire. They begin running toward the sound of the drowning musket fire. Immediately after the guards start their sprint, it falls quiet in the wilderness, excluding the frogs. A few minutes pass, and the two guards come across the dead. Musket smoke still floats in the air above the warm, lifeless bodies.

As the two redcoats get closer, they see a mutilated pile of twelve British regulars with a collection of arrows in each. One of the guards immediately vomited on the road. A combination of seldom sprinting and the defiled dead. Corporal Werdon, the taller redcoat, says unclenched,

"Bloody fucking hell, bear witness to slaughter, greenhorn."

"This is the work of savages! It had to be a column with their blasted arrows! Tormenting us from the shadows!" Lance Corporal Gill says deliriously, eyes wide, looking in all directions, dropping to the ground on his knees, seemingly losing his bearings, with vomit still on his chin.

"Bloody natives. Why scalp them? The red savages in these parts don't have a reputation for scalps," Corporal Werdon speculatively says, looking at the body as he rolls it over with his musket barrel.

The other redcoat was becoming delirious and quickly losing his sanity from the sights and smells.

"Disgraced war trophies, awful bloody things, we must leave now! Who knows how many more there are near?" Fear controls Lance Corporal Gill.

"We need to report this immediately. This will not be good for us," says Corporal Werdon, the collected recoat. "Get back on your feet! You're embarrassing the Crown!"

The two redcoats sprint back to the garrison as quickly as they left. A caravan is sent within minutes to ensure the men's story's legitimacy and collect bodies. Just before dawn, the procession of fifty British infantry regulars and horse-drawn wagons returned. It followed with dreadful news, carrying twelve scalped soldiers, confirming the two men's story.

The door opens from the headquarters building, and a gangling Major emerges with a war-hardened face. Before him was the entire garrison standing at attention, ready for his word about the attack.

"Men, we have been attacked. Targeted, one might say. We've been on the receiving end of a despicable disgrace to the Crown's men. There will be changes." As he speaks, his tone is stern; he pauses. The men know what he says goes.

He continues,

"Patrols will be doubled for rovers and doubled in size. You will no longer drink at local taverns until these savage culprits are brought to justice."

No matter their discipline, you can hear scoffs from the men throughout the formation.

"I will not have my men slaughtered by savages! Cease your griping," the Major snaps quickly and continues, "Captain, send a message to all local taverns and towns about this slaughter. Our men will not be subject to provocation and targeted attacks," he directs his words at the younger Captain and walks back into the headquarters building. The grumbling among the men is a dull roar, and within moments, they are released from their formation.

"See, I told you, Gill…" the Corporal looked to the younger man, "This attack will not be good for us," saying in a darker tone.

"After what I saw, I never wish that upon my worst enemy." Lance Corporal Gill replies.

"Don't be such a coward. You should be upset that we are stuck here to drink and cannot share festivities with the townswomen. What do they expect us to do? This place will eat itself in a fortnight." He angrily scoffs, walking off.

"Wait for me!" Gill says as he catches up with Corporal Werdon, who is grumbling under his breath. "You can smell it, Gill, the disorderly conduct reports being prepared while the men run out of suitable activities for solidified soldiers. This is a fucking mess. The next chance we get, we will request a transfer. I'm not being stuck with this timid regiment." Werdon says and goes back to under-his-breathe complaints.

Grumbling gripes are growing outside of every tent around all the fire pits, and complaints are ever-growing and quietly echoing throughout the British garrison. The men, now confined to their fort, are effective prisoners under their own flag.

**

Creeping over the horizon, the sun breaks the plane, disbursing light into the world. Dawn was Adahy's favorite time; the crisp, cool air from the black nights prior and the aroma of the fresh sun on the earth was perfect. Adahy sits atop Raven, riding toward the entrance of the Santee River Tavern. He unsaddles the black mare and ties her reigns to the hitching post. Adahy presses his forehead against the horse's head for a brief moment, collects his thoughts, and walks inside.

Mr. Mullan was awake, rummaging through some wooden crates behind the counter. No drunken fool was unconscious in the corner this morn, and the small wooden doors over the windows had been opened, letting in the beautiful early sunshine. The old barkeep speaks from behind the counter, still occupied,

"Weary traveler, may I offer you some crisp steaming coffee?"

"Many redcoats travel through these parts?" Adahy asks in a mimicked tone, like the first day he arrived.

Daniel, recognizing the voice, lifts his head, smiling, and comes around the bar, "Adahy, young man! I must shake your hand. The garrison redcoats are restricted from local establishments indefinitely due to some trouble with some Indians, said they scalped 'em." Daniel says slyly, with a look in his eye.

"It's a temporary fix, old man. Once they realize there are not any real natives taking advantage of their drunken soldiers, they will soon be back tormenting the local people."

"I know…" Daniel tells Adahy quietly, "I will use this peaceful time to contact my friends in the northeast and persuade them to come here and work if more issues arise about the garrison redcoats. A growing sentiment echoes in the shadows of taverns and meetinghouses. Men meet, men talk, and men plan. Soon, there might be enough collective support."

Adahy, never being one for politics, breezes over the words, "I'll take you up on that coffee if you don't mind," trying to change the subject.

"Right away. Would you like some forced eggs as well?" Daniel asks Adahy as he grabs the kettle for the coffee.

"No, thank you, coffee is fine."

The old barkeep rounds behind the counter, boiling the water over the fire. In what seemed like seconds, the distinct bean aroma filled the tavern quickly and was a welcoming scent to the journeying young man. Upon the coffee's completion, Daniel pours Adahy and himself two steaming mugs; together, they enjoy the silence and the piping black sludge.

Forty minutes pass, and Adahy stands up; his tall stature towers above the sitting Daniel,

"Well, old man, I'm off. Time to continue my path. This is *the best* coffee I have had in an exceptionally long time. Thank you, and your hospitality has been generous."

Daniel stands, "Aye, well, it was my pleasure. If you don't mind, where are you headed?" He asks as he takes the last sip of the coffee.

"Boston, by way of the king's highway," Adahy replies.

"What is a young man of your talent doing headed to Boston? You would be a perfect fit for the underground continental cause in Philadelphia. They need capable young men like yourself." Daniel Mullan says to him convincingly.

"You know, a fortnight ago, I would've never spoken to you of my travels or path, but after this week, I do believe we have gained a sense of trust and confinement in each other. Would you agree?"

"Aye," Daniel replies firmly,

"Before my mother died, she instructed me to find my father's brother, a man named '*Thomas Young*,' who could help me learn more about my father and that side of my family," Adahy says plainly and continues, "Mother died of yellow fever. According to her, my father was on the run for years by privateers, bounty hunters, and mercenaries, all hired by King George II before they eventually caught up to him and killed him. She rarely spoke his name."

Being taken aback, Daniel stands up, "Thomas Young was one of the most notorious officers in the French & Indian War. He's a well-known patriot."

"That is the man I need to find," Adahy replies smoothly to the old barkeep.

"Well, Adahy, I believe you will find who you are looking for. He is a leader in the city and doing great things for the continental cause, or so that's what my friends in Philadelphia have conveyed to me. My younger, well younger than me, Cousin Wilfred, owns '*Mug Tavern*' outside Boston in the small-town Brookline… if you ever need a good ale and a place to relax, that is the place to be."

Adahy listens to his words and remembers the names of his cousin and tavern in case he needs to refer to the resource later in life. It's always a good idea to keep in contact with trustworthy people and locations; Adahy learned this early in life. Daniel seemed happier or at least more at ease than he had been when Adahy first arrived, and seeing that made Adahy proud and filled him with gratification.

"It has been a busy few days, but I am glad to put your redcoat worries at ease. It does people no good to be bullied, harmed, or killed by their King and his men… I am always happy to help in that area when I can," Adahy conveys directly to Daniel Mullan.

"Aye, thank you. Your actions will spread through the colonies fast. It might even reach the ears of the clandestine cabals in Boston; you never know. Now, drink the rest of this coffee before you embark; you'll need it." Mr. Mullan fills the mug to the brim as Adahy sits back down, withdrawing his clay pipe and tobacco pouch for one last smoke before getting on the road.

By midday, the sun was at full brilliance with no clouds in the blue sky, a genuinely riveting sight. Adahy had left the Santee River Tavern but still couldn't get over that damn coffee. Before leaving, he had Mr. Mullan fill up one of his spare canteens with as much as it could carry. He grabs the gold talisman with his left hand and clutches it tightly, thinking of his mother. The sentiments fade from missing his mother to the mission and her wish for him. The road was long indeed, but the resilience within Adahy was great. He was optimistically steadfast and youthfully determined.

Solitude & Violence

Summer 1762

Native Country

"Knowledge is infinite, Adahy. Know this, learn this, live this. It is infinite. Having the ability to learn from every aspect of this earth is a privilege. Recognizing lessons nature provides means being a soul that lives an understood life," Wohali said, looking down on the eleven-year-old boy.

It was hot, and the temperature was rising as the sun did the same across the daytime sky. Adahy was exhausted and nearly out of breath. Yet, he was angry, unwilling to listen to his uncle preach. He lunges forward off the ground with his dull blade leading. With his right hand, Wohali snatches Adahy's wrist, twists it, and flips the teen back to his starting point.

"You are young, Adahy. Even though you have completed your pilgrimage and are considered by all in the tribe a man, you are still reckless with your emotions. You are quick-tempered and impetuous."

"Enough, uncle!" The young man says, lunging forward again, this time side-stepping to the right and slashing his uncle's thigh with the dull wooden blade; he pops up with youthful prowess and jumps upon his uncle's back, placing the wooden knife on the grown man's neck.

"I have you," Adahy states boldly.

"Do you?" Wohali asks, and with expert finesse, the grown man removes Adahy's grasp from around his neck and, with all his force, launches Adahy off his back, throwing him forward, back onto the ground.

"That is enough knife practice today. You need to save your energy for tomorrow. For we have stalking, and you will need to be well rested. We will be gone a fortnight," Wohali said to his nephew, reaching out his hand to help him up.

"I enjoy stalking. It allows me peace and the ability to focus," he says, grabbing his uncle's hand and standing up.

"You are very good at it, but you must recognize when to allow emotions to take hold. You must be stronger. Like today, you mustn't allow your emotions to control your fighting. It must be smooth, thought-out, and precise with each strike and each movement. You have the potential and abilities to be a great warrior, Adahy, but there is darkness within you. There is a storm that has never settled since your birth. You must harness this storm and use it. Do not allow it to bring you down. You are my nephew, Adahy. You have my blood... you are strong."

"I must be stronger," he says to his uncle, brushing off the pine needles and dirt.

"Mastery of one's strength is not a thing to be rushed or miscalculated. With time, your strength will grow, and you will become a master of your body and emotions," he says as the two begin their trek back to the tribal homestead.

Rustling in the trees, a large white owl screeched into the sky. Bringing a welcomed melody to the densely wooded forest. Adahy watched the bird for a moment before his mind brought him back to training,

Knowledge is infinite, he thinks to himself, trying to tap into his senses. Awakening them he sees the world vividly, for all its detail. Quickly noticing the smells, differentiating them. Every moment was a moment to train and learn.

Within a few short minutes, the two men were back within the boundary of the tribal homestead. It was the main concentration of tents, huts, gardens, and people. In the tribe's center was the shaman tent, where members attempted to speak to the gods. In a half-circular pattern, on the backside of the shaman tent laid multiple rows of crops and vegetables; each tribal member was responsible for sustaining their share of the garden. Sweet corn, squash, onions, carrots, beets, cabbage, tomatoes, beans, lettuce, and more all found their way into the garden. The crops were on the outer layer of the garden, and they housed cotton, wheat, and oats. The tribe itself had nearly 200 members, all hunting, foraging, and purposefully contributing to the tribe, ensuring generational success.

"Adahy!" the voice is familiar as Adahy looks at her.

"Mother!"

"How was he, Wohali? I hope he was good today."

"Mother, I always respect Uncle Wohali's teachings… even if they come across as haranguing," Adahy assures slickly.

"Ha! The humor in this one, Aryana… that is your son. *'Haranguing,'* are you even sure you know the definition of such language?" Wohali cheerfully replies.

"You have your father's humor, dry and sarcastic," she adds with a painful smile.

Adahy knew that after his father died, she detached herself from any aspect of her previous life and their shared life apart from Adahy, whom she loved dearly. The pain of the memories was too much; she constantly suppressed them. She would tell Adahy about her adventure, from leaving Nassau when he was an infant to traveling the seas and then through

La Florida to the tribe. It was a lengthy story he often heard throughout his life.

***

July 1771
The King's Highway

Adahy was raised to be self-reliant. It was a familiar place for him. He thrived in solitude and was accustomed to violence. He seldom enjoyed the company of others, and when he did, he did not show it often; Daniel Mullan was an exception via his coffee and hatred of bullies.

Being twenty years old, Adahy had many things to learn, but he had vast knowledge of many aspects of life that the tribal elders were willing to share throughout his time with the tribe. Taking a life was a coveted act where he's from. It is a personal commitment to yourself, and it was expected on life's journey as a tribal warrior.

Still, Adahy quickly allowed the dead spirits to occupy his mind. He was still young, filled with rage. He is not yet a master of his emotions. His mind drifts as the faces of the redcoats being slain flash in his mind.

"Ugh, Raven... it's pesky... these thoughts," his words carried a weight into the nighttime air.

She whines, seemingly in response.

"Aye, I'll smoke when we stop," he replies, deflecting his own thoughts.

Raven's hooves systematically impact the ground, bringing Adahy north along the King's Highway. Memories of his ritualistic training in his youth ran rampant in his mind. He knew nothing but solitude and violence. His heart was from

53

his mother, where his compassion and empathy still held a respectable space within his soul.

His mother kept Adahy attached to the tribe, as he always felt like an outsider. Wohali kept an eye on him throughout his childhood. When his mother passed, Wohali was exemplary, reinforcing the message from Aryana that was only meant for Adahy's ears,

"You must find your uncle, Adahy."

His uncle's words echo within his mind as they travel along the route. At the start of 1771, Adahy and Raven had left from the north Georgia hills to the coast. Quickly, they found the King's Highway and began the long journey in high spirits. The route to the sea was one Adahy had taken with his mother on trading trips as a boy, so it came with ease and familiarity, but they never ventured north. The road was an easy month-long trip with Raven when he took his time; he never rushed as they kept a good pace.

After leaving the '*Santee River Tavern,*' getting past the Georgetown checkpoint and through the actual city was easier than he thought it would be. During the dark hours of the night, anyone can go seemingly unnoticed in plain sight. Adahy was adept at this understanding. With the greatcoat buttoned to his nose, covering his face, leaving only his green eyes exposed, he made sure to stay as anonymous as possible.

"It's a nice night, isn't it, girl?"

With a short neigh and head bob, Raven replies.

"We just need to get out of this rain... even if it's a drizzle, it gathers. From the looks of these clouds, it's not going away anytime soon," he says with a light laugh.

Rain always helped with cover and concealment, covering up tracks, and overall was another valuable tool in the battlespace, much like confusion was.

Sounds of the gurgling and dying redcoats beings creeping back into Adahy's mind...

"Was it justified, Raven?"

She neighs sharply.

"Was that a needed endeavor?"

Raven gives no response.

"You're right... Redcoats, more times than not, are vile creatures with no regard for civilians."

The king's highway was a rough route to venture. Filled with highwaymen, bandits, drunkards, soldiers, and undesirables, it was a journey not meant for thin-skinned souls. The killing of redcoats, however poorly justified, leaves Adahy questioning his honor continuously. He thirsts for justice for the oppressed and fights for what he believes is the right decision. Still, he lets the killings weigh on his mind.

The black mare stops moving, abruptly halting, startling Adahy,

"Whoa, girl! What happened?"

With a sharp movement, Raven bucks slightly before settling back to normal.

"Should I have just let them continue?"

She neighs in response.

"You know I cannot. Bullies deserve the outcome that I provided those men that night. But I do recognize we need to be more cautious...Still, I enjoy the fight."

Raven exhales with a sudden snort.

"I know... I know... I will be careful."

A force consumed him while in combat. Even on the highway the other night, he enjoyed the violence. Focus flowed through him, as well as a warm, sensational form of vehemently precise rage. Adahy thrived in violence, not without its price. His mind cracked and constantly crashed between succeeding in brutal conflict or settling quietly and calmly in the woods. Adahy searched for clarity in oneself through violence. It is one of the only times he feels like he understands himself.

Puddles formed quickly, and the incoming raindrops muted the day's sounds. Once Adahy arrived in Alexandria, right off the Potomac, it began to downpour. He looked for the nearest trading post and headed there. Like others along the king's highway, this town was filled with degenerates and thieves. Dismounting Raven, he ties her reigns to a covered hitching post and walks inside.

"Welcome, wet traveler. Are ye lookin' for somethin' particular?" The merchant asks as Adahy walks through the door, dripping with water.

Adahy looks up; his stern face and piercing green eyes crash upon the merchant,

"I need Virginian tobacco and cannabis. Haven't had it in some time," he says, taking off his tricorn hat.

"Aye, we have a satchel of both. Sumthe best 'round here. Whatareye tradin' for it?"

"I have numerous bundles of deer jerky rations, several rabbit pelts, and a few crowns. Any or all of that should be suitable for a trade. I desire a heavy quantity."

"Aye, I'd sayso," he replies with wide eyes and, with two hands, lifts a satchel of Virginian tobacco and cannabis on the counter with a thud, "Are ye needin' anythin' else?"

Adahy puts on his tricorn and grabs the satchel bags, "Yeah, there is… what do you know of Thomas Young?"

The merchant's eyes jolt to the floor, and he becomes uneasy; Adahy senses the change, "Ye don't want to know that man," the merchant mentions eerily, looking back up toward Adahy.

With a closed fist, fierce power, and precise violence, Adahy slams his fist into the merchant's relaxed open hand on the counter.

"Why not?" he asks coolly.

"That man destroys lives. Yet the whole of Boston loves'em for it," he lets out quickly, wincing in pain.

"Why?" Adahy asks, pressing his fist harder.

"Thomas Young is a man who operates in the shadows, beyon' the sight of the law, beyon' the Crown!"

"What do you mean, he destroys lives?"

"It is unclear. A wave of death seems to follow him like a shadow! People die," Adahy removes his fist from the man's hand. As quickly as it's released, the merchant retracts his hand, "I know nothin' of Thomas Young other than the words from others and the stories one hears on the road and in Boston."

Sensing authenticity and truth, Adahy stops with the harsh tactics and heads toward the exit.

"Death follows ye too! Look at ye shadow, yoee'll know nothing but loss and pain!" The merchant shouts hysterically as Adahy walks out the door.

Crazy old loon, he thinks.

The rain impacting the porch roof was a pleasant and welcoming sound that quickly drowned out the shouting merchant. Adahy brought the herbs to his face, opened the satchels, and smelled the sweet aroma.

"Ahhhhh, sweet smoke," he says, directing his words at Raven, quickly shifting topics for his own sanity.

He then bundles the tobacco satchels in his greatcoat, protecting them from the rain, and takes the reigns mounting Raven. She was ready to keep moving north.

Before arriving in Alexandria, Adahy expended the last bit of his New Bern tobacco in Williamsburg one wet rainy night, and he was without it for a few days. He was happy to finally have his hands on some Virginian tobacco, which was a bit more tasteful than others.

Pipe smoking was a daily ritual among most tribal members. It was considered a mechanism for reaching peace within oneself. It calmed him. Rarely before sleep, Adahy blended the tobacco with another herb from the earth, hemp seed hops. The colonists called it 'cannabis.' Smoking cannabis was a rarity among the tribe, as it had psychoactive properties that enabled them to see the universe in dreams. It wasn't until after his pilgrimage that the tribe allowed Adahy access to the herb. Only the tribal war council grew the herb and used it for ritualistic activities.

As a boy, Adahy had spent many nights around the fire with the tribal leaders as they allowed him to smoke and hallucinate, trying to meet the source of existence. Good versus evil and light versus dark were frequent battles in elders' smoke. These were the times he felt a true sense of belonging with the tribe. A cool chill runs down his spine, and the memories are fleeting as the cold, wet night air brings him back to reality.

"This looks like a good place to stay for the night," he remarks to the beautiful black horse, swinging his right leg over Raven and putting his feet on the ground. Walking her over underneath a thick tree, Adahy ties her reigns to a low-hanging tree branch. Taking the saddlebags off Raven, he rests his musket's barrel up against a large rock.

"We need to get a fire going, girl."

Adahy looked around for what was needed to build an adequate perimeter around the small clearing where he intended to stay. Noticing some previous fallen dry branches amongst the wet ones, he grabs those for firewood. He collects the other wet fallen branches and builds a makeshift fence. He learned at a young age that good sleep requires security.

Although a musket and pistols can keep you safe, he knows it is best to set up preventative measures. Wohali never let him forget all the trouble within the wilderness. Bears, wolves, coyotes, but most of all… man.

The tent was a simple wool canvas draped on a rope line between trees and anchored with four wooden spikes. It was enough to keep Adahy dry in the twilight rain. Squatting just outside the opening of the newly set up tent, Adahy uses his old flint and steel, sparking the tinder and creating fire. The dry branches absorb the fire, giving it life, ever-growing the flames. Fixated on the elusive dancing fire, waving and contorting, his mind drifts, and the fire dances deeper into his eyes.

With only three days away from Boston, he was nervous about his plan to find his uncle. Adahy didn't know where to start his search in the large city. He figured going to an active brothel or tavern and asking about Thomas Young would hopefully be enough. It is a vague, poorly thought-out plan, but Adahy sees this as the quickest way to gain information about his uncle.

If it goes awry, violence.

After a few moments, he stands, stretches his back, walks to Raven, pets her neck, and grabs his haversack from the saddlebags on the ground.

"Not bad, right, girl? I do enjoy the quiet, and you've never been much of the talkative type. Quite the sensation."

Raven produces a soft whine, and Adahy laughs, sitting on the ground next to the flames. He pulls a body-sized linen sheet from his haversack and places his pistols and knives on it. He also removes some linen rags and oil for cleaning. His hands go to work, and the familiar tools move gracefully within the well-oiled rag. His mind drifts into a meditative state.

Hours pass, and the fire crackles and cracks, arguing with the night silence over the domain as Adahy diligently cleans his arsenal.

Mindset is everything.

His mother, Aryana, always said he was destined for more, to achieve great things. He never believed it. Since childhood, he was taught to be in the moment and focus on the present state of life. His uncle Wohali steadily tried to shape Adahy's mind to be fortified and tough.

"The body will break, but the mind must not," he always preached to Adahy, desperately trying to ensure he was raised strictly with discipline in the mind and to be independent and self-sufficient.

The stars in the sky have moved almost across the entire black canvas when Adahy is finished with his weapons. The plan for Boston is clear, and he knows what he needs to do. He packs the guns away as before, leaving the Dragoon on his chest while the blunderbuss and Charleville are close to his side. He pulls out his small pouch of hemp-seed-hops and tobacco, then mixes a deep bowl in his pipe. The end of the pipe is ignited with a piece of wick from Adahy's wick ball, which he uses explicitly for pipe smoking. The smokey fumes are inhaled and disperse a calming sensation throughout his body. A few more puffs and his eyelids become heavy as he drifts into a deep sleep. The wary half-native slept with both hands on his seasoned tomahawk.

**

The twilight rain has extinguished the fire for a few hours, and the cold seems to be compounding with the darkness. Silence sweeps the area, and Adahy awakens from the chilly air, shivering to the core.

"Fuck. It's cold," his words slice the ice air as the chill creeps down his spine, reminding him it is time to move.

After a moment, he exhales into his hands, rubbing them together to warm himself up. Removing his wool blanket, he gets up, leaves the tent, and bundles his greatcoat to his chin. The air was fresh off the coast in the form of a slight breeze, bringing the morning chill. He slept with all his clothing on, a precaution while traveling on the King's Highway.

The moon is low on the horizon as the sun begins illuminating the bluish-gray shadows. The night sky is now early morning, becoming a new day filled with noises, eradicating the silence. The sun was beginning its climb as the deep darkness was easing off, and the cold air was cutting to the core. Steadily shivering, Adahy begins packing away his gear.

Rustling trees catch the dawn breeze off the sea as the sky starts to warm itself, he thinks to himself, taking a deep breath of the morning air.

Adahy finishes packing his belongings when Raven claps her hooves against the floor, indicating her desire to move.

"I know, I know… you want to go. Don't worry, Raven. Soon enough, we will be on the move," Adahy says, connecting his head to her head.

As he mounts Raven, he clicks his teeth, and she slowly begins to head out. On the move, he adjusts his weaponry for riding and reaches for his tobacco pipe and pouch. The nine-inch clay pipe was a tool he crafted with his uncle Wohali when he was just a boy, and it had resonated with tobacco and hemp-seed shops from years past. The taste was distinct. Adahy wouldn't want it any other way. He firmly packs the Virginian tobacco in the pipe bowl as Raven slowly strides on the trail, getting back toward the main highway.

"Well, girl, I've prepared myself to puff some smoke, but I've gotten no fire," Adahy says, laughing at himself, knowing he packed away his flint and steel.

"I'll save this one for the next stop; how does that sound?" The horse neighs and Adahy pets her neck before putting his pipe and tobacco pouch in the greatcoat's inner pocket.

The crisp morning air is clean as he inhales deeply, knowing that his plan might not work, but it's all he can do now. Time passes the day as trees rustle in the wind; with the rhythm of Raven's hooves clopping against the ground, Adahy's mind starts to drift. With each passing tree, his mind wanders, and his mother's voice comforts him, retelling him the story of how she met his father.

"Soon"

December 1738

Native Country

Aryanna, unaware of the tribal tradition, today was scary and intimidating. She'd rather run in the fields, climb trees, and explore the rivers with her brothers.

"Come, now, girl... it is time," the female leader was taller, had midnight black hair, and a soft smile. Her wrists were filled with jangling bracelets, and her fingers were full of rings.

Looking up with her wide, bright green eyes, she knew she had to accept her fate and meet with the tribal shaman for her reading. Aryana extended her hand, and the older woman helped her stand.

"When the shamans read you, you will connect with a higher form of yourself, a higher form of life. Mother Earth will show you the way. She will guide you, show you your path, and you will be better for it," she told the girl.

"Orenda, you will frighten her. She is young and the Chief's daughter; please do not scare the child," one of the male leaders says softly.

"I am not scared," Aryana said confidently.

Collectively, the tribal leaders smile and walk the girl out of the tent; she looks back as the tent flap shuts behind her.

This is it. I must be strong.

The walk is short. It's one she's familiar with. The tribal shaman tent is a frequented place for young children as it is a place for stories and storytelling. Each of the tribal leaders leading the child comes to a stop and makes way for her to enter the tent. She notices smoke softly flowing out from under the tent flap and takes a deep breath.

I am ready, she tells herself.

Upon entering, the smoke crashes into her face like a wave crashing into the shore. There are two tribal shamans, Etrimok and Aadrika, sitting across from her. It is hard for her to see and hard to breathe. Immediately, she recognizes the smoke as hemp seed hops. She tried to resist but couldn't breathe. So, she welcomes the smoke with no other choice.

"Sit, Aryana," a voice says from across the smoke, coming from one of the shamans.

Within moments, her mind begins to find itself and begins to etch clarity into her psyche. She could see the seat and sat down accordingly.

"You are frightened, child?" the voice emerges from the female shaman, sitting across from her to the right. Her hair was bundled into a large knot atop her head, her eyes were dark brown, and inked markings adored her face in poetic ways.

"I am…" the young girl answers truthfully.

"We must explore the sky, child. We must meet the creator who enlightens us, illuminating a dark path," she replies.

"What Aadrika says is true. Consume the elixir and discover your path. Do not be scared. Let go. Trust yourself," the male shaman says to Aryana; his shadows reflectively dance upon the inner tent walls as he extends his arm over the flickering flames, offering the small clay bowl.

Timid but not hesitant, she leans toward the fire and grabs the clay bowl. Her shadows blend with Etrimok as their shadows reset. The two of them sit back in their spaces, her with the elixir and him without. She brings the bowl to her face, and the aroma is strong. She quickly drinks the lemon-scented, black concoction and hands the empty bowl back to the man.

Both shamans drink a bowl of the sludge and reach for their smoking pipes.

"Etrimok will burn the sacred spice... we will be here to guide you... do not be afraid," Aadrika says in a kind tone.

Her voice is angelic, Aryana thought.

The two shamans begin smoking heavily, and the tent is quickly consumed in it. Aryana continues to breathe it in, having no option but to go with the flow of the ritual with the shamans.

"Ugh," she groans and clutches her stomach, "it hurts!"

It's hot, the air is thick with smoke, and Aryana can barely see through the air. The fire cracks, getting louder, and everything is becoming more intense, overwhelming Aryana's senses. She manages to keep her eyes open long enough to see...

Sitting meditatively, the two tribal shamans were calm, staring at Aryana with wide, bright, ivory-white eyes. Aryana winces in pain

"Your eyes..." she groans and holds her hands around her waist.

Ethereal angelic tones that had never entered Aryana's ears nor a pitch that was of this earth began emanating from the mouths of the Etrimok and Aadrika... in unison, their words released,

"Soon, on the shores where spirits roam,
with flowing hair and time's embrace,
lightning dances, thunder drums,
seas enraged, the storm alive,
ripping trees from Mother Earth,
found will be the one you seek,
yet his time in the hourglass wanes,
in the sands, his fate is sealed,
by this chant, love's path revealed.
from love comes the son,
from the son comes—"

The words stop, and their eyes snap from a pure ivory white to an endless abyss of black. Aryana recognizes the change.

"Death comes for the son—"

The shaman's eyes snap back to an ivory white, and she begins foaming at the mouth. Bright red blood ran from her eyes. Her body collapses, and she falls to the ground with a hard thud. As she begins convulsing violently, her eyes collapse into her face,

"AAHHH!!" Aadrika screams in pain, grabbing her face with both hands. As she screams, she begins choking. The guttural noises seemingly consume Aryana's mind, and Aadrika begins unconsciously shaking on the ground.

"Ahhhhh!" Aryana shrieks, stunned by the situation; her body is motionless, and tears flow from her eyes as she notices pink and red spatter coming out of the foam in the shaman's mouth.

"Dear god!" Orenda shouts as she enters the densely smokey tent and quickly picks up a young Aryana, attempting to shield the child's eyes from witnessing this further.

Hearing the shrieks and cries from across the tribal homestead, Wohali panics, knowing his sister's reading was this night, and runs to her aid,

"What has happened?!" Her youthful brother asks, running from the darkness.

Petrified, Orenda can barely speak,

"Your sister... the shamans... something... something went wrong... terribly wrong..." she collapses to the ground. Her eyes are unable to void what they have just witnessed. She breaks down and cries, still holding a young Aryana in her arms.

***

October 1750
Nassau, New Providence

Jolts of lightning and thunder crash along the horizon, snapping Aryana's concentration, pulling her back to reality and far away from her ever-persistent day-drifting memories, no matter how distant the days grow.

Nassau in the fall was beautiful when there wasn't a thunderstorm rumbling overhead, but even then, she appreciated the grim beauty. Aryana is a stunning beauty in her own right. She has gorgeous green eyes with long lashes attached, and she sits atop high cheekbones with thick brown hair flowing to her lower back.

"Aryana, come now, the rain is near," Wohali hollers, concerned.

Scanning, she investigates the sky above and drops her eye-line to the horizon. The dark blue ocean ebbs and flows with the thunder crashing within the argumentative clouds. Not wanting to leave the shore, she replies,

"Soon, brother," her voice is relaxed.

"Soon? We must get in the cottage! This storm will tear this island in half!" he shouts as the wind picks up and the dark clouds consume the light sky.

"Soon," she repeats, and her mind drifts to the words she once heard,

> *'Soon, on the shores where spirits roam,*
> *with flowing hair and time's embrace,*
> *lightning dances, thunder drums,*
> *seas enraged, the storm alive,*
> *ripping trees from Mother Earth,*
> *found will be the one you seek,*
> *yet his time in the hourglass wanes,*
> *in the sands, his fate is sealed,*
> *by this chant, love's path revealed.'*

"Aryana, you're foolish! Nothing changes with you; these trading trips are not for you to stand in thunderstorms; how many times can you do this!?" He condemns her and walks inland toward the row of shore cottages.

Damned shamans and their sorcery scared her mind, he thought to himself as he challenged the wind with each step back to the cottage.

Piercing the ocean, lightning flashes, immediately followed by deep thunder crashes in the clouds as the rain falls. The storm's chaos is soothing the woman's soul as her feet embed themselves in the sand. To her right, she sees an odd image along the shore. A man lands a small rowboat on the beach, struggling to drag it through the sand.

Intrigued, Aryana bundles up her cloak and walks through the storm toward him. Moments later, she stopped a few yards away and watched the man. He smiles slightly as he notices her from the corner of his eye, not trying to display his exertion with the boat.

"Enjoying the struggle, are we?" His words navigate their way through the rain, still pulling the rowboat through the sand.

"Actually, yes," she answers shyly.

He chuckles,

"Well then, don't allow my interruption. Carry-on."

Blonde hair flows from under his black tricorn hat, resting atop his broad shoulders. His large frame showcased his strength as he hauled the 150-pound wooden rowboat further inshore. Aryana watched as he pulled it far enough inland that the tide wouldn't affect it, finally falling to his backside,

"Ah," he exhaustingly lets out.

"Stranger, may I ask why you are rowing in the rain?" she asks as she puts her cloak hood over her head.

"Well, *stranger*, it wasn't raining when I launched off the northeast island, just there," he says, lifting his arm through the raindrops, pointing at a smaller outer island northeast of Nassau.

"You've seemed to avoid my inquiry..."

The man lifts his head and looks up at her, unaffected by the wind and rain, completely dismayed at her statement but impressed by the beautiful and dynamic female; he laughs,

"Well, aren't you determined to know my business?"

"Not your business, but why go rowing when there is a storm on the horizon unless rowing is your business... in which case I'd say you're succeeding," she aptly answers with a slight smile.

Revealing his commanding figure, the man stands up at six-foot-three inches, entranced by the beautiful woman; he can barely let out the words,

"Why am I rowing in the rain? Indeed, that does require answering. But the more important question to me is why such a thing of beauty as yourself is standing on the beaches of Nassau in a disastrous storm, lurking over a man rowing ashore. There are vile men, drunkards, and vagrants running about... but no... I run into... you?"

The feeling between the two was immediately magnetic.

She smiles, "Indeed, that does require answering... but I wouldn't say I am lurking. I am merely interested in a man who chooses to travel in storms when it is clear that it could sink your vessel and leave its captain with nothing but an oar to float on."

"Aye; storms indeed swallow ships with regular persistence... but..."

He steps close to her, and his aura welcomes her in. Heavy raindrops falling from the black skies break apart as they land on him, ricocheting on her. The storm seems to pause, if only for a moment. Her green eyes shoot toward his, and they lock,

"I'm compelled to confess that I am being tracked by men who wish to see my end," he states calmly and frankly.

Unsure of his revealing comment but sure of his aura, trusting the man, she says, "Well, let's see that they fail their task."

He smiles, "Aye, let's see that they do."

She turned inland in the direction in which she had come just as the storm began to pick back up. Her brother was already inside their cottage, and she followed the path with the mysterious man trailing. The heavy rains and howling wind blend perfectly with the booming crashes of the shore waves. She looked back at the man and noticed he walked with a purpose. He was on alert and seemingly awaiting a fight.

The wooden door on the brick building is flung open from the wind, allowing rain to douse the entry. Aryana removes her cloak hood and makes way for the burly, blonde-haired man to enter. He closes the door behind him, shutting out the storm.

"Good to see your return," Wohali said to Aryana and looked at the man behind her, "I see you found some treasure in the sand." Clearly, he was displeased by her newfound companion.

"Treasure? That is yet to be determined." She replies with a sly smile, looking back at the soaking wet man.

She releases the knot of her hooded cloak and hangs it on the coat rack. Walking past her brother, she walks to the fireplace and sits near it, warming herself up.

"Who is this man?" Wohali asks Aryana in their native tongue, disregarding the blonde man standing near the door.

She looks at her brother and looks at the blonde man,

"He was rowing between the islands in the storm and needed somewhere to stay. I offered him shelter and food. He is harmless," she lies, trying to ease her older brother.

He scoffs at her, walks directly in front of the blonde man, and speaks clear English,

"I've yet to know your name," he says, annoyed, "Are you a King's man or a free soul?"

"I'd like to think I am a free soul, but we all serve someone or something, do we not? I believe in me, so I serve myself..." he pauses and looks at the woman, "but I sense that changing. My name is John Young, and I was once a lieutenant in the Royal Navy until I denied King George II an item I carry—"

"The King is a snake who speaks from his tail, so he may save his mouth for striking," Wohali adds dryly, watchfully looking at the man.

Recognizing he was saying too much, he stopped and spoke directly to the question,

"I am no king's man."

Aryana is genuinely taken aback by his statement, validating what he said on the shore.

"I am Aryana, and this is my brother Wohali. We are in Nassau for trade, departing from the north Georgia hills; we make this voyage every few years."

As she speaks, it's soft, and John notices she is well-spoken, with a sense of wisdom in her tone. He removes his tricorn, and the puddled water falls from the depressions on top of his hat as he places it over his heart and half bows.

"It is an honor to formally meet you, ma'am, although you never answered my question as to why you walked down the beach to watch me come ashore?" He smiles.

"The storm told me to wait. I did until I saw you in your rowboat, and it seemed I found what I was waiting for," she smiles back, determined to cover her true motivations; she carries her fate and experiences closer as she covets their secrecy.

"Eh," her brother sighs, turning back, "Sounds like nonsense to me. But then again, since we were children, everything was nonsense," Wohali says, extending his right hand to greet the man,

"Welcome, John Young."

A Meeting Unknown

August 1771

Boston, Massachusetts

The narrow, rough road leading into Boston, or the neck of Boston, was silent in the twilight hours. The black greatcoat is buttoned to his nose while the leather reins rest tightly between the musket and his fingers.

"Damned cold," he states to the black mare as a chill makes its way down his spine. He hated the cold.

The greatcoat has served multiple purposes since leaving home, but the most important one has been providing him warmth.

Upon entering the raucous town, he noticed pockets of prostitutes and off-duty soldiers huddled around the entrances of brothels on the back alley streets.

"Deviants thrive at night, and tonight is no different. Let's keep our wits about us," he reminds Raven.

He knows his plan is a bit pieced-together and not one of the most well-thought-out ideas... but he knows nothing of this town or its people, so inquiring about a prominent city leader shouldn't be too much of a stress. And if any information were to be spread around, it would be at one of these brothels or taverns.

Once through the neck, the city opened up. '*Orange Street*,' Adahy read on the street sign as he maneuvers Raven through the people. Homes with shops mixed between became more apparent as he furthered deeper into the populated city. It had a certain feel to it, as if there was a looming cloud, eternally graying the atmosphere and chilling the air.

"Whoa, girl, here is good," he tells the black mare, looking at a densely populated tavern. Adahy guides Raven to the hitching post and dismounts.

Once off the mighty horse, he secured his gear in the saddlebags and ensured he was armed for anything. He places his forehead on Raven's head and sarcastically smiles, saying,

"Cover me, girl."

The horse neighs, seemingly replying to Adahy. He unbuttons the top button of his greatcoat, opens it up to his chin, and walks toward the tavern entrance. '*The Green Dragon Tavern,*' he read as he approached. The group of redcoats and women are outside drunkenly, frolicking as he slips into the hall unnoticed.

Inside, the tavern was clouded with pipe smoke, laughter, and constant cheers. Bicorns and tricorns blended with powdered wigs between the men and women. The atmosphere couldn't have been richer, a contrasting difference to the calm atmosphere of the late-night outside. Adahy made his way to a space at the bar top. Before he could get his hand up to order, the barkeep spoke,

"Coffee, tea, ale, cider, rum, Madeira? We tend to carry it all."

"Madeira," Adahy replies, immediately recognizing the tavern's political alignment by the man offering coffee before all else. In his experiences, those who offer tea before rum or coffee are Tories or loyalists.

Adahy unbuttons a second button on his greatcoat, allowing him to drink smoothly. He has been craving the subtly sweet Portuguese wine since Charleston.

"Aye, sir, coming right up," the barkeep answers with a spirited tone and grabs a bottle of wine, emptying the remaining contents into a large mug for Adahy, "I am Alan Bismarck, the barkeep and local observant of all in this here tavern. If you don't mind the inquiry, what brings you to Boston, young patron?"

"I do mind," Adahy replies plainly, becoming slightly annoyed.

"Well, sir, my apologies," Alan adds as he tosses the empty bottle onto the ground.

"But you might know how to help me, or at least point me to the person who can," Adahy states, resting two schillings on the bar top.

Confused but interested, the unpleasant-looking barkeep stops his cleaning and leans on the bar toward Adahy with his eyes on the coin, "You have my attention."

Cautiously but firmly, Adahy speaks, "Where can I find a man named Thomas Young?"

With the slightest wince, the barkeep shifts his body slightly and softly speaks, moving his eyes from the coin to Adahy, "Do you mean retired Major, now local committee leader, Thomas Young?"

"Yes, I do," Adahy responds directly, pulling his tobacco pouch and pipe out of the greatcoat side pocket.

"The information I have might be worth some coin... If you're willing to pay for one question or one would assume," Alan Bismarck adds slyly.

"This would be true if I were dim. Unfortunately, barkeep, I am not and will not pay you more than I offered.

You have profited nicely from me in these last moments. Do not let them be your last," he suggests sternly to the barkeep, lighting his pipe with a candle.

"Right, you are. I know of a man who knows him. Lives down the street, and I can get him tonight. Meet me out back in 20 minutes," his voice cracked while he spoke, eyeing his coin.

"Very well," Adahy replies, and with his next breath, pipe firmly wedged in the corner of his mouth, he pulls the long-awaited smoke into his lungs.

The exchange of information was rough. Adahy knew he couldn't trust the barkeep. Immediately, Adahy was cautious about exposing himself to the barkeep and others around, but the tavern patrons were all drunk, and it was a late night. It was a risk Adahy was willing to take for no other reason than he had no specific starting point for locating Thomas Young.

The smoke brings inner peace within him, and he finally feels some semblance of nearing the completion of his task. Adahy spends the next several minutes finishing his tobacco bowl and Madeira before walking to the side door and avoiding the congested front entrance. Once outside, the chilly night air is prominent, and Adahy rebuttons his greatcoat to the top.

This isn't right; he notices an object move sharply in his peripherals.

SMACK

Darkness envelops his mind as he falls to the ground, unconscious.

***

Faneuil Hall

With youthful vigor and optimistic endeavor, he replies, "Thomas, I think what you're trying to say is that we need to be more selective?"

The larger-built, silver-haired man replies, "I think you need to be more thorough on your selection process of whom you associate your dealings with. That last thing we need is a rat or hole in your operations on the wharf..."

A middle-aged man with light brown hair interjects, "Thomas, the Hancock Wharf is a valuable asset to the continental cause... you often use it for your own operations."

"Aye, Joseph, you are not wrong. But John..." Thomas pauses and looks at the man, "We need Boston to stay a tinderbox... our operations must continue, and you must keep the veil in place."

"I know, Thomas... that's how it's been, and that's how we will keep it. The protection you have afforded over the years and your willingness to subvert the Crown loyalists has been remarkable... I do not intend to lose ground where we have earned it."

"Good, then you shall not," Thomas replies, satisfied with the man's answer.

Knock, *Knock*

"Who is it?" Joseph asks sharply.

"Sir, there is a runner here who claims he needs to speak to Thomas," his nearly muffled words come from outside the room.

Thomas leans over and opens the door, "What is it? What do they want?"

"He said Alan Bismarck has apprehended an odd-looking native Indian who was asking for you... He knows your entire name," the younger man in the doorway replied calmly.

A *Native, for me?* he thinks, as a peculiar look emerges on his face as he looks oddly at the others in the room.

"I'll be there shortly; have them question him until I arrive."

"Yes, sir," the man replies and closes the door.

The room became quiet as the newly arrived news settled on the three men's ears. John is the first to speak,

"A native? What do you make of this?"

"Aye... cautious and careful approach. Ensure no one speaks of this upon my leave until I have a full understanding of the motivations of this native."

"Of course," Joseph replies.

"You know your requests are always respected," John adds.

Sunlight breaks through the linen cloth, and Thomas stands, "All right, John... Joseph... I will see you soon, be safe."

"Stay safe, Thomas," Joseph's words are filled with sincerity.

"Aye, be safe out there, Top," John adds as Thomas nods to the two men and exits the room.

***

Tavern Barn
Boston, Massachusetts

Ugh, fuck, my head, he thinks, as the pain throbs the back of his skull.

A muffled wool bag covered his head holding within pig shit smell and hay scent filling his nose. As he tries to move, he recognizes immediately that he is tied tightly to a wooden post. Trying to stand, his feet are conjoined by a securely fastened rope. Aggressively trying to wriggle free, his wrists are too tightly constrained.

"Psst, he's awake, I see," one of the fuzzy figures remarks to the other.

Both figures disrupt the filtered, bronzed light coming through the wool bag as he attempts to open his eyes.

"Fuck you," his voice cracks, mixing with a cough.

"Shut your mouth!" One of the captors shouts, aggressively snatching the wool bag off Adahy's head.

"Wake up, sunshine!" The other captor shouts with a crooked smile, tossing a bucket of rainwater on his newly exposed face.

"Fuck!" he shouts and is immediately silenced with a quick thrust to the ribs from the fatter man's musket buttstock.

Adahy began to gain his bearings and recognized it was the morning. The sun's position told him that immediately. He also noticed that his weapons and tools were nowhere to be found. Panicking, he shrugged his shoulders, trying to wiggle enough to feel the talisman chain on his neck; he did. Relief then wafts over him. It doesn't linger as he thinks of Raven. Panic ensues again,

"If you harmed my mare, I will rip your internals from out of your anus and hang you by your balls," Adahy declares sternly, furiously looking up at the two worthless militiamen.

"Listen here, you fucking Injin! I don't know who told you—"

Light from outside immediately canvasses the small barn, and standing in the light is a man. He's taller than most, with a silver beard and broad shoulders. His square face carried a prominent scar. No doubt from his time in the wars prior. It was nearly from his forehead to his chin, being thickest just above and under his left eye. A look of indignation scowled upon the room, resting on the old man's hardened face. Immediately, he noticed blood along the backside of the tied-up man's neck and blood dripping from his mouth.

With force, the older man grabs both men by their jacket collars angrily,

"You fucking imbeciles. This man was to be questioned… that is all. Now, you have harmed the probity of Massachusetts with your hasty actions… you should be ashamed of yourselves," he states rigidly, looking to them for nonexistent answers he knows they do not have.

Humiliation covers their faces as they look toward the floor.

"We… we were questioning—" one of them tries to mouse out of his mouth.

"You may both take your leave. Incompetent disgraces… you're lucky I don't have you on a transport ship tonight headed to the African coast," the old man says, thrusting them out of the barn door and into the morning light.

"Yes, sir. Sorry, sir," they say in unison as the man closes the door.

"Fucking savages. These militiamen get more torpid with each new wave of recruitment. And they say the natives are the savages, but I've yet to see the natives beat a man that's tied up," the old, silver-bearded man proclaims with genuine benevolence.

"Then you've never met true savages," Adahy utters viciously, spitting out the remaining blood in his mouth.

It's the back of his head that still is throbbing, establishing a pounding headache. A thick rope is wrapped tightly around his ankles, and his wrists become burned and bloody from his countless movements trying to wiggle free.

'*They must've caught up with me from the Santee River Tavern,*' he thought.

The man is well-dressed in exquisite clothing, his hair is well-maintained, and he comes off educated and affluent. Adahy, unsure how to feel, watches him grab a small barrel and sit in front of him,

"First off, let me apologize for those men's behavior. Their treatment of you was not my intention nor my wishes. I am sorry," he said genuinely and continued with a half-smile, measuring the tied-up man. He examined him, and there was a familiarity to him, "Well, you're either dumb or brave. Who sent you, young man? Who is your employer, and why are you inquiring about Thomas Young in Boston?"

Still thinking of Raven, Adahy quickly spews out with a murderous undertone, "If you touch my horse, I am going to kill you and whoever you employ."

"The black mare is untouched, still hitched where you left her," he affirms plainly but deepens his voice, becoming firmer, "Now answer my question, boy. Who sent you, and why are you inquiring about Thomas Young?" The words leave the scarred, silver-bearded man's mouth in a tone of increasing impatience.

"I have no employer. I am a man of my own trade and skill. Thomas Young is my father's brother and my blood uncle... I intend to seek him out and uncover the truths about my father," Adahy says, hoping the truth is his best route to his uncle.

The man stops moving and sits straight up, fixing his posture, clearly becoming uneasy and uncomfortable,

"I assure you; you must be mistaken," he states directly.

Adahy looks at him, slowly realizing the older man he's speaking with is Thomas Young. He was tall before he sat down and carried himself well. He stood in black leather knee-high boots with tan trousers and his linen work shirt was cleanly tucked in, all being secured with a three-inch gold buckle with a leather belt. The elegant overcoat was an emerald color and finely made and slightly bunched as the older man sat in near disbelief with his eyes falling victim to a lost trance...

"Thomas," Adahy says plainly, attempting to seize the momentary lull in the man's attention and get a reaction from him.

He flinches and looks at Adahy.

He is the right age and right build, and he has an aura to him, Adahy thinks.

"You are Thomas..." the young man implies.

With a deep breath, almost unwilling to admit Adahy is correct, he exhales and speaks, "I am."

As the words leave his mouth, Adahy inspects every detail of the man as if he were seeing his father for the first time. Acknowledging and analyzing his features, unable to ignore how similar they were to his own. Adahy, never seeing his father or his father's side of the family can see a clear resemblance with Thomas before him.

"I have no nephew, and I have no time for tricks and games! Give up this ruse and explain yourself," he says, his tone becoming darker.

Thomas, not wanting to accept Adahy's statement, is adamant about getting the true intentions out of the captive. Still, there is a familiarity with the young man that he cannot remove from his mind.

"I am the son of John Young."

"That is impossible!" he shouts, standing abruptly, kicking the small barrel he was sitting on.

"I sit here before you, tied up like a pig. Your nephew. I was born in Nassau in 1751," Adahy replies adamantly, unphased by the man's demonstrative demeanor.

"Lieutenant John Young was killed in 1751, so it would be wise of you to stop talking," the man asserts, now with his face red and angry.

"My Charleville 1728 was my fathers and his fathers before him... your father, if you are Thomas Young, like you claim you are, your brother is John Young, sons of Edward Young. I speak no lies. I am here, clearly, with honest intentions."

The prominent Bostonian stood silent for moments upon hearing his long-dead father's name,

"How do you know this information?"

"Again, sir, my father is John Young. I do not lie," Adahy says firmly.

Frustrated, the older man walks out of the barn, turns to the prisoner's muskets, and grabs the Charleville. To his surprise, there is an engraved *"E.Y."* on the buttstock plate. Thomas then grabs the captive's gear, goes through it, finds a black tricorn, eerily familiar with the one his brother wore,

Interesting... he thought and snatched up the woven leather chest rig; within it securely fastened is a 1739 sea-service pistol, engraved on the pistol grip, *"J.Y."*

Is it possible? he questions himself, admiring the long-forgotten musket that was once his father's and holding the two pieces that were once his younger brothers.

Inside the barn, Adahy's head was throbbing. Regardless of being tied up, he was relieved he was in the presence of his uncle. Even if he was hogtied to a post, he still was youthfully optimistic about the outcome of the day.

Blinding light breaks apart his thoughts, and the door shuts behind the large Thomas Young. He is holding Adahy's tricorn, pistol, and musket and walks over, setting up the smaller barrel again to sit down upon. Once down, the man places the faded black tricorn atop Adahy's head.

"In the name of Elmir N., my god, boy…" Thomas exclaims with a smile on his face, "You…" he chuckles a bit before continuing, "You look like John," he admits.

At that moment, he stood up, removed a small blade, and cut the thick rope restraints around Adahy's wrists and ankles. Once finished, he sits back down in front of Adahy.

"What is your name?" He asks smoothly.

"Adahy," he states, grabbing his wrists, rubbing his wounds, and getting all the excess rope off his skin.

"Tell me everything you know about John Young, Adahy."

"He's my father, but I only know of him through the brief stories my mother and Uncle Wohali told. He died a few full moons after my birth. He was a sailor of sorts and loved my mother. That is all I know," Adahy answers firmly.

"His attitude resonates in you, Adahy. It is good to meet you formally. I am, indeed, Thomas Young. You know… It's uncanny. Now that I see it, I cannot unsee it," Thomas tells Adahy with a soft chuckle.

"Walk with me, Adahy. I want to know what you know of John Young and of yourself and where you come from. Uncovering a newly found relative is a new experience for me. I don't want to lose the opportunity," Thomas says, walking toward the barn door exit.

Looking around the barn to see if there is anything of his on the ground, he scans the area, then follows his uncle and exits the barn.

Boston City was much more alive in the daytime than its nighttime counterpart. Shops were open; apothecaries, shoemakers, and more were all receiving business. Small but loud paperboys were on the corners, soldiers were marching to and from outposts, and people were everywhere, all types of people; it was a living and breathing city. Ropemakers, blacksmiths, and saddlers all worked their tools, ensuring productive trade and commerce for the city.

Carts and wagons rumble past, wheels groaning over the uneven streets as merchants call out their wares—fishmongers sell fresh-caught cod and lobster while farmers display bunches of carrots, apples, and squashes. Shops spill their goods out into the street—tailors' bolts of homespun fabric, blacksmiths' displays of nails and tools, and apothecaries' jars of powdered herbs and elixirs. Lively chatter fills the air as tradesmen haggle over prices and news of the day, often murmuring about "the British" with wary glances, whether the topic is taxes, soldiers, or the occasional brawl that breaks out over the latest decree from London.

Thomas leans down to pick up all of Adahy's gear, weapons, and tools, handing them to the young man,

"I apologize for my men and their treatment of you… when strangers appear inquiring about me… well, I must see it through. Too many assassins, schemers, and agents of evil roaming these streets to take inquiries lightly," he replies apologetically to Adahy, genuinely upset that his nephew was treated so harshly.

"Aye, thank you for that, but it is nothing I cannot handle or haven't already handled in the past," Adahy says keenly, reaching for his gear from Thomas.

Taking the leather chest rig, he begins to fashion it back to his body, placing his head through the neck loop and buckling the two straps on his backside, fastening it tightly to his body. He smoothly holsters the 1739 Sea Service pistol into the empty holster across his chest; now, both of his Sea Service pistols sit tightly secured across his rig. Next, he straps his belt around his waist; it carries his tomahawk, a few secured flying talon blades, and some smaller musket tools on a silenced key ring. Finally, he takes the greatcoat from his uncle's extended hand and throws it on. Almost immediately, it conceals his chest rig.

"Where is all this from?" Thomas asks, curiously examining the chest rig and its design.

"My tribe. They gifted it all to me before my expedition," he said casually, already becoming more comfortable around his uncle.

"I am impressed. It looks useful and efficient," Thomas says, now with empty hands.

"It is… I have grown to being forgetful it is on most days, it also allows me to conceal my pistols and knives without drawing attention to myself," Adahy replies proudly.

Impressed with the young man's ability to let go and move, Thomas thought Adahy admirable, and he was truly happy for the first time in a long time.

"Come with me; let's take a walk," Thomas motions for Adahy to follow him as he begins walking into the heart of the city.

Before Adahy steps off, he makes it a point to see Raven, "They didn't harm you, did they, girl?" Adahy asks the mare, petting her neck as she's noticeably happy to be back in his presence.

"I know, I'm okay. I'll be back in a bit," he speaks to the horse, pressing his forehead against hers, and rubs her snout before turning around to catch up to Thomas.

"Adahy, I must confess, I am not sure where your path leads you, but Boston is no place to settle down and start a family. Well, at least not these days. The crown has taxed so many items trying to clear their debt that it is straining the people. And the people are getting angry," Thomas remarks.

"I have no intentions of starting a family. My aim is to uncover who my father was and why he is no longer alive. That is my sole purpose, to know why."

"The story of your father is a long one. He was infamous, Adahy. Have you ever heard of '*Sailor Johnnie*?' or heard the shanty?" Thomas asks Adahy as they walk through the bustling streets of Boston.

Sailor Johnnie, Adahy thought, *what in the world?*

"No, I have not," Adahy answers smoothly.

"Your father was a magnificent sailor. He sailed nearly across every ocean on the run from bounty hunters and privateers hired by King George II. His journey became a legend among the Royal Navy and civilian sailors alike… he was a great man, Adahy," Thomas explains and continues, "He was cunning, witty, and sarcastic when he wasn't supposed to be. Always pushing the envelope, trying to explore more, go higher, sail faster, shoot better… he challenged me many times as an adolescent. Truly, a remarkable human being, and I don't just say that because he is my brother," Thomas admits.

Adahy had never heard anyone explain his father like this to him before, outside of the brief mentions from his mother, and smiled, ecstatic to hear more.

"And you know?" Thomas stops walking and looks at Adahy, "You are the spitting image of John! His thin, stringy blond hair, square jaw, broad shoulders, and tall, strong frame… as well as your seemingly carefree attitude, resembles his more than I think I'd like to admit!" Thomas says with an authentic smile, knowing it was more than he led on; the young man had a look in his eye, a look that heavily imitated John…

"Adahy—" he begins to speak but is interrupted swiftly by a young rider. The man is brown and not of English descent. His skin was nearer to Adahy's color. He approached on horseback with a spare horse in tow.

"Mr. Young!" The young rider shouts, pulling his tan horse to a stop, causing the second horse to stop, "You are needed… now, sir," in a seemingly cheerful tone.

Noticing his uncle's demeanor shifting, he can tell this is an uncommon occurrence. Looking at the young rider, Adahy notices the man's eyes are speaking to Thomas with a concerned look.

"Ah, Nimish, my noble companion, why are you here, in the streets? Why am I needed?"

"Oi, good day, sir. We have a complication," Nimish replies in a now more serious, authentic tone.

"Aye, all right, I'll be there; tell the others," Thomas says to the young rider; he turns to Adahy,

"I must go. Please grab your horse and gear from the old barn and meet me back at my home. It is a three-story property on the corner of Green Lane and Lyna Street. You cannot miss it," Thomas tells his newfound nephew.

"I will," he agrees.

Thomas had a stern visage, nodded to Adahy, and turned with Nimish, the young rider, and his tan horse. In one seamless motion, Thomas mounted the spare steed, and away they went. Adahy watched as they rounded the corner of the nearest brick building rapidly.

He was a bit thrown off by the abrupt end to the conversation, but he knew Thomas must be a busy man... As he roamed through Boston back to Raven, his mind filled with wonderment and intrigue about his father sailing his ship, unfurling the sails, loosely hanging on the shrouds, and eyeing the incoming day. The young man's mind roamed, thinking of all the things *'Sailor Johnnie'* must've done to accrue such a legend.

Elegance in Evil

Spring, 1756

Mayfair, London

"Agador! Make your way to me this instant!" She shouted into the large estate, her echoes trapped within the myriads of rooms and hallways, "That damned boy will be the death of me," she said quietly.

"Your parents will return today from their trans-Atlantic business trip, and we must leave to see them! Now is not the time to be troublesome," her shrill voice echoes throughout the estate.

Grayish-blue clouds allowed little sunlight to make its way, creating a dismal day.

"Agador!! Stop hiding and reveal yourself! This is not a time for games; we must depart with haste!" The young woman shouted as she walked frantically looking for the young boy.

As she rounds a nearby corner, the boy, with thick black hair, bright blue eyes, and pale skin, jumps out from behind a study chair, "Boo!"

Startled, the young housemaid falls backward, "Bloody hell, Agador!"

Her face glows red with anger, and her eyes glare at the boy, "That will be the last time you ever scare me! You have wasted too much time with your trivial games!"

She stands, brushes herself off, and, with force, grabs the young man by the hair, "We must leave!"

"Let go of me!" he shouts, violently trying to wiggle free of her grasp.

"No! You will adhere to my rule and listen when I say it is time to depart."

The boy, in pain from her tight grasp on his hair, removes his small blade from his waist and, with as much force as he can muster, swings his arm into the housemaid's body repeatedly. After the second or third swing, his hair is released, and she begins stumbling,

"Agador, what?" She asks, horrified, coughing up blood.

Out of breath, Agador looks up and sees her holding her stomach. Blood begins turning her white dress red, and her face is unsure of what has happened. His artic-blue eyes watch her stumble, watch her bleed, and a sensation overwhelms his body.

"You'll not touch me again!" He says softly, with a slight grin.

Her eyes swell up with tears, and she falls to her knees; she's trying to speak, but nothing comes out. Enraged, Agador tightens his grip on the blade, running at full force toward the maid. Agador stabs the maid repeatedly.

It's warm. This feeling, the blood, the hatred.

Moments went by, but his gaze upon the dead body didn't cease. The boy did not blink. Slowly, his eyes look to his small hands, covered in her warm blood, and he smiles.

Minutes passed, becoming hours, and the sun retired for the day, making way for nightfall. The Ivey Estate was quiet, and Agador enjoyed the silence. Hooves impacting the cobblestone road outside intercepted this silence, and within moments, his parents were standing with Agador, appalled by what they were seeing.

"My boy!" she shouts, dropping to her knees and grabbing the young Agador for a hug.

His father, a royal cousin to the King, a member of the King's Guard, and a prominent military commander, was not one for Agador's pity.

"Annabel, this is the second housemaid he has now bled out in our estate. Leave the boy be! He is a demon walking," Abraham says spitefully, "I refuse to have you feed him with sympathy when he commits these atrocious acts."

"You will stop, boy," his father says as his voice rises, grabbing a young Agador by the hair, "You will stop! You are an Ivey! Royalty, not evil, is in your blood, boy!" He says forcefully, lifting the boy up to stand on his feet.

"Abraham, stop!!" Annabel screams, trying to stop her husband from killing their son.

With his open palm, the man violently smacks Agador across the face. With enough force, the boy goes unconscious.

Abraham disdainfully looks at his son and back to Annabel, "The King need not know of this. I will have to speak to Henry again to ensure it does not spill over into the palace and become the focus of conversation," his deep voice dominates as Annabel lowers her head in acceptance.

***

July 1771
London, England

His quarters within St. James Palace were an intimate place where he often entertained others. Oddities, sexual deviants, and Agador's vices were found being exercised in this room. Two women exit his room and make their way into the main hallways of the palace, trying to hide their clearly visible wounds.

"Another day... ugh," he groans as the door closes behind the two women. A faint sound creeps into his quarters, and he hears approaching footsteps. His rage stoked,

More company after the whores left. Fuck, he thinks.

His annoyance grew. With each step echoing outside his chamber in the hall, his chest gets hot, and his blood boils hotter the louder and closer the steps get.

Disturbing my peace. Disturbing me. For what? Nuisances.

"Major General Ivey, sir," the young corporal says, half out of breath, coming to a halt in the doorway of the major general's quarters. Rolling his legs over his bed, he stands. Agador Ivey did not have time for indulgences, especially if those indulgences didn't include violence.

This better be good, he thinks to himself.

Quickly stretching, he walks to the door and opens it.

"We have a problem," the young corporal said to the stern major general,

"For bloody fucking's sake, what is the fucking issue now, boy!? Stop eluding around the subject. Be direct and concise with your words," Agador shouts.

"There is a situation with your cousin, Sir Alec. He has been found…. Has been found stea--"

"Spit it out! God dammit, man!"

"Been found stealing from the king's palace, and his majesty preferred you handled this task personally."

"Sir Alec… cancerous scum," his words carry a disgusted tone, and he takes a sip from his tea from the night prior. His eyes move swiftly to his weapon table, followed by words cold as ice,

"I'm on my way."

A smile slowly creases onto his freshly shaven face as he admires the contents on the table.

"Which one of you is deserving of play today?" He whispers to the handful of sharp knives, loaded pistols, and torture tools.

Agador's arctic blue eyes get lost in the steel's form, shape, and possibilities. He studied the sharpness and every detail of each blade. Reality falls away as his mind wanders. Thinking back on his boyhood memories, they pulled him to it, and he chose the smallest blade on the table. It was one he rarely used anymore at this age, but his memories pulled him to it, a tortured experience from his childhood.

"Yes, you will do," he says as he picks up the smaller, more intimate blade.

With the blade in hand, he stood up in his chambers and exited the room, making his way to the Throne room.

As an average-sized young Englishman born in 1745 in western London, he had to fight a lot. His name demanded respect, but most feared his unexpected nature. Most times, he would gain it through violence. Early on, he made his way up the ranks in the shadows as the King's fiercely loyal attack dog. His thirst for violence fueled his hatred, and his childhood fueled the violence he imposed on others; with this, he thrived on the fear he incited.

The crown was the reference point for the foundation of Agador's existence. Whatever His Majesty requests, he fulfills. His reputation was well-known throughout the royal ranks as a ruthless and bloodthirsty officer who would kill his own blood before betraying the crown, for in Agador's mind, without the crown, there would be no blood, and there would be no family, no country, or God. Ensuring the crown's safety and its success throughout time was his sole purpose and life's mission. The crown allowed Agador an outlet for his dark and evil desires; the King knew this all too well.

Sir Alec, what a waste of space, of life, riding the King's coattails for too long, and now what, stealing? Petty scoundrel, I am happy to be of service to my King.

***

Throne Room
St. James Palace, London

The King's throne room was extravagant and ever so grand, desperately trying to mimic the architecture of the French. As the Major-General entered the elegant space, King George III sat with a face full of anger and disposition. Two of the palace guards open the doors, and the Major General enters quickly with a purpose and bows to the King.

"Your Majesty, you requested me."

"Yes, Major-General Ivey. It seems Sir Alec has once again proved his worthlessness in this world. You'd think he would learn after so many mistakes," the King pauses…. And smacks his teeth,

"I would hang him in front of the palace for the little people to see that even royalty dies when you cross the Crown. Yet, I deferred and told the guards you would handle this situation since he is your cousin. End his petty existence, Agador," The King commands smoothly and directly.

"Yes, Your Majesty. It will be done." Agador replies with ice in his voice. He bows and turns around. Out of the corner of his eye, the glass case containing the Crown's royal artifact collection catches his eye.

Curious artifacts…

Of all the King's collections, the royal artifacts collection is one that the Major-General has always been skeptical of. Ever since being a boy, watching the hunters return. St. James Palace became divided between believers and non-believers. Rampant skepticism has been prominent in the palace since they returned with their relic, yet the ears of the King have seemingly avoided such conversations.

The Aureum Pentagonum… or is it? Only one shard was found and presented… could the child's stories be true?

As the King's Guard Commander, learning and exploring the Crown's history and artifact missions was his nature. But there was an ominously dark tone that followed the hunters since they arrived back from their hunt. They never seemed authentic. This moment is brief, and then his mind reverts back to the mission: Sir Alec.

Pathetic, he thinks, as he walks out of the throne room, looking forward to his meeting with Sir Alec.

***

Dungeon Gaol
St. James Palace, London

The staircase was dark and wet. When Agador arrives at the palace dungeon gaol, he finds Sir Alec sleeping in shackles. The pathetic man lies covered in hay in the barred cell.

"You two, fetch some air. It smells like shit down here," Agador tells the two sentry guards.

"Yes, sir!" They respond sharply and walk up the stone staircase to the courtyard.

He unlocks the door with one of the keys on his personal key ring, steps inside the cell, and closes the door behind him, locking it. The closing cell door wakes Sir Alec.

"What are you doing? Who are you? I swear it won't happen again!" Alec proclaims in a cracking, fearful voice with his eyes barely open.

Agador turns to face the man lying in the hay, revealing himself.

"Fuck… you frightened me, cousin. I thought you were someone else to do the King's bidding." He says, letting out a sigh of relief.

"Precisely. You should know better than to think relief upon seeing me. For I am the King's retribution." He says calmly, in an eerie tone, tightening his riding gloves and towering over the man in the hay with a look of death on his face.

"We are family, Agador! Your father is my blood!" Sir Alec proclaims, finally seeing the real Agador that people murmur in the shadows about.

"None of that matters, Alec; none of that has ever mattered. You are worthless scum, and it is time to cease your little life. You will not have a knight's funeral. You will not have a legacy to leave behind. You will not see tomorrow," Agador says calmly, squatting to get closer to Sir Alec in the hay.

"You see, it will be the highlight of my day, sliding this blade into your throat and watching the empty life leave your body."

Fear consumes him, and it shows on Sir Alec's face, which is more apparent than ever.

"Agador, please, you don't have to---"

The sharp edge enters the lower left side of Sir Alec's neck, and he stops talking, stunned, his eyes widen. The sound of the blade tearing through his throat reverberates through his open mouth.

"I always despised your soft little, pathetic life."

Agador thrusts the dagger to the opposite side of his neck, slicing his vertebrae and nearly decapitating the man. Blood sprays the immediate area and stains the Major-General's sleeve. After seconds, the blood stops pumping from the dead man's body, and Agador is relieved.

He cleans the blade on Sir Alec's robes and sheaths the weapon, standing up. He composes himself and collectedly turns around to the cell door, and with the key, he opens it, letting himself out of the cell. The ruthless man walks up the stone staircase, revealing the dreary, overcast day.

"You two, make sure your prisoner finds his way to the river," Agador commands the two sentry guards.

"Aye, sir!" They respond, then head downstairs.

The day has just reached noon, and Agador Ivey was set to meet with a Rear Admiral at the pub shortly.

No officer need be seen in a blood-stained uniform, he thinks.

With haste, he returned to his sleeping quarters to change his coat as Sir Alec's blood had stained most of his left sleeve.

The staunch officer didn't think twice about Sir Alec and his decision. The King made it easy for Agador. Any command from his majesty was an order from God. At least, that's how Agador viewed it, and he wasn't going to sway his beliefs. Within minutes, the Major-General was on horseback and traveling to the pub on the damp streets of London.

***

King's Royal Observatory
Greenwich, London

Lately, the King was found in solitude, ever curious and infatuated by the cosmos. Being overly meticulous, he found it a great outlet for his leisure to plot and chart the stars. It fostered a deep connection to prior rulers and kings. It was his space for peace and a space that brought him tranquility. It was just past nightfall, and he had come upstairs to view the star-filled sky through his telescope.

*Knock, Knock. *

"Oh, what is it?! I am busy!"

"Your Majesty, I bring you news from the colonies," Baron Richard Ashford says from his small, thin-lipped mouth, standing in the doorway.

"Do not disturb me with news from those 13 ungrateful things. I give them life, and they grouse, gripe, and whine at every chance they get," he says, calming his tone.

"I do believe you will want to hear this news, your Grace," he says to the King.

Annoyed by the intrusion, "Ugh, well, do tell Lord Chamberlain!"

"As you know, Ms. Napier was scheduled to depart Brookline Bay port with her son…" he stops, "Ahem, your son…"

"And where are they now? Downstairs?" The King asks carelessly, still eye to glass with his telescope.

The Baron swallows, "No, Your Majesty… they are missing…" he stops and continues, "If whispers are true, then they are believed to be dead."

His focus shifts, and he takes his face off the telescope, looking at the Lord Chamberlain of the King's Council, "Repeat the words you just spoke," he says sternly, hoping the words he just heard were untrue or misspoken.

"Ms. Napier and the child you fathered with her are missing. They are believed to be dead," the Lord Chamberlain states clearly.

They are believed to be dead, he thinks to himself, repeating the words over and over and over again.

"I do believe you are mistaken!" he shouts with fury.

"I will leave you to it then, your Grace," the Baron says as he slithers out of the observatory room.

Bewildered by what the old man said, the young King stands up; his blood begins to boil as his mind races, thinking of all the outcomes that could be the reality. Anxious and unable to contain himself, he snaps,

"Where is Major-General Agador Ivey?!!"

Furious with rage, his words carry weight and travel quickly, echoing throughout the Royal Observatory.

***

London, England

"As you said earlier, Major-General, the colonies are a tempered bunch, but by no means do they have the ability or mental wherewithal to mount a legitimate revolution against the crown and all its might." The older Rear-Admiral says confidently from across the table.

The pub is one for military officers and dates back a couple of hundred years. The stone walls blend well with the candlelight, creating a decent atmosphere in which to discuss business. The front door swings open, bringing in the natural overcast light and a royal guard walking into the pub. Silence fills the area. He enters, and with swift distinction, he notices whom he is looking for: the black-haired, blue-eyed King's Guard Commander.

"Major General Ivey, the King requests your presence immediately," the stern royal guard says.

Agador looks to the Rear Admiral, "Let us finish this conversation another time," He stands up, and the entire pub shifts its eyes in his direction. With purpose, the British officer exited the tavern.

Quickly, Agador rode, arriving in minutes. The palace gate opens as they notice his arrival. Royal hands take the reins from the Major General and hitch his horse to the hitching post. Agador swings his leg over and lands on the ground. Looking up,

"For you, I live," he says to himself and walks into the large entryway.

His life started as a young man fighting for King George II in far-off lands. Over the years, his fiery rage paid off in the business of violence. He surpassed his mentors and earned the rank of Major-General within the shortest time in British military history. At 26 years of age, he had the King's ear and was a close confidant and advisor to his majesty. His position near the King was controversial for the court, but the King insisted. His Majesty enjoyed the benefits of having a faithful guard dog.

The palace doors open, and Agador enters the throne room, "Your Majesty," he says as he bows his head gracefully.

"Yes, Major-General. I was pleased to hear that poor Sir Alec had found his way to the other side...." A slight smile creases his face, "good riddance if you ask me. Let us discuss why I called you here during your pub meeting." The King says, standing up from the throne and walking toward Agador. "There is ... a problem in the colonies."

"The colonies themselves are the problem, Your Majesty," Agador says with a full chest and a mind clouded with hate.

George III laughs, "Yes, they are," his genuine laughter ends, and his voice turns sinister,

"But we have a disturbing problem. A band of rebels has been sabotaging shipments leaving ports in the Massachusetts colony. An insubordinate cabal."

The King drops his head, and his tone changes from sinister to sorrowful,

"Whispers say they are 'the King's Bane,' although I have never given attention before because… well, why would a lion give any attention to a fly? This time, they have crossed a personal line…." He pauses, and Agador notices a tear run down his cheek,

"They killed my son…" The words clumsily fall out of his mouth, and the weight of them lands upon Agador like a boulder.

"Regardless, if he was never going to rule or even have any title, I wanted him. I wanted him in my life. He was my son. My son!" the King shouts angrily and continues,

"Before anything else that the courts say about adultery, he is my blood. And now he is dead… he *was* my blood!" He says as the anger mounts within him.

"I'll find them for you, and whatever you want me to do, I'll do. I am forever at your service, Your Majesty." Agador says, bowing again, feeling bad for his long-time friends' loss.

"Go to the colonies and find this band of rebels that call themselves the *'King's Bane'* and show them what a bane truly is, Major-General Ivey. You have my full support with whatever you need. I will see that you are untethered, unleashed, and can work freely to resolve this matter expeditiously. You have the King's Council blessing as well." The King's tone is dark and fierce as he knows Agador will handle the task.

"Yes, Your Majesty. I will not fail you, and I will take the personal best from the King's Guard to Boston to ensure this is handled properly." Agador says calmly. The mention of the King's Guard increases the Sovereign's tone.

"Good. See, it ended properly. You have my faith, Major-General," he says, walking back to his throne and sitting down.

The doors open behind Agador, and a few royal advisors enter the room. With them, the King's Council. *A filthy bunch, loaded with too much influence and not enough common smarts*, Agador thought, as he despised their existence. They were a group of old men who would corrupt their great king if it were not for the King's Guard, who had such a prominent role in his majesty's life. Agador bows and turns toward the exit. Thankful to be away from the council and with a new mission: Ending the '*King's Bane.*'

Family Ties

Boston, Massachusetts

Overlooking the mill dam on the North end of Boston, opposite the neck entering the city, sat a large property with various trees and enough space for gardens. Dissimilar to most properties in Boston. On the corners of Green Lane and Lyna Street was a three-story magnificent Georgian style with large glass pane windows, green window shutters, and a half wrap-around porch.

It was quite the home, Adahy thought. Out front, a small waist-high fence wrapped around the property, and it was a significant plot of land for such a compacted city.

Just outside the fence to the left was a covered hitching post with two militiamen standing guard outside the property gate. Neither of them was the men from earlier; Adahy discerned that immediately. He dismounted Raven and hitched her smoothly,

"That's it, girl, take a break," he says, placing his head on hers.

Turning to the brick home, Adahy walks toward the guarded gate.

"Good evening, sir," the one guard says, opening the wooden gate and allowing Adahy access to the walkway. He follows it, arriving at the front door, grabs the copper door knocker, and knocks.

A stunning middle-aged woman answers the door, not an inch past five feet in height, with light brown hair.

"Good evening, Adahy! Come on in," she politely welcomes him into the home, closing the door as he enters. Her attitude was that of genuine hospitality.

"Happy to meet you, Adahy. I am Mary Young, Thomas's wife," she said kindly, "Thomas will arrive shortly. He is ever engrossed in his work," she said politely, smiling.

"Likewise, but how do you know my name?" Adahy inquires, unsure of how the woman would already know who he was.

She laughs, "Well, you look like John, except those eyes, those you must take after your mother."

Adahy is filled with confusion. And his face shows it.

In a friendly tone with a smile,

"Ah, I know, he's always running around. Thomas was here about 15 minutes ago. He briefly explained the situation, and then he was off. Come with me. I'll see to it you get some food in you," she motions for him to follow her, and he does.

It has a warm atmosphere with white walls, wooden floors, and finely detailed carpentry, making up the beautiful home. Ornate crown molding hugs the walls in the corners, displaying their lavish taste. Shelves with trinkets, flowers, and random items Adahy has never seen sit atop them.

Following her into the kitchen area, he subtly inspects the home interior. Adahy notices a few hearthstones supporting an iron stove and brick oven. Copper pots and kettles hang from hooks on a rack connected to the ceiling.

As they enter the kitchen area. Mary makes her way to the wall of cabinets,

"Coffee?" She asks, grabbing the pot and coffee jar.

Sitting down at the nearest chair, his reply is happy, knowing the black water lifts his mood, alleviating his headache.

"Yes, ma'am, you have a beautiful home," he says, looking at the residence's interior.

"Thomas built it in 1745. We are proud to live here," she replies, finishing prepping the coffee.

Adahy could hear the front door of the house open and close, followed by approaching footsteps. Naturally, he was uneasy by the anticipation. As he sees the shadow approaching, he notices Mary smile and walk toward the hallway. *Thomas has returned*, he thought.

"Welcome home, dear," she says happily, giving Thomas an affectionate hug.

Thomas warmly embraces her back, and with a deep inhale, he speaks, "Ahhhhh, someone is making coffee!"

Mary steps back to the brewing drink, "Yes, I was just making Adahy here a cup of it. I'll pour you one, too."

"Thank you, my love, you are ever so thoughtful," he says sincerely.

It was clear they were in love, but it was more than that. Adahy noticed they had a true friendship and genuine appreciation for each other that was apparent.

"Adahy, I must apologize for hastily departing you earlier. I was needed on business. We were talking about your father, and well…" he stops and looks at Mary. She nods as if to tell Thomas he needs to be transparent, and he sits in the chair next to Adahy,

"Your father was in trouble and being rigorously pursued by the previous monarch, King George II," Thomas says, leveling his tone to match the seriousness of the words.

Mary leans over the table and places two steaming mugs of coffee for them to drink, "Adahy, it was a pleasure meeting you. I will leave you both to your discussion," she says and leaves the room.

Grabbing his mug and taking a sip, Adahy opens up about his knowledge of his father, "My mother told me he was hunted for years, but upon arriving in Nassau, he committed to settling down, but they eventually caught up to him and killed him. That's what I know from my mother,"

Thomas motioned for Adahy to follow him as he stood up from the chair and began walking toward one of the front rooms.

"Aye; it is true, but do you know why he was hunted, why the King of England wanted him?" Thomas inquires, leading the two men into the library room.

As Adahy enters, there is a crackling fire beyond the hearth, with leatherbound books neatly organized along the wall shelves that encased the fireplace. Thomas finds the chair on the far side of the room and sits, situating himself comfortably. Adahy finds a chair and does the same.

Upon sitting, a beautifully made wooden case catches Adahy's eye.

It is elegantly made, he thinks. The polished rectangular wooden box had an elegance to it that Adahy had rarely seen in craftsmanship. On a golden baseplate, there are the same initials his musket carried, 'E.Y.,' and he immediately assumed it was his grandfather's old musket or sword. His mind quickly moves on and back to the current conversation.

"Truthfully, I do not know why my father was hunted," Adahy answers smoothly, taking another sip from the steaming mug, "to be honest, I never gave it much thought. I assumed he committed a crime or some form of treason; he was seldom the topic of conversation."

"My brother, your father, was an honorable man. He served the Crown faithfully for a long time…" Thomas begins.

***

1748
Massachusetts

Snow wisps through the air, coming off the sea breeze and falling into the harbor. Boston in the winter was rough for all who endured it season after season. The heart of the city was filled with people most nights, but tonight, there was a murderous chill in the air, slicing and cutting those who traveled in it like knives. Warm amber lighting emanated from the three-story newly built home, showcasing the warmth within.

Mary was sitting by the hearth, staying warm, reading a book, when a tapping came from a side window.

Tap *Tap*

"Thomas!" The young woman screams in terror, jolting up from the hearth.

Without hesitation, the large man rounds the corner to the room. Stronger in his youth, much more hardened and anxious for a fight,

"Stand back, dear," he says calmly as he guides her to the stairwell.

"I'll see what the noise is," he says confidently, grabbing his musket and exiting the home rapidly.

Cold hit him immediately, and a chill covers his body, *fuck, it's cold*, he thinks and puts the musket buttstock into his right shoulder and raises the barrel up, ready to fire. After a few steps, he sees movement.

"I don't know what you're doing on my property, but I will shoot you dead where you stand!" He shouts aggressively to the shadowy figure standing under the apple tree that was on the side of the house.

Under the tree, the indistinct figure puts his hands up; his gloves are worn with some of the fingertips missing, and the man's clothing is ragged and beaten.

"Is that how you treat blood?" a low-toned, familiar voice states from the darkness.

Thomas drops his stance, and the barrel of his musket falls, "John?!" he asks excitedly.

From out of the darkness of the fruit tree's moonlit shadows, a man with a black tricorn hat atop a cloak hood emerges; removing his hat and then pulling off his cloak hood, revealing his identity,

"Aye, brother, it is me," he confirms and begins walking toward Thomas. His hair is blonde, tied in the back, and his square jaw and broad stature are prominent in the moonlight.

Thomas opens his arms with the musket in his right hand, and the two men embrace each other,

"It's been too long, brother," Thomas says, stepping back and looking at his fatigued kin.

"That it has, brother. And I must say, what a beautiful property you've found yourself," John says, motioning to the larger home.

Unable to give his brother's words much thought, he was enveloped by the mere sight of his brother before him; for too long, they'd been separated.

"Come inside, get warm, let me feed you and give you coffee," Thomas says to John, happy to be with his younger brother again.

"Aye, that sounds good," John replies, entering the warm home.

It took a few minutes, but the two brothers were settled inside the house, and John had removed his gear and weapons while Thomas brewed coffee. Crackles and snaps stem from the burning fire, warmly enveloping the room.

"You know, it was not my intention to startle Mary, brother, but I had no recourse, and it's cold, so I did what I did. I apologize for my approach," John says, genuinely placing his hands near the dancing flames.

Thomas rounds the room corner with two steam-filled mugs of black coffee; he hands one to John and sits in the opposite chair as him.

"John, I am just happy you are alive, happy you are here!" Thomas exclaims, placing his right hand on John's left shoulder, "I am glad to see you," his tone gets sober, "The whispers on the road, on the sea, in the cities and streets, John, they speak about you, they tarnish your name. Royal guards have questioned me myself… in this very home you sit now. Why are you being pursued, John? What has happened?"

As any caring older sibling would, he was worried for John and knew this was not going to end well if John couldn't resolve this issue with the Crown. Steadily sipping his hot coffee, John nods to what his brother says but does not look away from the dancing flames.

"Do you remember when father would read us folk tales and nursery rhymes from Elmir N. when we were children?"

"John, I am asking you, directly, what has happened with you and our King," Thomas says, disregarding John's question.

"Thomas, I do not merely ask you for nostalgia. I am asking for a purpose. Now, do you remember the tales or not?" John snaps away from the flames, looking at his older brother.

"Of course I do," Thomas replies, examining his brother's disconnected demeanor.

Knowing the information he carries would incriminate his brother, he is reluctant to speak,

"What does that have to do with my inquiry?" He asks his younger brother.

John inhales deeply and exhales before taking a large sip of the coffee and speaks, "Do you remember the story of the Golden Five?"

"Ah, father loved telling that one before bed, *The Legend of the Aureum Pentagonum,'* didn't he? God sent the five Roman soldiers to carry the five golden shards to the five corners of the earth. To stay hidden and secret, lost in the sands of time…" Thomas says, reciting some of the passages, "Truly a tale full of honor, perseverance, and strength."

"Aye, he did. Thomas, but it is more than a children's folk tale…" He speaks, unflinching, "I believe it actually happened…I believe I found one of the golden shards…" John says in a deadly serious tone.

Thomas's face becomes stern, and he looks to John, "John… they are tales for children, written to engage children's minds with wonderment and possibility," he says, overlooking his brother's heartfelt words.

"Thomas… I am deathly resolute in my thinking. I am correct."

Taken aback and unsure how to approach these next moments, Thomas is confused, "How do you know? How can you be sure about this?"

"Thomas!" John shouts angrily and stands up, filled with passion, "I've been nearly killed four times since '38, hunted by the King's best men. I cannot show my face to anyone without the threat of being taken prisoner… do you think I am insane? Look at me, brother, you know me. Why would I be hunted like I am? I have uncovered an artifact lost to history… it is powerful. I know it! This item he wants… and he cannot get his hands on it…" He pauses.

"Thomas, you know the story. You know why I must keep it safe and secure. For those reasons, I will give my life to ensure it does not fall into his hands," John says fiercely.

Thomas analyzes his irritated brother. John is different now. He is paranoid, scared, and in fear for his own life. This wasn't the carefree brother he knew John to be. He was more grave and sober in his words, thoughtful in his actions, and seemingly nervous or on edge. Thomas began to notice after the elevated nature of his attitude settled upon initially seeing his long-lost brother.

"I see..." Thomas says.

"You don't believe me, do you?"

"John, I do. Trust me, I do... I can see you have changed... this has changed you. I want to help. What can I do?"

"Find me safe passage through the colonies... I can find my way from there, but I doubt I will be able to navigate the heavily guarded ports and towns without being recognized and detained. I need to leave tonight," John says, looking at Thomas.

"I can do that, brother."

"You know how the King is, Thomas, you know his obsessive ways, he won't stop until he has what he wants..."

"This is true, John, this is true," he replies grimly to his brother.

"This is it," he says, removing a necklace and holding it before Thomas."

It shimmers gold. The pennant was triangular, with the two closer corners wrapped in thin string connecting to the tip, securing the golden shard tightly to the chain.

Immediately, Thomas sees a familiar shape, one that was drawn on the page of children's books. The talisman brilliantly shimmers like the stars, even with the film of time and history upon it. Thomas's eyes are locked... becoming entranced. It is beyond captivating. The rough surface of the triangle catches and reflects light. The shard glimmered, creating a subtle interplay of shadows and highlights, accentuating its geometric form.

Thomas's eyes widened, and he was captured by it. The talisman required attention when it was shown, and John placed it back around his neck, tucking it underneath his clothing. Thomas knew, from that moment, that he needed to help his brother.

"I will see you have safe passage, John. Stay here, eat, drink, and we will see to it you are quietly on your way," Thomas says to his younger brother, knowing there isn't much he can do for him. Plans are in motion, men currently pursue John, and he's clearly been scarred by this hunt.

Thomas makes his way to the library room in his house, where Mary is currently reading. It's a larger room, with shelves across the walls filled with all types of books and candelabras attached to the walls holding lit candles, providing the woman ample light for reading.

"Mary, it's John," he said, as if she wasn't already aware.

"I know, dear, I have ears…" she replies sarcastically, "How do you want to help him?"

"We need to get him fed, clothed, new gear, and he needs maps and currency for his travels," his words are pure as they leave his mouth.

"Then we will see to it, Thomas," she says softer, knowing her brother-in-law has been missing from their lives and Thomas was willing to do anything for John.

Thomas rummages through the kitchen area, "Dear, I will gather the food and clothing, you facilitate the remaining items," she says, relieving him of the unfamiliarity of searching the kitchen.

"Aye, you're not wrong," he says, leaning in to kiss her, "I love you, dear,"

She meets him, and they kiss briefly, "I love you, too," she replies.

Moments pass as Thomas makes a ton of noise in the equipment room getting the gear ready to give to John, as Mary prepped potatoes, carrots, onions, a satchel of dried deer jerky, and a small wool bag of apples. Thomas got out his father's musket, with the engraving, 'E.Y.' for Edward Young, on the buttstock, as well as a stack of year-old colonial maps and older maps of numerous Caribbean islands. Thomas walks all of this to the room with John and gently drops it into the chair he was sitting on earlier.

"Father's musket, newly minted maps of the colonies with the latest roads and rivers, some maps of Cuba, Hispaniola, and others, and Mary is prepping you some food for your travels."

Feeling a sense of relief, John exhales, looking at his brother with grateful and appreciative eyes.

"Brother, you don't need to do any of this. I didn't know where to go. I apologize again—"

"John, stop. You are my blood. Never apologize to me for needing help… I am here for you, always," Thomas says with an assured tone.

With reluctance, John grabs the gear in haversacks, throws them over his shoulder, and prepares himself to move out and move on with his journey,

"Brother, I know… but staying here for longer than necessary opens possibilities for your involvement and collusion. I need to go. Overall, it is not safe for you or your wife."

He secures his inscribed 1739 sea-service pistol into his waistband.

John places his cloak on, concealing his haversacks and pistol, and then places his tricorn back atop his head.

"Wait, wait…" Mary's soft voice emerges from the kitchen area, followed by her carrying rolls and a vessel for soup.

"Can't forget that!" John smiles.

"No, you do not. Make sure you eat that soon. You're too thin these days," Thomas adds, placing his hand on John's shoulder.

"Well, Brother, and Mary, I am forever grateful for your hospitality and generosity. Truly, I am in your debt," John says, ready to go, standing in the hall.

"Please, take this. Thomas never wears it now that we moved into the city," Mary says, extending a thick coat to John.

John looks to Thomas, "Take it," Thomas says smiling, "she's right, I haven't touched it years, plus… you need it."

"Aye; it is cold," he says, taking the coat from Mary.

Quickly, John puts the coat on and wears his cloak over it. The added warmth was more appreciated than he anticipated.

"There is one more thing," Thomas says, grabbing the smaller wooden chest off the hallway chair, "What of your half of father's estate?"

Looking at the chest, John steps to it and opens the smaller wooden box. Inside is a felt liner and a magnificent amount of currency, gold, silver, small jewels, and gems.

"Do you have a coinbag?" John asks abruptly.

"There is one in the library," Mary says, running to the room and returning with the item in her hand. She extends it to John.

"I will take a generous handful. I am sure it will be of use on the road," he half-smiles, putting a hearty handful of the chest's contents into the newly acquired moleskin coinbag.

"Thank you both, again, I can't say it enough," he says, wrapping his arms around Thomas and proceeding to hug Mary, telling them both farewell,

"John, please, be safe. Take care of yourself and figure out whatever you need to do to rid yourself of such elaborately devilish schemes… I wish there were more I could do…"

**

Completely entranced by his uncle's ability to orate and emote, he was enthralled by the story of his father. Fire danced in the pit, flickering shadows upon the room walls.

"I took him outside to our small barn, gave him one of my, then, fastest horses, and we said our goodbyes. He thanked us again, and his figure on the horse, with that tricorn on his head, was the last I saw of him.

"The talisman…" Adahy says ominously and pulls the necklace out from under his shirt and leather chest rig.

"This is the item he found." The gold talisman glimmers like twilight stars in the reflections of dancing flames.

The distinctly shaped golden shard was beautiful. It was triangle looking with sharp edges, polished and smooth. It was wide, with the two points at the top going down to one final point at the bottom. The shard was encased and held to Adahy's chain by thin metal wire, wrapping the edges to the top and securing it.

Immediately, Thomas is astounded to see the item his brother once held before him in this exact room.

"Adahy…." Thomas's voice almost stammers, "That is exactly the item your father carried and was hunted for…"

The young man's mind races, trying to make sense of all this information. His mind attempts to connect the pieces,

"You would think they would still be searching for it," Adahy says heedfully.

"They may, but the manic King George II is dead, and his meticulous and calculating son, King George III, sits atop the throne. As far as he is concerned, the supernatural, mythological mission died with his father. What you hold has been lost to history. As far as the Crown is concerned, they have it on display in the King's Palace. Unknowing of this one around your neck," Thomas says and pauses, looking at the fire.

"Your father believed it with all his heart that this item was the true piece of the Aureum Pentagonum… and he was killed for that thinking. You must keep it safe, and it can never fall into the hands of crown loyalists or even let it be known that you are the son of John Young."

"What do I do?" Adahy unselfishly asks, "There is no going backward."

"You can stay in the second-level guest quarters until you settle your mind and find your true path."

Adahy looks to the man, "This relic, this *'shard,'* needs to be protected, and no matter what I do or wherever my path leads, I will keep it secure."

"Aye, that is evident," Thomas replies, knowing his brother's intrepid spirit lives with Adahy.

Moments pass, allowing the crackling fire to interrupt the silence. The atmosphere in the room is clear as Mary stands up and exits through the doorway to the library. Adahy, unsure of what comes next, lifts his head out of his hands, glancing around the room, and looks at the elongated locked wooden box once more.

What's in the box? He thinks, analyzing the wood-stained box. Thomas stands and walks to the fire, sitting in the chair opposite Adahy.

The elder figure leans toward his nephew with his elbows on his knees as the fire reflects on his face, highlighting his facial scar. In a low, more serious tone,

"In your travels, have you ever heard of the *'King's Bane?'*"

Motivations & Liberty

September 1771

Boston, Massachusetts

Roosters crow outside as the lavender-pink dawn sky begins illuminating the shadows in Boston. The once-large fire beyond the hearth has been reduced to coals and ash as Adahy and Thomas Young finish their night-long conversation.

"There is one more thing," Thomas says, standing up, "Your father's inheritance."

A wave of confusion consumes Adahy, and his voice mirrors his feelings,

"My father's inheritance?"

"Yes, dear boy. Our family comes from a long line of smugglers, privateers, military men, and men of means. In my father's will, he left behind myself and John large amounts of coin, and I am giving you your father's share. I am happy to be relieved of it," he says, walking out of the room.

Inheritance? I've never needed large amounts of currency...

Many thoughts and feelings crash over Adahy as his uncle returns quickly, holding a smaller-sized wooden box. It is easily carriable but not concealable. The smaller wooden box had two hinges on the backside connected to the top. Opposite the hinges was a latch with a loop and lock. Thomas places the box on the table, removes his key ring with multiple keys, and grabs a distinct key. With a smooth movement, he removes the lock from the chest. He opens it and displays the internals to Adahy.

"Silver? Gold? British pounds? This is a treasure chest!" Adahy says, youthfully excited, having never seen this much money before.

Thomas laughs, "That's right. I suggest leaving the chest somewhere hidden and safe. You should fill your coinbag and replenish it when necessary, but that shouldn't happen anytime soon. Keep it discreet, and most importantly, use it sparingly only when needed," he says sincerely to his nephew.

The gift is impressive. Adahy knows he needs to keep it safe. His uncle was right and he understood money had no place being flaunted or disregarded as expendable.

"When you get upstairs, you will see the guest quarters are quite sufficient, and I am sure you'll enjoy all the amenities comparatively to the wilderness," Thomas says, stretching his back as the shadows of the fire dance off his body.

Adahy stands, holding the chest, "Thank you, Uncle Thomas, I am grateful to have found you."

"I feel the same," Thomas says, leading Adahy out of the room, "Now, go get some rest, unpack your things, get comfortable, and come see me when you're ready."

"Will do," Adahy replies.

Thomas looks to his nephew, "Hmm," he smiles, "I am so happy you're here."

"Me too," Adahy says and heads up the staircase.

Thomas walks down the hall to his bedroom. Taking off his boots before he enters, Mary opens the door,

"Thomas, you need to sleep. Many avenues need addressing tomorrow, well, today, my dear," she says softly to the man.

"I know... I am," he replies tiredly.

"How is he?"

"He is like John, but not... it's strange but familiar," Thomas says.

"Did you tell him about the others?"

"I mentioned it and asked him if he'd ever heard of them while traveling to Boston; he had not. But he seems eager to be involved, and he looks capable," Thomas says to Mary with a smile.

"Well, get some rest and bring him to the others in the evening," she says.

"Aye, woman, you know my thinking," his smile widens, and he leans down, kissing her on the lips.

"I do, old man. Now go rest. I'm off to brew some coffee," she says, walking down the hall and around the corner into the kitchen area.

Thomas undresses and crawls into the bed.

His thoughts become louder in his mind, ever-growing, thinking of his brother. *Odd, he's so much like John, so eager for purpose... let's hope the others take to him,* he thinks. The others enter his thoughts; *they're all good people, and they'll see the value in adding Adahy.* His mind reassures itself of the confidence behind his idea, and silence follows, drifting him into a deep sleep.

**

For Adahy, it was almost too soft, but he crashed into the deepest sleep upon entering the bed. His mind raced and crashed thinking of all the new information he'd been given, but exhaustion quickly overpowered his mind, and he succumbed. Darkness ensues as he drifts off.

Knock, *Knock*

Immediately, his mind welcomes the sound, and his green eyes open. Adahy was up, and his mind turned on, though a bit groggy. He peered at the door, remembering he was in his uncle's home, and spoke,

"Aye, come in!"

Thomas opens the door and enters the guest quarters with an eager look on his face,

"I apologize for the intrusion. Mary told me to let you rest, but it's been nearly 24 hours since you've been asleep," he laughs and continues, "Your father never liked me bothering his sleep, but I am eager to show you around."

"Aye, I am eager to see the city," Adahy replies cheerfully.

"When you're ready, come downstairs with your gear. Mary has made forced eggs with strips of bacon. It'll be a great meal for the day," Thomas says and makes his way back out of the room, closing the door behind him.

Well, he's in a good mood, it seems, he thinks.

He removes the blankets, gets himself out of bed, and quickly dresses himself. His white long-sleeve shirt first, tucked into black pants. He puts his socks on, followed by his deer-skin shoes, and then his tan leg gaiters. After tying off his leg gaiters above his knees, he secures his leather chest rig to his body. Finally, he throws on his great coat and grabs his faded black tricorn before leaving his room.

Entering the downstairs area, Adahy was enveloped by a tantalizing aroma.

"The food smells so good," he says, rounding his way into the kitchen.

Mary and Thomas sat at the smaller nook-style table in the corner under a glass-pane window. Adahy could see much better with the assistance of sunlight peering through each window throughout the home.

"It is good! Take a seat, and I'll make you a plate," Thomas says, inviting Adahy to sit.

"Aye, thank you," he replies, sitting down.

"I'll make it, Thomas, you sit," Mary says, smiling.

She makes her way to the food, grabs a tin plate, and fills it with adequate proportions for a man of Adahy's age. She then places a large coffee-filled mug next to the plate.

"Here you go," Mary says, placing the plate before the man.

"Thank you," Adahy says as he starts to eat, "Ugh, this is delicious. I haven't had a meal like this in months," he says with a half mouth full of food.

"It is my pleasure, and I am glad you are enjoying it," she says with a chuckle, "You'll need all the energy for today. Thomas has a good day planned," she finishes and returns to her spot at the table.

"Aye, I do," he affirms.

Adahy nods while continuing to eat the food, "Thank you again. Forced eggs and bacon are always a welcomed treat."

"They are easy to make, and I'm glad you enjoy it. It's funny... the way you eat, you look like him," she says to Adahy.

"Aye. You do." Thomas affirms heartfeltly.

Adahy stops eating, "I am hopeful to continue his journey... but I am happy just being here with you both. It seems family is rare, and I am happy to have you both."

"We are happy to have you with us, Adahy," Thomas adds.

"Well, truth be told, I am ready for the next adventure," Adahy says, taking large gulps of the black coffee.

"Tell me, and I forget; teach me, and I remember; involve me, and I learn..." Thomas quotes and continues, "Today, Adahy, I will involve you with my life here in Boston."

"Who said that?" Adahy asks, standing up.

"A good friend of mine from Philadelphia, Mr. Benjamin Franklin... One day we will go there, and I'll introduce you. Now, let's get a move on. There is a lot to cover," Thomas says, standing up and fixing his personal gear.

"Aye, let's do it," Adahy agrees.

"Thomas..." Mary stands and walks to her husband, "I am sure Adahy would love to see the Liberty Tree in the common. Take him there. It will be nice today."

"Yes, ma'am, that is a marvelous suggestion. We will find ourselves there by the end of the day," he says, leaning down to kiss her.

Within moments, the men are outside, walking along the path toward the gate. The two guards are new guards and not the same men from the night Adahy arrived. One of them opens the gate, and immediately, Raven neighs and gets excited to see Adahy.

"Hey, girl... shhh," Adahy says to her, petting her snout, "I'll be back later."

Thomas and Adahy stroll down Green Lane, away from the property and toward the city docks. Boston was busy. Once far enough away from Thomas's home, the city was awake. Merchants were attempting sales to all. Newspaper boys were shouting headlines while horses and carriages moved throughout the streets with purpose. Everyone seemingly has a destination to be and work to do. It was the busiest city he'd ever seen.

"Down there are the docks..." Thomas points to the wharf, "Lots of commerce and trade happening down there, ropemakers, shipbuilders, maintenance workers, and sailors, among others."

Adahy paid attention to everything his uncle pointed out, but one thing stood out to him more than anything else: the abundance of redcoat troops marching and roving throughout the city in small ten-man elements.

"What about the Redcoats?" Adahy asks as he notices more redcoats as he has traveled north during his journey since leaving home.

"Aye, they're everywhere. Here in Boston, the term '*Redcoat*' is a rebel term, considered a slur. It will gain attention from the British regulars, officers, and Tories alike if it's heard. It will invite interrogation," Thomas says, in a lower tone, making sure he is discreet in his words.

"I see. I'll be sure to keep that in mind," Adahy says coolly.

As they walked, Thomas showed Adahy all the local taverns and shops, pointing out all the places to avoid and places to go. Familiarity was paramount for Thomas as he explained the city.

"Remember these locations, memorize the city streets, the flow of people, and pay attention to the small details…" Thomas sporadically repeated to him as they walked.

Adahy did. He made mental notes of all the Tory taverns that Thomas would point out, with an emphasis on George's Tavern. The morning became afternoon as the two men walked and explored Boston. Adahy shared some stories of his adventures on the King's Highway of raining nights, and swampy days. Thomas regaled Adahy with stories of his father in his adolescence, stealing horses and running from their father when in trouble. Adahy was enthralled and enjoyed hearing about his father, whom he never met or knew.

"Adahy… let me ask you… what do you know of the politics here in Boston or the colonies, I should say," Thomas asks directly.

"I know politics from the tribe. I have seen the elders."

"And what was learned from them?"

"I learned only one point: Politics is power."

"Aye, this is true. That is a great perspective and outlook, but I am curious to know if you understand the politics that has been unfolding as of late, here in Boston and the murmurs across the colonies."

"I understand what I see. And what I see is troubling. Just along my journey from the tribe to here, anti-British sentiment has been rising among the people. Unique taxes are imposed, and just today, I've seen pockets of British soldiers roaming nearly every street here," Adahy replies with a more serious tone and continues, "I can feel the tensions... truth be told, Uncle... I fear I have fueled these tensions with my actions."

Thomas takes his eyes off the water, looking at Adahy, intrigued, "How do you mean?"

Their conversation was much heavier than anything they'd discussed prior; Adahy could feel the weight.

He's my uncle, he can know, he has to know... he thought.

"In South Carolina, early on my expedition, I killed twelve soldiers that were looting locals..."

Knowing when someone confided in him, Thomas recognized that his nephew was comfortable opening up and sharing his experiences. This triggers the older city leader.

"We could use you..." Thomas says ominously, disregarding the admission Adahy just supplied.

Use me? Did he not hear what I just said? He thought curiously.

"I don't understand."

With a slight smile, Thomas leans forward, "Adahy, you possess certain *vocational skills...*"

"Vocational skills? What is a vocational skill?"

"A vocation is a trade, a skillset. It is artistry you learn, practice, and employ. The King's Bane operates within a certain vocation, which I believe you understand as well...Violence is a vocation, my boy. I believe you understand it... I believe you recognize it is a tool to be wielded."

Adjusting his coat, Adahy knows he's right.

"I heard of the massacre near Santee River... word spreads fast of the killing of British regulars. Some say it is a conspiracy. Some believe we must improve relations with our native neighbors since the incident. Either way, it was well executed and just the type of thing we need in the King's Bane," Thomas says directly.

"The King's Bane?"

"Yes... you've said you haven't heard of it, which is a good thing; it is a system... or rather, a collective of individuals who, like yourself, are students of the vocation of violence. Masters of subterfuge and pupils of evasion. Men and women who have committed to the skill of subtly and the art of killing," Thomas says to Adahy with true eyes, "this is the King's Bane... sending these men and women to disrupt the Crown's tax shipments, currency shipments, and anything directly related to the King's purse. We do not harm trade shipments, nor do we aim to kill civilians or kill unjustly."

"Why only Crown and tax shipments?" Adahy asks.

"The Crown killed your father," Thomas says, looking out over the water, "the Crown is the reason for many financial difficulties and struggles for so many colonists."

"Why does the Crown work this way? I've heard of these unique taxes?" Adahy asks, not understanding the Crown or colonial politics, but he did know what a tax was.

"The Crown went into debt after the French and Indian War. I witnessed first-hand their expansive operations. It took the Empire a lot to ensure victory. A great cost..." Thomas pauses and continues,

"Over the years, taxes have been introduced. With the Sugar Act, Stamp Act, and Townshend Acts, the people are becoming exhausted from their money being taken. I am but a small piece of the colonial resistance puzzle. Growing sentiments stretch across the entirety of the colonies, from farmers to prominent people in positions of power. The crown crossed too many lines too many times."

"I've seen it myself as a child when the tribe would venture to the nearest town for trade. But as I've gotten older, I have noticed it has gotten worse for the colonies," Adahy says and continues,

"I've heard the whispers on the road to Boston. The crown has been squeezing the colonies for work and supplies for too long, and the people gather in the shadows to discuss revolution and revolt. This attitude was prominent among most citizens and people I ran into thus far."

"You are lucky then," Thomas says, smiling, "Many Crown loyalists are out there. They hide as Patriot sentiment grows stronger, but they are there. The Crown's presence is stronger now than ever, and we must stay vigilant. Spies are under every rock. Children are spies. Women, the retarded, blind, deaf, and ugly are spies. Every color and designation can be the enemy, able to convey information given a chance. You must be cautious, always," Thomas pauses and looks to Adahy,

"You must understand the King's Bane operates in secrecy, in the shadows, and is not a real entity that can be uncovered. Once you join, you must become a ghost in Boston, no longer in need of public taverns and brothels. You must become a shadow with no name, as the danger and threat will be too high, and the risk of your face being known or your name will get you and anyone you care about killed."

"Uncle Thomas, how have you been able to stay in the open as yourself?"

"Well, my dear boy, it is a secret," he smiles, looking at Adahy, "plus, no one in this city actually believes the King's Bane is real. Small pockets of anti-British sentiment have grown into large populations of the city, which has bled to other colonies. The King's Bane is more of an ideology and spirit in the minds of the people. What they believe is in the idea of standing up to the Crown. The King's Bane, in essence, allows people to believe anyone can stand and fight against injustice. At least, that's what I choose to believe, and that's how I justify my actions. Allowing this idea to fester and take hold helps us operate in the shadows. That, my boy, helps us in staying hidden," Thomas says slyly and continues,

"I also uphold my ties to both realms, Patriot and Crown... one of the many perks of serving in the British military during the war."

"Aye, I respect the cause, and I will join you, under one condition..." he pauses and pulls out the gold talisman from under his white shirt,

"Help me figure out why this was so important?"

"Of course I will. I helped your father as much as I could at the time, and I will do the same for you," he says authentically to Adahy.

"The Crown did kill my father... When do I start?"

Thomas smiles, resting his right hand on his nephew's left shoulder. The sun was reaching beyond the forest to the west, tinting the dusk sky orange. Boston was a rowdy city, but now it seemed almost quiet.

"It is not like that," Thomas said, smirking, "I'll introduce you to the others. But first, let us take in the glory of the ole Liberty Tree!"

Interweaving between all the civilians, redcoats, and beggars, the two men walk through the cobblestoned streets toward the bustling Boston Common, where the large elm tree stands proudly.

The King's Bane

Boston, Massachusetts

"Back-alley hideaways and dingy streets are the battlefields for the King's Bane," Thomas explained to Adahy, "It is where we live, operate, and use our talents."

The air was stale within the dense brick corridors. Each turn led down another cobblestone alley that lengthened their journey deeper into the heart of Boston.

"Hmm... enemies are everywhere."

"Correct you are. You must assume you will always be outnumbered, and you will always be outgunned."

"Aye... That I can understand."

"I believe you can," Thomas adds heartfeltly.

Smiling and enjoying his time with his uncle, Adahy says, "You'd get along with my other uncle, Wohali."

"I am sure he is a skilled master within many violent arts."

"He is. The reason I am the way I am is because of him."

"I know it must seem that way, Adahy... but I see John in you. John's attitude lives in you, whether you recognize it or not."

The further they walked, the void of lantern light seemed to grow, and the less the city seemed alive. At last, Thomas slows his pace, coming to a halt in front of what looks like an old tavern no longer in service.

"Look there," the silver-bearded man points to the large square door sitting in the barn-like structure.

"What is it?" Adahy inquired.

"There is our stable. You can put your mare there... forgive me, what is her name?"

"Raven."

"Raven! Beautiful. She can live there while you live here," he says, turning to the building nearest to them. It is a large, multi-leveled, vacant brick tavern.

"Does anyone live here?"

"God, no. This part of the city is empty."

"It's quiet," Adahy says, eyeing the surrounding area.

"Aye, that's by design, my boy," Thomas says, walking toward the entrance door,

"Here we are," Thomas says, looking up to the rundown tavern entrance, "You must ensure no one, and I mean no one, sees you enter here. It is the entranceway into the safe house."

He bypasses the main door and walks to a set of stairs on the right-hand side, nearly hidden in the shadows, leading to an underground corridor.

Adahy follows.

"Mind your feet and where you step, it's going to be dark," Thomas says as he gets to the bottom of the steps.

Hearing distinct noises in the corridor tunnel, Adahy whispers, "Uncle Thomas, stop. There is someone at the end of the corridor. I can hear them."

Surprised by this, Thomas stops and listens...

"Oi, is that you, Thomas?" a young voice shouts across the muted darkness of the long corridor.

"Ah, Nimish. Why are you in the entrance corridor?" Thomas asks and begins walking toward the man.

"Waiting on the others," Nimish replies to Thomas.

"Good ears, Adahy," Thomas softly admits to his nephew and continues walking in the darkness.

Adahy could make out the man's figure in the darkness as they walked down the blacked-out corridor. It helped that there was a little amount of light outlining the door the man was seemingly guarding. As they got closer, the man opened the door, and the light from inside the room illuminated the dark corridor. Adahy could see the man for the first time, and he recognized him as the young man who came to Thomas on the first day they met.

He was youthful, a few inches shorter than Adahy, with brown skin and brown eyes. He wore traditional militiaman garb. Which was a typical earth-tone gray coat, tan britches, cross-chested haversacks, and a musket slung on his left shoulder. *Rather ordinary*, Adahy thought.

"Nimish, this is Adahy," Thomas says, introducing the two men.

"Oi, so this the nephew who showed up asking questions?" Nimish asks, sticking his right hand out for Adahy to shake.

"I am," Adahy replies, greeting the man.

"You were with Thomas just recently... I guess Thomas was giving you a tour of the city," the young man chuckles, closes the door, and strolls toward a chair near the hearth.

"Welcome!" a bellowing deep voice projects out of the corner of the room.

It was his frame, which Adahy immediately noticed, towered over all as he stood up. He is bald, with a light beard that is aged gray. Adahy saw he was wearing a long white work shirt with rolled sleeves and black britches. His belt was thick with a three-inch buckle. Attached to the belt, he carried a drop holster for his pistol on his left side and a saber sheathed on his right.

"Ah, James, good to be here, and I am pleased to have brought Adahy with me," Thomas says cheerfully, shaking the man's hand and giving him a half hug.

"Aye, Adahy, good to meet you! I am James 'Robbie' Robinson," he says strongly, outstretching his colossal hand.

"It is a pleasure meeting you as well, James, and you too, Nimish," Adahy replies with a firm handshake.

"Where are Ester and Elias?" Thomas asks with concern to the other two members.

"The redcoat has finally awakened out of the coma, and—" James stops talking and looks to Thomas as if he had spoken words he was not supposed to.

"Aye, it's okay, James. I briefed Adahy on our cabal. He should hear it."

James nods his head, "They moved him, so Elias and Ester are following to see where they take him, as well as assess the security of the location."

"Very good, then we shall wait here for their return," Thomas states, walking toward a finely crafted wooden chair near the hearth.

As he looks around the room, he takes it all in. To his right was a wall with a doorway leading to another room. In front of him, about ten feet or so was a large wooden table with five chairs. Along the wall on the far side were multiple sets of stacked beds. Next to them sat wooden racks with muskets and swords hanging from the pegs. As his eyes traveled along the wooden racks, they flowed into a countertop with three toolboxes filled with useful tools. Three wooden barrels sat next to the tool bench; Adahy presumed they were filled with powder. As he kept scanning the room, Thomas walked to the hearth and sat down in a rocking chair next to the fire.

"Adahy, get comfortable. This is the King's Bane headquarters, so to speak. A surgeon in Charlestown owns the property. No direct connection to anyone in Boston."

"It is very spacious. How old is it?"

"I used it in the 60s while secretly smuggling on the side. It has become invaluable in the years since."

Completely immersed in the trinkets hanging along the walls and the space of the room, Adahy stands still in the room, taking it all in. The table was larger than most and sat proudly as the centerpiece. Atop, it carried a Union Jack draped tablecloth. The red and blue wool-type flag was large enough for a frigate.

"Oi, Adahy, are you enjoying Boston?" Nimish asked as he leaned against the wall near the hearth.

"I am. It's the busiest city I've visited on my journey," he replies.

"And how's that journey going for ya?" James interjects.

"Well, I found my blood uncle, Thomas, and now I am here with you."

"And with us you shall be!" Thomas says proudly.

Several moments went by with mild banter between the three men. The fire danced along the walls, illuminating the dark spaces of the room. Adahy found himself a chair near the fireplace, relaxing. The door opens, and everyone sitting turns to see. Adahy sees two individuals walk in; one is female, and she's older. The other was a man with salt and pepper hair who was also older, near Thomas's age. Each is carrying a musket slung on their right shoulder. The man has a navy blue military coat on; it seems old and used but personalized with regalia and finery. On the left lapel, he has woven a Wisk and Pick that sits permanently in his clothing. Wearing dark brown trousers, tan leg gaiters, and black leather boots, he lets out a relieved exhale.

The woman was shorter, and petite, but Adahy could see her body was hardened. In an emerald coat and dark brown trousers with knee-high black leather boots. Her hair was whiter than snow, and she was wrinkled in the face. Adahy noticed quickly that nearly her entire neck carried a small burn mark a few inches below her chin. She was very rugged and carried herself strongly, but her smokey-gray eyes told Adahy she had seen a lot in her time.

"Ah, Welcome, Ester and Elias!" Thomas says, standing and walking to greet his compatriots.

"Ah, Nyx. The Goddess of Night, how appropriate for you to arrive at such late hours." James says to the woman affectionately.

She smiles at the large man's words from across the room. Her teeth are nearly perfect, and she is well-kept.

"Ah, Mr. Robinson... it is appropriate, isn't it? Thomas, did Nemo or Robbie tell you about the survivor from Watertown?" Ester asks Thomas plainly.

"Aye, they said you were coming with new information. What's the word?"

"They transported him to the Watertown's ammo magazine. Four nurses and two roving guards outside, more inside. The magazine is challenging to get to without being seen, but it is possible...." Elias said, with a thick English accent, "Our best bet is sending one of us to get inside and ensure the man is... properly killed," he said with a patronizing undertone, looking to James and Ester.

"No one would've guessed he would've survived our attack," James said seriously.

"I am teasing, but we do need to finish the job. He knows, if he remembers that night, the name of you...

Thomas… it's imperative he's dealt with hastily," Elias says with sound judgment.

"Then we will see that it is done," Thomas says and then looks to Adahy, "the others have met him already, but this is my nephew, Adahy."

"Bloody hell, Sailor Johnnie's boy!?" Elias proclaims loudly with excitement.

"Aye, that's him," Thomas says, putting his hand on Adahy's shoulder.

"Delighted to meet you. I'm Adahy," he said, extending his hand toward the two King's Bane members.

"Likewise, Adahy. I am Elias 'Shakespeare' Owen. You can call me Elias," he said, strongly shaking the young man's hand.

"You knew my father?" Adahy asks.

"No, I never met him, but I saw him when I was younger. He had a large property on the western reaches of Nassau. Working at the rum distillery afforded me ample opportunities to deliver rum around the island. He was a good man and known on the island to be so. He was such a good man that he gave the previous King a stroke," Elias says, laughing.

"Hello, Adahy, I am Ester Webb. I go by Nyx, I'm the one female here… as you can see, I don't take their shit," the older woman said with a bright smile, shaking Adahy's hand.

Adahy yearned for more stories and information about his father. He enjoyed hearing about his adventures. Being around his uncle made him feel good, and he enjoyed being connected to Thomas. Having a family beyond the tribe felt powerful, and Adahy was quickly taken by the attitudes and characters of Thomas's rebel cabal.

"That is quite the setup you have there, Adahy," Ester says as she points to his leather chest rig.

"Aye, it's unique in allowing me to configure whatever weapons, pistols, knives, tomahawks, to fit on me for what is required for the mission. I was gifted it from my tribe when I left."

"It's beautiful," James says respectfully.

"Thank you, I find it overly useful," Adahy replies, "I am curious though…" he stops and looks around the room, "Why not call you by the other names?"

Thomas smiles, "We need to communicate while we are on a mission, and if we used our normal given names, well… that would… that wouldn't be good," Thomas smiles and continues, "it is merely a form of concealment."

"I see…" Adahy says, looking around the room. He knew he needed to make an impression, "Considering we know the location of the wounded man, let me go. I want to help however I can," Adahy adds, commenting on the information he overheard when he initially walked in.

"No," Thomas spouts immediately.

"Aye, he seems capable enough… we could use him…" Ester says, looking around the room.

"He's your nephew, Top, what you say goes," Elias said firmly, looking to Thomas.

After not speaking for a while, Nimish recognizes the tense atmosphere and attempts to cut the tension, finally speaking up, "Oi, Thomas, you brought him here, you have welcomed him to our group, and he is eager to help… let's see what he has to offer. I think he can do it, but then again… I just met him," the young brown man says to the others and continues speaking, "You brought us all together, and we are capable as well, no different than him."

"Exactly. Why not send me? Because I am of blood relation? Even more of a reason for me to go and put my loyalty into action," Adahy argues passionately.

Knowing Adahy could handle the mission, Thomas begins to entertain the idea.

"I'm with Nimish. You brought all of us together; look at us; we trust you, Thomas… now trust him," James says strongly.

"Aye, thank you, but I must say, I am not sure I feel safe sending my newfound nephew to go on a job that may bring you harm… It is disrespectful to John," Thomas says to the group.

"I want to help you. This is my path, helping you, joining the King's Bane, and avenging my father. This is my fate," Adahy says seriously, taking a step toward Thomas.

Knowing his nephew and the other King's Bane members have valid points. He still feels a way about sending his nephew away on this mission. The atmosphere of the King's Bane headquarters filled with palpable anxiety as they awaited their leader's response.

"Okay, the mission is yours," Thomas says, knowing his nephew is eager for inclusion.

A smile emerges across Adahy's tan face, "Thank you, Uncle Thomas. I will not fail you or the group."

"I know," Thomas asserts.

Within moments, Ester is rummaging through supplies and pulls out a map. She walks over to the large Union Jack-covered table in the room, unrolls her map, and places goblets and mugs on the corners to hold it down.

"Here is Watertown," Ester points out on the canvas map.

Adahy steps to the table and analyzes the map. Immediately, he recognized the map's orientation and moved to the other side of the table. Now standing next to Ester and facing North, he points to Boston and slides his finger from the neck where the route connected to Watertown.

"It doesn't seem too far. It will be a quick ride for Raven," Adahy asserts firmly.

"Aye, Watertown is just a quick fifteen-minute ride on horseback. What you will need to be careful of are the bystanders who may or may not see you; let's hope the latter," Thomas adds.

"I do not want to hope. I want to ensure no one sees me, no one hears me, and most of all, no one even realizes what has happened until I am fully clear of the town," Adahy says clearly, understanding what he needs to do.

"You will need to use a blade," James says, stepping toward the map and towering over everyone in the room.

"Agreed, no pistols. A blade is quiet... intimate," Elias says peacefully.

"A blade I have," Adahy says with a smile, removing one of the medium-sized blades.

"That's the spirit," Elias retorts happily.

The great hall room was well-lit, and all the members of the King's Bane's faces held hope for Adahy.

"It is best to ride quickly with the night air and hitch your horse to the hitching post on the fringes of the town's borders. There will be one. Keep an eye out for it," James said strongly.

"Aye, the ride to Watertown is brief, but it gets quiet out there... so a quiet approach is needed, Adahy," Thomas says smoothly.

"Survey the town. Count the people walking around and ensure that when you move into the town, you are cautious beyond understanding... you will be alone, and they have him secured well. You must understand the importance of stealth. Think like a thief," Elias says with an eerie smile.

"The town's magazine is in the center of the main square. It is the town's ammunition and weapons cache. They moved him there, thinking he would be hidden and safe. There will be two guards roving outside the magazine, and there will be nurses and guards inside the magazine. This is where you *MUST* be quick and silent. There is one door to get in and one to get out," Ester adds to the discussion.

"I will leave my muskets and pistols here. They will only slow me down, make noise, and get in the way as I try to get inside the magazine. I do not want to worry about any of that while I am there. My focus needs to be the mission," Adahy says as he removes his pistol holsters from his leather chest rig.

"Right you are, you seem okay with doing this work…" James said, almost in the form of a question.

Stillness and quiet consumed the room and everyone seemingly turned to Adahy for his response.

"Violence is a tool, and I am adept to its intricacies… I have no qualms with using my abilities within the tool of violence, especially if that means it protects this group," the authentic words are projected in a genuine tone to the others.

"Adahy, you must be careful and cautious with your approach and execution of the plan and of the survivor. I am weary about you doing this, but I know you want to help, and for all intents and purposes, this is a relatively simple mission. But oftentimes, simplicity disguises itself as complexity. You must move with caution," Thomas says to Adahy passionately.

"I will, Uncle Thomas," Adahy replies.

"Right. So, we understand the mission?" Elias asks Adahy.

"I am. When do I ride out?"

"We need to wait until after midnight," Ester adds to the discussion.

"At 2 am, we will have you ride out to Watertown," Thomas says, looking at his Bagnall pocket watch, "that gives us a couple of hours to spare until then."

Everyone settles, and an air of relief wafts through the King's Bane demeanor as the tension is removed from them. Having now volunteered for the mission, it seems the tension has now embraced Adahy, and he feels a wave of responsibility land upon his shoulders. *Can I complete the task before me?* He thought.

A strong hand lands on Adahy's shoulder, "You got this," James said in a low, affirming tone, leaning in toward Adahy. He pats Adahy's shoulder one more time and gives him a wink of assurance.

"Now, let's have a drink!" Elias suggests cheerfully.

"None for me. I need to have a clear mind," Adahy replies strongly.

Elias pauses with a stale face and turns to Adahy, "Killing sober? What kind of beast are you?"

"The kind of beast we need!" Nimish shouts happily, reaching out his empty mug toward Elias.

"So, Adahy, you are the only one of us who purposefully sought out Thomas. Thomas found the rest of us," Ester says after taking a swig of her rum.

"Yes, the *'children'* I never had!" Thomas laughs with the group.

"How did you all find Thomas?" Adahy asks the room.

"Ha! Now that is a story!" Elias shouts.

"Is it?" Thomas sarcastically asks Elias, "I found you in a tavern, drunk in the corner telling war stories, upset you couldn't go home to London."

"And who listened to those stories?" Elias smiles leaning his head toward Thomas, seemingly disregarding the London comment.

"Ya, ya ya… I felt bad for you," Thomas says with a big smile.

Elias smiles larger and taps Adahy's arm, "Ya, he felt so bad he offered me a job and a place to stay… gave me purpose again—"

"Thomas shows you he cares; he doesn't tell ya!" Nimish says to the room.

"The boy!" James says loudly in an endearing tone, "Tell Adahy how Thomas found you… or I should say how *WE* found you!"

Adahy's attention shifts from the middle-aged Elias to the youthful brown man who seems to be around his own age.

"No, you don't want to hear that. It's boring," Nimish says bashfully.

Getting more comfortable around Thomas's cabal, Adahy adds to the atmosphere,

"It can't be much more boring than drunk talking shit in a tavern!" Adahy has a shit grin as he looks over at Elias.

"You!! He's your nephew, Thomas, that's for bloody fucking sure!" he says, laughing and swigging his rum.

"He's a quick one, that's for sure," Thomas replies and continues, "Go on, Nimish, we are all family here."

Adahy sees that Nimish is nervous, and clearly does not do well speaking in front of others.

"I was a boy… my father left our homeland, and by the time we arrived in the colonies, he was dead… died of exhaustion. Luckily, Thomas, James, and Ester rescued me on the water that day."

"I remember that day as if it were yesterday…" James says smoothly and calmly in his deep voice and continues, "We were running some arms and ammunition to some privateers in Virginia. Just after dawn, we spotted the rowboat and, within moments, got you both on board the ship. You were barely breathing, Nimish."

He turns to Adahy, "See, I told you it was boring,"

"I am happy you survived, and you have been... like a son to us all, Nimish," Thomas says, assuring the boy he was and is an important aspect in his life and in the life of the King's Bane.

"Why do you smoke that shit?" James Robinson asks, still looking into the fire.

"Tastes good, relaxes my nerves, and helps me not snap from foolish questions like that," Adahy says, smiling at James as his gaze breaks and he looks over at him.

"That's why I like you, Adahy, your audacity." James laughs and turns back to the fire.

Adahy laughs and reaches for the nearest candle on the table, lighting the end of the wickball. He leans back into the chair and sparks the pipe bowl, puffing until it's lit.

"So, Adahy, why are you here? Other than Thomas, is your uncle?" James Robinson asks.

"My father was hunted and killed by King George II, and my mother raised me with our tribe. Once she passed away, I headed here to find my path... I guess you could say that I'm on it." Adahy says as he releases a puff of smoke.

"My condolences to your parents, Adahy. I, too, earned a rough past. My father went bankrupt in my childhood, losing his theater in London. The banks seized the theater within months, and his health issues became too much." Elias says sadly and continues, "My father despised the colonies, and when he died with nothing, I figured it seemed a good place to start over."

"Rough, my friend," Adahy says genuinely.

"You want to hear rough? Tell him what happen to you both!" Elias says toward James and Ester.

"What, you want to hear how I got the scar? Another time, Elias, okay?" Her words are filled with contempt.

"Fine, be that way. How about you, James? Care to tell Adahy where you come from?" Elias keeps poking.

"Fuck off, we're not in the mood," his deep voice replies.

"Elias… Mr. Robinson and I are two sides to the same coin. You know why we never mention my scar… it is the same reason no one mentions your father's legacy or James's past. It's too rough," she pauses, looks into the fire, and continues with a lighter tone, "So, can we please shift the conversation?"

"Of course we can," Elias responds sincerely, "It is no issue for me."

Interjecting, Nimish eagerly leans forward in his chair, "Tells us about you, Adahy."

Era of Folly

St. James Palace
London, England

Leaving most of the King's Council outside the throne room, the two leaders of the council entered. As they walked into the throne room, they could feel the Major General's hateful gaze. With his brash attitude, he marches past them toward the main door. Agador Ivey, the King's Guard Commander and second cousin to the King, thought he knew what was best for the Crown since he was raised with the King.

He's mad; he always has been, the old man thought as the arrogant officer walked out of the room.

"Ah, Lord Chamberlain Ashford," King George III says, sitting back down, "What melancholy whispers have you brought with you this day?"

Baron Richard Ashford held the title of Lord Chamberlain, Executive of the King's Council, since the early days of King George II. In his elder years now, he walked slower, with a narrow frame, and slightly hunched from a bad back. He bows,

"Your Majesty. No melancholy whispers, but I must ask, do you think it is necessary to send your beast to kill these petty bandits?" He asks presumptuously.

The words jaggedly enter the King's ear and burn his soul. He grips the armrest with hate,

"Lord Chamberlain, repeatedly, you have come to me with arrows through my heart with your news, poison in my stew with your proposals, and hanging me by my balls with your complaints!" He shouts to the old man, "I refuse to have it!"

In a vexed tone, the old man replies immediately, "I am not your dog."

The atmosphere of the Throne Room shifted from general salutations to hostile, as the older Lord Chamberlain was not backing down.

"Baron Ashford, you will reevaluate your tone with me! You come to me and bring me news of my son and his mother being murdered, and now you criticize my sending away of Agador to find them and kill them?! Blasphemy!" King George III stands aggressively, stepping toward the two men.

The Lord Chamberlain takes one step back, "Your Majesty, you send away the best sword the Empire has... to the Colonies... Do you not think that this, strategically, is folly?"

The King's face is still.

"Your Majesty, send the German. Keep your King's Guard Commander here, guarding you, the King..."

"The German," his words carry clear disgust, turning away from the men, "I cannot trust this mission to anyone outside my inner circle. I refuse. This must be done for all colonial eyes to see. It needs to be known that the Crown can handle a petty band of rebels."

"I understand, Your Majesty. If you do not want to use the German, at least consider the potential fallout of Agador's actions. His penchant for violence could inadvertently turn moderates into rebels," the older Lord Chamberlain says, and as he does, the younger Lord High Chancellor Nathanial

Hawke steps forward next to the Lord Chamberlain, immediately easing tensions.

"Indeed. The last thing we need is to galvanize more colonies against the Crown. Commander Ivey's actions could be the spark that ignites a wider rebellion," the middle-aged Chancellor Hawke says calmly. He had auburn hair, green eyes, and pale skin.

The King pushes out a fake chuckle, "Agador is not a brute. He understands the subtleties of power and the necessity of decisive action. This... *King's Bane group* is a disease that must be excised, and Major General Ivey is the right surgeon for the job."

"Even so, Your Majesty, the people of the colonies may not take kindly to Ivey's approach. We risk losing their support entirely," Lord Chamberlain Ashford says in a wise tone.

"Yes, Your Majesty. We need a diplomat as much as a soldier. Someone who can offer an olive branch with one hand and hold a sword in the other," the High Chancellor says convincingly.

Visibly frustrated with the two Councilmen's words, the King resets his emotions, "I do appreciate your concerns, but I believe you underestimate Agador's abilities. He can be both forceful and strategic. We must show strength if we are to maintain order."

"Your Majesty's confidence in Ivey is noted, but we must tread carefully. The balance of power in the colonies is delicate," the auburn-haired man said firmly.

The Lord Chamberlain clears his throat, "Perhaps, Your Majesty, we could pair Ivey with a more diplomatic envoy. This way, we could leverage his strengths while mitigating risks."

Getting more annoyed by the second, the King sits back in his chair, "A fair suggestion, Lord Chamberlain. I shall consider it. But let us be clear: the King's Bane must be dealt with decisively. Agador will play his part, and we shall ensure it is tempered with prudence. Now, I wish to be rid of your voices and be alone in my silence."

Both men bow to their King, "Your Majesty's guidance will surely guide us through these troubled times," Chancellor Hawke says assuredly.

"Indeed, Your Majesty. Together, we shall find a way to maintain order and loyalty in the colonies," Lord Ashford says smoothly and turns around, leading the King's Council out of the Throne Room.

As the large door shuts, the Lord Chamberlain takes a few steps and pauses, turning to the others.

"Chancellor Hawke, come with me. The rest of you disperse. I will send for you when we meet again."

The remaining King's Council members nod their heads, turn toward the corridor, and walk briskly into the stillness of the hall.

"Walk with me," Lord Ashford directs his words to the other man as they begin walking down the opposite hallway as their counterparts.

"Do you remember the search for the shard of the Golden Five and hunt for John Young? I know it was before your appointment to High Chancellor, but it is well known."

"I do; that was a difficult time. Conflicts spread across the globe, as well as the hunt for John Young. Many resources spent on the hunt, nearly a decade," the green-eyed, regal chancellor says as the two men walk further into St. James Palace.

"Correct. Difficult times, indeed. I am afraid we are nearing difficult times again. The French are always causing problems. The colonies are defiant, uncivil, and foul. Now, the King sends away his King's Guard commander with a contingent of good men for what? To quell the King's Bane?

A folly if there ever was one. This will not end well for us or the colonies," Lord Ashford says sternly, steadily walking at a quick but smooth pace.

"Aye, but what does this have to do with the shard and the hunt?"

"All in good time," Lord Ashford says, stopping before an inconspicuous door, "Chancellor Hawke, do you believe that shard that was presented to King George II by the hunters sent to find the elusive sailor is indeed the true shard that was found?"

Lord Ashford asks as he opens the door for Chancellor Hawke. The two men enter a room through a short tunnel and a spiral staircase winding upward, intertwining itself to the top of the tower.

"I have never once thought about it, Lord Chamberlain," the auburn-haired man says as he follows up the staircase.

"Precisely. The relic in the King's Throne Room within the artifact case bears no resemblance to the descriptions documented when John Young found the original shard. Those with him that day were interrogated and interviewed, and their accounts were meticulously recorded. The drawings and statements depict entirely different relic…"

Concerned by the words and their implication, the High Chancellor speaks, "Are you saying King George II was given a forgery?"

"The integrity of the shard lends itself to showcasing the incompetence of the previous members of the King's Council. If it is a forgery, this shard casts doubt on the integrity of King George II's expeditions and our capacity for discernment. We must tread carefully," Lord Ashford says solemnly, continuously stepping upward along the spiraled staircase.

"Now that Agador Ivey is headed to the colonies, and given his reputation, I fear this may be another fruitless endeavor," Chancellor Hawke says placidly.

"I agree, he and his men would better be allocated toward a more tangible threat. This small rebel group, the King's Bane, is nothing more than aggravated colonists doing their best to undermine the King. When in all reality, they mainly conduct little damage to our Empire, it is a drop in the bucket," the older, wiser King's Councilman says as he continues up the stairs.

"Agador is a capable man, angry, precise, and violent when needed, no doubt, but his talents are wasted on a fool's errand. The colonies are volatile, and sending him there on a dubious quest could be a grave mistake. It echoes too closely the reckless abandon of our late King's pursuits," Chancellor Hawke says in an understanding tone.

"Precisely. We must learn from the past if we are to succeed in these coming troubled times. The council grows wary of these endless quests that drain our coffers and morale. The tale of Sailor Johnnie is a testament to our failures as keepers of the King's interests. His escape and the subsequent loss and damage to our ships only emphasize our need for caution," Lord Chamberlain says, arriving at the top of the stairwell.

Upon reaching the end of the stairs, there is another door and one opening along the wall to let in exterior lighting, whether moonlight or daylight. Lord Ashford removed a key ring and set aside one specific key; walking to the door, he unlocked the lock, opened it, and motioned for the High Chancellor to walk through. He does.

"I agree, Lord Chamberlain, the Council must present a united front in advising our King. We cannot afford to squander our resources on reckless missions. Let us focus on strengthening our defenses and stability of the Empire," the pale green-eyed man says; his words are firm.

"Together, we can steer the Empire towards a future grounded in wisdom and fortitude. It's time to end these pointless endeavors once and for all. We will send someone to keep an eye on Major General Ivey, ensuring his success... or if his mission proves to be as fruitless as we fear, we will be well-informed and can intervene before more resources are wasted," Lord Ashford says strongly, walking into the room behind the Chancellor, locking the door.

"A wise precaution. We must remain vigilant and proactive in our council to the King. The era of folly must end here," a riled-up Chancellor Hawke says passionately, examining the room, and continues, "Is this the Shadow Room, Lord Ashford? It looks rather stale," Chancellor Hawke says wryly.

"You've been within your appointment for nearly five years now, and you have a higher intellect than the others, an adept understanding of deception, and you are pragmatic in your strategy. I feel this needs rewarding... other King's Council members are not privy to such areas of the palace," Lord Chamberlain says, sitting at the head of the table.

"I do what is best for the Crown," he adds.

"As do we all," Lord Ashford replies in a darker tone, "please take a seat."

The room is large, like a great hall, and is abundant with oil lamps adorned on the walls. In the center, hanging from the ceiling is a regal chandelier with magnificent details. On the far side of the room are smaller rooms with no doors, each having a bed and chairs. On the left-hand side, the center room was a magnificently detailed fireplace. Large dark wooden bookshelves lined a portion of the wall opposite the magnificently made fireplace.

"One of the oldest constructed rooms in the palace, Chancellor Hawke, take a seat and enjoy the finer spirits the Empire offers. Here is where we can truly discuss Crown matters without peering ears from the King's men. Here, we can discuss the five shards in confidence," Lord Chamberlain Ashford says with an eerie, subtle smile.

**

Several days passed since he received the news that he would depart for the colonies, and he was eager to leave. He had one thing on his mind: hunting and killing the King's Bane.

My patience runs thin... the hunt must begin. He thinks, looking out the glass-paned windows.

His demeanor was that of suppressed rage, ever waiting to burst, but this new mission shifted his attitude. He was finally headed to the colonies and felt reinvigorated with enthusiasm to hunt new game.

Throughout the palace, the evening bell rang, illuminating the courtyards and halls with its sound.

"The time is now," he says to himself, looking at the wall clock as the hands hit 05:00.

Gathering his personal belongings, he departs his royal chambers. In moments, he is outside, making his way to the royal horse stable. A palace guard has his horse ready as he arrives. In one seamless motion, the commander of the King's Guard mounted his horse and quickly spurred it into motion. He rode quickly to the docks as his housemaids prepared his belongings for the trip in the days leading up.

Agador did not waste time. Earlier in the week, he gathered his men and instructed them to be at the docks on this day. A mission laid ahead of them that was of the utmost secrecy. They were to be gone away from home for nearly twelve months if they were to succeed.

Success is the only option, he thinks, as he rides.

He trusted his men more than he trusted many people. They were his weapons and instruments of death. They needed to be loyal, or they were useless to him. As he arrived at the dock, the sun was headed beyond the horizon, and Agador spotted a rugged, familiar face.

"Ah, Colonel Valles, how good of you to be seeing me off," the gritty Major General says.

Standing, in his dress uniform and bicorn hat, was Colonel Francis Valles, an older man in his fifties but built strong with a large frame. Without his formal education, he would be considered a brute, but Francis Valles was a cunning man and loyal to the Crown through all his honorable years of service since his teens.

"Aye, I've decided I cannot allow merely Captain Bates and a company of Sentry Rangers to go with you alone...No, I fear the colonies grow ever dangerous, and you are, in fact, the Kings Guard Commander from the Royal House Ivey. I do not want to be the one who has to explain to the King if you are hurt or killed," Colonel Valles says dearly, with genuine sentiments.

Agador, not having many genuine people around him in the King's court, felt some form of comfort in knowing that his longtime friend was joining the hunt.

The Colonel was Major-General Ivey's closest confidant, knowing the young Major-General from his first year in the king's service in the British Army. Francis Valles was a shorter man who knew only violence and used it expertly. His ability to kill made him a natural asset early in his career, and Major-General Ivey plucked him from his regiment, repurposing him to be on his personal squad. Their bond over bloodshed on various battlefields united these two on a closer level than most of the rest of the 30-man platoon.

"Francis, my dear friend, this will be the hunt to end all hunts. These rebels think they are clever, but we will be two steps ahead of them. They aim to hinder Crown shipments and Crown caravans... good... we shall give them Crown shipments and Crown caravans to hinder. When they show themselves, we capture them," the malicious Major General says coolly.

"Aye, we shall plan it accordingly and capture the rebels. I have no doubt," Colonel Valles responds in spirit.

"Yes, we shall."

"Let us inspect the men before departing. We cannot have unfit soldiers and gear if we are to be successful," the Colonel tells Agador amiably.

Placing his right hand on the Colonel's shoulder, carrying a seldom smile, "Aye, I am glad you are coming."

Grim Omens

Neck of Boston, Massachusetts

Shadows attach themselves to the branches, leaves, Raven, and Adahy, amalgamating into a ghostly presence projected by the illuminating moon. Thomas, draped in darkness, stands under the covered doorway in the alley, never letting himself into the moonlight,

"Now you know the route to Watertown. You know the target. Good luck."

"I do, thank you. I'll see it through." Adahy replies with assurance. Ducking away, Thomas disappears into the blackness of the alley.

Adahy clicks his teeth and pulls the reins, moving Raven away from the alley and onto the main street.

"It's silent," he said softly to Raven as her hooves clopped and clacked along the street, seemingly making for the loudest aspect of the night. Moving inconspicuously is the key objective when moving toward a target, and in the city, there are spies and eyes around every corner. They take their time, moving merely as a traveler and his horse. Moments pass, and the two find themselves on the neck, leading out of the city.

"Yah!" Adahy shouts. She picks up her pace and strides into a run. Adahy's gear is fastened tightly to Raven's saddle as they begin their ride, only quickly impacting hooves for local acoustics as the two make their way toward Watertown with haste.

Adahy thinks about his approach, execution, and withdrawal from the town's magazine; *it must be flawless... I must move within the draped shadows and be smooth in my actions.*

Moonlight reaches all corners of the road and shines brightly into the forest as they move quickly. A few more of Raven's strides and Adahy could finally see the lanterns in Watertown. The forest around him was thinning out, and corn fields lined the road instead of trees.

"There it is, girl,"

Raven neighs, and he clicks his teeth, bringing her to a slower pace.

"Let's take a pass around the town, shall we?"

She neighs again.

"That's my girl," he says to her, patting her on the neck.

He lowers his tricorn and buttons his greatcoat to the top button, covering half his face. As he's doing so, the two of them pass a hitching post,

"That's where you'll wait for me, girl. Let me get a good lay of the land first," Adahy says to Raven.

"We don't want any surprises, do we now?" He asks, lowering his voice to a whisper. The mare's impacting hooves blend with the nighttime noises as they maneuver on the outskirts of the town perimeter.

Given the ample moonlight, the entirety of Watertown can be seen easily. There aren't too many buildings, and each has enough space between them so that Adahy can adequately assess the town square from the outskirts. The town's magazine is an oddly shaped building with one door and two roving guards outside. Raven moves slowly, and Adahy sees the two roving guards have a moment to themselves... it is a brief moment when they do not have the other guard in their eyesight. *That's the moment*, he thinks, *that's when I strike.*

He keeps moving and eventually reaches the far side of the small, quiet town.

"One more pass, and you can relax for a few minutes," he whispers to Raven, pulling the reigns to navigate the mare back to the opposite side of Watertown.

He notices that each of the roving guards carries a musket, a pistol on their waist, and a bayonet sheathed on their hip. One of the guards yawns heavily and slows his pace. *They're tired, and with speed and accuracy, I can deal with them quickly*, he thinks to himself. Moments later, he and his horse are nearing the furthest hitching post on the outskirts of the town.

"All right, girl, now my work begins," he says to the horse, placing his head on her head and petting her snout.

Analyzing his gear, Adahy grabs his tomahawk and leaves his muskets and pistols; he knows this needs to be silent. The bow, arrows, and quiver were safely secured to the saddlebag, and he wouldn't need them either.

With his face concealed, he begins the walk into Watertown, and as he gets closer to the lantern's glow, he lowers his stance and begins stalking, utilizing the shadows from the illuminating moon.

Like a hummingbird moving from flower to flower, Adahy moves with the shadows he can find, furthering him to his target with each step. Quietly, he arrives a few meters from the town's magazine, squatting behind a stack of crates. Noticing this is not the ideal kill box, he scans the area. *There, in the tree line, it's a perfect spot for both guards to rove within,* he thinks, and moves expertly to the location undetected. Under the waving branches, he waits. Each leafy shadow moves with the wind, allowing Adahy some form of noise concealment, and he slowly readies his tomahawk.

He waits for the perfect moment as the second guard begins his walk around to the front side of the magazine. About twenty seconds pass, and the first guard roves into the darkness, entering Adahy's kill box. As the first guard turns his back on the tree line, Adahy stands with the tomahawk gripped in his right hand and throws it.

Crack

With a fierce splintering crack, Adahy's tomahawk severed the first guard's spine in two. The kill is instant. The sound of the tomahawk slicing and severing the guard's spinal cord was nearly muted under the rustling trees. Adahy places his left foot on the dead guard with the tomahawk stuck in his back and releases the wedged tomahawk from the broken spinal cord. *Only a few seconds; I need to move fast*, he thinks, as he moves to drag the lifeless guard into the dark shadows.

As Adahy is pulling the dead guard, the second guard rounds the corner. It was a brief moment before the guard would notice his companion was no longer roving, so he needed to act. Adahy releases the blade for a second throw. Fiercely rotating in the night sky, the tomahawk slams into the upper half of the guard's chest, dropping his body to the ground. The motions are quick. *Fuck*, he thinks as he arrives at the man. He's still alive, with the tomahawk sticking out of his chest, gurgling and choking on his blood.

"May the earth receive your blessing," he says, unsheathing his smaller blade and quickly slicing the guard's throat, ending his suffering. Adahy repeats the tomahawk removal process before cleaning his blade. Quietly, he drags and hides the body beyond the tree line. In moments, both roving sentry guards were removed wholly from the operation.

Adahy moved in quickly and quietly toward the front of the town Magazine. The town was quiet as most of the townsfolk were sleeping, and he peered around all corners to ensure no one was watching him. Seeing and hearing no one, he opens the door quietly and moves in.

It's warm, and Adahy can hear more than one person in this magazine. *Taking caution is key,* he thinks. As he begins scoping the layout of the room, he notices the wounded man must be in a separate room. As this thought enters Adahy's mind, a door opens, and he stands up straight, trying to conceal himself behind it against the wall. A woman walks out with bloodied bandages on a tray and heads out of the other room, not noticing Adahy. With the door closing slowly, he silently holds it and moves expertly behind her and into the room, not making a sound. With his back to the bed, he shuts and locks the door. Adahy unbuttons one button in the midsection of his greatcoat, then withdraws his smaller blade from the opening.

"You're...." a weak voice says, coughing, "you're here to kill me?"

"I am," Adahy says softly, turning around to face the man.

"Killing me won't..." his coughs are rough,

"Won't stop what's coming. You think you're damaging our majesty with minor caravan attacks and shipment disruptions?" He whispers, followed by a few violent coughs.

"Nothing will matter for you soon," Adahy says coldly with an eerie stillness in his eyes.

"Death comes for us all. That I can take...." The coughing erupts again, "but death won't save you from the man who will eventually come for you. Killing me doesn't change the outcome for you or him...." He tries to finish without coughing.

Adahy doesn't care what or who is coming; *this is taking too long,* he thinks to himself.

"Whoever is coming is irrelevant," Adahy says, forcing the blade into the man's chest under his arm in the soft spot.

"It will be…" he gasps, staring through Adahy.

Removing the knife, Adahy cleans it on the sheets and sheaths it back into this leather chest rig. He turns toward the door, buttoning the greatcoat. Peering into the candlelit magazine, the voices still murmur in the other room, but he sees no one. Quietly and carefully, he moves out of the room and into the open magazine and slips unseen out the front door. His green eyes scan Watertown, and it's still quiet, all but the wind. Following the shadows out of the town, he sees Raven and sprints to her.

"Ahhhhhhhhh!!" the female nurse shouts from inside the Magazine; her high-pitched shrill could be heard throughout the town.

"And that means we must ride like the wind, girl!" Adahy says to Raven as he unhitches her and smoothly saddles up.

In a seamless motion, the two become one and are quickly on the road back to Boston. As he looks back to Watertown, he notices there is commotion, and his mission has awakened the sleepy town, turning it into a nighttime frenzy. With Adahy in a forward, aggressive stance, Raven moved quickly, seemingly becoming one with the offshore winds.

Corn fields blend back into thick wooded forests, with the bright moon lighting up the open spaces as they travel down the road back to Boston. Shadows and light, shadows and light, repeated as they move quickly.

The dead man's words populate Adahy's mind: *Killing me doesn't change the outcome for you or for him…* Adahy tries to brush it off and focuses on the ride, brief as it is.

Soon, he sees Boston. The dimly lit city sat just down the road. From here, he could see its size. The abundance of lanterns creates a warm glow blanketing the town. Adahy clicks his teeth, and Raven sprints down the hill toward Boston's neck.

Late hours in the night make for interesting characters out and about. Adahy notices drunkards and beggars awakening, disheveled, and returning to their vices. Horses are being taken from their stables and saddled up, getting into carriage harnesses, and being prepped for the nearing day that's on the horizon. Minutes later, they arrive at the dank alley hiding the entrance to the King's Bane great room.

Adahy quickly dismounts Raven and opens the barn door. He moves her in and closes the door. Placing her in an open stable, he ties her reins to secure her and exits the barn.

Adahy takes a few quick glances to ensure he is unseen and crosses the alley. He quickly heads down the stairs into the entrance corridor. It is dimly lit by one near-expended candle in the corner, just enough light for Adahy to see the outline of the door leading to the great room.

"He returns!" Elias proclaims loudly as Adahy enters the room, closing the door behind him.

Scanning the room, Adahy noticed most of his companions were asleep, all but Thomas and Elias. Ester, James, and Nimish quietly slept in the stacked beds against the far wall.

Standing up from the chair in front of the fireplace, Thomas looks at Adahy,

"Is it done?"

"Everything went according to the plan," he replies, removing his tricorn and his greatcoat.

"Was he awake?" Asks Thomas.

"Yes. He had a lot to say when I arrived. Barely could speak with his coughing, but he spoke of someone he was afraid of. Someone that we should fear. It initially seemed senseless, but his words entered my mind on my ride back, and

I haven't been able to shake it..." Adahy says, visibly frustrated, and sits in the empty chair beside Shakespeare.

"Bloody lobsters always trying to stall the inevitable!" Elias says with alcohol on his breath.

"What are the words he spoke?" Thomas asks intriguingly.

"*Killing me won't stop what is coming… death won't save you from the man who will eventually come for you…. Killing me doesn't change the outcome for you or for him….*" Adahy says in an emulated tone as the man.

"Sounds like horse shit to me," Elias says roughly.

"No," Thomas says with authority, "these words must be carefully considered. There is one man I wish to never see on this side of the Atlantic…" he seemingly dazes into the fire and sits back in his chair.

"Who?" Adahy asks, looking at his uncle.

"Major-General Agador Ivey," Thomas says grimly, keeping his blue eyes on the frolicking flames.

The Wolf & The Bear

September 1771

Outside Boston Harbor

Controlled chaos mingling with disdain, ever fights for the top position within Agador's mind. Dark, malicious thoughts enveloped his reasoning in all platitudes of his life.

With fiery edges, not dissimilar to the yellowish-oranges of the blanket flower, the quickly rising sun warmed all it touched.

The time spent on the ship was one that he despised. Being confined to the sea and ship was terribly mundane for the Major General. Having the ability to exercise his violence restricted infuriated him to no end.

Killing and death then enter his mind, and his focus is razor sharp: *I will find you, and I will kill you all… King's Bane.*

"Land Ho!" A sailor from the crow's nest shouts to the deck, interrupting the Major General's thoughts.

Quickly, his mind moved to the mission, "Colonel Valles!" Agador shouts to his second in command, looking out at the peaking waves and rising sun.

"Yes, sir?"

"Let's wake the beautiful bastards, shall we?"

"When you are ready, sir."

The month-long journey was coming to a head, and the Major-General could not be more relieved. He handpicked the 30-man element from the King's Guard headquarters at the royal palace. These men would earn a new title, *'Sentry Rangers.'* Most, if not all, accepted that this could be a one-way trip. Dedicated to operating among the shadows in order to locate enemies of the Crown, his elite unit of men had the full endorsement of King George III.

"Let's go," Agador replies to Colonel Valles, and the two set off toward the descending stairs. The ship's interior was dank and smelled of rotten food, stagnant water, and human shit.

"Wake up, my heathens!" He endearingly shouts to his men.

Between the thick wooden beams, all the swinging cloth hammocks rock back and forth. Each revealing men's legs, followed by a collection of soldiers standing on the deck. Each of them carries an eager yet aggressive look on their faces, knowing they'll soon be going to work.

"Gentlemen, we have been sent by King George III to personally take care of and dispose of the rebel extremist group so aptly named the *'King's Bane.'* Our mission is to find and kill these bandits before they create more sympathizers for their petty, rebellious cause. These insurgents will be hunted down and killed. That was my promise to our King, and I intend to keep my promise. Is that understood?"

"Aye, sir!" The elite soldiers shout in unison.

"Good, now gather your gear and prepare for landfall, you bloody heathens!"

They do as they are instructed, and they are the best of the best under the Crown. Satisfied, Agador makes his way to the top deck. The men were his pride, and as a Major-General, he undoubtedly had all respect for his rank. But these men... these select men... his men, respected the man, not the rank, and they would all gladly give their lives for his.

**

Eyeing the wharf as they get closer, the Major General is the first man off the longboat and steps onto the wooden dock as it nears. A pudgy man begins making his way toward them with a curious scowl. Agador inhales heavily,

"Ah, I remember why I despise this land."

Within moments, the rest of the men unload from the four longboats and follow him onto the docks. Their presence is known immediately.

"Captain Bates, get the men and their equipment situated off the docks."

"Aye, sir! Sentry Rangers! In a single-file line, move off the docks!" The brown-haired Captain shouts, and the disciplined men move with purpose.

"Ah, Major-General Ivey, we were not expecting you—"

"Of course, you weren't. You will not find us on the manifest. Now point me toward the highest-ranking official in the city," the notorious Major-General demands.

"Right, you are, sir. Follow me, please," the dock worker replies in shock, trying to appease. He leads the Commander of the King's Guard off the docks, and they bypass the Sentry Rangers forming up.

"Captain, once you have them formed up, follow me. Let us make ourselves known," Agador smiles with a side-eye to the captain.

"Aye, sir! Platoon! Attention!" Captain Bates shouts to the rangers.

Agador and the pudgy dock worker start making their way toward the city. Captain Bates shouts and begins marching the Sentry Rangers in tow,

"Move out!"

Salty air breaks through the ships docked at separated wharves, and conversations permeate through like wildfire about the new crimson coats that have just arrived.

Standing next to a crate of glass bottles, an older gentleman extends one toward the seemingly annoyed Major General,

"Jackson's Spa Bottled Water! One copper per quart! Take a bottle- I promise you'll come back for more!"

"Carrying a bottle of water? Outrageous," the Commander replies dismissively.

Absolutely disgusting, he thinks, looking at the city and its people. The poverty and pure haggardness of the harbor town reminded him it had not changed since his time in the latter year of the wars. Muddy roads and pathways with street dogs and drunkards sleeping in the spaces they can find, with bustling commerce and trade happening all around, are the sights that fill Agador's walk. After a few moments, they begin walking toward Green Lane.

The dock worker stops and points to the three-story house, "There you are, sir, Thomas Young's residence."

"Good, now go back to the docks and get to work," Agador commands, walking toward the gate leading to the porch.

The Boston militiamen stood tall in a worn dark blue overcoat and acknowledged the Major General as he approached Thomas's porch. He passes the Militiaman in a dark blue overcoat. As he comes under the porch awning, he raises his hand to knock, and the door opens. In the doorway stood a tall figure, silver hair and scar running down his cheek, in tan britches and dark green coat,

"Major-General Agador Ivey, Welcome back to Boston."

"Major... or Privateer Captain... or?" Agador replies smugly to his counterpart. "I see you're poorly handling the insurrectionists that hide and sneak around throughout these little colonies, Thomas."

"The title is City Leader," Thomas lightly chuckles, "I see you're still our Majesties precious hound dog; how far has he lengthened your leash this time?"

Agador smiles, letting out a quiet breath through his nose, almost a silent laugh.

"Now, now, Thomas. We are here to handle problems *you* seemingly cannot control. Am I wrong?" Agador asks Thomas, not biting the older man's bait. If this were his younger years, Agador would have acted much differently, but with his age came wisdom and the ability to choose his battles.

"Right and wrong are only a matter of perception. Mr. Ivey, have you ever considered your King to be... a bit mad in his mind?" Thomas knew this line of inquiry would aggravate his guest.

Rage consumes Agador's body, and his face becomes hot,

"He is *OUR* King."

"Yes. Right... *Our* King. Perhaps you are right, Major-General," Thomas says, seemingly patronizing the man.

How dare he!? In seconds, he has insulted our King... refocus... the mission, the King's Bane, he thinks and refocuses his thoughts. Thomas was Thomas, and the British Major-General knew the old privateer was cunning.

"You are getting too old to handle a small band of rebels? I will make quick work of this. No need to worry any longer," Agador adds with an eerie smile creasing on his face.

"I do not believe in conspiracies, Major-General. There are many individuals who call themselves rebels nowadays. Any one person could be harboring ill will toward the King."

"Enough to kill his child?" Commander Ivey stares through Thomas.

Unflinching, Thomas blankly stares in return, "I was unaware our Majesty suffered such loss?"

With a short breath from his nose, seemingly recognizing Thomas's cutting tone, "In April, our King's child was on a transport ship with his mother, leaving from a port just north of here…" Agador's eyes are focused, "Several cannon shots sank it. Do you recall any talk in the city of this?"

"I do not."

"Hhmm," Agador takes a step back, "We need housing, *City Leader.*"

"Very well. The empty squad barracks are currently housing wine and grain. Remove them, and you and your men can find housing there."

"Very good, Thomas. My personal Sentry Rangers will find this accommodation satisfactory. When we are settled, you and I need to sit down soon about these rebels and the new strategy to remove them."

"So, we shall," Thomas nods in acceptance.

Agador knew his tumultuous career within the British Army was a well-known story, but the stories of Major Thomas Young's bravery and ruthlessness shook the most brutal of men.

In a genuine tone, Thomas adds, "You'll find the colonies are not how you last left them in '62, *Major-General,* but I offer you all my resources to find these so-called rebels."

"I'm sure I'll find the colonies just how they were when I left *Major…* full of savages, belligerents, and drunks so unprepared for a life they wither and die upon trying," Agador shakes his head, "Wasteful, really, the entire lot."

Smoothly, the King's Guard Commander, in his blood-red coat, turns and walks off the porch.

"Move out!" Captain Bates shouts to the Sentry Rangers as their Commander returns to the street.

The atmosphere was how he expected it to be: hostile. He didn't acquire the rank of Major-General if he cowered away from hostilities; it was a challenge he eagerly anticipated. Soon enough, the rebel cabal would be brought down, and he could make his way back to London. The men move in formation to their new home, and within minutes, the King's Guard Commander and his Sentry Rangers would arrive at their harbor-front barracks.

**

As they arrived in the harbor, the rising sun was now settled beyond the horizon of rolling hills with pockets of thick forest patchwork throughout. Inside the barracks, the Sentry Rangers cleared out and built defenses from the excess wood and materials gathered. The second floor became the headquarters office.

From behind the large oak desk, Major-General Ivey called for three volunteers. Within moments, the three soldiers stood at attention outside the office.

"You three, come in," he directs his voice outside the door.

"Yes, sir," the Corporal reports.

"You three will be my instruments," Agador says strongly, looking out a second-story window as the three elite soldiers enter the office.

"I need you three to gather information… to be… my…" his mind drifts to the violent possibilities, quickly returning to the moment, turning around to face the three soldiers.

"I need you three to be my eyes and ears…. You each have a role to fulfill. One of you needs to map the town. Find me the pockets where no one lives, where the vagrants roam, and explore the routes in and out. One of you needs to survey locals. You need to see the patterns, recognize who is in charge, and find the holes ripe for bribery. Finally, Rooney, I need you to follow the suspicious town leader, Thomas Young. You, Corporal Rooney, must be as cautious as possible… to be careful is an understatement… I cannot stress this enough. He is a slippery snake. He will be cautious. Know this, and use this," the ruthless major general elaborates.

"Yes, sir."

"Move quickly, and be silent," the Major General endearingly tells his men.

The three, led by Corporal Rooney, intentionally move out of the office. Agador moves back to the window and, through the glass pane, has a proper view over a few streets and then the harbor. Scanning over what he can see, he has an idea: go to Thomas Young's house. Quickly, he grabs his jacket and leaves the newly established headquarters.

As he went to Thomas Young's home, the new moon darkened the sky over Boston. He thought of all the weak spots within the city the men would notice and all the new questions he would have for one of the highest authorities in the harbor. But before that, he needed to ask Thomas directly about local groups and specifics of colonial sympathizers. *As a leading town authority, Thomas would, or should, have information on suspicious groups and individuals,* Agador thought.

Passing the two militiamen at the front gate, the King's Guard Commander arrives at the front door and knocks.

"Who is it?" A softer female voice says from inside the house.

"Ma'am, this is Major-General Ivey. I've come to speak with Thomas Young."

"He's out. Return tomorrow," she sternly and quickly replies.

"What time tomorrow, ma'am?"

"Return in the evening," she replies.

"I will. Thank you," he says and turns around.

Odd, he thinks, exiting the porch and heading back toward the barracks.

Agador's walk back was a bit slower. *Why wasn't Thomas home? A prominent leader, not being readily available for the people... was he merely busy with more pressing matters? Yet, he was not available within the town where he was needed. Or are there more sinister reasons he is not free?* His mind was spinning to new possibilities and alternative theories of the rebel situation in Boston. Agador knew all too well that Thomas Young's cunningness was deadly, but to what extent, he questioned. Agador had to approach this situation in Boston carefully if he were to complete his mission and return to London in splendid gratification.

**

With both hands on the office doorframe and his head popping through,

"Colonel Valles!" Major-General Ivey shouts into the squad bay of the barracks.

"Yes, Sir?" The man replies from the opposite end.

"Come into my office," he says and walks back toward his large oak desk. With a smooth motion, he rounds the desk and sits in the elegant leather chair.

"I want you to tail Corporal Rooney. He is gaining a foundational understanding of Thomas Young, but I sense the city leader knows more than he lets on. I inquired with him about the sinking, yet he didn't seem affected. I do believe, though, that he knows someone who has information about the incident. Also, I want you there because Rooney will not be able to see it all, for he is also young and impetuous."

"Aye, Sir. These youngsters have vigor but not patience. And that Thomas Young has always been slippery."

As they spoke, the Colonel removed his bright-red Officer coat and placed it on the coat rack before grabbing an older walnut-tanned cossack.

"Right, you are, dear friend. Justifications for your companionship on this mission are indeed plenty and full. I want to know what is said in the shadows."

"I'll get it done, Commander."

"Be safe, and do not be seen," Agador insists in a respectful tone.

As he finishes changing, he looks like a normal, unsuspecting civilian, "Of course, sir," he says as he places the cossack hood over his head.

Major General Ivey, with an eager look across his face, seemingly satisfied. Colonel Valles exits the room and makes his way toward the rear exit. He mustn't be seen leaving the front entrance. As the crowds of civilians bustled through the streets and alleys, Colonel Valles expertly blended with them and approached Corporal Rooney's last known position.

Tunnel Rats

Faneuil Hall

Boston, Massachusetts

"He's older now, that's evident," the large African man said impartially, looking through the crowd at the Major General.

"When did you see him?" Adahy asked curiously, looking up to James.

"During the war. He was a boy then and with his father, Abraham Ivey. But he is a man now."

Adahy turned and looked forward through the crowd, seeing him. He looked strong; he could see that. His posture was firm, and he stood with pride. His blue eyes and black hair pulled back were prominent features. A square jaw supported an annoyed look that was louder than the man announcing the Major General.

"What is that medallion on his black and gold sash?"

James squints his eyes, "That is worn by the Commander of the King's Guard."

"He looks irritated," Adahy laughs.

James smiles, looking down at Adahy, "That's because he doesn't know what he's looking for. C'mon, I've had enough of this exhibition. Let's make some coffee and see what the others are up to."

Passersby stared a lot at James as they walked through the city market. Adahy didn't blame them. Not only was James twice as tall as anyone else, but he was also a free man. James was so huge that he parted the crowd easily; all Adahy had to do was keep close in tow. He quickly gathered that people knew James was not a person to engage with unless you knew how to handle him. His aura was standoffish, but so was Adahy's, and James led the others when his uncle wasn't around... or at least, that's how Adahy was interpreting things.

Walking behind James, Adahy asks carefully,

"What's it like knowing all these people are terrified of you?"

"Excuse me?"

"Yeah, you know, you are not a slave... so they can't really do anything to you... and you're... you know... huge."

He stops and turns around. Looking down at the native with a puzzled look on his face, "Let me ask you... Do you think, at my age, or my attitude, or even the color of my skin enables me to give any god dammed care about what these people have to say, think, or feel about me?"

Adahy could see he was deathly serious, "No, I guess not."

"That's right. I am too old to worry if they are terrified or not... I can't worry... I must just be me and live the life I have before me."

"What life did you live before meeting Thomas?"

As the two men walked through the city and further away from the town hall, the pockets of people were thinning out.

"It's not a good story."

"Neither is mine... but it is *your* story."

Thinking about it, James reluctantly starts speaking,

"He was an old man, Mr. Robinson. He was kind, took care of me, and he freed me, along with other slaves he would purchase. Mr. Robinson only purchased people with the sole intention of freeing them. An *old righteous scallywag*, as he would often call himself..."

Adahy glanced up at James, and he could see it was emotionally affecting him to articulate the story. Reluctantly, the massive man continued,

"Naturally, this gained the attention of others with different attitudes toward the idea. He paid me, so I stayed working for him, but after a few years, they came and killed him..." he pauses with a sigh but continues,

"So, I killed them. Every single last one of them..." He adds coldly.

"Good. I am glad you did."

"For years, I was hunted by slavers and bounty hunters... It's okay, though, because I dealt with them all.... Mr. Robinson took me in, freed me, taught me how to read and write, and showed me true compassion. I'll be forever grateful to him... he was the father that was taken from me."

"I understand. My father was killed before I was able to walk... but at least we have Thomas?!" Adahy adds somewhat sarcastically, shifting the tone of the conversation.

James smiles, "Yeah, we do, don't we?"

"And we have each other!" Adahy's falsely optimistic tone doesn't go unnoticed.

"Yeah, you're not so bad, kid," he chuckles lightly and playfully punches Adahy's left shoulder.

The two men walk casually through the streets of Boston, passing multi-storied brick buildings and merchants selling wares. Drunks beg for coins, and prostitutes do their best to rope in paying customers. The atmosphere is rich with flavor in all sensory aspects.

"How are you taking to Boston? Much different than the wilderness, I'm sure," his deep voice growls in a positive tone.

"It's a city," Adahy replies stalely.

"Aye, that it is, isn't it?" James lightly chuckles.

"It is nice being with Thomas and him allowing me to join you all."

"Well… you carry certain skills, and they are needed for this line of work."

"Thomas has mentioned…" Adahy smiles.

***

Liberty Tree
Boston, Massachusetts

"I'm not doing that!" One teen said to the others as they stood near the old elm tree, smoking their pipes.

"Don't be a pansy!" Another replied.

As Thomas approached the group of young people, they all shushed each other, trying to quiet their conversation.

"Shh."

Damned kids, he thought as he passed them, turning right off Orange Street onto Essex, leaving the crowds. Then, another instinctual thought consumed him. One he's familiar with, a darker thought.

I'm being followed. The feeling overcame Thomas entirely. Immediately and subtly, he shifted his movements and began moving toward the north.

This isn't good, he thinks, as he begins to formulate a way to lose the tail.

He could not go the usual way to the King's Bane headquarters but knew Boston was a dynamic city with resourceful routes scattered within.

"John's old smuggling routes," he said to himself under his breath, "Yes, under the city in the dank tunnels. They would be perfect to move unseen."

Thomas notices the small hand-drawn triangle in red chalk on one of the bricks and knows he's near one of the tunnel entrances.

"The Major General is more cunning than I initially assumed," he said to himself as he walked through the multi-storied brick buildings lining the streets, keeping track of his tail.

Thomas knew he needed to be more cautious and quicker wherever possible. Noticing the opening to a small alley upcoming on his right and a pocket of merchants, Thomas moved slyly into the alley, ducking behind a stack of barrels.

Peering through an opening on the stack, he notices the British soldier walk by the alley, unaware of his movements,

Damn, Brit. A few moments go by, and he notices another... *Why are there two?* His blue eyes follow the second man slithering between the crowds, following the first tail.

Once clear, Thomas stood up and followed the alley deeper until it opened to a clearing between the buildings. It is filled with laundry hanging out to dry. *Around here is the opening,* he thought. Carefully, he looks around the base of the buildings and notices the collection of symbols drawn on the bricks above the run-down wooden cellar-style door: a triangle, a 5-point star, and a diamond. All are drawn the size of a coin.

Thomas notices that the wood is old, and the doors haven't seen much use in the last several years. He grabs the handles and opens the doors. It's dark, and the dank underground stench rises.

"Now, let's see if I remember how to get to the great room from here," Thomas mutters to himself softly.

Stepping onto the wooden step ladder, he makes his way underground and into the rancid tunnel. He closes the doors as he gets to the bottom. Faint beams of light pierced through the darkness, slipping through the narrow cracks in the stone above. The walls of the tunnels, damp and rugged, caught the glimmer, casting long shadows that danced with every flicker. As Thomas walked through the tunnel, his memory returned to him. He recognizes familiar pathways as he furthers into the smuggling corridors.

Several minutes go by as Thomas navigates the darkened smuggling tunnels, eventually finding the door that will lead him to the King's Bane great room. The old door hasn't been opened in decades, and Thomas has to lean into it with all his strength to pry it open. He does, and on the other side is a new room that he's seen before. It was a storage room for his crew. He is correct; this is the door he is looking for. Closing the door and securing it tightly, Thomas turns and exits the storage room and enters the great room.

Withdrawing his pistol, Adahy stands, turning his body to face the storage door.

A scared-faced and gray-haired man emerges from the edge of the door, and Adahy relaxes his stance.

"Uncle Thomas! What are you doing?"

"Is this because of this King's Guard Commander? You are using the old tunnels?" Elias asks snobbishly.

In a deadly serious tone, Thomas snaps, "I am using these tunnels because you all sank the King's child!"

Silence consumes the space. Elias's usually plucky face dropped to a petrified stillness it hadn't held in years.

"What are you saying, Thomas?" Ester regrettably interjects.

"So, the transport ship was *important*," James grimly adds.

Thomas scoffs, "Unbelievable, you three. I have created monsters out of you all. There were women and children on that ship…"

Adahy can feel the tension as the dead silence envelops the room.

Elias speaks, "Thomas… the redcoat carried your name—"

"It needed to be done…" Her soft voice carried regret. Ester stood from the chair near the hearth and walked to Thomas,

"We couldn't let them uncover your role."

She rests her small, weathered hand on his chest. Thomas's body eases, and he seemingly becomes a bit more relaxed.

Adahy's eyes are wide. He looks back and forth as the tension seemingly dissipates, and he speaks to change the subject,

"We were out today. At Faneuil Hall, watching them announce the Major General."

"You're lucky… it's exhausting having to throw them off," Thomas says, shifting his tone and mood, and Ester follows,

"Are you sure they didn't follow you into the tunnels?" Ester asks with a slight chuckle and walks back to the hearth.

"Well, this King's Guard Commander is cunning and calculated. Agador Ivey is no pushover, nor is he someone that you want to cross. The King has now sent his best weapon to hunt us down and kill us or, at the very least, try to hunt us and kill us. That is why we must be more careful than ever before; we must stay in the shadows," he tells his crew.

"You've given them the old squad barracks. We can watch who goes in and out. We can hunt them, too," Adahy says, excitedly leaning forward in his chair.

"Aye, and Nimish is currently doing just that," Thomas confirms, sitting in one of the rocking chairs and removing his gloves.

"That kid can get in and out of anywhere, I swear to Odin," Ester says after taking a sip from her ale.

"Aye. He's a natural at subterfuge," Thomas adds.

"He blends well into the population and is not an overthinker. Good skills to have in today's world," Elias adds.

"Aye... today's world requires stealth, violence, and the right mind to act appropriately with such tools," Thomas replies strongly.

"Speaking of tools, how much did you make on the last cannon sale from the hilltop perch to the privateers?" Elias inquires with Thomas.

"Not enough," the old man grumbles.

"Shame, we could've used them now," Elias states, looking into the fire.

"It's fine; we have another shipment of powder and cannon coming soon... we will turn that over quickly to our friends in Philadelphia and make some money," Thomas adds confidently.

"When is that arriving, Top?" Asks Elias.

"They should arrive within the next week or two. Etienne is coming with his nephew Lucian, and we will provide him and the shipment security to Robert at Tun."

With a deep inhale, James adds, "Ahhhh, I love a good trip to Philadelphia."

"It should run smoothly," Thomas asserts.

"Aye, it will. Etienne is a good man."

"That he is, Elias," silence follows Thomas's words.

Taking advantage of the break in the conversation, Adahy interjects,

"When is Nimish returning?"

"Soon. There are specifics I need answers to," he sighs, followed by a deep inhale and slow exhale.

Shadows from the flames in the fireplace glow upon the faces of the King's Bane members as the group of them sit around the great room. Each carries a different attitude between them.

***

1752
London, England

Agador's small hand was secured within his father's hand as the two reached the throne room.

"The hunters have returned, Agador," Abraham Ivey says to his son with a collection of steps making for great acoustics in the hallway.

"What were they hunting, father?"

"The Aureum Pentagonum, my dear son."

"The children's fairytale story?"

"Yes, Agador… some believe it is more than a story and believe it holds validity and truth. Others have even dedicated their lives to searching for the five golden shards."

"Someone has found a golden shard of the Aureum Pentagonum, Father?"

"Aye, that's right. Or at least that is what we've been told. Which is why we are here today… the hunters have returned with one of the golden shards."

"How did they get it?"

"Well... from all accounts, a Royal Navy Lieutenant initially found it while on an expedition. He refused to hand it over, when prompted, to give it to our King. Thus, kicking off a decade-long manhunt for him."

"How did he come to find it, Father?"

"That is complicated because conflicting narratives surround how the Lieutenant came across the shard. But you remember the stories, son. History claims that God chose five Roman Legionaries to carry the five golden shards to the far corners of the known world, keeping their identity and location hidden... ensuring no one would ever find the shards," Abraham said, looking down toward Agador.

Agador's youthful mind races in awe, "Who is the Lieutenant that found it?"

"A man named John Young...but history will remember him as *Sailor Johnnie*. After denying the King, he killed several compatriots after they tried to arrest him. He revolted and went on the run from the Crown," says Abraham in an elevated tone, almost excited to listen to the men who returned.

"Why did he deny the King the shard?"

"Not sure, maybe he believed the stories... or maybe he is a lunatic who went insane on the expedition... but you never deny the Crown."

"How can someone deny our King? He is the will of God," Agador asks with loyalty.

"That he is. To deny him would be blasphemous. This is why the lieutenant was hunted and killed. No one denies the Crown. Given that our King is the will of God, you will do right by him and his son, your cousin," Abraham stops walking, disregarding all passersby going to the Throne Room, and squats to his son's level.

"You will be a tool for our King. You are an Ivey. This means you do as the Crown instructs, and you do it with grace, dignity, and force. This is your path, Agador," Abraham says with conviction

He grabs his son's hand and continues walking toward the throne room. Everyone is making their way. Agador notices familiar faces and people he has seen around St. James Palace. *This must be important*, he thought. Women and men were all moving toward the Throne Room in the finest clothing and best jewels. Barons, Chancellors, and even some high-ranking soldiers were in the hallways making their way. As the two of them entered the Throne Room, conversations hummed throughout, filled with excitement that the hunters had returned. The smell of beeswax, perfumes, and candle smoke permeated throughout the room. *It is magnificent*, he thought.

The room was grand, with high ceilings, painted murals across the walls, and woven tapestries flowing between. It was large enough to hold everyone comfortably, including everyone from the London High Society awaiting the King.

As the heavier oak doors swung open, the throne room fell silent. Baron Richard Ashford, the Lord Chamberlain, stepped forward, his voice echoing throughout the throne room,

"His Majesty, King George the Second, by the Grace of God, King of Great Britain, and Defender of the Faith."

A ripple movement followed throughout the crowd as every standing person turned their head toward the doors, and those sitting stood up and faced the doors. As King George II entered the room, the only sound that was heard was the soft rustle of clothing as he walked to the throne flanked by his King's Guardsmen.

"Now, bring forward the heroes! I have waited long enough! For a decade, I have been yearning for this moment, bring forth the men and the artifact. Display it to the Court and Crown. For we are the ones who funded such a lengthy and gratifying expedition," the King says loudly.

"Laurence Carbis and William Davies, step forward with His Majesty's artifact," the Lord Chamberlain directs the men.

The room is quiet. Everyone is following along. William Davies and Laurence Carbis stood tall within the crowded room, stepping through the people making their way before the King. The silence is deafening. Each man bows toward their king, and Agador notices William Davies shift his eyes to his partner for a brief moment. When they return to their normal stance, the shorter one, Laurence Carbis, steps forward and removes an item from his greatcoat chest pocket. Slowly, he removes the cloth protecting the item.

One flap after the other, he uncovers the artifact. No one can see it. The object is too tiny to be seen within the palm of the man.

It's gold, he thinks, as he watches the worn-down-looking man pass the item to the King.

"Fascinating!" the King exclaims, nearly entranced with the relic, "At long last, the golden shard of the Aureum Pentagonum is mine!"

The room erupted into cheers, and the King was undeniably happy and filled with joy, totally consumed. Agador notices Davies and Carbis exchange a quick side-eye look, nearly imperceptible, but there. Most cheered and clapped while others did not, sparking conversations between them. Sidelong looks between nobles were lightly blended between the cheers and elation. Agador and his father were next to a group that began talking amongst themselves.

"They've been gone for years," a smaller, balder military man adds, "and they return now, with this? They couldn't capture the traitor when he was under their noses numerous times, and we are expected to believe they accomplished their mission. Doubtful at best!"

"Indeed, Admiral Griffin, the gold does not shimmer as described within the texts of Elmir N. The *'shards to shimmer like the stars,'* and this is no star," another taller man adds to the group, still speaking below the hum and cheers in the room.

"A decade of searching for the traitor, and they return with nothing more than what?... A trinket from the market," Abraham Ivey adds to the discourse.

"This is a momentous occasion, and we will celebrate accordingly! Lord Ashford, ready the banquet hall. I want every table filled with pheasants, fruit, bread, cheeses…. I want it all! And you," the King snaps his fingers at the Palace Guard,

"Bring down my son. He needs to join me on this day!"

King George II's voice echoed as he walked out of the throne room, never taking his eyes off the relic.

"Your Majesty!" The taller man in the group stepped forward, "Might we have the royal scholars inspect the relic in the spirit of scholarship? The text descriptions of Elmir N. are complex, and I believe additional studies could offer new insights, your Majesty."

The King stopped moving, and his smile faltered only slightly, and he waved his hand dismissingly toward the man,

"In due time," he said in a firm tone. "For now, we shall celebrate. Let us feast!"

Flanked by the King's Guardsman, the King made his way out of the throne room. Portions of the crowd followed. Slowly, the remaining crowd, not going to the banquet hall, began making their way into the palace hallways, and more conversations were being had about the relic, the men's adventure, and the feast to come. In the shadows, others spoke of more conniving topics, swirling rumors and beginning tales that would linger in the halls for years to come.

"Father..." young Agador says, looking up at his weathered father.

"What is it?"

"Just now... the conversation you had with the others..."

"Yes? What of it?"

"Why does the King refuse an examination of the item?"

Stunned by the awareness of the boy, Abraham smiles, "So, you were listening?"

Dropping his head, "I assumed you would not have brought me if you did not want me to learn of crown politics."

"Very good," a proud Abraham states, and continues, "The King is an obsessive man."

"Are you allowed to say that?" Agador questions.

"Aye, my son... you have a great deal to learn about Palace Politics."

"Why did he refuse the examination?" Agador asks again.

"Well... Loyalty is not merely blind obedience to the Crown. Loyalty is an internal compass... a guide if you will. I serve King George II, absolutely, but even more than that, I serve the British Empire, the Crown itself," the man stops walking and squats to the boy's level, "These are not always in alignment."

"But he is the King..."

"This is true, but he is still a man. And a powerful man must have checks and balances to maintain the Empire. This is what duty looks like, Agador... not blindly following orders, but ensuring that those orders reflect the best possible outcome for the Crown," his words are heavy as he finishes and stands back up, continuing the walk.

"In instances like today, what if the King refuses to listen?"

"Then you serve in whatever ways you can and remain steady. True loyalty does not flee, my boy," his father's words reverberate through his mind.

***

1771
September

Knock, Knock

As he snaps out of his daze, the world seems to recreate itself around Agador. Looking around the room, he notices the book in his lap, his latest endeavor, '*Candide*' by Voltaire. Returning to reality, the Major General snaps the book closed and places it on his desk.

"Yes, what is it? Open the door," his fiery tone never ceased, even in his relaxed state.

Opening the door, the guard speaks, "Corporal Rooney has returned, sir."

The hooded Corporal Rooney walks into the commander's quarters and stands at attention before his superior.

Agador Ivey stood from behind his desk, revealing his bulldog-like stature,

"At ease, Corporal. What news do you have?"

Removing his hood, he rests his body and speaks,

"He arrived home, sir."

"Perfect. I will go see him now," Agador smiles and walks from behind his desk.

"But sir…" Corporal Rooney adds.

"What?"

"The target's activity is peculiar. He moves in patterns. I followed him by the wharves, and he somehow evaded my sight and seemingly disappeared. It is almost as if he knows he is being watched... I will keep my eyes on him."

"Hmm. Interesting," the Major-General says slyly, "Regardless of his dealings, we will keep our eyes on him. The old, retired Major is just a paranoid old man stuck in his ways. He is not the concern. Keep an eye on him just in case... but remember, Corporal... people lie. People will lie to survive. Never forget that when you're watching a target," the Major General cautions sternly and continues,

"You see, Corporal, we will kill these bandits and return to London, leaving this wretched land behind, never to set foot here again, bringing our King some form of closure with these wretched rats."

"Aye, Sir! They will die, and we will not fail."

"No, we will not," Commander Ivey replies, grabbing his coat from the coat rack and putting it on, "I am going to Thomas Young's residence. Pick back up with him in the morning, Corporal."

"Aye, sir!"

**

The walk from the barracks to Thomas's home was rather short but long enough for the Major General to become annoyed. Outside the gate stood a militiaman with one musket slung over his left shoulder.

"You there, I am here to see Thomas Young."

"Yes, sir. Of course," he replies, opening the gate.

Agador made his way onto the porch and removed his tricorn. With black leather gloves, he curls his left hand to knock on the door. As he does, the door opens, revealing Thomas.

"Ah, Major General. How is Boston treating you?"

In a serious tone, not one for back-and-forth, the King's Guard Commander replies,

"Boston is Boston. I am here because I am curious to learn how a rebel cabal...if you can call it that, has been able to fester here like a disease?"

"I am remised to admit that there are many gatherings of men, women, and children every day around the city. Many people have collective interests and enjoy the company of like-minded souls," Thomas's words are smooth.

"If King George III has acknowledged their existence... you shall as well, Thomas," he replies with a quick breath out of his sharp nose.

"And do you believe such a cabal does exist?"

"They must. The King's blood was murdered."

A slight breeze rode through the air between the men, seemingly slicing the tension.

"The King has many enemies. You, most of all should understand this. As the King's Guard Commander, it is your duty to protect the King and Crown from all threats, should they arise," replied Thomas, unflinching.

"Do not patronize me, Thoma—"

"And do you think your time is best spent here, in these... as you say, '*godforsaken colonies*' or do you think they sent you away for a reason... on a fruitless hunt searching for ghosts?"

"I am not here to listen to this bullshit. I know you know of the treachery that has been manifesting here in Boston. There is more happening in these streets, and I will uncover it... Mark my words!"

"If you say so. But I would not be a bit surprised if you uncover that your King and his whispering King's Council sent you away to distract you...I do hope you have a great night tonight."

"This is not over, Thomas. I will find out what is happening here."

"It is a beautiful September night... I do believe one gains a better appreciation for the city in the nighttime hours. Now, thank you for stopping by; it is a bit late. Goodnight, Commander Ivey; good luck!"

In one movement, Thomas closes the door, and the lantern from behind the home window is extinguished.

Send me away... he doesn't know what he's saying, he thinks as he turns to face the road.

"Pfft," Agador mutters, putting his tricorn back on and stepping off the porch onto the path. He passes the militiamen and starts off down the street.

"I'll find the King's Bane. My King asks of it, and I will deliver," he grumbles as he begins his aimless walk into the city.

Grasping Shadows

Tuesday, October 2nd, 1771

Hancock's Wharf

7:30 AM

Unlike most mornings in Boston, this morning was quiet. Murmurs of the people surrounding the wharf die down as he arrives. Major General Agador Ivey and a handful of his Sentry Rangers, the elite of the King's Guard.

"What did the man say again?"

"Murders on the Wharf, Commander," Captain Bates replies.

"Ah, I bet these are the murders committed by the ghosts Thomas was speaking of."

The men come around the corner of the warehouse on their horses and see it. Just on the horizon was the sun, reaching from the depths to illuminate the day. Agador smoothly analyzes the area, and he looks across. He sees the morning mist canvassing the harbor's still waters. His keen eyes sweep the scene as the sea-salted air scent melds with the faint metallic smell of blood. Lifeless soldiers lie scattered with pools of blood and mud. Glinting off the dead men's brass gear, sunlight begins spreading and filling the dark pockets on the wharf.

"Absolutely pathetic," groans Commander Ivey as he loathsomely takes in the massacre.

The Major General smoothly unsaddles his horse as his black leather boots land on the damp wooden dock.

"Tell them not to touch the bodies anymore. Leave them for the Rangers. Although, we will need their services when it's time to move them from the scene," the Major General instructs his captain.

"Yes, sir."

"The kills look clean," he says softly as he crouches beside one of the corpses, his hand brushing against the corporal's torn coat. A clean arrow wound to the neck. He touches the blood, still somewhat fresh,

"Whoever did this wasn't far ahead of them."

Agador Ivey surveys the dock, the crates still stashed away in corners, hastily covered by tarps, up against the wharf warehouse. Within his black glove, his fingers trace the faint, muddy tracks leading toward the heart of the city.

They were here, he thinks, his mind already piecing together the movements of the elusive King's Bane.

"Arrows and blades again," Agador mutters to himself.

"What are your thoughts, sir?" Captain Bates asks.

"A group of five, maybe six…."

"Do you believe it to be the King's Bane?"

Commander Ivey sighs,

"The King's Bane… If it is, they're getting bold. And whoever's helping them is keeping them supplied with the best."

Agador rises, his eyes narrowing as he calls over one of the Sentry Rangers, a seasoned scout named Gage,

"Gage, tell me what you've gathered."

The younger soldier moved with purpose and spoke directly,

"Commander, it's as we suspected; cannons were being offloaded last night. You can see the crates of powder up against the warehouse over there," he says, pointing to the crates.

"And they hitched cannon to their wagons... there," the young Sentry Ranger points to the tracks in the mud.

"The soldiers must've stumbled upon the deal— didn't make it out," Gage says smoothly.

"French... there is no doubt about it," the Major General says to Gage.

"The French, sir?"

"Look at the tracks, Gage... they are not British cannon. The wheelbase is of French design," he says, pointing to the muddy ground, "It's a thinner wheel design than English design."

"I would have never noticed, sir."

"When you've killed Frenchmen around the world, you tend to learn their weapon systems," he said with a smile.

The French connection wasn't new to him—rumors had swirled since his arrival—but the brazenness of this operation was. The enemy grows more daring by the day.

"Bates! Find me Hancock and bring him to the barracks to have him provide an answer about why the King's men are dead in his wharf!" the Major General says sternly to Captain Bates.

"Aye, sir!" he replies, taking a squad of soldiers with him and marching toward the city's heart.

Agador takes a deep breath and looks around again... *None of the people are speaking, French munitions, and dead King's men,* he thinks to himself, perplexed on how this early morning event unfolded.

"Gage, follow these cart tracks… see where they go," Agador instructs his Sentry Ranger.

"Aye, sir," he replies.

Moments pass as Agador assesses more of the scene of blood puddles with salt water littered across the dock. *No large slashes on the bodies, smaller blades, and no gunshots… hmm*, he thinks, scanning around.

"Major General, sir!"

"What did you find, Gage?" the Major General asks the man as he arrives back to the docks.

"Nothing, sir. The tracks blend into multiple others around the city. It becomes indistinguishable," the man's resultless words cut through the air like a tumbling tomahawk.

Visibly frustrated, the Major General exhales smoothly,

"I see…I want squads on the King's Highway, and I want them there immediately. They aren't keeping the French munitions here in the harbor city. They're selling them, so we need men inspecting all caravans and carts on the roads. They won't stay hidden. We will find them," Agador says definitively and mounts his horse. With one disgusted look, he rides back to the barracks.

***

London, England

The lantern lighting was abundant, illuminating all the historical tapestries along the walls and books on the shelves. Candles drip wax onto their candelabras as the night moves on. The Lord Chamberlain and Chancellor Hawke were eating dinner when the conversation suddenly shifted to Agador's expedition.

"Have you heard any word on our young King's Guard Commander and his Sentry Rangers?"

"Ah, Chancellor Hawke, how good of you to ask. As a matter of fact, we have received some valuable information on the latest shipment from the colonies," the Lord Chamberlain said, taking a bite into his food, chewing and swallowing it,

"Colonel Valles says they are settling into an old militia barracks. They are actively hunting the rebel cabal, the King's Bane, and the young Commander Ivey, who is playing his role to perfection, is leading the charge, ever unaware of our Colonel's true intentions…"

"What news of colonial matters? Any spaces within to disrupt?" Chancellor Hawke asks impetuously.

"Well… we all know of the Massacre that occurred last year, and if that sort of situation unfolds again, we can simply shift the blame to our hot-headed Major General," Lord Chamberlain Ashford says with a slick smile.

"I see…" the Chancellor says slowly, seemingly connecting the dots.

"You see, Chancellor Hawke… there are more than brute force ways to spark dissent in the minds of the people… showing our King that it is required of him to rid the world of these petty colonies," the older man says cunningly.

"Without young Agador here in the King's ear, we can shift his priorities… a war would be good for business, would it not?"

Nodding his head in agreement, Chancellor Hawke says, "Yes, it would… we could sell our old reserves to make room for new and updated artillery, muskets, and better-quality powder. Getting production started on new weaponry could bolster the economy. We know the Seven Years' War weapons are sitting, rotting away. A refreshing of our munitions stock and weapons reserve will properly line the right pockets."

With a devilish smile, the Lord Chamberlain replies, "Precisely. You understand the process, Chancellor. There is a reason you are here, in the Shadow Room, and not with the others on the base level of the palace... low-level minds require low-level living."

"I am thankful for the invitation to be here and continued faith in my loyalty," he says gratefully and continues, "As much as I do not want to see our soldiers in yet another war, it is advantageous for us to have one... the weapons market will flourish undoubtedly, and the money will be spent in the streets of the British Empire, filling the coffers of British Parliament."

"Once the colonies realize that it is futile to fight with the Empire, they will stop the blatant disrespect and will bend to our will. After that, they will be taxed even harder to repay the debts from all wars on that horrendous land," the Lord Chamberlain says after he sips his Portuguese wine.

"They will not be able to compete with the might of our King's empire. We will roll over their spirit. It will not take longer than a single year to get them subdued," Chancellor Hawke confidently said smoothly.

"That is the spirit, Hawke. The colonies have always been a rowdy bunch, but with Commander Ivey there... we have the opportunity to pin their violent uprisings on his actions or inability to act. Whichever one prevails first, we shall see..."

His voice echoes against the Palace walls, with the candelabras spread evenly in the stone. The two men's shadows dance with the candle flames as their night fills with elation and talk of dark possibilities across the Atlantic.

The French Connection

Tuesday, October 2nd, 1771
Hancock's Wharf
2:35 am

Out of the darkness came the shrill, haunting cry of a large white owl—"Keeek!" Its screech reverberated off the silent water and still brick buildings, catching the attention of the King's Bane members. Adahy's eyes dart to the flying creature and watch it circle twice and land on a nearby rooftop.

Reminds me when I was a boy back home with Wohali, he thinks, and the frosty air brings his mind back to the wharf. It's cold, and the chill finds its way down Adahy's greatcoat, causing a shiver.

"Fuck, it's cold," he mentions to the others.

"Fucking southerners, shit," Elias replies with a smile.

"Fuck off, Shakespeare, you hail from England, the land of the heartless and cold bastards," Adahy adds lovingly.

"Yeah, yeah, yeah…" he replies, taking the ridicule.

"James, I know you need no reminder, but we need to stop at George's Tavern on the way out of the city," Thomas mentions.

"That's right... Barratt has the information of the next coin shipment from Cambridge," James devilishly smiles.

"Aye, hopefully, he does."

"Hopefully, Top," James says, looking into the darkness of the harbor, "When are they supposed to arrive, Thomas?" James asks impatiently, sitting on a barrel top.

"Soon, they will be here, and we can get this done and over with... the sooner, the better," Thomas states as he stands on the edge of the wharf looking into the harbor.

"They need to hurry. That squad of Regulars keeps patrolling closer and closer to us... I thought you said John cleared this area, and it would be void of redcoat activity?" Elias adds with inquiry.

"Aye, he did say they wouldn't be here, but they are... we will have to just work around it...." Thomas says and stops mid-sentence, turning toward the darkened harbor, "They're here," he finishes to the others in a lower tone, trying to stay as quiet as possible.

As the words leave Thomas's mouth, Adahy looks into the blackened harbor and sees it... a well-maintained frigate emerges from the darkness. The lanterns from the docks allow some form of illumination and light up the white-furled sails and ropes strung across the masts. The size was average, but Adahy had never been near or up close to a well-built ship like this. It moved slowly on the water, graciously entering into the wharf.

"Oi, Monsieur Young!" a voice emerges happily on the ship's deck.

"Is that Etienne Turenne I hear?!" Thomas replies, looking up from the dock.

"Mon Ami, it is great to see your beautiful face again!" Etienne jokes playfully with Thomas, knowing the scar is his identifier.

A plank with iron and rope rails connected the frigate to the dock, emplaced as the ship became still. The Frenchman that walked onto the dock was not what Adahy was expecting to see. Etienne was taller, had sharp facial features, and had a smaller mouth. He was dressed in the finest French fashion but not over the top.

"Thomas, my friend… it is great to see you in one piece… I heard they sent the King's dog here to sniff you out," Etienne smiles.

"Indeed, the young King's Guard Commander is here… but we have done a solid job at keeping our distance, ever-steadily working toward the overall goal," Thomas replies smoothly.

His smile is cold but welcoming, yet Etienne's eyes are calculating, giving Adahy the impression that he's assessing every person at the wharf.

"Monsieur Young, I have always admired your ambition. However, ambition does not pay for cannons. We both know what's at stake here, and I trust you'll see the value in maintaining our arrangeme—"

Before finishing his sentence, Thomas extended his hand with a bag full of coins. Etienne takes it with a subtle smile,

"You never conneries with me. I appreciate that the most," Etienne compliments.

"And I never will, my friend. We are bound by liberty, Etienne," Thomas adds and turns to the other King's Bane members, motioning for them to help unload the equipment.

Adahy, James, Ester, Elias, and Nimish hastily move and begin rolling powder barrels off the ship. Once on the dock, they rolled the barrels to the empty wagon and loaded one full wagon with powder. The barrels are heavy, but Adahy enjoyed the work. Working carried a gratification with it. Several minutes pass, and all the barrels are staged next to the cart.

"Who is the cheveux blonds peau rouge?" Etienne asks Thomas as the King's Bane unloads the powder barrels.

Thomas smiles, "That is my nephew… and he finds no joy in being called a redskin,"

"Que diable, Thomas! Why did you not lead with that?" Etienne laughs and continues, "Lucien, the boy going with the shipment, is my nephew… he's young, like yours. Although I must admit, he's a bit of *a bête*," he finishes.

"Aye, well, I am sure he's lovely, like you," Thomas sarcastically adds with a smirk.

"Hahaha Thomas! You are a funny fils de pute, old friend," Etienne replies, laughing with Thomas.

"Oi, what's goin' on here?" an unfamiliar English voice asks.

Silence follows his words, falling onto the wharf, halting everyone's movement. Adahy, James, Elias, Nimish, and Ester, all still, slowly turn and look at Thomas. Etienne looks at Thomas, too, puzzled at what this disruption is doing. Thomas looks the most stunned out of all, and Adahy notices.

I thought Handcock's men were supposed to keep the Redcoats out. Adahy thinks to himself as he scans back to the redcoats.

Tension fills the atmosphere, replacing the sarcastic and fond relations from moments ago. Several Regulars follow the lieutenant past the carts and fill into the open spaces where the others stand.

James stood behind the cannon with a puzzled yet ferocious look on his face, with Elias and Nimish holding the ropes attached to the front of the cannon chassis with similar looks, watching the redcoats enter the area. Each redcoat walks with their 14-inch bayonet-tipped muskets off their shoulder and in an aggressive stance.

"I asked, what's goin' on her—"

"We heard you, lobster... what are you going to do?" Thomas says, as his words slice man's second inquiry. clearly antagonizing the man.

With an impatient and stern tone, "Oi, this is the King's land, and you will adhere to the law..." the redcoat lieutenant says and begins looking around at what they are doing, "and it seems you deviants are smuggling weapons."

I know what I'm going to do, Adahy thinks, knowing they need to get rid of the disturbance.

Picking up a barrel of powder, he drops it on the back of the cart heavily.

Bang

Startling the redcoats within the wharf area, they all have a look of fear and uneasiness.

A smile creases under his green eyes, and with ferocious one motion, Adahy grabs his knife from his leather chest rig and springs to the nearest redcoat. Leaping through the air, he lunges with the blade leading.

"What the—" the man says as the smooth-edged steel enters his brainstem from under his chin. Blood flows onto his hand, and Adahy falls to the ground with the lifeless body, aggressively looking to the next redcoat to his left. He pounces on him.

"Here we go," Thomas says coolly, nudging Etienne's arm with his eyes wide.

James jumps from behind the cannon like a lion and lands on his nearest redcoat with a blade in each of his hands, landing with each in the man's chest,

"Urrgggll," the man tries to speak but is immediately overwhelmed by the large man.

In one hard motion, James pulls the man up with the steel in his chest and slams him down into the muddy cobblestone ground.

The Lieutenant tries cocking his musket to a full load, but Elias stops him and grabs the redcoat's hand with his right hand, snapping his bones with a quick twist of the wrist.

"Aaagghh—" he shouts but is silenced when Elias quickly, with his left hand, slams a ten-inch dagger into the redcoat's skull, going through his tongue.

"Bloody King's Bane!" A redcoat shouts nervously, trying to full-load his Brown Bess. Ester removes her blade and slings it side-arm into his chest.

"Ugh," the air escapes his throat.

With a few steps, she moves quickly to remove her blade, letting the man's body fall to the wet floor. Ester jumps to the next redcoat with the blood-soaked blade, landing on his back, bringing him to the ground, and his face smacks hard into the ground. His teeth shatter upon impact. With her left hand, she grabs a handful of the redcoat's hair and, with her right hand, opens his neck from ear to ear with her blade, spraying his blood into a puddle under his face.

"Thomas, they are like a pack of wild wolves," Etienne says laughingly as the King's Bane members move with intentionality and ferocity.

Adahy moves quickly with his blade in his hand and an ecstatic look in his eyes, moving to nullify the prying redcoats.

"Come here, you," Adahy says playfully, removing his bow and one arrow from his quiver. Readying his bow and nocking an arrow, he steadies it, aiming at the redcoat, trying to run off the wharf…

"Hel—"

Thwipt

The arrow is loose and, within half of a second, enters the backside of the redcoat's neck, with the arrowhead rupturing through his esophagus. He gurgles blood and quickly stumbles to the ground, reaching for his neck. As he hits the wet, muddy deck, he is dead. Adahy turns around to the others. Each of the King's Bane members is finishing their final kills with multiple redcoat bodies scattered around the wharf.

"I am getting too old to be snuck up on," James growls, on one knee, removing his blade from the lifeless redcoat.

"That you are! For age is but a number in which we hold a mutual agreement with time, and you, my friend, are stretching that agreement," Elias adds playfully.

Retorting quickly, Ester snaps, "You are too, old man!"

"Me?! Old!"

"Now, now... you are all old!" Nimish cleverly interjects.

James sighs with a slight smile, "To you, everyone is old."

"Oi, none of y'all have changed one bit since as far back as I can remember," the younger man adds.

Thomas takes a step forward, "We need to move these now to the cart. Attach the cannon carriages to the two wagons and let them move. Leave whatever barrels that aren't already loaded."

"Aye, we need to depart quickly... there will be another patrol, and they will soon be inquiring where this squad is," James cautions.

Adahy moves purposefully and helps hitch the cannon carriage to the wagons with James, Elias, and Nimish. Ester grabs an older canvas tarp and drapes it over the three remaining barrels against the brick warehouse wall.

"Well, Thomas, I must say... that was a great show... I am happy about the trouble this will bring to your city, but I'm sure you will handle it," Etienne says with a cold smile.

"Eh. It's nothing we haven't handled before," Thomas replies, taking a step back toward his friend.

"As we discussed previously, I will give you Lucien. He will follow the cannon to Philadelphia, and I will pick him up there in a few days' time," Etienne says, putting out his hand to shake Thomas's hand.

"My old friend, we will gladly take him to ensure they arrive at their destination accordingly," Thomas adds with assurance.

"No, no, Thomas… you misinterpret my words. I only want him going with the cannon because he needs to take over my business eventually… Do you see me? I am too old to be doing this much longer," the well-dressed Frenchman laughs.

"You and me both, my old friend."

"Lucien, garçon, come here!" Etienne shouts up toward the frigate's deck.

In the dead of night, the boy's footsteps can be heard on the deck, approaching quickly to the plank connecting the frigate to the dock.

"Tonton, de quoi as-tu besoin?" The teenager asks as he emerges from the shadows and under the moonlight with a musket slung. He is youthful, with bright and observant eyes, like his uncle.

"English, you imbécile!" Etienne shouts.

"Mon Ami, I am sorry! We don't like the King's tongue on this ship," Lucien says with a cunning smile.

"Pfft, it does not matter… Are you ready? It's time to go," Etienne says to his nephew.

"I am," he says, grabbing a haversack from the deck and slinging it around his body. Quickly, he walks off the frigate's deck onto the plank and then onto the wharf dock.

Lucien walks past Thomas to the closest wagon cart and loads up in the back with the powder barrels.

"Well... my friend... no time to lose. You best be off before the next squad of Redcoats comes and alerts the harbor master to your arrival," Thomas tells his longtime friend fondly.

"You've always been a true partner," Etienne says as he boards his frigate, "I will see you again, Thomas. Au Revoir!"

The two wagon carts are filled with powder, along with the two cannon pieces hitched to the wagons, and the King's Bane is moving off the wharf. Adahy looks back just before the carts make the left turn onto Middle Street. Disappearing into the harbor fog, Etienne's frigate smoothly glides into the darkened twilight night. Quickly, his eyes shift toward the ground.

Damn redcoats, why'd they show up? His green eyes shifted forward, and his mind shifted to the present.

The sound of the large wagon wheels moving through the muddy section of the street pulled with them the air of death. Behind the carts, stationary, are the lifeless men on the wet, dirty ground. Some floating next to the dock. The sounds of the wheels soon drifted from the wharf and all was still.

Where Light Fades

Wednesday, October 3rd, 1771

The King's Highway

4:20 pm

Birds and crickets chirp within the tall grass and thick trees along the edges of the King's Highway. The overhanging trees create a covered layer protecting from the bright sun on this warm fall day. Leading his men down the road, the Major General sits tall on his horse with his shoulders back. Within the birds and crickets, there is another noise in the distance. He recognizes the faint sound immediately... musket fire, but more distinctly, loads of British Brown Bess, and it was coming from the south along the road.

Our road scouts have them, he thinks with exhilaration.

"Ride faster! The King's men are in danger!" He shouts backward and picks up the horse's pace with a hard kick.

Setting the pace, Major General Ivey rode intensely as his men followed. Trees became blurs. The elite Sentry Rangers moved expertly on the highway toward their destination. Mirroring a stampede, the horses rode hard, creating a jarring acoustic. In an aggressive stance, the King's Guard Commander focuses his thoughts.

I can hear the musket fire...I have them now; they are close, he thinks joyfully as they ride hard to get to the skirmish.

Rounding the next corner, they arrive, and Commander Ivey throws up his left fist into the air. His men see the scene and stop their horses.

How many were there? He thinks to himself.

Cautiously, the Commander dismounts his horse, removing his pistol from his waistband. With his right thumb, he cocks the pistol twice into a full load. His eyes are still scanning and analyzing the gruesome scene before him.

Thick musket smoke still consumed the air under the tree canopy. Gunpowder lingered in the air as if it were resting in the nothingness. Within seconds, the smoke began thinning out, slithering into dissolution. Fire cracks and crackles through the musket smoke, revealing the burning wagon splintered and overturned in the tall grass. Agador cautiously looks around in the tree line on both sides. His eyes drop from the trees to the dead men. Inspecting the bodies, he connects the dots

"Gage, these soldiers have similar blade markings as the soldiers on the wharf," the Major General says to his Ranger.

The seasoned soldier approaches his Commander, "Aye, sir... they do. What do you make of it, sir?"

He notices a nearby tree riddled with arrows. Recognizing the arrows passed through some of the soldiers, killing them and then making their way to the tree. He moves through the tall grass and removes an arrow from the tree,

"Look... the arrows... Too fine for ordinary militiamen... this took craftsmanship to make... a skilled hand," he says to his men, inspecting the evidence.

"Fan out, scout the perimeter! They are not far!" Agador shouts to his men, walking back through the tall grass and returning onto the road.

As the Commander walks among the dead, his boot nudges the body of a slain soldier face down in the dirt. The dead man's eyes still open, his hand outstretched toward the road as if trying to crawl away from death itself. Agador squats next to the body and notices the cuts on the man's neck and chest.

These kills are deliberate, quick, and done with skill, he thinks; *there was no panic in their attack... only efficiency. It's beautiful... the violence of it all.*

"Major General Ivey, sir?" Captain Bates shouts.

"What is it, Captain?" Agador responds in an agitated tone and stands back up.

"Each musket shot is a headshot, sir. These are expert marksmen," the captain says after inspecting several musket shots on the dead.

"The King's Bane are not amateurs, Captain," he says and continues, "They strike hard and fast, knowing exactly where to hit," he says, seemingly thinking to himself as he scans the areas and bodies.

"Someone must be organizing them... or training them. There must be more participants at play here," he says with a curious look in his eye.

"Major General, you believe this is the work of the King's Bane?" Gage asks.

"I do... and I believe it has a direct connection to the events on the wharf," the ice-blue-eyed Commander adds.

"How so, sir?"

"It seems they are attempting to move their recent shipment. They didn't know there would be any patrols on the highway today and got caught up. I sense familiarity with these rebel tactics. They take advantage of the covered roadway and thick vegetation to conceal their positions. I would do the same. They are hunters...like us. They understand the importance of never wasting movements and striking precisely and accurately. They are trained shooters…" Agador asserts coldly and mounts his horse.

As the sun begins its journey to rest, Agador sits on his horse in silence, piecing together what he knows of the elusive King's Bane. *These aren't just fighters*, he thinks; *they're building toward a goal. They slip through my grasp each time, becoming more dangerous and killing more of the King's men.* The conflict weighs on his shoulders.

"Listen, men," he calls out to his Sentry Rangers as they are piling the bodies of the slain British soldiers, "we are not chasing apparitions anymore! The King's Bane is real, and we will eradicate them from this existence!"

The words leave his mouth with sincerity, truth, and responsibility. The Major General thoroughly believed his words, and his confidence radiated to his men because, after a sight like this week, the men needed a resolving boost from their commander.

"Captain Bates, clean this up and return these bodies to Boston. Gage, you ride with me. I need to meet with Colonel Valles at Headquarters," Agador commands before turning his horse and spurring it, moving forward to Boston.

So, you want to hunt… very well… we shall hunt, Agador thinks to himself with a devilish smirk on his face as he rides quickly back to the harbor town.

***

George's Tavern

Barratt Cassius cleaned a mug with his rag as the bargoers enjoyed their drinks around George's Tavern. His rough, seasoned hands expertly prepare the latest collection of cleaned mugs. The audible murmurs around the bar filled the warm atmosphere.

Ding

The door opens, ringing the small hanging bell, alerting Barratt of newly arrived guests. The middle-aged man looks up with his brown eyes and sees the city leader, Thomas Young, standing tall before him.

"Fuck," he muttered gloomily, "What did I do now?"

"What did you do?" Thomas asks patronizingly.

The man sucks his teeth as his head drops, "I haven't done anything, Thomas..." the fear in his voice is loud.

"Oh, I know... I am here because I need information from you..." he casually drops some coins on the bar top, "When is the King's next coin shipment leaving Cambridge?"

Visibly frustrated, Barratt exhales an exhausted breath, "Thomas, you know I no longer have that connection. My cousin, the governor, doesn't allow me in his meetings anymore. I believe he has become privy to my motivations..."

"I disagree, Barratt. You *will* find me the date and time of the next coin shipment, or else you know what I'll do," Thomas assures dryly with a sadistic undertone.

"I do... I haven't forgotten the words you spoke to me that day," he replies, shaken.

"Good," Thomas answers with a satisfied look on his face, "Then bring me the information I demand."

Shakily, Barratt replies, "I will, it will be done..."

"Good. That is what I wanted to hear," Thomas softly knocks his knuckles onto the bar top, "Pour me some rum, will ya?"

Without thinking and expert movement, Barratt takes the mug from under the wooden bar top and slams it down. In his other hand, he reaches for and grabs the bottle of rum in his hand, places it in front of Thomas, and begins pouring the dark fluid into the mug.

Within a sharp movement, Thomas swigs the entire drink in one motion,

"Ahhh… you have great rum here, Barratt, that I can appreciate."

His scar is worn proudly, and he puts his tricorn on, making his way out of the tavern with a tune whistling from his lips.

Ugh, fucking hell, Barratt thinks as the tavern door closes behind Thomas.

His mind swirled with possibilities of how he would go about trying to gain this information that Thomas was inquiring about. He knows Thomas is valid in his questioning because Cambridge has halted the larger shipments due to them being attacked by the King's Bane.

There will be a shipment, he tries to focus. *Eventually, they must bring the coin, gold, and trappings to London. But when?* He thinks.

A plan begins to swirl in Barratt's mind. Within minutes, the roaring audible inside the tavern is muted by his thoughts, and he goes back to cleaning his drinking wares and bar top.

***

Hancock's Wharf

Overlooking Hancock's wharf sat a three-story brick building that was freshly built, owned by the same man who's wharf it stood. A warm lantern glow stemmed from the second floor as the two men discussed recent operations.

"That is horseshit, Thomas, and you know it!" the well-dressed, handsome man said passionately.

"The redcoats were there, they interrupted the shipment, and you fucking said the wharf would be good to go, off-limits to any British soldiers…" Thomas replies to him ferociously, pointing his finger into the man's chest, and keeps going, "Now you need to deal with the mess, John. That's the way it goes."

With a genuine tone, John replies, "Aye. I can deal with that. But what I cannot deal with is how this even happened?! I had my men block off the entire section of the town, ensuring the wharf was cleared and ready for you."

"We own the buildings, John. There shouldn't be a need to clear the roads! They should be clear, regardless!"

"Thomas… truthfully, I do not know how they knew to be there… but I will correct this error," he was genuinely worried, and the older city leader could see there was an authentic concern about the wharf's operations in his protégés voice.

"These British bastards are getting thicker since the massacre. We must remove them from this land," John adds.

"This may be true, and this may come to pass, but all I know is you will be the one facing charges for what happens on your wharf. Hopefully, your cousin can help if that comes to pass. I don't pay you the amount of coin I pay you for these types of mishaps and bloodshed in the city, let alone your wharf. That being said, you, as well as I, know that what I'm doing here cannot come undone or found out. You must take the hit for this if it comes to pass. The movement here and in Philadelphia and across the hearts of patriots needs to live and breathe… know your role in this machine, John," Thomas's words are stern, almost fatherly, to the man.

"I understand, Thomas," John accepts.

"Now, what will you tell Commander Ivey of the King's Guard when he comes questioning you with his Sentry Rangers?"

John begins pacing, placing his hands behind his back, "I will say French fur traders got into a squabble with the soldiers as they were processing out... it should settle his appetite. If that doesn't, then... I will offer some coin."

"That could work," crossing his arms and stepping to the thick glass window overlooking the wharf, "But I caution you, John. Agador Ivey will expect more than a tall tale about impetuously violent fur traders on your wharf. He is also not keen on bribery... if you go that route, it might end badly. Be cautious."

Still pacing, "Aye... I am good with my words... Either way, he will accept the story as the truth, or he will hold speculation and not take the coin."

"If he speculates, he will tighten his grip on me... which is fine... there are more than enough smuggling tunnels and hideaways in the city," Thomas pauses and continues, "Tell me though, John, why is it you believe the redcoats were patrolling the area and not stopped by your men?"

John stops pacing and looks to Thomas, "That needs to be investigated... if my men are compromised or the Commander of the King's Guard is enforcing new rules, we need to be privy to that... I will find the reasoning for this disruption."

"He's getting closer... he has tails following me... he is disrupting our shipments, or at the very least, his arrival here has shifted their directives, it seems. We need to be more careful... find out why the redcoats were there and how they got inside the perimeter of our operation and make sure it is not repeated, John."

Thomas's countenance was that of frustration and rage. His old eyes glare out the glass window, trying to make sense of the events that unfolded.

The Crimson Highway

Wednesday, October 3rd, 1771

The King's Highway

4:05 pm

Sunlight peers through the overhanging canopy along the King's Highway, creating pillars of light that drop to the ground. The two wagons were filled with powder barrels, and two cannons within carriages were hitched to the back of the wagons. Adahy was next to Ester on the second wagon, with Nimish in the back. Elias rode with James on the first wagon with Lucien in the back with the barrels. Thomas was still in Boston, handling his business, knowing he couldn't leave the city on missions with a tail.

From the first wagon, Elias's voice bellows,

"A sailor Johnnie escaped King Geoooorge in the HMS Oooocean... The King sent beasts to hunt the man and kill him where he sleeps, ya... The sailor Johnnie escaped againnn, this time through the Ottoman... The King sent beasts for his head, unknowing where they're lookin'... The sailor Johnnie traveled on and made his way round all seven

213

seas... The King caught on and found dear Johnnie, sinking him in the Ooooocean... They killed sailor Johnnie, yet his name lives on, and the King passed in sixtyyyyy-two... The song we sing for the sailor Johnnie, the Spanish say lives in Biru.... Sailor Johnnie outwitted the King, now we sing his song for you, ya..."

The tune follows the first wagon to the second, and Adahy enjoys the tune.

"Elias knows all the shanties," she smiles, looking over.

"It is unbelievable his story... my mother never said much... wait," Adahy's eyes pick up a crimson blur out of the ordinary and normal green vegetation up ahead,

"Ester, there is a British squad coming up... I can see the sharp red through the trees..."

"Are you sure?"

"I am. Stop the wagon..." he says, shouting lowly to the cart in front of them, "James! Stop the wagon!"

He does it without reaction. Ester halts their cart as well. Upon stopping, Adahy jumps out onto the road, making his way in front of the first wagon, smoothly readying his bow.

"What do ya smell, dog?" Elias says jokingly to Adahy.

"Hush, Shakespeare, if you were paying attention, you'd see the redcoats around the bend," Adahy says in a snarky response.

"Ha, he's not wrong," James laughs and nudges Elias's shoulder.

"Ugh... I am an old man. You have the youthful vision!" Elias says, jumping off the wagon and readying his daggers.

James drops the reigns, turning his body, and knocks on the closest barrel, "Lucien, we have company. Get out."

As he finishes, he hops off the wagon, squints his eyes, and sees the bright red blurs in the vegetation around the corner a few hundred meters away. He sees a covered cart and a squad of redcoats escorting it. *We can't have disruptions on the highway*, he thinks.

"Adahy, we must neutralize them... Nock an arrow and rain hell from the tall grass... the rest of us will move like fire, spreading our blades to one and the next until they are dead," James says with authority.

"I'm on it, boss," Adahy replies, nocking an arrow. The youthful green-eyed native squats and begins stalking lowly in the tall grass, getting closer to the bend in the road.

Coming to the front of the wagon is Lucien, "Bunch of fucking salissants," he says in his youthful voice, seemingly excited to get his hands dirty.

"Shh," Ester says intensely, removing her cutlass and walking toward the front of the first wagon, "we want them to be surprised, Frenchman."

"Mon Cherie, I'm here to help," Lucien says with a smile, throwing his hands up.

"Then you better get a kill," Nimish says with a smile, patting Lucian on the back.

The two of them walk up with the rest of them to the front of the wagon. James is still watching the redcoat squad with intentionality, "Adahy will be in the tall grass... We need to hide and blend in with the foliage... we attack the moment the entire patrol passes the bend... it will be a perfect kill box for us. Wait on my shot. I'll take out the highest-ranking officer... and then we move like wildfire to kill the rest as quickly and as smoothly as possible."

The King's Bane doesn't respond, and they instinctively move into hidden positions. Adahy moves slowly to the bend in the road, using the tall grass to hide his position. Ester looks around and quickly runs to an easily climbable tree and expertly gets to a perched position. Nimish and Lucian move to the tree line and begin settling into covered positions, hiding away with their blades ready. Elias quickly moves to the opposite side of Adahy on the road and smiles devilishly at him, seemingly excited about the coming ambush. *Fucking maniac*, Adahy thinks to himself and smiles back in response, shaking his head.

James stood in the road next to the horses. Intentionally hiding his right hand in the horse's mane, concealing his sea-service pistol. Within a few moments, the first redcoat soldiers emerge from around the bend. A few moments later, the entire squad and covered wagon are entirely across the bend.

A lieutenant stands on the wagon and shouts to James, "Boy... what in the world are you doing alone on the King's Highway?"

James, disapproving of the words, looks up and down at himself, "Boy?! Before you is a man! A free man at that!"

With a quick, short breath through his nose, he gets visibly frustrated with James's response, "Listen here, black..." The redcoat begins and jumps off the wagon, walking toward James.

Four steps later, he is within accurate range of James's pistol. The two horses attached to the cart neigh and flick their heads up and down. The redcoat briefly looks to the horses and in one swift motion, the larger African man brandishes his pistol, bringing the barrel to the redcoat's eye level, and fires. The powder sparks in the flash pan, and a well-rounded lead ball moves through the air, impacting the lieutenant's face. His lifeless body impacts the dirt road without a face and a wide hole in the back of his skull.

Quickly, James holsters his pistol and removes two large daggers from the sheaths on his waist, moving quickly to the nearest redcoat.

Adahy lets his arrow go, and it slices the neck of one of the rear redcoats on the patrol. The man gurgles, grabbing at his neck, and falls to the ground with the warm outflow of blood stemming from his new wound. Without thinking, Adahy nocks another arrow, aims at the next redcoat, and lets it loose.

As James's trigger is pulled, Ester leaps ferociously out of the tree. The unassumed redcoat hears the branches move and looks up. For a brief moment, he is stunned at what he sees: the white-haired Ester with a devilish smile, seemingly floating above him with her blade leading toward his face. Her cutlass inserts into the man's face through his eye. He dies instantly. The dead man's bones snap as he crumbles into the ground as she uses his body to break her fall. She tumbles into a roll and pops back up with the next redcoat target in mind.

He's taking a knee, trying to reload. In three steps, she's within striking range. With a strong backswing, she slashes. Her sharp blade slices through the redcoat's neck with ease, never once getting caught up on his bones, muscles, or tendons. Expertly, she moves to the next redcoat as his head hits the dirt road, spraying blood into the air

Running swiftly from the tall grass, Nimish throws his tomahawk to the nearest redcoat as he tries to fire his musket at the young King's Bane member, missing as the tomahawk blade slams into his diaphragm. He quickly steps on the man's body to leverage the tomahawk out of his chest. As he does, he smoothly regrips the handle and accurately throws it to the next fumbling redcoat. Folding over itself in the air, the sharp tomahawk slams into the redcoat. His musket fires into the tree canopy, and Nimish tackles the man, bringing them both to the ground. He removes his tomahawk and looks up to the rest of his compatriots.

Snap

Adahy feels the force of an incoming musket round whiz beside him and hears his glass water bottle shatter. Looking down, he sees the broken neck of the bottle still attached to the rope slung over his chest.

"Fuck!"

"You hit!?" Elias responds concernedly.

"Yeah, my fucking bottle of water I picked up on the docks from Jacksons Spa. Absolute horseshit using glass."

"So, you're not hit?"

"No. I've lost my water, though. You know, on tribal land, if my hide Blatter was damaged, it could be repaired. There's no way I'll be able to repair this broken glass."

"You should go back to your tribe then!" Elias adds sarcastically.

"Eh, fuck off, Shakespeare."

The thick musket smoke disrupts everyone's vision within the confined spaces of the King's Highway under the tree canopy. The rest of the Redcoats fall all around Nimish as his compatriots move like apparitions within the peering-sunlight smoke.

"Fuck," Nimish mutters under his breath, startled at the violence unfolding between his friends.

Within moments, there are no more muskets firing off; it quickly becomes silent, just as quickly as the commotion started.

"Report!" James shouts from within the smoke.

"I'm good, just lost my water bottle," Adahy's voice calls out.

"I'm good to go," Elias replies.

"I told you not to bring that on missions," James adds to Adahy.

"I can't just drink rum or Maderia all day," Adahy smiles.

"Eh, point taken."

"Almost got me, but he missed," Ester adds, walking through the smoke toward Nimish.

"Nimish, are you good?" James asks, emerging through the smoke as it rises into the tree canopy above them.

"I'm good... We must move our wagons and get out of here now," Nimish replies with urgency.

"Whew! That was palpitant!" Lucian adds happily, holstering his pistol.

As Adahy walks back to the wagons,

"I agree... that was loud, and if anyone was around, they most definitely heard this."

"I agree," James says, climbing back on the first wagon and grabbing the reigns, "Light their wagon up, Adahy."

"Consider it done," Adahy says, placing his bow back into his quiver.

"Yaah!" James shouts to the horses as he snaps the reigns. Elias smiled and winked at Adahy before jumping into the wagon next to James as it moved toward the bend.

Fucking Shakespeare, he thinks, and leans over, grabbing a handful of the dry tall grass, throwing the bundle in the back of the redcoat wagon. Adahy then removes his flint and steel and begins smacking the two together, sparking the grass until it catches into a flame.

Adahy blows on the fire, growing it until it catches on the wagon's wood.

"Let's go!" He shouts as the fire spreads to the canvas wagon cover; he turns to catch up to Ester and the wagon.

As he climbs back in, he situates his gear and sits down, "Your arrows were precise and perfect," she compliments the young man.

"Thank you, Nyx. I saw you too... leaping from the trees," he remarks with a slight chuckle.

She smiles, "Ever since my incident as a kid... I have carried an intrinsic connection to the forest, to the trees... I find them fascinating. Each tree tells a new story, ever reaching and twisting toward the heavens."

"Living in the wilderness as a boy, I've always loved utilizing trees for the hunt."

"Aye... the hunt is a bit different now, I suppose."

"Indeed..." Adahy replies softly, looking out at the passing trees. His mind goes back to the fight, and his excitement returns,

"I let loose my second arrow, and I saw you out of the corner of my eyes. You looked like a fucking flying squirrel!"

"Shut up, you!" Ester shouts sarcastically, smacking Adahy in the chest with her right arm.

Adahy enjoyed Ester. She reminded him of his mother; *maybe it was her age*, he thought, *maybe it's her aura...* his mind drifts as the two king's bane carts pass by the burning wagon and dead bodies along the road. Within minutes, the group was moving at a good pace. The further they were from the newly killed redcoats, the better they would be. Adahy enjoyed the ones he was with and took in every moment as they made their way to Philadelphia. Minutes became hours, and the fight became another moment passed.

"Ester... I have a question," Adahy states, seemingly randomly to the older woman next to him on the wagon.

"Oh ya? What is it?"

"Your neck scar..."

She laughs, "You want to know how I got the scar?"

Cautious with his answer, he slowly looks to her, seemingly for approval, "Yes?"

"Everyone always wants to know... like it's some conversation piece," she responds, slightly annoyed, looking out into the passing trees, "just know they tried to kill me, but I killed them instead," she growls, glaring at Adahy.

Fuck, he thought, *I shouldn't have asked.*

"I'm sorry for opening old wounds."

"Eh... you're young and curious... plus, your Thomas's blood. That means your family... I won't take your balls for asking me about it," her tone is serious as she finishes, still glaring at Adahy.

Adahy laughs lightly, "Thank you."

She half smiles and brings her smokey-gray eyes back to the front, focusing on the horses and route, "You're all right, kid."

Silence then refills the wagon, only being broken by the creaking wood wheels rotating along the dirt highway. Some time passes, and the nighttime glow from the city starts emerging in the distance. Philadelphia is a large city that is structured well, and Adahy appreciates the atmosphere.

Upon arriving at the large city, the King's Bane members began maneuvering through the pockets of people, "We're looking for the Tun Tavern... the property owners are allies with Thomas," Ester says to Adahy.

"It's busy," he says to Ester, looking around the city, "much like Boston, but a lot less Redcoats, if any..." Adahy finishes, seemingly inspecting the atmosphere, and not seeing any British soldiers.

"We may disrupt the King's coin shipments and be an annoyance for the Crown, but in Philadelphia, these colonists... they are the real *King's Bane*... if they can figure their shit out, they could do much damage to the British Empire," Ester says confidently.

After several minutes, Adahy knows where they're going. They approach a distinctly looking two-story building on a soft hill. A man emerges from the front door. Moments later, the two wagons with hitched cannons arrive at the tavern. A strong, youthful man with a dark beard and dark blue greatcoat steps forward with a large smile.

"Ah, James, you gigantic black fucker!" the man says with admiration.

"Robert, you smooth-talking son of a bitch!" James replies with a wide smile, jumping off his cart.

The two men embrace each other with a hug.

"How's ole scarface?" Robert asks through his smile.

"Eh, you know Thomas... he always has a lot going on up in that brain of his," James says smoothly.

"Yeah, y'all got that Major General up your ass... how's that going?"

James laughs dryly, "He is slowly becoming a nuisance but still filled with blinding arrogance, as always."

"So, his reputation precedes him? Fucking King's Guard... bunch of pansies," Robert says, and then looks to the rest of the King's Bane, "All right, let's get the wagons to the warehouse in the back. We can offload there."

When he finishes, he turns and leads the horse-pulled wagons around the building and to the rear warehouse. The tavern itself is fairly large and looks impressive from the outside. Arriving at the warehouse, Robert pulls out a key ring from his greatcoat and unlocks the doors, pushing them open, making enough room for the wagons to enter.

As soon as both wagons fully enter, Robert closes the doors, and the King's Bane members hop off their carts and begin offloading the supplies. Nimish and Adahy begin unhitching the cannon carriage that is attached to their cart, and James and Elias do the same to theirs.

"Lucian, this is where you'll stay when we leave," James says to the young Frenchman.

"Ya, where is Etienne's nephew!?" Robert shouts.

"He's here," James responds, and Robert walks over.

"Etienne should be here in a day or two. You can stay in the Tun until he arrives. There will be food and drink in abundance," Robert says to the young Frenchman before turning to the others, "Let me grab a bottle of rum to celebrate, and then you'll be off."

"That does sound good, Robert; I'll come with you," James says as the two men walk out of the warehouse.

Ester, Elias, and Nimish are all standing together between the two empty wagons as Adahy makes his way to them.

"So, Lucian, are you ready to take over your uncle Etienne's smuggling business?" Ester says sarcastically.

Lucian turns to the group, "You know, in Paris, we often say the best way to understand a man's motives is to see what he fears. Fear, after all, is the sharpest motivator…do you know what my uncle fears?"

Each of the King's Bane members looks at each other with curious faces; Adahy interjects, breaking the silence, "He fears your riddles!" Adahy laughs as the others break down in laughter, too.

Lucian sucks his teeth and throws his hand at them, waving them off, "C'est ça, bien sûr, you King's Bane!"

"Oh c'mon, don't get mad; we are just teasing you," Ester adds, smiling.

"Yeah, that's how you know we like you!" Says Nimish spritely.

Laughing with the others, Adahy removes his pipe and tobacco pouch. Quickly, he blends some cannabis with his tobacco and packs a large bowl in his clay pipe. Adahy takes a couple of steps to the nearest candle. He sparks the end of his wick and starts torching his bowl. The herbs burn and subtly crack as he inhales the warming smoke, holds it for a second, and releases it. The overwhelming sensation consumes him, and he feels invigoration throughout his body.

"Shit smells like a skunk spraying his ass," the youthful Frenchman says, smiling, "May I have a puff?"

Adahy smiles, "If it smells that bad, it must be good!" He extends his hand with the pipe within, and Lucian grabs it carefully, bringing it to his lips and inhaling.

Cough, Cough

"Yeah... you don't have that in France," Elias says lightly, laughing at Lucian's inability to smoke the herbs.

Coughing over and over again, Lucian tries to defend himself, "We smoke tobacco... but Mon Ami, what in god's name is that?"

"That is a little gift from our native brethren here... he smokes the hops that grow on hemp," Ester says, looking at Adahy.

"Damn good smoke, that's for sure," Adahy adds as the wave of relaxation and carefreeness wafts over his body.

He knew he was happy.

This is my home; these are my friends... my family... he thinks. As the pipe gets passed around the circle of friends, Adahy takes the moment to appreciate what he has.

"Can I say something? I know Thomas is my uncle, but you all are my family, too."

"This herb makes you melt, huh?" Elias smiles, "We are a family, Adahy... we are the King's Bane. That means family."

"That's right," Ester adds and nudges Adahy.

Admiration and gratitude for his new chosen family and their collective path warmed him. This warmth brought some sliver of happiness to his otherwise cold and brutal life.

Eyeing Adahy's pipe, Lucian smiles, "Let me smoke that again."

Birds of A Feather

November 1771

Boston, Massachusetts

Adahy stood out in the city, with no help from his blonde hair and tribal garb, but no one looked too long at one thing in the city anyway. Daytime in Boston was lively. Especially today, but it was cold, and the clouds overhead indicated to Adahy that snow would soon arrive.

Along the streets, beggars and drunkards mingled with proper businessmen, trying to manipulate and steer conversations in their favor. After a few minutes alone on King Street, he notices a small 'x' written within a square in red chalk on the brick wall.

Thomas needs me. Word needs to be passed along, or a new shipment, he thinks, as he shifts his path, now walking toward Thomas's home.

After a short detour away from the main road, Adahy makes his way through the bushes and through a small slit in a wooden fence. The entrance was undetectable to the untrained eye. Thomas stood in the city's public garden under the apple tree, his head nearly touching the branch he was under. He wore a long dark blue greatcoat with fancier, well-paid clothing underneath... but his facial scar was always his most prominent feature.

"Adahy, come quickly, under the tree," he says sharply to his nephew.

"Uncle Thomas, what is it? I noticed the red x by Kings Street," Adahy says, walking up to the man.

"I have good word that there will be a large shipment of coin leaving from Cambridge and heading to Boston harbor in the third week of January. I didn't call a meeting with the others because I still need to verify the source... but I need you to stay alert," Thomas says smoothly.

"I understand, Uncle. I will stay ready for anything, as always," Adahy replies strongly.

"Aye... there is a man. He's been following me all day, and now he stands in the warehouse across the street. Do not look back," Thomas says, still looking around, "He is on the second floor of the abandoned warehouse. I am assuming he will follow you now once you leave. Be careful."

Adahy doesn't look back, "Who is it?"

"I am not sure; it is most likely a Sentry Ranger Officer. There have been two of them following me since the King's Guard and the Sentry Rangers arrived."

"I can handle this pursuer if he follows me," Adahy assures his uncle.

"No, they have only been here a short while. We do not want them in a frenzy or roaming the city in a more aggressive posture," Thomas replies with directness as he stands from under the apple tree.

"I want to see what they do. Now, go out the way you came. Ensure no one sees you, or try not to, at least. We will hold a meeting tomorrow evening; tell the others when you see them," Thomas instructs lowly, almost in a whisper.

"Aye. I will," Adahy replies, turning around and leaving the garden the same cautious, inconspicuous way he entered.

**

Colonel Valles followed Corporal Rooney all day long, watching the Boston City Leader, Thomas Young. He noticed the King's Guard soldier was adept at stalking. But he also recognized that the youthful Corporal never once noticed the older officer following him. This concerned the stern Colonel, yet the thought didn't linger. If he wanted Corporal Rooney to notice him, he would've.

Several hours had passed with no movements, as Thomas stayed inside his home. Out of the corner of his left eye, he notices the young Corporal emerging from the alley.

"Is he heading back to the barracks?" He asks himself softly. Seemingly done for the day, the youthful Rooney casually makes his way south toward their auxiliary headquarters.

Bloody youth... always assuming they're done when they're not. It is barely the evening, he thinks.

Scanning from the second floor of an abandoned warehouse, the Colonel watches the surrounding areas of Thomas Young's home. The militiaman standing guard in front of the property stood alert, and Francis stayed looking for clues to help his reconnaissance.

Thomas, brother to a thief, manages to stay within parliament's good graces, he thinks to himself as he watches the city leader's home.

After some time, the cooling night sky begins, allowing for a light snowfall. The Colonel scans the sky from the window, admiring the snowfall and he sees Thomas exit his house. Carefully, the older city leader, in a blue great coat, walks across the street to a public garden, posting himself under the apple tree.

"What are we up to, Thomas Young," he whispers to himself, watching tentatively.

Several minutes go by and he notices a man enter the same garden. *A redskin… What business would the city leader have with a redskin?* He thought. Within minutes, the native man exited the garden the same way he had entered. *Curious… I think I'll start tailing the redskin and leave Thomas for Rooney… the city leader isn't the one we are looking for,* he thinks.

Quickly and quietly, the King's Guard Colonel made his way down the stairs. Through the door of the empty warehouse, the colonel peers through the gaps in the slotted wood. His eyes follow the young native, letting him get enough distance away. *Now,* he thinks. At that moment, the colonel exits the warehouse and expertly begins pursuing the native.

**

The northeastern air was chilly into late fall, with a light layer of snow that began falling only a few moments ago. The storm off the coast had begun, if only lightly. As he walked the streets, the brisk air pierced his open pockets of skin.

"Fucking snow…" he growls under his breath as the cold air blows in.

It rarely would snow with the tribe, and now I'm consumed in it, he thinks to himself in an upset mood.

It's been some time since Adahy arrived in Boston, and he seemed to enjoy the city with minimal interaction with the people. They weren't friendly and kept to themselves mostly; Adahy enjoyed that. He often found himself alone in the streets at night, but he was never truly alone in the city. As he makes a right onto Cambridge Street, he notices a peculiar movement, a mirrored movement to his,

Who is that? Is this the extra tail Thomas was speaking of? Let's see, he thinks as he begins moving with intentionality.

The red bricks of Faneuil Hall were quickly approaching, and he knew he needed to lose the newly attached tail.

Let's go for a walk, shall we? He makes a right, heading south on Marlborough Street, passing the Green Dragon Tavern.

Out front sat a young boy, halfway dirty, with holes in his clothing, "Fresh apples! Get your fresh apples! Good sir, care for an apple?"

"Hey, kid, take this!" Adahy pulls out a schilling from his pocket and flicks it toward the boy.

He catches it in midair, "Thank you, kind sir! Take 2 apples!"

"Aye, I'll only need one," Adahy says with a smile as the boy tosses an apple to him.

Now, let's see how far you're willing to go, Adahy thinks, with the tail in mind, placing the new apple in his pocket.

Emerging through the crowds, Adahy could see the leaves from the large elm tree near the neck.

The Liberty Tree. Yes, I'll lose him there.

Coming up to the large tree, there are more large pockets of people, and he darts between them. Quickly, he lowers his stance, bending at the knees, and glides through the crowd. Seeing the sign for Essex Street, he follows it with haste. Moments later, he is near the docks at the end of Essex, and he slows his pace,

"Lost him," Adahy says softly with confidence.

Emerging from the crowds, Adahy notices him again.

What? He thinks… *Is he still there? Okay, let's try again, shall we?*

In frustration, Adahy picks up his walking pace as he heads north along the docks.

He turns left onto Summer Street, and his pace quickens from a quick walk to a light jog.

"Let's see you keep up," he mutters softly.

After several moments, Adahy has jogged nearly through Boston as he arrives at Hancock's Wharf. It is quiet, and no one is around. Snow drifts down, pecking Adahy's open pockets of skin, and he scans the sky. *It's picking up,* he thinks, as the light snowfall has turned heavier, with patches of buildup on the ground.

Getting closer to the water, the clatter from the heart of the city began to drift in the distance, and he noticed an additional sound.

God dammit, is he still here?! Adahy thinks with rage. *I need to get back. If I can't lose him, I will end him.* Thomas's words are muted in his mind as Adahy's annoyance grows with the inescapable tail.

As the echoes fade, the sound of falling snow blends with the following nearby footsteps, exposing the pursuer to Adahy's trained ears. As the shadows move with the scattered storm clouds, the impetuous half-native moves smoothly to the furthest and darkest dock before boarding an unsupervised 22-gun frigate.

Removing his musket, Adahy darts to black shadows and hides, awaiting the tail. As he settles into his space, the extra footsteps grow louder and more cautious. *He knows it's a trap*, he thinks. Peering through the gap, his eyes are focused on the snowy deck, and a man's foot impacts the snow. With swift action, Adahy stands and forcibly slams his musket buttstock into the man's nose. He hears a hard crack, and the man falls to the deck unconscious.

Standing over his body, Adahy analyzes his pursuer. *He's an old man...* he thought. He flipped his musket around and used the end of the barrel to flip back the man's coat. A *Redcoat*, he thought, *Thomas was right.*

The almost hidden red fabric was bright amongst the darker articles of clothing. Quickly, Adahy searches the deck for spare rope. Immediately, he finds it, moves the unconscious redcoat to the main mast, and begins tying him to it. After securing his pursuer, Adahy leaves the ship to ensure no one else is coming down the dock. It's empty.

Next, Adahy finds a barrel tilt-rolls to a good position and drops it, never emerging from the dark shadows. Standing beside the barrel, he removes his tobacco pouch, tinderbox, and pipe and sets them on the flattened top. The unconscious man begins to come to slowly. Attempting to open his eyes, his nose and forehead were swollen with bloody patches.

"Ah, good of you to join," Adahy says from the shadows calmly.

"Wha... what the fuck is this?" The redcoat spits out, coming to.

"I wouldn't know?" Adahy says, seemingly dumbfounded, and continues, "You are the one following me. I caught you... that is all," he finishes directly. His breath is the only visible indicator of his presence on the ship.

"Fuck you!" the redcoat says loudly, spitting out blood and a tooth.

"I get it. But I want to know what you know and why you're following me," Adahy replies in a darker tone.

"Fuck you."

"You keep insulting me... I'm simply trying to have a conversation... I will take your tongue and do it with a smile," he says coldly.

"You are redskin! A native… a savage from another time. Your kind do not belong," the bloodied man says with conviction and spits out more blood and mucus.

"Thank you. You just made this much easier," Adahy says smoothly.

A shadowed silhouette breaks the light snowfall directly before the tied-up redcoat. Adahy emerges from under cover of darkness. In his right hand is a smaller blade glimmering in the moonlight. The green-eyed native recognizes a shift in the man's facial tone as he reveals himself.

Coward, Adahy thinks.

"You see, I need you to talk, not insult me.," the young man says, squatting to the redcoat's eye level.

"Fuck you, you dirty redskin," the man spits blood on his last word.

Exhaling in disappointment, "A tough coward. When I take your tongue, don't scream," Adahy says mindfully.

The tied-up man clenches his jaw and begins squirming to get away from Adahy, but the binding is so tight he can barely move. Adahy violently grabs the man's jaw and squeezes it tightly until he forces some of his hand into his mouth, grabbing his tongue.

"Stop moving so much. You'll make it worse," he says, smiling.

The man tries to become free of Adahy's firm grasp but fails. Adahy takes his other hand in control of the blade and severs most of the man's tongue. He doesn't scream but squirms as much as the binds let him.

"Well, what you didn't want to tell me you can keep forever now…." Adahy says softly, still squatting beside the man holding his tongue, "You see, I am the reason you are here," he says, standing up.

Adahy places the tongue and blade next to the smoking materials, wipes his hands on his greatcoat, and then dumps a small pile of tobacco on the barrel top. He pinches the wad and evenly packs the clay pipe bowl with the tobacco.

"You know, my uncle said you all were tough sons of a bitches. I believe him." Adahy says as he walks off the frigate to the closest candlelight and sparks his wickball.

He returns to the deck using the wick to spark his pipe. He puffs several times, getting the bowl lit,

"I didn't want to remove your tongue, but you really gave me no options," he says, looking down at the bloodied and exhausted tied-up man.

The blood flow from his mouth created a red staining stream on the rope binds, dripping to the ship's deck. The pain of his tongue being removed exhausted Colonel Valles to no end. He could barely stay awake.

"Now you will answer my questions, reply with a head nod. You understand? Or, don't reply, and I'll remove your fingernails. We can go further down this painful rabbit hole if you wish. The choice is yours," Adahy says definitively, inhaling and releasing tobacco smoke casually. The man nods his head reluctantly.

"Are you following me, per instructions from Major General Ivey?"

Bloodied and bruised, the man with a disdained look in his eyes nods his head yes.

"Very good. Do you have any reason to believe Thomas Young is connected to or part of the King's Bane?"

The tied-up man looks up slowly at Adahy in confusion.

"Answer the question," Adahy directs.

Reluctantly, the man shakes his head no.

"Is that an honest answer?"

The tied-up man, still with a look of disdain mixed with confusion on his face, slowly nods his head yes.

"You know, having you follow me from the garden was your first mistake… you should've stayed with Thomas," Adahy says, inhaling the smoke from his pipe before releasing it into the tied-up man's face.

As the snow lightly falls, Adahy and his captive are in near silence, with the slight humming of the heart of the city in the distance. This blended perfectly with the sporadic harbor wave splashes and creaking wood.

Adahy stands, "Your second mistake was calling me *redskin*…" he says, looking upward and placing his pipe on the barrel top.

With his right hand, he grabs the knife used to cut the man's tongue and squats back in front of the man's face,

"You know, my mother, a *redskin*, as you so aptly put it, was a beautiful woman… so beautiful, in fact, that an Englishman… a white man, like yourself… loved her, built a home for her, dedicated his life to her, and at some point, men like you killed him…"

The tied-up man sighs, and his head drops.

"Do you think I'm going to let you survive?" Adahy's tone drops and his words match the cold night air.

The tied-up man honestly shakes his head no.

"Unfortunately, my bloody and tied-up friend… I'm using you as a statement. You've been honorable." Adahy says as he swiftly inserts his blade into the man's neck, reaching his brain. The man's eyelids briefly flicker as his eyes roll, releasing his life.

"May the earth repurpose your soul," Adahy whispers, quarter-turning the knife and removing it from the man's head as the warm outflow of blood sprays onto a snow-covered deck.

After a few minutes, there was no more blood left to spill from the dead man. Adahy finished his tobacco bowl and cleaned his pipe, reflecting on the night. Looking up on the front mast, he sees a large white owl. It flaps its wings and leaps off the mast toward the green-eyed native.

"Keeek!"

Adahy dismisses the bird and quickly moves out of the way, "Blind fucking owl," he growls.

With a glance at the ship's deck, Adahy sees the dead redcoat, and his mind snaps to.

He decides to throw the body into the harbor. Using the same blade he's used all night, he cuts the rope bindings. Quickly he removed the man's cossack, revealing his rank, *Fuck,* he thought, *a Colonel…. Fuck…*

Quickly, Adahy placed the cossack back on the dead colonel, propped his body up, and began dragging him off the ship. After a few minutes, Adahy was along another dock and rolled the body into the chilly harbor waters.

**

Sitting upstairs, Thomas finally closes his eyes,

*Knock, Knock. *

Fuck, what is it now? I just want to sleep.

Jumping up, he rushed to see who banged on the door so hard at night. His mind immediately skips to the darkest possibilities.

"Who is it!?" The older man shouts from behind the front door.

"Adahy."

The door opens, and Adahy's emotions are clearly visible on his face. The young man walked into the home hastily, not to be seen.

"We have a problem."

"Why are you coming to the front door? What about the tail?" Thomas asks as he shuts the door behind him.

"That's why I'm here. He's dead."

"Who is dead, exactly, Adahy?" Thomas asks in a sterner tone.

"The tail... The redcoat that was following me," Adahy explains quickly.

"Okay... it was most likely some Corporal or junior Sentry Ranger. What did he look like?"

"Uncle Thomas, he wasn't young, and he wasn't a junior Ranger..." Adahy says, softer in a more reluctant tone.

Sensing an ashamed inflection and recognizing that Adahy's attitude is off, Thomas takes a step toward his nephew and, in a slower, softer tone, "Who did you kill?"

"He was older... he was a Colonel," Adahy states directly.

Thomas stops moving, trying to process the words that Adahy had just released from his mouth. Quickly, he realizes Adahy has killed Francis Valles.

"Colonel Valles is dead!?"

"Is there only one Colonel with Major General Ivey?" Adahy asks in a panic.

"There is only one Colonel within the whole King's Guard... and you killed him," Thomas replies.

Fuck, Adahy thinks, lowering his head. Shame, disappointment, and embarrassment consume his body.

"I was unaware he was an officer until after the fact, Uncle," Adahy says.

"You are unaware of more than just that!"

"I understand—"

"No, Adahy! I do not think you do. You are so similar to your father that it is frustrating. We are not *savages* living in the wilderness!" Thomas shouts, knowing the words are harsh as they leave his mouth.

He pauses, and his tone settles,

"You know, I've been here in Boston since 1749, before you were born, while your father was still on the run from our previous King. We must be patient... waiting for the right moments to strike." Thomas says calmly to Adahy and continues,

"I aim to bring down the crown from the inside like a disease, eating away until we are free. We cannot achieve this with blatant, brutal killings of British officers, especially ones that have just arrived," Thomas takes a breath,

"We achieve this by denying the crown our services and our exports. We achieve enormous successes with minor triumphs, culminating in a more collective cause within the colonies." Thomas stops his passionate rant and slows down,

"That is what we are doing here, Adahy. We are creating an idea beyond either of us. We perpetuate sacrifices in the shadows," he says before entering his first-floor study and sitting in front of the fire.

Adahy follows his uncle, realizing the disappointment but still feeling justified in his actions, and sits across from Thomas. His eyes wandered to the elongated, beautiful wooden box above the fireplace, which had always drawn his eyes.

"If they hunted down my father and killed him, they all deserve to die. Colonel Valles was a snake that needed bleeding." Adahy says youthfully before looking away from the mantle and to Thomas.

"I agree that they are swine who deserve to die, but you need to realize the bigger picture, Adahy. I need you to understand. We must stay vigilant and not make mistakes like tonight."

"I do understand, and I am sorry," Adahy says respectfully.

"The corporal in Watertown is not the same as the killing of Colonel Valles. Colonel Valles is the right-hand man to the King's Bane's newest threat, Major-General Agador Ivey, which will send him into a brutal frenzy. On top of that, he was a well-known soldier in the King's Army. This is not good. We need to suspend King's Bane operations until January. Let us resume operations then," Thomas says coldly, staring into the fire.

Adahy stands, "I'll inform the others," he says lowly as he walks out of the room.

"Adahy..." Thomas says in a quieter tone, then continues, "Colonel Valles brutally murdered women and children during the French and Indian War. He deserved his fate... but I wish you were a bit more organized and thought out in handling it... We live in a time of nuance and patience... these are things you still need to learn, clearly," Thomas adds, still staring into the dancing flames.

Adahy knows his uncle is right, needs no reply, and walks out of the house under a light blanket of shame and into the heavy blanket of snowfall.

Floating Revelations

King's Guard Auxiliary Headquarters
Boston, Massachusetts

Dancing off the brick walls, the shadows from the flickering flames twist and contort devilishly beyond the hearth. Uncharacteristically slouched, the Major General's attention on the flames is unbroken. His elegant redcoat with his gold and black sash is bunched on his chest and waist. His arms rest on the leather upholstered armrests that are secured with brass tacks along the edges as the rest of the chair's frame is polished with a deep luster.

"Sir, there is a vagrant here... he claims he has information about Colonel Valles," the sentry ranger announced to his superior.

His forehead was hot, and he was in no mood to speak to drunkard vagrants, "Tell him to share his findings with Captain Bates!"

"Aye, sir!" The sentry ranger replies before closing the door and turning around to walk out of the barracks.

"Fucking drunks, I hate this wretched land… crooks, criminals, vagrants, drunkards, and cowards… the entirety!" the blue-eyed, black-haired man shouted into the air in his office, never taking his eyes off the flames.

Wood crackled and snapped in the hearth as the fire danced within, illuminating leaping shadows across the walls. The large, polished oak desk was the largest piece of furniture in the room, but with Major General Ivey sitting behind it, no British soldier would think so. He carried a weight, a legacy, and an aura most feared.

The door opened again, "Bloody hell, what is the fucking issue now!?"

"Sir, I believe you need to hear this," Captain Bates asserts strongly.

In his early twenties, the younger Captain was taller and built stronger. He carried dark brown hair with lighter eyes and fair skin. The man turns and motions for the two sentry rangers to bring the drunkard into the office. Seconds go by, and the two rangers help walk the drunk man into the office and quickly exit.

It hits his nose immediately, "My God, what is that smell?"

"Sir, he has urinated himself multiple times since his arrival," Captain Bates states irritatingly.

"God dammit. What do you know of Colonel Francis Valles?" The Major General asks the man as he stands up behind his desk, his ice-blue eyes stern, "Do not waste my time!"

"I know more…" *Cough, Cough*, "than you," he says in a cracked, old, worn-down voice and continues, "The ones you hunt are why your Colonel is dead," the drunkard says plainly, looking at the King's Guard Commander.

Baffled, Agador shoots a look at Captain Bates and back to the rank vagrant.

"Speak on what you know..." he replied, growing impatient, "I promise you I will only find pleasure in coming around... or over this bureau to remove your life from that feeble pun of a body you live your life through," the black-haired commander said blithely.

"Not long ago, a native arrived in town..." the drunkard begins, coughing as he speaks, "he didn't just pass through..." *Cough*,*Cough* "he stayed in town... he has lighter, blonde hair," *Cough* "And rides a black horse..." *Cough*,*Cough* "I never asked around... but the other night, I was sleeping off a spell at the docks, trying to keep warm," *Cough* "Near dock lamps... you know..." *Cough* The drunkard spits out a wad of bloody mucus on the office floor.

Captain Bates glances at the Major General, and they exchange understood looks.

"I woke up to a large splash and saw the blonde native walking in the opposite direction... No one else was around," *Cough**Cough* "He walked off the docks, and I went to where I heard the splash," *Cough* "Where I saw him, your Colonel... floating there, already dead," the old man stumbled and caught himself with the chair.

"A blonde-haired native?" Major-General Ivey asks with a curious look on his face.

"Aye... a dist—" *Cough* "-inctive-looking man," he says before seemingly choking.

"How have we not noticed this man since our arrival? We have eyes everywhere, and if this man is as distinctive as you say, he would be easily found..." the King's Guard Commander adds interrogatively.

"It seems your Colonel took notice..." *Cough* "Do not underestimate the ability of a redskin to blend in..." *Cough*, *Cough*

Agador shoots another look at Captain Bates and back to the drunkard and says, "Is there anything else you need to tell us about this man?" Captain Bates smoothly closes the door, leaving only the three men in the office.

"No... but can you have sentry ranger walk me to George's Tavern? I need a drink, and Barratt imports some of the best Madeira," the drunk man says, looking up at the King's Guard Commander before coughing.

Captain Bates doesn't move, with his back up against the door facing his superior. Lifting his fists off the oak desk, Agador stands up straight. Lightly, he flattens out his dress uniform. Bright red and immaculate, carrying the black and golden sash, indicating his command over the King's Guard, the man walks from behind the desk. The fire cracks, and the flames dance as he makes his way to the drunk man. Smoothly, he walks with each step gracefully touching and leaving the floor.

"It seems this cough will be the death of you..." Agador says hollowly.

Cough, *Cough* "I just need some Madeira..."

With a slight chuckle, Agador says,

"Madeira, eh? What you need is to stop breathing," with a swift motion, the King's Guard Commander snatches the man off his feet. Staring up at him,

"Putrid little man," he squeezes harder. Anger overwhelms the Major General as the blood pumps through his tightening hand. In one aggressive motion, he slams the drunk man into the ground. Within Agador's hand, he feels the man's esophagus crack as he hits the office floor.

"Now, you die."

The drunkard's yellowy and bloodshot eyes showcase that he wasn't prepared or expecting this, and he tries to grasp for air. Agador stands, grips both chairs before the desk, gains momentum, and slams his right knee through the man's diaphragm. Splitting his chest in two, with his lungs rupturing air and blood out each side of the Major General's knee.

Dirty fucking vagrant, useful for this information... he thinks to himself, looking down at the man's lifeless face.

"As a consolation, I'll get the Madeira for you," he says softly and lightly double-smacks the drunkard's dead face. He stands, and he wipes the blood off his leg. Agador's blue eyes shoot over to the bottles of Madeira.

"I'll get the sentry rangers to get him out of here and to clean this up," Captain Bates adds, halfway smiling with what he's just witnessed, and continues,

"I am also going to put out a handbill to all merchants and to be read at the town hall. This *blonde-haired* native will be captured and killed for the death of Colonel Valles."

"Good, get my horse ready too; we're going to George's Tavern," Agador says smoothly as he walks to the counter.

"Aye, sir," Captain Bates replies and opens the doors, "two of you, now, come here!"

Two sentry rangers come running, and the noise of their arrival becomes blended audible with the fire. Agador grabs a glass and fills it with sweet Portuguese wine.

"Cheers," he nods and tilts his glass toward the dead man as the two Sentry Rangers begin to drag him out of the office.

"Seems like I am the one in need of the Maderia."

As he rounds the large, polished oak desk, he slouches back into the finely crafted chair. His eyes focus back to a daze in the fire, and he sips his drink, waiting for Captain Bates to bring him his horse.

**

City Market
Boston, Massachusetts

"Hear ye, hear ye!" the recoat droned on as other redcoat soldiers passed out the handbill to crowdgoers. Ester toned the man's voice out, and her smokey-gray eyes began to read the contents within.

WANTED
For the Murder of Colonel Francis Valles

A native savage known to walk the line between the wilderness and the streets of Boston. His origin is believed to be far from the city, yet his presence here signals danger to all loyal subjects of His Majesty.

DESCRIPTION:
Of native blood yet bearing a most unusual and unnatural feature—his hair is pale as flax, a striking contrast to the dark locks of his people. Tall and strong, he is easily recognized by this shock of blonde hair. He moves with the silence of a forest creature, vanishing as quickly as he appears. He is known to ride a Black horse.

Armed with the tools of the frontier—bow, tomahawk, muskets, and knives. His loyalty is to no known cause, though he has shown no mercy to those loyal to the Crown.

A REWARD of 150 pounds sterling is offered for his capture, dead or alive. He is to be considered armed and dangerous. Approach with the utmost caution.

By order of Major General Agador Ivey, Commander of the King's Guard, Boston, 1771.

"Fuck", she mutters.

"This is not good, Ester," James adds in a mirrored, worried tone. He crumbles the handbill after reading his own copy and tosses it onto the cobblestone street.

With sadness in her smokey-gray eyes, she turns to James with a low, worried tone, "No, it's not. That poor boy. No mother, no father, and now he must leave Boston."

"His path is not one of ease," James sighs.

"We must support him. If we can get him to Robert in Philadelphia, I believe he will integrate well and lose this attention."

"Aye, he's a smart kid. We will do all we can to assist him, my love," his words carry a semblance of comfort for her.

"And we both know the feeling of being hunted," melancholy fills her words.

"Aye, we do. Luckily, we don't carry that worry any longer, and those days are far in our past," he replies, extending his large arm and curling the woman inward.

"They are, but Adahy…."

"He has us, and we will help the boy."

The two walk within the crowd together, moving toward the hitching post. She half-smiles, "You always have a way of soothing my wicked soul."

"That is because you've soothed mine," he half smiles and continues, "Let's go tell the others."

She led the way out of the massive crowd. Moments later, they were at the hitching post on the outskirts of the market. They unhitched their horses and mounted them quickly. It was busy today, and the crowds were thick, all exchanging opinions and gossip about the handbill that was shared and read.

Ester rode her horse as quickly as she could down Fish Street. James did his best to keep up; being larger, he was usually the tail. Urgency filled their movements.

"Move," she mutters, as people awkwardly shuffle in Boston's streets as they swiftly maneuver through.

Soon, they arrived at the vacant alley near North Street. James hops off his horse and opens the large wooden barn door where they housed their horses.

"Ester... before you rush down there... remember, we need to be careful... who knows who has seen him with us," James replies, walking his steed in and hitching the animal.

"I understand... but his burden is now ours, James. Close the door, and let's go," she says, walking to the semi-hidden tunnel doors and opening them, revealing several steps leading to a tunnel.

James closes and locks the barn doors. He follows Ester quickly, and the two of them move deeper into the tunnel. The bald African man pulls the doors closed, wedging them tight.

"This isn't good, James..." Ester says in a continued worried tone to the man.

"I know... it is not... but we must not scurry or run... we find a better way to operate, and we get Adahy to Philadelphia," he says, in a confirming tone. Reaching his hand to Ester, she takes it, and he pulls her toward him, lovingly holding her, looking down at her, "My dear, where you go... I go... and where we go, we go together. Do not be scared."

Sadly, she looks at James, "They know what he looks like... and the King's Guard Commander..."

"Shh.... It will be okay," he says, comforting her.

"I know... but Adahy... he's just a lad..."

"That's why we will help him... Let us move. We need to tell the others," he says, followed by a kiss on Ester's forehead.

James can see her white hair when the sunlight breaks through the tunnel cracks and, within a few moments, are at the great room tunnel door. Upon entering, Nimish and Adahy sat by the fire, laughing and talking. Elias was sharpening a blade on a wet stone at the table, and Thomas was nowhere to be seen. James and Ester move quickly, getting through the door and closing it.

"Adahy!" Ester calls into the great hall while closing the door.

Adahy, hearing the stress in her voice, turns, "Ester, what's wrong?"

"Our new friend, the King's Guard Commander, had the Towncrier read a handbill that contained a description that nearly matched you..." James said in his deeply toned voice.

"Aye... not many *'blond-haired natives'* around these parts," she said regrettably.

Not sure how to handle the words, Adahy sits there in silence... thinking... *how... or who?*...

The door opens, seemingly breaking everyone's undivided attention on Adahy. They all look over to see Thomas entering the great room. The flickering flames illuminated his silver beard and scar.

"We have a mission," he says dismally.

Thomas brings a spare chair to the group around the fire and sits down.

"All right. I know what they read at the town hall this afternoon... and well... Adahy... I told you not to kill him, at least not yet," he says, and his head drops into his hands.

"Uncle Thomas... I know I made a mistake..." Adahy proclaims.

With a side-eye, Thomas's ice-blue eyes dart to his nephew, and with the most serious face, "Now you are their number one target. And you will have to deal with the consequences that come... but for now... we have a mission to complete. After that, we can move you to Philadelphia. I have friends who can keep you hidden while we eliminate the King's Guard Sentry Rangers."

Thomas continues with confirmed glances from all the King's Bane members,

"I have received verified intelligence of a troop caravan transporting King George III's latest coin shipment. The King hasn't been struck in a long time. I think it's time we correct that error. The caravan is leaving Cambridge four days from today and will be carrying two full wagons of coin and fur headed to Boston harbor. We know once the caravan is inside the city, it is almost impossible to attack. We need to hit it outside the city." Thomas says firmly.

"Oi, how about The Muddy River," Nimish says softly.

"What was that?" The Londoner replied to Nimish.

"He said the Muddy River," Ester adds shortly.

"Ahh… that is a good spot. The King's Highway has a perfect section between Brookline and Boston," Elias states.

"Aye… there is a path that can only be found by those looking that leads to the King's Highway. But we will need to leave the same way," James adds.

"Aye, we've used that path before; it's a good one," Ester replies, seconding the man's statement.

"Exactly; remember in '68, we ran those Charleville's up from Connecticut, and we were being followed?" The younger Nimish asks fondly.

"Of course! I remember now. That was a good path."

"You'll need to get there hours before the shipment arrives… concealment and surprise are imperative. I want this done quickly, quietly, and most importantly… I want you all to be safe in execution," the older Boston leader adds.

"I want to get back to work." James Robinson states strongly, followed by Ester's voice,

"I'm on board."

Thomas looks at Adahy, and Elias speaks,

"Me too."

"Same here," Nimish adds lastly.

"That settles it, then. We ambush this caravan take the Muddy River as our escape," the scared-faced, gray-haired man says, looking at his King's Bane compatriots.

With her petite frame and white hair, Ester stands carrying a devilish smile, "Let's get the bastards."

False Tales & Eager Hearts

December 1771

King's Guard Auxiliary Headquarters

Boston, Massachusetts

Since Agador arrived in Boston, he has made no real progress regarding locating and killing the King's Bane. They have avoided his grasp with annoyingly no issues.

I will not fail. I will not result into failing my mission… failing my king, he thinks as the flame shadows dance on his determined face.

"Captain Bates!"

"Yes, sir?" he replies, entering the Major General's office.

"Get my horse ready, I am going to George's Tavern!"

"Aye, sir!" he replies and moves with haste to complete the task.

Killing my Colonel? Killing the King's men? No world in existence will be able to hide them from me… I will kill them. The King will get what he has asked of me... I shall not fail.

Agador's mind wanders to achievement and accomplishment in approval from his cousin, the King.

Moments later, Captain Bates returned, "Commander, your horse is prepped."

The shorter, stockier Major General stood up from his chair. His coat was in immaculate order, and the gold and black sash sat perfectly across his chest. He snags his tricorn cap from the cap rack on the wall as he exits the room. Outside, his horse is equally pristine; he mounted it quickly and, within seconds, was on his way to George's Tavern. The ride through Boson was quick. A couple of gallops, and the Major General arrived at his destination.

He entered 'George's Tavern' alone. All seeing eyes around the tavern, mainly British loyalists, have seen the new Major-General in town, and rumors have been spreading about his purpose here in Boston. Agador has purposely been silent for security reasons after losing Colonel Valles.

"Good evening, sir. What can I get you? Some tea?" The younger barkeep asks as the Major-General approaches the bar top.

"Holland gin," Agador replies in his deep, cold tone.

"Right, you are, Sir," the barkeep says, pouring the liquor into a glass, "Rumors have it you are the crown's cutthroats in search of the King's Bane—"

"What do you know of the King's Bane?" Agador asks sharply, cutting the barkeep off, awaiting an answer with a mean look in his ice-blue eyes.

"Bunch of heathens!" The barkeep says excitedly.

"What is your name, barkeep?"

"Barratt Cassius... sir...." The man responds, shaken.

"What do you know, Barratt?" The Major-General asks the man, trying not to lose his temper.

"There's not much to know. They are faceless devils who deserve a traitor's death. Some people in town support the savages and think they are justified. A whole mess of shit if you ask me...." Barratt says loudly, then quiets down, leans toward Agador, and whispers, "Have you the right size purse… I might have a little more to say… but if not… I think I may have forgotten…"

The immaculate Major General leans in with a smirk across his face, and Barratt seemingly gets excited. With a quick snatch, Agador grabs the barkeep's collar and slams his face into the bar top.

"You will give me what I need, or I will take your head… your choice," the Major General says sternly in the man's ear and drinks the gin with his free hand.

"Aye," Barratt replies and the King's Guard Commander releases his clothing.

"Meet me outside near the horse trough. I have the information you want… too many eyes and ears in here," he says calmly to Agador.

"Thanks for the gin," Agador says with a cold look across his face.

All the tavern patrons seemed to pay no mind to the Major General and his antics at the bar.

Good, he thought… *good loyalists never interfere with the King's bidding.*

The nighttime air hit his skin as he exited the tavern, welcoming the chill. He preferred the cold and snow over everything else. The cold reminded him of London, the one thing he had warmth in his heart for. Cautiously, he maneuvered to the back of the building, anticipating any movement, trap, or indication he would be harmed. With his hand on his sword, Agador noticed motion, and a thin figure rounded the corner, cutting the shadows in the darkness. Removing himself from the shadows, Barratt Cassius emerges.

"What information do you carry, barkeep?" The Major-General asks, purposely ignoring his name.

"The King's Bane is quite the small group of bandits. Their outfit is maybe four to eight men—"

"Stop... four to eight men? Is this an honest assessment of this cabal?" the Major General asks in disbelief.

"Aye... I have personally seen them in action. They are no more than eight men, sir," Barratt replies.

"Keep going, tell me more."

"Their musket fire gives away their positions during the attack. Then they move like apparitions. And... when they do attack, they attack personal crown shipments or coin caravans. They try to hit the King where it hurts...his purse." The man says, nearly shivering.

"Where have you seen them? What were you doing?"

"I was coming back from a rum run, and we were offloading the rum barrels when the vessel to our left began getting attacked... It was fast, it was loud, and within minutes, they had killed over 30 British soldiers and sailors who were getting the coin shipment prepared for transport. This was a few years ago... maybe around the same time as the Stamp Act," Barratt answers and rubs his hands together, breathing into them.

"I want more information... I need to know where they are, who they are, where they go!" Agador says, getting visibly frustrated with the barkeep's answers.

"Yes, sir... I understand... but they are near ghosts.... But... A coin shipment is leaving Cambridge and heading for Boston in a few days. This is where you can assume to find them," Barratt says confidently.

"And how would you know this or have knowledge of this?"

"At George's, people talk... and I listen..." he replies.

"That is not verified or valid. How can you give me information I am supposed to act on without verification or any form of validity other than what you tell me?" Agador asks as he takes a step closer to the man.

"I would not tell you this if I did not believe this is where the King's Bane will strike next..."

Sensing authenticity in the man's voice, he takes this man's word. Knowing that putting several men in the coin caravan would be a simple execution, he doesn't want to waste the King's resources.

"I must be sure, barkeep..."

"Aye... I understand. I would not lie to a King's man, and I most certainly wouldn't lie to you," Barratt shutters, genuinely to the intimidating King's Guard Commander.

"You know if this is a lie, I will have my men burn your house down with your family inside, and you will be forced to watch... do not cross me, *Barratt the Barkeep*," Agador says to the terrified man, putting his finger on his chest, "Do not cross me."

Speechless, Barratt stands there shocked, and the Major General turns and begins walking into the shadows the way he came. He pauses and turns slightly, extending a coinbag,

"Your service to the crown will be rewarded with 50 schillings."

The barkeep reaches for the bag, and Agador drops it to the ground and says directly, "Upon taking this coin, you are entering into my service, and you will work for me."

The barkeep looks down at the fallen bag and nods,

"I'll do whatever you ask," he replies and squats, picking up the coin that had fallen from the coinbag.

**

December in Boston meant snowfall and chilly drifts off the sea. None of that really bothered Corporal Rooney as he moved with haste through the populated city streets. He didn't move with any British markings or uniform, making it more difficult to traverse the city, but nonetheless, he was making his way quickly. *The Major General needs to know*, he thinks, moving with purpose.

"Grab the Gazette! Fresh copies are available! Get your hands on a copy!" the young boy shouts, standing on a flipped-over crate with a stack of Boston Gazettes at his feet.

The headline grabs Rooney's attention: *The King's Bane: Real or Propaganda?*

"Horseshit," he says under his breath.

Scanning intently, he is getting closer to the barracks where the Sentry Rangers are staying for the time being. Maneuvering through the pockets of people, Corporal Rooney finally arrives at his destination after several minutes. The two Sentry Rangers that stand guard outside recognize the man quickly, nod, and give the man the proper greeting,

"Good afternoon, Corporal," they say collectively as he opens the doors, walking into the barracks.

Quickly, he went to the Major General's office, exhaled, and knocked on the door.

Knock, Knock

"Fuck, what now?!" the distinct voice shouts from behind the door, "Come in!"

He grabs the door handle and enters the room, closing the door behind him,

"Ah, Corporal Rooney, why didn't you say it was you? What news do you bring?"

"Well, sir, I do carry news. It seems Thomas Young knows he is being tailed. He is in a pattern now… He wakes up, leaves his home around 7:00 am, and walks the city until about 9:00 am; he then moves back and forth between Faneuil Hall and his home. Usually working longer hours in the town hall building, but nothing is out of the ordinary."

"Thomas is a slippery snake… keep watching him… His attitude and outlook are off. I have a deep feeling he has not been as forthcoming as he should be. I do believe he is withholding information about the rebels," the Major General's tone drops as his topic shifts, "What of the blonde native?"

"There have been no sightings, sir," Rooney replies.

Commander Ivey slams his fist into the desk, "God fucking dammit, Corporal!" he exhales and inhales heavily for a few moments,

"We need to find him. I do not care what requires his discovery… we will systematically go through each household… one by one until we find him. Whoever is aiding him, we will kill also…" he finishes as his ice-blue eyes look up from the desk and to the door, "Captain Bates!"

Footsteps come running from outside the Major General's office, and the door opens as the captain enters the room.

"Aye, sir," the youthful brown-haired man says, standing at attention.

"At ease, Captain. I need you to take the platoon of Sentry Rangers to find this blonde native. Search every home and business. Leave no stone unturned… and disregard the people; they may be helping this degenerate. When you return, we shall discuss the latest coin shipment," Commander Ivey finishes sternly.

"Aye, sir, I will get it done, sir," Bates replies automatically and leaves the office with a determined look on his face.

"Now, what other news, Corporal?" The Commander looks back to Corporal Rooney.

"Well, sir, while I was sitting outside Faneuil Hall, I heard whispers of a new shipment of gold and coin coming from Cambridge. Most of the people are staying off the highway the week it departs Cambridge," he says to the cunning Major General.

"And why would they do that?"

"The people do not want to disturb or interrupt the King's Bane… even if most people do not believe they exist… they believe it's better not to take the chance."

"We will be with the coin shipment from Cambridge and ensure we surprise the King's Bane… We shall await what findings Captain Bates uncovers in his searches, and we will move forward with formulating a plan when he returns. I am done taking chances. They will not slip through my fingers a third time!"

**

"Major General, sir,"

Releasing an aggressive sigh, "What is it, Lieutenant?"

"The last of Colonel Valles's personal effects are here, sir. What shall we do with it? Shall we send it back with his body?"

"No. Bring them to me," Commander Ivey says darkly, never removing his eyes from the window.

Shuffling into his office, two sentry rangers, each carrying one side of a wooden footlocker, carefully ease it onto the floor. The two men exit the room, followed by Lieutenant Gage closing the wooden door, leaving only their Commander.

After several moments of being alone, Agador removes his eyes from the window. A couple of steps and he is before the footlocker.

"Let's see what you carried, Valles."

In his calf-high black leather boots, he rests his knee on the floor. The black front-flapped trousers bunched up as he bends forward toward the footlocker. His left hand extends, and the bright red wool jacket covers his arm with elegance as he opens the case. His ice-blue eyes uncover all of the Colonel's possessions for this mission. With his hand, he shuffles around and sees a letter. He grabs it, revealing the contents, and slowly, he begins reading it to himself.

"King's Council... the young Major General is playing his part... he knows nothing but shortsightedness and rage... it is perfectly designed," he mutters with scrutiny.

He ceases reading the remainder, too hurt. Quickly, he crumbles the paper, throwing it to the floor.

Thumping faster and faster, his chest burns, and the blood surges in his veins,

"Bloody cowards!"

Curling his fists, he slams both into the topside of his oak desk, shaking the floor.

Mingling with the sentiment of betrayal, the Commander's words fall heavily, "Colonel Valles... a... spy?"

Creating a noise from nothing, the silence reverberates off the items and walls in the room. Darkness drapes over the Commander as the treachery of his long-time friend becomes his new reality. Questions of motivations swirl as the rage intensifies.

"Lieutenant Gage!"

Scurrying from the hall, the younger officer comes running.

Opening the office door, "Yes, sir?"

"This coin shipment from Cambridge... we need to embed Sentry Rangers within. If the rumors and chatter of the King's Bane focus on this shipment are correct, we will ensure these pieces of filth are destroyed!"

"Aye, sir."

"I will await the ambush near the neck with a squad of troops. Once the Sentry Rangers initiate the fight, we will intervene with haste."

"Yes, sir."

Ensnare the Hare

January 1772

The King's Highway

Above the five King's Bane members, a deep lavender sky welcomed the rising sun. Pink and purple clouds littered the morning sky, a patchwork of deep and bright hues. Frozen blades of grass crunch with each step in the snow, and icicles hang from the tree branches as they walk one behind another along the hidden footpath.

"You cold, Adahy?" Elias jokes with Adahy.

"Fuck off, Shakespeare," he replies, shivering.

"You baby."

Looking over, Adahy watches as he removed gray fingerless wool gloves,

"Here, take my spare gloves," Elias tosses them to Adahy.

"Thanks, old man."

"Enough... we are getting near the road," the larger James asserts over the others.

Coming to the end of the thick tree line, the King's Bane halts their movements. Leading the group, James steps out beyond the tree line into the open. Crouching and cautiously approaching, he nears the road and looks both ways, inspecting for travelers. Within seconds, he returned to the group.

"All right. Here's the play: Adahy, I want you up front on the corner of the road. You will be the furthest point. No one gets past you. Shakespeare and Ester, I want you both on the far side of the road. When it's time to attack, fire all your muskets and move in with blades. Nimish and I will be doing the same on this side."

"Who is initiating the fight?" the stringy white-haired woman asks.

"Adahy," James replies confidently.

"Me?"

"Yes. With your first arrow, hit the lead officers on horseback. This will shift the attention of the rest of the soldiers, and we will eliminate them one after the other. I don't want them moving into the woods... I want them to stay on the road."

Adahy nods in agreement.

"Okay... okay... quick and easy," Elias adds.

"This operation is going to require all of us to be concealed expertly. Use the trees, use the grass... but remain unseen. Once Adahy releases his first arrow, we will begin. Get to your positions and dig in."

Adahy felt the burden of initiating the fight. He could feel the weight in his chest, and immediately, he began walking to his position. The cold air seeped through Adahy's jacket and clothing, biting to his core. But the idea of taking down this coin shipment has his mind racing, and it's enough to keep him warm. Arriving at the corner of the road, he looks at the empty road winding and twisting toward Boston. Overgrown trees draped the highway, creating a sort of arched way cover. *Beautiful*, he thinks, taking in the nature and beauty of the earth.

Adahy finds it after taking a few moments to inspect the area for the best position possible. A shallow dip in the ground a few yards away from where the road curves. There are fallen trees and high grass surrounding it. *I need more concealment*, he thinks, after analyzing the spot. Looking to the tree line he sees a nearly broken branch barely hanging to the tree. Quickly, he snaps it off, drags the large, cold branch to his position, and lays it over a fallen tree. *Perfect*, he thinks and maneuvers himself underneath it.

He removes his quiver filled with arrows and his well-made bow. Taking out the bow and mimicking firing an arrow, Adahy ensures he can be effective in his position.

Satisfied with his construction, he settles in. *This is perfect... they'll never see me.*

As Adahy gets comfortable, he looks out to the highway where the soon-to-be ambushed redcoats will be and sees the others settling into their concealment.

**

Travelers, traders, soldiers, and undesirables frequented the King's Highway outside Boston, but none traveled today. The caravan from Cambridge would cross the Muddy River soon, in the hours before noon.

Birds chirp in the chilly mid-day air as he looks out at the quiet highway. In times like these, Adahy was always wary of deafening silence in the wilderness. Today, his wariness was intense.

The stillness of the area was peaceful, and the others were so well concealed that he could barely determine their locations.

"Psst, Psst," James's sounds from trees are heard, and Adahy knew the time was nearing quickly.

An eagerness consumed him as the caravan could be heard nearing their positions. Through the pines and birch coming into view, Adahy could see them.

The element comprises three officers on horseback leading the caravan, followed by two large horse-drawn wagons controlled by one soldier a piece. In the rear were two Officers on horseback, and 12 British light infantrymen were between the wagons.

Adahy ensured he counted five officers on horseback and 12-foot soldiers, and they each carried a Brown Bess with a cartridge container and bayonet. With each breath, the caravan inched closer and closer.

The tension began rising over the area, and he watched the British soldiers as they neared their soon-to-be permanent home. *Here we go*, he thinks. Slowly, he pulls back on the drawstring, and with the arrowhead nearly touching the bow, he releases.

Thwipt

Collect your reward, death, Adahy thinks as he watches the first arrow fly through the chilly air.

Impacting the lead Officer's chest, the sharp arrow slices through the top half of his chest. The momentum from the arrow brings him off his horse and to the ground, quickly creating a pool of warm blood.

From their concealed positions, the King's Bane fires on the unsuspecting redcoats. Each shot is perfectly placed to achieve a kill. Confused, the British soldiers shoot aimlessly into the tree line on both sides of the highway.

Adahy expertly rips three accurate arrows into the air, one after the next.

Thwipt, *Thwipt*, *Thwipt*

Each arrow finds its intended target. The first two arrows find the upper half of the other lead officers on horseback, killing them as they slump over their dazed horses. The last arrow impacts the lead wagon driver in the abdomen, and he keels over, bringing the first wagon to a halt.

They are organizing, he thinks as he sees the redcoats begin to situate themselves into a defensive position.

British soldiers exit the openings of the two wagons. One after the other, redcoat after redcoat, until the road was nearly covered with them. Adahy counted 15 soldiers flowing out of each of the wagons.

Fuck, that's not coin or fur, Adahy quickly thought, looking around at the scene that was unfolding.

He promptly noticed the enemy multiplied from 18 soldiers to 48 in a matter of moments. The redcoat numbers amassed quickly, and the King's Bane found themselves outgunned.

"It's a trap!"

Adahy could make out James's voice among the chaos. He is right. They're trapped.

Both sides of the wagons now had defensive wedge formations formed. Each contained two rows of redcoats, the first row on one knee, firing. The second row stood just behind the others, firing when the first row reloaded. Quickly, the highway becomes thick with musket smoke, and Adahy knows now is the time to move and disrupt the redcoats.

Emerging from his concealment, he quickly secures his bow into his quiver and his quiver to his back. In the same motion, he removes his tomahawk and medium-sized dagger. In a crouched position, he uses the chaos and smoke to conceal his movement toward Elias and Ester.

"Nyx! Shakespeare!" he shouts as he sees them firing behind a thick section of trees.

"Here!" Shakespeare's voice clamors through the destruction and violence.

Adahy jumps into their concealment position as the lead ball rounds fly into the vegetation around him, impacting the front side of the trees. The noise is incredible.

"I bet you're not cold anymore!"

With a light laugh and a smile, Adahy replies, "No... no, I'm not, old man."

"That's the spirit!"

Blending shouts from dying redcoats and redcoat officers trying to coordinate the attack can be heard between musket shots and their end impacts on trees and bushes.

The light infantry are skilled killers as they begin timing their shots synchronously, allowing one to reload while one to shoot until there is no space between them.

Once finished reloading, she fires the well-aimed shot but recognizes their particular uniforms, "Those aren't normal infantry! That's Sentry Rangers!"

"What?" Elias exclaims, "We need to get the fuck out of here, now!" he roars, trying to be heard over the chaos.

"We will... Cover me, Shakespeare."

Elias looks at the young man in confidence and nods. Adahy climbs out of the concealment position and runs between the congested trees toward the road. As he moves like an apparition, he can feel Elias and Ester's shots passing by him, impacting their intended targets.

The musket fire is intense, and British lead ball rounds impact the trees around Adahy, snapping into branches and nearly missing him. His breathing is smooth and steady.

Gripping his tomahawk hard, he rears it back and throws it precisely. Through the musket smoke, the native's tool rotates until it reaches a redcoat chest. The soldier groans and falls backward with the force of Adahy's throw. This creates an opening in the wedge formation for Adahy to break through.

He leaps through the opening of the wedge with his medium-sized blade in hand and thrusts it into the neck of the next closest soldier, bringing him down to the ground and snapping his neck in the process.

The other soldiers of the wedge are taken by surprise and scatter from their defensive position. Clarity controls his thoughts, and he moves with precision unmatched. Like a routine dance, Adahy slices and stabs to kill.

"Die, you bloody redskin!" One of the soldiers with a loaded shot fire, barely missing Adahy's face.

"Not today," Adahy replies, shoving the blade in his right hand into the man's esophagus.

With his empty hand, he pushes the lifeless redcoat off his blade. Then, he moves to his tomahawk and removes it from the dead soldier's chest. Avoiding a charging soldier, he quickly steps forward, inserting the blade underneath the chin of the charging soldier. The man's body stiffens, and Adahy removes his knife. Instantly, an outflow of blood follows, spraying the immediate area. He finely resets his stance.

Two more Sentry Rangers are reloading, and one gets shot in the back by Elias and falls to the cold, hard ground.

With insufficient time to reload, the second redcoat improvises, uses his musket like an ax, and swings at Adahy's head. Using the tomahawk, Adahy blocks the incoming musket thrust. Turning around quickly, the green-eyed native stabs him with the sharp steel knife. The musket fire from the other British defensive positions still deafens the day. *Death is rich today*, he thinks aggressively.

Adahy sprints back to the concealment position where Elias and Ester are located. Shots still erupt on the road, but no shots impact this sector.

"What a mess, Shakespeare," Adahy says as he returns to the concealment position.

"You said it. They came prepared to the nines. Why were there so many men? How would they know?" Shakespeare asks quickly as the words seem to rush out of his mouth.

266

"Who knows, but we need to get out of here alive," Adahy replies as he takes a knee, peering over from behind the tree and surveying the carnage.

"Robbie and Nemo are going to get swallowed up soon by the musket fire if we do not move and get across the road," Ester adds, firing another shot and earning another kill.

"Agreed. We need to get the fuck out of here, now!" the older Londoner spits out quickly.

"We need to establish a new sector of fire and eliminate these rangers," Adahy says as he removes one of his muskets, fully cocks the weapon, takes aim, and fires at one of the further soldiers. Quickly, he reloads and secures the musket back on his back.

In the same motion, he removes his quiver, "This is a great spot to rain hell on that wedge," he says, nocking an arrow.

"There," he pinpoints a cluster of men and rapidly sends accurate arrows toward the enemy.

Thwipt, *Thwipt*, *Thwipt*, *Thwipt*, *Thwipt*, *Thwipt*, *Thwipt*

"Now, let's move," Ester says on the release of Adahy's seventh arrow.

Each of the arrows impacts a soldier one after the other, dropping their bodies. Adahy was deathly precise with his bow shots.

**

Major-General Agador Ivey heard the musket fire erupting directionally west, close to the Muddy River. He knew immediately that his trap had sprung. His team of 10 horseback riders move into action, following their commanding officer. The men move quickly toward the chaos stemming from the wilderness.

They will not get away this time, he thinks, as his horse moves with haste.

He knew a handful of rebels wouldn't be able to survive the ambush of 40+ British infantry and Sentry Rangers, and he was excited about the results. He eagerly raced quickly to where the lure took place, the riders behind him trying to catch up.

**

Crossing the road, Adahy, Ester, and Elias moved cautiously through the dead and dying redcoats. Arriving between the two wagons, the three of them take cover. As they approach, the opposite side of the road is erupting in fire.

"Robbie is pinned down; we need to get over there," Ester frantically adds to the chaotic noise.

Adahy looks up, trying to locate James. Two aggressively moving Sentry Rangers are creeping toward a thick tree. To Adahy's surprise, James rounds the tree, revealing himself to the redcoats. Almost touching the soldier's face with the tip of his two pistols, he fires. Killing both men instantly, James tucks back behind the tree and reloads his handhelds expertly.

"I think he's okay," Elias says with a half-smile.

"Where is Nemo?!" Adahy diverts his attention to locating Nimish.

Down the road was a wedge formation with four redcoats creeping toward the tree line, "There!" Elias points out.

Elias and Adahy sprint toward Nimish. Musket fire continues, targeting James. Seeing vulnerabilities, the British corporal calls for a regroup in defensive positions.

"Sentry Rangers, form a column—" the man attempts to give the command, and Ester's cutlass interrupts, decapitating the redcoat. Blood sprays into the air as she moves to the nearest soldier, ready to kill.

Avoiding the lead ball rounds, the two men arrive at Nimish's position behind a large, felled tree.

Taking aim, Adahy pulls out his flintlock and quickly fires into the closest cluster of soldiers.

"Oi, Shakespeare, you slow bastard," Nimish says, half smiling.

"How are you holding up, kid?"

"Gentleman, I believe I've been hit," the young man says, unfortunately, looking down at his abdomen.

"What? Where?!" Elias questions quickly, examining his friend.

Nimish's right hand holds his bloodied abdomen, trying to keep pressure on the wound.

"I've lost too much blood, Shakespeare; I know that is certain. Death is near; let us finish today and worry about me tomorrow," he says weakly with a dulled smile.

"Unfortunately, he's right."

Confused, Elias looks to Adahy, "What the fuck do you mean he's right? We are not leaving him!"

"That's not what I said, Shakespeare... I'm saying he's right about focusing on getting out of this mess. We need to get Nemo up, and we need to leave. This whole thing was a trap for *us*. We need to leave now." Adahy says, determined, looking at Nimish,

"Let's make it happen, boys," Nimish says strongly, trying to stand.

Elias throws Nimish's arm around his neck and lifts the young man up.

"Let's go!"

Nimish and Elias start moving through the thick forest toward James's position, with Adahy behind them. Using his

Charleville and timely reloads, Adahy quickly fires off two expertly placed rounds, killing two more Sentry Rangers.

Ester and James notice the three men nearing their positions and tactically begin to retreat toward them. The two are deadly in their final shots, covering the other three men as they move deeper into the thick woods.

**

"Whoa!" Agador pulls back the reigns, halting his steed.

How are these many men dead?! He thinks to himself, infuriated.

Dismounting his horse, the King's Guard Commander removes his pistol, fully cocking it. His approach is with caution, as the musket smoke is still thick, and the groaning, dying men litter the cold road. Raising his right hand, he motions for the men behind him to move along the sides of the road behind him.

"Be wary, men."

A wedge was still formed on the far side of the road, near the tree line, still firing off shots.

"Gage!"

"Yes, sir!" the younger Gage replies, standing in the formation.

"Where are they?"

"We have them on the run, sir. They went there," he says, pointing to the thick trees.

"Then do inform me why you are still firing and not giving chase?!" The black-haired Major General shouts angrily and darts into the woods. Keeping his pistol high, he moves ferociously through the frosted forest, trying to end the hunt.

**

"C'mon, Nimish, stay with us; we're getting in the boat now," the words leave Elias's mouth filled with noticeable hope.

Ester throws her muskets into the boat and hops in, carefully helping Elias lay Nimish on the rowboat's deck.

"Stop talking," James insists as they climb into the vessel, trying to stay silent and looking at the path from which they all came.

With a hard push, Adahy shoves the rowboat off the bank. In the same momentum, he leaps into the boat. Elias and Ester begin situating Nimish and the gear. Adahy and James Robinson grab the oars and begin power rowing, trying to reach the mouth of the river as quickly as they can. After a few solid rows, they are off, moving swiftly down the river.

Snap

A lead ball round impacts the aft of the rowboat, splintering wood into the air.

"Fuck! Who the fuck is that?" Adahy shouts, startled by the incoming shot.

Snap

Another ball round impacts the aft of the rowboat, this time lower.

"Make no mistake. I will not miss next time!" A faded, deep voice shouts as a shorter but larger frame emerges from the trees.

All four of them look in the shot's direction, Nimish still lying down. Through the pistol smoke, they finally see him. A bright, blood-red overcoat first broke through the mist. His coat was pristine, carrying a black and gold sash across his chest. Standing tall and proud, getting revealed through the smoke, he smiles.

"Major General Agador Ivey," Adahy muttered.

Uncannily waving goodbye to them from the riverbank, "I see you, King's Bane! There isn't anywhere in the colonies you can go where I will not find you now!"

"Fuck," Elias mutters, dropping his head.

"I shall see you again, and you will die!" The Major General's tone is cheerful, but his voice fades as they hurry down the Muddy River. Through the thicker fog, he stands unbothered, waving.

"Look, he's still waving… he's smiling too," Adahy lowly grunts, subtly looking up as he rows harder with each pull.

Each of them took their time to look back, and the last thing the King's Bane saw of him was the flintlock pistol in hand and an eerie half-smile he carried. The imagery seared into their minds.

A Day to Remember

Boston, Massachusetts

Thomas always despised when British officers would force themselves into his home for meetings, an instance that happens more than he would like to admit. He especially disliked the arrogant continuance resting upon Major-General Agador Ivey's satisfied face.

With clear annoyance, "Welcome to my home. Don't make yourselves comfortable."

Stepping into the open room, the Major General looks around, "Hm."

"Take a seat," Thomas motions to the chair.

The worked-up British officer takes a seat. His captain stands near the door.

"Why do you look so accomplished, Agador?" Thomas asks, taking a sip of the warm coffee.

"It's Major General Ivey, or Commander Ivey, to you, colonist," he croaks out directly.

Visibly annoyed, Thomas knows it best to give them ample opportunity to assert themselves when faced with overtly disrespectful officers.

Little, egotistical prick, he thinks with a now calmed look resting on his face.

Looking around the room, the blue-eyed British officer isn't impressed, "What a quant home…"

"Aye, why are you here?"

"Escaping formalities today, are we, Thomas?"

"Tell me why you're in my home… or else, I will have to ask you to leave."

The high-class officer let out a quiet breath through his nose, "You know… I find it rather odd that a blonde-haired native murdered Colonel Francis Valles, and then just today… I see that exact native on the rowboat with a white-haired bitch, a rather impressively large negro, and some other unfortunately ordinary man with grayish hair."

Thomas does well not to move or make any indication that this worries him,

FUCK, he thinks.

With his eerie smile growing larger, "I saw them… the bloody King's Bane!"

"I have never believed such conspiracies. That is not a real thing, Major General."

Standing up from the chair, he adjusts his black and gold sash; he brings his blue eyes to Thomas, "Oh, but they are real. I saw them… they killed many of my men. I can assure you. They are as real as you and I sitting here now. The King's vengeance will soon come to pass."

Thomas leans into the officer's attitude and says, "Now you have the proof. What are your intentions?"

"I will hunt them. Find their scent and root them out. There is no space within the British Empire they will be able to move freely and openly. This leaves everywhere else, and the arms of the Crown endlessly reach… I will find them," he says coldly and takes a step toward Thomas, "And I will kill them."

"Well, I wish you the best of luck," Thomas says, motioning to the front door.

Captain Bates opens the door and exits. Before Major General Ivey exits the home, he stops, "Apparently, they were the spectacle to see, dashing and slicing, stabbing and shooting. The survivors are genuinely shaken and most likely have to spend their years in an asylum being eaten away by rats…." he sucks his teeth, "Poor souls. Mark my words, Thomas, the King's Bane, will not escape me. I have ordered Captain Bates and newly promoted Lieutenant Gage to search every single structure in the city," the words leave his smug lips.

"And you will do this after the Massacre in '70? The people of this city will not appreciate nor welcome you into their homes willingly," the scarred-face city leader says to the youthful Major General.

"They need not be willing… they are subjects of the Crown, and I am doing the King's bidding," he says, smiling.

"I see," Thomas responds questioningly, standing in the doorway, "Be safe out there, Major-General."

"Safety is for the weak," the agitated officer scoffs with a side-eye and half-smiles, exiting the old city leader's home.

***

Dr. Warren's Office
Charleston, Massachusetts

"Arrrggh!" Nimish cries out as the physician digs deeper with the forceps, trying to remove the lead ball round from his abdomen.

Thomas enters the room urgently, shutting and locking the door behind him, "I came as quickly as I could. Is anyone else hurt?"

"No, but he saw us," the deep-toned voice says, disappointed, from the corner of the physician's office.

"He told me. He was mighty eager to tell me, too."

"What all did he say, Thomas?" a worried Elias asks.

"Well... for one, he thinks there are four of you... he didn't see Nimish for whatever reason."

Looking worriedly at the physician doing work, Adahy adds, "We laid him in the rowboat. There was no way for him to see Nimish—"

"God dammit," the physician says softly as Nimish groans.

"Joseph, tell me he is going to live?" Thomas leans toward the physician, shifting his focus to Nimish.

"By grace, the wound in his abdomen will heal with time, but he will need to rest and recover for the next eighteen months or so," the middle-aged physician assures Thomas.

"Thank god," James mutters, speaking for the group.

Reaching for his bloodied hand, Thomas grabbed it, "Nimish, hold on, Doc Warren is going to get you patched up, and you will be fresh as a spring day."

"Yeah... and this is the exact reason why I need to get out of this line of work," Joseph states bluntly.

"Arrrrgghhh, fuck!" Nimish winces and cries out.

"Almost done," the middle-aged physician says, pulling the bloodied round out with the forceps.

Upon the round being removed, an exhausted Nimish passes out. Joseph then stitches his wound closed and begins to wrap his abdomen with linen bandages expertly.

Looking at the King's Bane, "The blood on your clothes is not yours?" Thomas asks.

"It was a massacre..." James's deep voice comes from the corner of the office, "Although your nephew sure did handle himself well, Thomas."

"It was an ambush. They were waiting for us to attack the column," the green-eyed native says strongly.

Elias steps forward, "It's true. They multiplied in a matter of seconds. For our part, I'd say it was a bloody masterpiece."

Adahy removes his tobacco pouch, clay pipe, wick ball, and hemp-seed-hops pouch. He mixes the hemp-seed-hops and tobacco before pinching a large amount and packing his clay pipe bowl. Lighting the wick's end, he torches the bowl, puffing the pipe until it is lit, and begins inhaling the smoke.

Ah, relief, he thinks as the smoke fills his lungs.

"If you call that a masterpiece," Ester says, visibly upset, pointing to Nimish on Joseph's wooden examination table.

"No, of course not. But we killed a lot of redcoats... and that's the masterpiece..." he pauses, and his tone drops, "Any time we get to kill a redcoat is a masterful piece of art, my friend."

"Ugh, never serious," she replies.

"Well... we are all fucked, truthfully," the smoke leaves his mouth with the words, "I was already on the Major General's list because of the Colonel... now we all are. Are we all going to Philadelphia now?"

Each pair of eyes that belonged to the King's Bane looked at each other for confirmation or approval or any indicator of what to do... before all turning to the old, gray-haired, scarred-faced Boston city leader.

In a defeated tone, Thomas replies, "Yes. Philadelphia, it is."

Joseph walks forward into the conversation, "I have a home in Charleston, across the bay, where I can have Nimish stay and recuperate. No one, especially a redcoat, will be there. It will be safe."

"Joseph, thank you for your services. As always, you've been incredible. I will have one of my militiamen bring your payment," Thomas says to the physician, shaking his hand, "We will get out of your hair. Take care of Nemo. He's like a son to me."

"He's like a son to us all, Thomas. I'll ensure he is well cared after, and when he is healed, I will send him to you," Joseph responds.

Thomas motions for the King's Bane to exit, "All right, let's go. Doc, please send a runner when Nimish wakes up. Thank you again."

"Thank you, Doctor," Ester says heartfeltly and exits.

"Yeah, thanks, Doc," Elias adds, following Ester out the door.

Walking slowly toward the door, James's frame towered over most, "Listen, Joseph, genuinely, thank you for always being there for us… you didn't have to, but you were, and I… we appreciate you."

His large hand nearly swallows Joseph's hand, and he exits the office. Thomas winks and nods toward the door to Adahy.

Exhaling smoke, "Thank you, Doc, you've been honorable," he says, exiting the office.

"He reminds me of you," Joseph says to Thomas as the door closes.

Thomas half smiles and lets out a quick breath out of his nostrils, "he *is* my nephew."

A large smile creases on Joseph's face, "Really?"

"My kid brother somehow managed to become a father and not tell anyone.... How inconsiderate?" he asks sarcastically.

Knowing Thomas for many years, he could tell when Thomas was sarcastic and not, "The stories the world could tell about your brother would be grand, my friend; rest his soul," he says, dropping his head in grief.

"All jests aside, I am thankful to have him here. Regardless of the mess, we are with the Sentry Rangers and the King's Guard. I am happy my brother's blood still runs... and truth be told, Adahy is a great kid... a bit rash and filled with rage, but he has a good heart."

"Indeed. That is clear," Joseph agrees.

Knowing he had to leave, "Thank you, again and again, forever... take care of Nimish. I'll see you soon," Thomas says genuinely, exiting the physician's office.

***

Boston, Massachusetts

The city was alive in the hours following the ambush at the Muddy River. Every merchant, sailor, soldier, militiaman, and civilian was alerted to the existence of the King's Bane. Murmurs, conversations, and everything in between floated throughout the crowds in the city. All day, squads of redcoats passed out newly printed wanted handbills with details of the King's Bane descriptions and rewards for information. Walking through the North End, after easily losing his tail, he sees it slowly drifting along the street. Leaning over, Thomas picks up the discarded handbill.

"What is this shit?"

WANTED
For High Crimes Against the Crown and Threats to His Majesty's
Peace

Be on guard for a ruthless and dangerous band of rebels who have come to be known by loyal subjects as **The King's Bane**. *These outlaws operate as one and have sown discord across Boston, inciting rebellion, disrupting trade, and targeting those loyal to the throne. Together, they threaten to tear apart the order and security of His Majesty's territories. Each individual within this group is as treacherous as they are distinctive. Approach with extreme caution.*

DESCRIPTION OF INDIVIDUALS:

— The **Blonde-Haired Native** *– Wanted for the Murder of Colonel Valles- Associate and Member of The King's Bane. Approach with caution.*

— A **White-Haired Woman,** *Older, though her appearance may suggest refinement, she is armed and dangerous, known for cruelty and unflinching resolve.*

— A **Large Negro** *of notable strength and stature, unmatched in size. He is considered extremely dangerous and is likely to overpower any man who crosses him.*

— A man of **Unremarkable Appearance** *with gray hair who may blend easily into the crowd but should not be underestimated.*

A REWARD of 500 pounds sterling is offered for information leading to the capture, dead or alive, of any member of The King's Bane. Loyal

subjects are encouraged to report any sighting of these individuals and to avoid engaging them directly. They are to be considered armed, dangerous, and without mercy.
By order of Major General Agador Ivey, Commander of the King's Guard, Boston, 1772.

"Fuck, I need to get them out of here," he mutters to himself, crumbling the pamphlet.

This side of Boston was quiet, and that was by design. Between Thomas, Hancock, and Dr. Warren, the three men owned a lot of the properties that were empty. In a smooth, quick motion, the gray-haired man moved unseen to the run-down, vacant tavern entrance. With familiarity, the scarred-faced man glides down the steps into the dank corridor, reaching the opposite end smoothly. He opens the heavy wooden door.

Inside, the King's Bane are packing their belongings.

"I need my cossack," Elias frantically says, rummaging through a chest.

"I have my things ready," the deeply toned voice says, sitting in the chair with nothing more than his muskets and clothing on his body.

"James, come now, pack a haversack with your things," Ester tells the man.

Gazing into the fire, "We were so close…."

Hearing the words, Thomas walks to James, "So close to what?"

Keeping his eyes on the dancing flames, "to getting away and not being seen… now look," he says, turning back to the others packing their things.

"I know… it hurts," he says, placing his hand on the man's shoulder, "the fight isn't over, and Boston is just one location within the tinderbox that is the colonies."

"This isn't the end, James. We will go to Philadelphia and keep up the fight," Ester says from the room reassuringly.

"Mhm," he groans, visibly disappointed at the events unfolding.

Search & Seizure

City Center,

Boston, Massachusetts

"Move out of my way, woman!" Captain Bates growls at the woman in the doorway.

"You have no right!" she shouts angrily, her breath being seen in the chilly New Year air.

With a swift motion, the youthful brown-haired captain backhands the woman across the face, "You are subjects of His Majesty King George III, and you will adhere to the search, or you will be tried as a traitor and criminal to the Crown!"

Gasps and breaths can be heard from the gathering crowds outside the residence buildings. The woman grabs the red part of her face. She cowers out of the doorway, crunching a pile of snow, allowing the captain and several soldiers into her home.

Violently, the British soldiers flipped the inside of the woman's home upside down. They searched in every crack and crevasse within the home. In a matter of five minutes, they were done and moving on to the next house. Systematically, they had begun their search for the King's Bane.

"Come one, come all! See the ill-justifications of the Crown!" Hancock shouts, clearly trying to evoke the crowd.

283

"What sense do you make of this, John?"

Quickly turning to the voice, the boisterous man sees the middle-aged physician bundled in a thick coat.

"Ah, Joseph… can you believe this? They're searching civilian homes."

"Absolutely pathetic," Joseph replies coldly.

John turns back to the redcoats, "Unwarranted search and seizure! It is ungodly to invade a person's living space. What you are doing is against the very fabric of God and human decency!" the loud, charismatic man berates the redcoats.

"Yeah!" a voice seconds.

"Is this how King George repays his subjects?! With a strong arm across the face and destroyed property?!" John shouts with passion toward the redcoats as the crowd draws larger.

"Is that John Hancock, I hear? Shouting like a madman?" an older, familiar voice asks.

"Ah, Thomas…" Joseph turns to Thomas with an inquiring look, "Good of you to join."

"Thomas! Finally, you can see what their truths are… look… they go from door to door, forcing themselves into the homes of the people," John shouts fervently, pointing to the redcoats.

Each time he shouts, the crowd murmur thickens, and the people begin to speak about taking action.

"They are scum. This is certain," Thomas adds surely, but the weight of the home searches directly results from the King's Bane actions.

John was clearly in a joyous mood, and Thomas did not want to dampen it. The man continued berating the redcoats with a smile, "Where is the justification? Where is the proof of these so-called 'killers?'- where?"

More voices in the crowd begin to repeat John's shouts. The anger within the crowd grows, and a woman throws her fist into the air, shouting,

"Where is the justification?"

"It seems you've gotten them going, John," Thomas says, looking around at the crowd becoming increasingly hostile.

"Good. We need the crowd behind us… on our side… Lord knows we have the numbers here to swamp them."

"Do you think it's best for us to pursue that route?" Joseph asks intently.

"I do. And I know Thomas does, too," John replies, overly confident in his words.

"Aye…" Thomas responds, watching the redcoats force themselves into a new home, "I believe we are headed for a major shift…. The massacre in '70 was too much for the people. They've been scarred and grown tired of the Crown's overreaching…, and now this. We are headed down a path where we have manipulated the course to end up where we are now. War will happen… it is only a matter of time."

"War is good. Liberty… and dare I say, independence…" John eerily half smiles at Thomas.

"Dare you say?" Joseph asks rhetorically, "INDEPENDENCE!" His voice carries in the cold air and travels throughout the crowd.

The spectacle of Joseph Warren shouting the word brought a slight smile to Thomas's scared face, "Where would Boston be without you two?"

With a satisfied look resting upon his face, John replies, "Boston, by the Grace of God, would still be here… but would it be the city we love, bled for, and sacrificed so much for? I doubt it… but we owe many thanks to you, Thomas… you have been a leader here for decades."

"I appreciate you, and I am not leaving any time soon."

"What about the others?" Joseph inquires in a softer tone.

"They are leaving town as we speak," Thomas calmly assures the man.

Both John and Joseph nod, understanding that the King's Bane, as elusive as they are, still have too many eyes on them. They would be hunted indefinitely and needed to depart the city as soon as possible. Noticing the British soldiers exiting a home and moving to the next one, John starts his criticizing,

"What are you searching for, Sentry Rangers? What in heavens do these people have for you? Why do you treat them with such ferocity and destruction? These are Your Majesty's loyal subjects! Why would they be abused and their homes tossed?!"

His words entice the crowd, and they cheer when they end. The atmosphere in the square is hostile and loud, with cries and cheers reverberating from the multi-leveled brick buildings. It is becoming a nightmare scenario for the British Sentry Rangers.

**

"The crowds are heavy by Faneuil Hall. They must've started their door-to-door search campaign," James says, peering out of a broken section of the barn.

"Fuck 'em," Ester says coldly, tightening the stirrup strap to her saddle.

"Are we almost ready?" James asks the crew, turning away and looking down into the barn.

It was quiet, all but for the prepping and movements of the King's Bane and their horses. The barn was larger, with three levels, and vacant. It was their unofficial horse stable for the last several years, and now they were being pushed out of their city. The veteran members all had a visible distaste for leaving their city.

"Aye, I am ready, boss," the English-accented man replies with acceptance.

Sitting atop Raven, Adahy replies, "I am ready. Should we travel two at a time while we're in the city? They may be looking for four travelers."

Ester stops with her saddle, "That's smart, kid. You and Elias will go first, and James and I will go second. We will meet back up outside the neck."

Using a rope, James slides down from the third floor. Walking to his strong horse, he mounts the animal, "That works. We will link up outside the Neck. Be safe and stay unnoticed." His tone is deathly serious, and they all know he is right; going unnoticed is key.

"I'll let you out," the white-haired woman says, opening the large barn door and allowing them to depart.

"Hey, kid, why don't you tie your hair up? They know the blonde, and they'll be looking for it. That's why mine is in a knot. There aren't many white-haired women like me... same as you... not many or any blonde-haired natives. Don't throw caution to the wind now."

He knows she's right, and he knots up his hair. Buttoning his greatcoat to his nose, Adahy was fully bundled with his hair hidden under his tricorn, using a scarf to wrap his head and neck.

Both muskets are secured in the leather holsters, draped on both sides of Raven's neck, and Adahy's gear in the saddlebags. He left home with just enough supplies, and he's barely gathered more during his time in the city.

He clicks his teeth, and Raven starts to move. Elias and his white horse follow. Emerging into the vacant alley, Raven and Adahy enter the bright but chilly sunlight.

"We will see you outside the neck," Ester winks at Adahy and Elias.

"See ya out there, Nyx," Shakespeare replies endearingly to the woman as she closes the door behind him.

Looking back to Elias, "You ready, old man?"

With a side-eye and a smile, "More ready than you can possibly imagine... I love the city, but it feels nice to have a shift in scenery," he says, having his horse slowly trot to Adahy's side.

On their horses, both men ride side-by-side, rounding the corner of the vacant alley, coming into view of the crowd's edges in front of Faneuil Hall. Pockets of civilians are walking, seemingly collectively, toward the town hall. As the two navigate through the dense city, the cold air hits the open sections of their skin, and Adahy shivers.

"You are absolutely absurd," Elias laughs at Adahy, "If I hadn't seen you kill redcoats with such violence, I would swear you are the most fragile little flower I've ever seen!"

Shaking his head, Adahy keeps shivering, "Fuck off."

The murmurs and crowd audible were roaring as the two men moved closer to the collected mass of people. Raven and Elias's white horse's hooves are drowned out by the noise.

"Look, John is doing his best to taunt the redcoats!" Elias laughs, motioning his head toward the loud man in the crowd.

From a distance, the popular merchant's voice cried out, "Is this what His Majesty gifts us? I do say, the people shan't forget today's events, my dear soldiers!"

"Look, Thomas is with him," Adahy points out.

"Let's not pay too much attention. The less we do, the better we will be going unnoticed," Elias states but continues, "that John Hancock is unparalleled in his ability to irritate redcoats," he finishes with a smile.

"He seems to be a good man," Adahy replies, "but I wonder when we will see Thomas again."

Knowing Adahy's past, Elias's blue eyes dart to the younger half-native, "Your Uncle is the smartest man I know. He knows where to meet us, and we will see him at Mug Tavern. Trust me," Elias assures the young man.

I hope he's right, Adahy thinks.

"Thanks, Elias, you're a great friend."

"Oh, don't get all mushy on me… you shivering cat!" He laughs and clicks his teeth.

Both men pick up the pace, moving past the large crowds. Quickly riding past the multi-storied brick buildings, they move past George's Tavern and within another few gallops, are out of Boston and moving along the neck.

**

"All right, I think it's been enough time," her voice was steady and calm as she opened the barn door.

The chilly air slices her wool jacket, and she shivers lightly. Bundling her coat, she mounts her horse.

"Let's move out," the deep voice says, leading the two out of the barn into the narrow, vacant alley.

The horse's hooves impact the cobbled road, and the chilly salty breeze comes in from the harbor. It was a cold afternoon with the sun getting captured behind pesky clouds, keeping a cool shade over the day.

"It's bittersweet," her voice carries over the horses.

"It is. But we will return. I have no doubt about that," James replies optimistically.

As they round the corner the crowd ahead of them is steadily growing. More and more people are gathering to watch the redcoats and listen to other civilians criticize them.

With her memories flooding her mind, Ester tightens the grip on her reins, "Do you remember when we first met, James?"

The larger man turns his head right, "My dear... it's one of my fondest memories." His smile can be seen even through his scarf. The roars of the growing crowd filled with shouts and cries toward the redcoats.

"You were with Thomas, coming in off a shipment, and I was sleeping on the dock," she smiled and continued, "I was such a vagrant back then."

His deep laugh barrels through the air between them, "You are still a vagrant! You just learned how to bathe."

"Oh, you hush!"

"I just remember getting off the dock and being mad some old drunk was sleeping where we needed to offload the cargo... turns out under that white hair... was you."

She smiles, "You scared me half to death... but in your eyes, I found a calm that welcomed me."

"I am glad you didn't have a heart attack when you saw me, and I just wanted to help. You were .... You are still so tiny," he says with endearment toward Ester.

With sincerity and love,

"You've helped more than you'll ever know, James."

"The feeling is mutual," he replies in kind.

Ahead of the two riders, the crowd thickened, and many people began shouting insults and threats, more than before, at the redcoats going in and out of the homes.

"There is no King here!" a raspy voice shouts from deep in the crowd.

"Another massacre waiting to happen!" another shouts from the front of the crowd.

With a worried look, Ester's smokey-gray eyes meet James, and he knows she's worried about the city... about Thomas and Mary.

"It will all work out, my dear. Thomas is more capable than he looks, and you know his reach is far... no one will ever suspect him, and he will be okay here," the large man assures the white-haired woman.

"I know... I know.... I am just sad we are being forced out of our city."

"It's never been *our* city, Ester, you know that. This is a perfect opportunity to make new roots in Philadelphia."

With a strong inhale, exhale, seemingly accepting the outcome, "You're right. Let's go."

Two spurs later the strong horses are galloping with ease toward the neck of the city. As they ride, an unaccompanied feeling of new beginnings overwhelms Ester, and she looks to James.

"Never worry, Ester, we have each other," he happily assures.

"We do."

To their back is the past, their history, and they know this is the shift needed for their survival.

London's Thoughts

St. James Palace
London, England

With each step, the winding stairwell seemed to further itself from the shadow room. Lord Chamberlain Ashford rushed to the Council Chambers with news from the colonies. Crumbled in his left hand, he carries a letter.

"Not good... not good, indeed," he mutters.

Each step echoes into the darkness of the hallways as he frantically makes his way through the bowels of the St. James Palace. The cloak drapes, almost touching the floor, nearly snagging on every corner he sharply rounded. The hallways and rooms were empty on this side of the Palace, but as he moved further toward the center, the more frequently he would come across a random palace worker.

Soon, he was before the Throne Room. Before entering, he pauses, takes a deep breath, and opens the large wooden doors.

"Please, do not bring me more dismal news."

"Aye, your Majesty. It's just—"

"No," he cuts off Lord Chamberlain, "I just said, do not bring me more dismal news... and it seems you are about to announce dismal news, gloomy and void of happiness. I have heard enough *news*. I refuse," King George III says, waving his hand at the man, "Not today. You are the King's Council… solve the issue."

"Yes, your Majesty," he replies, bowing.

In seconds, a stunned Lord Chamberlain is back in the palace hallway.

Fucking King, same as his father, he thinks and storms off the way he came.

Wait… he thinks and pauses. *I should seek out old man Henry. Yes, old man Henry will have the answers.* Quickly, Lord Chamberlain Ashford moves in the opposite direction now.

The older man moved with purpose through the elegant and artistic hallways. His footsteps echo into each corridor as he makes his way to the far side of the palace. After several minutes, he arrives at the hallway he is seeking. In one smooth motion, he knocks on the wooden door.

"Who is it?!" a voice shouts from the room.

"Lord Chamberlain Ashford."

The door unlocks and opens, revealing a much older man who is hunched over, "Ah, Lord Chamberlain, how good of you to stop by," his voice quivers with age.

Entering the chambers, the Lord Chamberlain sits at an empty chair, "Let's talk Henry."

"What plagues you so? I can see it in your face," the elderly man stated weakly as he closed the door.

"Colonel Valles has been killed. He was our eyes and ears. This cabal in the colonies has been irritating, and now the King refuses an audience."

After a few slow steps, Henry sits in the empty chair across from the Lord Chamberlain, "The king is young, and like you, the cabal in the colonies irritates him, and you bringing him news of Colonel Valles's death will not help. I am but an old man, having conversations with death, so I am not one to be giving guidance," the elderly man states.

"Henry, you were the longest-serving Lord Chamberlain before me. Do not be clever."

With a smile creasing, he said, "This is quite simple, my boy. First, you need to let the King be. Then you will need to inquire with the German. Once you do, consider introducing him into the colonies with the Major General without the knowledge of the King," pausing, he drinks water from his mug on the table. With a devilish smile, he continues,

"Let the young Commander Ivey deal with the German. Or don't. They might not be as cohesive as you think... or they will be, and then you'll be to blame when they massacre civilians. The land is filled with incidents of violence and death. These are all considerations to be given attention to."

Lord Chamberlain Ashford nods his head in understanding.

Henry continues, "But...you should have confidence in the young Commander. He is quite the animal. Even when he was a boy, I remember his family having issues with his... let's say... attractions."

"Major General Ivey's exploits around the globe are well-known. But what do you mean his attractions?"

With a pleased look, Henry continues, "The young Commander Ivey has been ill-tempered his entire life. As a boy, he brutally murdered a handful of his housemaids. He was only six when he started. They were horrifying scenes, but King George always suppressed them from getting out. The Ivey family is powerful, and Agador is the culmination of generations of intelligently violent men."

Shifting in his chair, with a more curious ear, Lord Chamberlain leans forward.

"You had been Lord Chamberlain for nearly 2 years when the final one occurred, around the same time as when Davies and Carbis arrived back from their hunt. He is a vicious boy. You could instruct the German to assist Commander Ivey, but… then you might miss out on a marvelous display of precise violence. He can accomplish a lot when he puts his mind to it."

"I see. So maybe I let him be…"

Henry nods his head, "Why add the German when you can use Colonel Valles's death as the wind in your mission's sails? This is just the opportunity needed for Commander Ivey to snap."

Lord Chamberlain Ashford nods his head as well, "I will allow the situation to unfold without assistance."

"Wise decision, Lord Chamberlain."

"We both know you are the wise one," Chamberlain Ashford smirks.

"Wisdom comes when you realize morals and religion are mere words with no meaning," Henry's wrinkly face smooths a resting smile.

Lord Chamberlain stands from the chair, "Thank you, Henry, you're a beacon of light."

"No, I am but an old man nearing my end," Henry replies, laughing, and continues, "Now get out of here and stop worrying so much. Everything will work itself out."

Opening the door and walking out, the Lord Chamberlain turns to the elderly man, "Good day, Henry."

"Good day, Lord Chamberlain," he replies and closes the door.

Immediately, the dreariness of the palace swamped over him as he stood alone in the quiet hallway. But the feeling settled and blended into a more welcoming sensation. A wave of calm and assuredness consumed him.

I will have some tea, he thinks. And casually walks down the hallway with a new perspective on the situation in the colonies.

***

King's Guard Auxiliary Headquarters Boston, Massachusetts

"Gage! Get in here!"

"Yes, Commander," Gage answers, entering the office.

"Where are we with the searches? Any leads?"

"No, sir."

"God dammit!" He throws his glass across the room and stands, "I want these fucking degenerates found!"

"They are well-hidden or no longer in the city, Commander. We searched nearly every building except the empty north end. They are all rundown buildings. Captain Bates is there now with a squad of Sentry Rangers."

"Rundown buildings would be the perfect hideaway..." Commander Ivey says in a lower, calmer tone, "Let's pay the captain a visit. I have a good feeling about this."

Reaching for his bright red overcoat, Agador smoothly puts it on and buttons it shut. He grabs the gold and black satin sash and throws it over his shoulder. Rounding the desk, Gage hands him his sword belt. Agador tightens it and is ready to go.

In moments, both men are out of the barracks and on their horses, moving toward the quiet north end of the city. Snow covered the ground with smaller ice patches littered between. It was mighty cold, and Agador enjoyed it this way. Seeing his Sentry Rangers a few hundred meters out, he brings his horse to a slower pace. Arriving at his men, he does not see Captain Bates.

"Where is Captain Bates?"

"Sir, he is in the cellar over there," the Ranger says, pointing to the doors protruding from the ground.

"It goes underground?"

"Right there, sir, that is one entrance. We have discovered several," the Ranger continues to his Commander, "it is possible there are connecting tunnels."

A smile creases on the young Major General's face, "Tunnels for the rats."

The smaller cellar-style doors broke open with a large bang, revealing the brown-haired Captain Bates. His eyes meet the Commander, "Welcome, Sir! We have uncovered the bandit's hideaway."

"Where are they?"

"Gone, sir. The entire space has been cleared out. It is clear they aren't in the city anymore," the captain expresses.

"Cowards," he mutters.

"What was that, sir?"

"The King's Bane are fucking cowards, Bates," and in a fit of rage, the Major General snaps,

"Aargh!!! FUCK!"

"What do you think London thinks about the situation, sir?"

"Captain... they are not here, are they?" the Commander asks, looking around patronizingly, and steps toward the junior officer, "I care not of London's thoughts or their wanted outcomes. They are all liars and cheats. What I care for is about retribution for *MY* King."

Captain Bates nods, "Aye, sir. My mistake."

"A stupid one, Captain. Now, show me what you've found," he says, calming down, motioning for the captain to go back down the stairs.

Without words, he turns around and leads the Commander to a dark tunnel with a door on the far end.

"The whole area is cleared out, sir," the captain says opening the door, revealing the open space once occupied by the King's Bane.

Entering the room, the Major General scans the space. Quickly, the first item he notices is the large wooden table with the draped Union Jack.

"Shameful," he mutters under his breath.

His eyes move from item to item as he slowly walks in, analyzing every inch. He starts with the far wall and notices a door, seemingly hidden, and then shelves along the wall leading to a couple of bunks attached to the wall. On the opposite end of the door and shelves sat a fireplace with several chairs stationed around it. He could feel it was recently lived in.

"They were here recently, Captain…" the Commander says softly, still looking around the room, "Interesting…" he reaches up and grabs a clay mug from the shelf.

"We have gathered all the supplies left behind, sir, and there is nothing more than a few empty haversacks, old powder horns, and miscellaneous tools," Captain Bates added.

His blue eyes snap toward the captain, "Hmm, and you think that is all that is here?"

"Aye, sir. It is all we could find."

"Where does that hidden door lead to, Captain?" the Commander points to the hidden door by the shelves.

Captain Bates looks up at the door, confused.

"I thought so. Follow that path and see where it leads. If it is a tunnel, it might lead to more findings…"

"Aye, si—"

"And make it hasty. I do not have all night, nor all day tomorrow. If they have departed from the city, we need all the information we can get to begin our search outside the city limits."

"Aye, sir. I will get it done," Captain Bates replies as he moves with purpose to the hidden door.

"I will be back at headquarters by the time you finish. Bring me the routes of the tunnels, and we will formulate the next steps in the plan."

"Aye, sir."

Commander Ivey looks at the room and scoffs before turning around and leaving the way he came. Emerging on the vacant alley, he finds his horse and mounts it. *Nothing is normal. This whole situation is off,* he thinks.

Quickly, the Commander is off, with a hard spur and a loud shout, "Yah!"

Snow and dirt kick off the cobblestone road as the commander's horse intensely gallops toward the headquarters building. As the light snowfall blankets the city, Agador's mind drifts.

They've had help; they must've. But who? Hancock? Adams? Or Young? All suspicious indeed, but still... I am not sure,... he thinks as his mind wanders.

Spies, & Lies

February 10, 1772

Brookline, Massachusetts

Just outside the small town of Brookline sat Mug Tavern. An older establishment that welcomed many guests from all over. A constant hum of conversation filled the air as the tavern pulsed with life. Chairs scrape against the floor while the low murmur of hushed gossip makes for atmosphere acoustics.

The ale is top-notch tonight, he thinks. With no care in the world, he sits back and drinks his worries away.

"You know, Barratt... you should leave Boston," the man across from him says smoothly.

"Aye, I did!" he replies loudly, holding up his mug.

"I am serious... the city is no longer safe. They are going house-to-house looking for those bandits."

"That is none of my concern; I am loyal to the Crown," Barratt slurs.

"Shhh! This is not the place to say that too loudly."

"It'll be fine," Barratt remarks casually, swigging back his ale.

He slams his empty mug on the table, and he sees them. His eyes recognize the blonde hair from earlier in the previous year... *the native who came looking for Thomas Young*, he thinks, focusing his gaze. Immediately, he becomes tense.

As he focuses on the native walking down the stairs, he notices he is followed by three others: a large black man, a smaller white-haired woman, and a middle-aged-looking man.

Becoming frantic, "Hey, do you still have that handbill the King's Guard Commander read at town hall?"

With a peculiar look, "I do, Barratt." Reaching into his greatcoat pocket, the man removes the pamphlet.

Snatching almost immediately, Barratt reads it over, "Fuck," he whispers to himself.

"What is it?"

Slowly looking up to his friend, "The four wanted individuals on this handbill are..." he suspiciously looks around, "Here."

The man's eyes widen, "Wait... are you saying the..."

"Yes, I am... the King's Bane is here," Barratt smiles devilishly.

"We need to alert someone," the friend adds.

"Aye. I Agree. The young King's Guard Commander will be thrilled to hear it," the semi-drunk Barratt smiles smoothly as he stands up.

Making an honest attempt at moving unseen by the members of the King's Bane, Barratt turns toward the front door and makes his way out. Both men exit the warm tavern and enter the chilly outdoor air. Alan shivers and rubs his hands together,

"Let's get there fast!" His words carry his hot breath into the cold air, and the two men move hastily to the horse barn just behind the tavern.

**

"Thank you so much, Wilfred," James says in his deep voice, cutting clearly through the audible conversations in the tavern.

Adahy turns to Wilfred as they make their way to the back room. The man was older and looked similar to Daniel Mullan, but some things were a bit different,

"Your generosity has been gracious, especially with the horses. Thank you for allowing Raven to stay in your stable while we figure this out.

"It's no issue. The horse stable is one of the better parts of the property...even if it is a decent walk, it's always worth it," he smiles.

"Aye, we are eternally grateful," the scratchy white-haired woman adds in a heartfelt tone to the tavern owner.

As they enter the back room, Adahy notices the wooden beams are high into the ceiling. With his left hand, he pulls out a chair and sits.

"It's like Ester said earlier... the city is too hot right now... they have redcoats flipping civilian residences upside down looking for us," Elias says in a worried tone, and continues, "It's not good, and in doing so, the Major General is making a lot of new enemies..."

In a deep, experience-driven tone, Wilfred speaks, "Aye... that is okay. King George III sent his dog over here to root you out, and they are doing exactly what they planned on... if he creates more enemies for the Crown, it might end up being complicated for the King."

"How so?" Adahy asks.

Wilfred looks at the young half-native,

"We are already a tinderbox, my boy. The people can only take so much before we fight back... they can only do so much damage before we stand up and refuse to take it. It's tragic, truly. There is no King here... why do we pay him? For what? His war debts? Pfffffft! Horseshit!" he finishes loudly and impassioned.

"I agree," James adds, "The more this King's Guard Commander causes a stir, the more the people will come to resist him and his actions. It is a good thing he is hunting us... we will lead him away from Boston."

"Aye. Philadelphia has many resources and connections we can use when we arrive," Ester says as she sits down at the large table in the back room.

A young woman with high cheeks and beautiful brown eyes enters as everyone is situated, "Ales all around then?"

"Aye, and bring me some jerky," Wilfred replies.

A long pause follows as the young woman leaves the room.

Looking around and deciding to cut the silence, James speaks, "We won't be here long, Wilfred."

"I don't mind if you are, Mr. Robinson. You all can stay as long as you need."

As he finishes the words, the young woman enters the room again with five mugs of ale and a plate of jerky for Wilfred.

"Thank you, Alexandria. Everyone, this is my daughter, Alexandria. She's been helping me run the tavern as of late."

Each King's Bane member nods and says hello, and she smiles cordially, accepting their salutations before exiting the room. As she shuts the wooden door, Wilfred takes a sip from his ale and then looks at James,

"So, tell me how you were ambushed?"

***

King's Guard Auxiliary Headquarters
Boston, Massachusetts

Rage and hate consumed the inner parts of Agador Ivey. *Wherever they are... I will find them, and I will kill them,* he thinks to himself as he paces back and forth in his office. Confidence in himself radiated from the anger, and his emotions simmered.

I will eventually gain the upper hand in this chess game of death with the King's Bane, he thinks as he stops moving to look out the window. The winter pleased him as the snowfall fell from gray skies.

"Captain Bates, the killing of 42 of his majesty's men gives us a solid narrative for the troops to rally behind if they need one. Colonel Valles being openly murdered does nothing but strengthen this stance. These bloody damned degenerates are going to die," his tone is dark, mirroring the empty look carried in his eyes.

"Aye, sir. The men are still ready to go at a moment's notice. They need no more motivation outside of serving you and their King."

A sense of assurance wafted over the Commander, and his mind drifted to Colonel Valles, "It makes sense why the blonde native killed the Colonel... Valles must have realized he was uncovering a lead to the King's Bane."

Quickly, his mind moves on from the traitorous Valles, "He was following Corporal Rooney... Captain, get me, Corporal Rooney!"

"Aye, sir!" the captain replies, swiftly exiting the office.

Moments later, the door opens, and Corporal Rooney and Captain Bates are in tow.

"Major General Ivey, sir!" The corporal says, saluting and standing at attention.

"At ease, Corporal. I need some information that I have been too busy to ask for. You were tailing Thomas Young, correct?"

"Aye, sir. Per your instruction, I tailed Thomas Young for several weeks and picked up nothing of significance that would indicate he was connected to any illegal or nefarious dealings."

"Aye... So how did Colonel Valles come to be murdered by the blonde native who is part of the King's Bane? He was instructed to follow you..."

"It was directed to me that I merely needed to follow the target until he fell asleep, indicated by the lighting in his home. I would arrive before the sunrise each morning, seemingly before he was even awake, and follow the target throughout the day."

"The night Colonel Valles was killed, was there anything out of the ordinary at the Young residence?" Commander Ivey asks intently.

"No, sir. It was the same as it had been each night prior."

Slamming his fist into the table, he lets out an exhaustive exhale, "Fuck."

"Thomas Young knows what is going on in this city. I can feel it in my bones. Ever since the Crown hunted and killed his brother, he's changed."

"Do you think he knows where they are?"

"I think he carries valued information... if not their location, he knows the person who does," Commander Ivey answers coldly.

'*Whatever is necessary.*' The King's words repeated in Agador's mind. He knew the King was being humiliated by the King's Bane rebels, and he was sent from God to destroy them, the crown being the hand of God. Agador was on spiritual awakening to restore order to Boston and bring pride upon the crown once more.

"We will go to Thomas and ask him directly... his response will tell us everything we need to know."

Knock*, *Knock*

"Come in," Commander Ivey shouts toward the door.

"Sir," the Sentry Ranger says, opening the door to the office.

"What is it?" The vile Major-General spits out.

"There is someone here to see you. They claim to know the King's Bane's current location as of a few hours ago." The sentry guard shouts quickly.

"Send them in."

Two King's Guard Sentry Rangers quickly escort the man into the office. Commander Ivey stood, leaning over his large desk, while Captain Bates and Corporal Rooney stood off to the side.

The doors close behind the man, and he speaks,

"I can help you."

"Is that so?" Agador replies, still not looking away from the fire.

"I know the King's Bane. Some claim they are merely conversations of patriotism in taverns... but I know the truth. I've seen them," the skittish man says.

Intrigued by the familiar man's words, Commander Ivey leans forward,

"Is that Barratt Cassius I hear?"

"Aye, it is, Major General..."

"I, too, have seen the elusive King's Bane."

"So, you know they are a collection of eclectic and violent individuals who have spent their life killing British Regulars—"

"They are no more intimidating than a rabid dog that needs a solid lead ball to the brain… a nuisance if you will," Commander Ivey interjects swiftly.

A smile creases on Barratt's face, "I will require coin for this information."

"You will be paid when you tell me what you know… for I will determine if it warrants my coin."

"Aye… what I saw and what I know are worth many coins… but I was having a drink at Mug Tavern in Brookline. And what I saw was a large African man who was middle-aged, a young native with numerous muskets, a white man with hair who looked middle-aged, and a woman with white stringy hair with a large scar on her neck. The four of them were in the Tavern this day, breaking fast and drinking spirits," he says coolly.

Commander Ivey's attitude loosens as the man describes the four individuals he witnessed on the river that fateful day.

"The native… did he have blonde hair?" Commander Ivey asks.

"Aye, he does."

Captain Bates swiftly looks to Commander Ivey, and they know they have them.

Seeing the British officers exchange looks, the man speaks again, "The blonde native came into the city in the summer of '71."

With a skeptical look on his face, the Commander motions for him to continue.

"From a few accounts, he came searching for Thomas Young."

Another quick look is exchanged between the Commander and the Captain. This time, each holding a minor grin.

"Did he say why he was interested in locating Thomas Young?" Commander Ivey inquires.

"I was not there, sir. I only heard after the fact."

"Truthfully, you have given me more than the King's Bane location; you've connected the dots for us," Commander Ivey says coldly and continues, "Captain, see, this man is paid and paid well. When you return, we need to discuss the plan of attack for this tavern in Brookline."

"Aye, sir. I will get it done. Do you say they are in Brookline? At Mug Tavern, do you?" Captain Bates turns to Barratt.

"Uh, yes, sir," he shakenly replies.

"Very good. You will be well rewarded. Captain Bates, take this man to the dispensary and reward him," the Major-General commands with a distinctly dark undertone.

**

Candles slowly drip used wax down their candelabras, illuminating the Commander's quarters with a golden sheen resting upon the room. The Major-General's mind is steadily focused on organizing an ambush from which these petty rebels will not walk away. The menacing looks on his face sit familiar as he contemplates his next move.

The doors open abruptly to the Commander's quarters, and Captain Bates walks with a gratifying look in his eyes.

"It is done?" The Commander asks his officer without disconnecting his focus from the map he analyzes.

"Yes, sir." Captain Bates replies coldly.

"Odd that a blonde native comes into Boston looking for Thomas Young, manages to murder Colonel Valles, and then I see the blonde native on the river as part of the King's Bane…" the Commander looks to his Captain.

"It seems Thomas knows much more than we ever expected."

"That is what it seems, Captain."

"What of Thomas Young?"

"I will take care of him when I return from Brookline. For now, we will move forward with ensuring these elusive rats are properly caught in a trap."

"What sort of trap, sir?"

"Well, if they are within Mug Tavern, I will bring two squads of Sentry Rangers, set it ablaze, and shoot whoever exits. They will not escape again."

Commander Ivey places the canvas map of Brookline on the table, and with a satisfied look on his face, his eyes dart up to his Captain,

"With any resolution, we will return to London in the coming days."

"Yes, sir, we will see it through. I will get the men ready."

Mug Tavern Massacre

February 14, 1772

Mug Tavern

Brookline, Massachusetts

Inside Mug Tavern, the ceiling was higher, and large wooden beams were interconnected. *What a glorious work of artisanship*, Adahy thought as his mind wandered looking around the tavern. It was energetic, full of traders, farmers, drunkards, craftsmen, and craftswomen, and a variety of sorts intermingled, making for an eclectic atmosphere. Adahy enjoyed it.

The sturdy wooden building stood for decades, being handed down through the Mullan family. As Wilfred explained, his grandfather built it. Tonight, they were in the main tavern hall in the midst of the joyous and loud atmosphere. His daughter, Alexandria, is running around with the bulk of the work.

"Mr. Mullan, thank you again for having us stay in your guest quarters this last week," Adahy says to the man competing with the volume of the tavern.

"It's not a burden, young man. You all are welcome here at any point and time."

"We do appreciate that, Wilfred," James adds.

"You know, when Thomas would frequent this tavern, he would come to me with his stories and resentment for the Crown. I am glad to see that he made good use of his anger... you all have been doing a lot for the continental cause we all believe in."

"It is a cause we can get behind. It carries posterity and hope for liberty," Elias says confidently to the group.

"Aye, you're not wrong. You know, Adahy, it seems your father's sacrifice may have led your uncle to this path..."

"Aye, my father was hunted like a dog and murdered for nothing more than a folk story in a book."

"That may be my boy, but I'm glad I can help you. Your father's spirit means a lot to your uncle, and your uncle means a lot to the movement within the colonies. Without him, we wouldn't have been able to gain a real narrative foothold in Boston and the towns surrounding these last several years. He has been a key asset to the movement while retaining his office as city leader in Boston. He's a silent hero." Wilfred takes another sip of his ale and asks Adahy and the others, "Do you want some supper? We made a roast with potatoes, carrots, and cabbage."

Elias shifts in his chair, and his face produces a smile, "I would love some food."

With a side eye at Elias, Ester half smiles and looks to Wilfred, "That will be great; we will all have some."

Standing up, his chair scrapes against the floor, "Alexandria, grab four bowls of roast!"

Being on the far side of the tavern hall, she cannot hear him and begins walking toward the table. With a few steps taken, loud crashes shatter the glass-pane windows of the tavern, hurtling lead ball rounds in every direction.

Snap, *Snap*, *Snap*, *Snap*, *Snap*,

Adahy looks up, and in one chaotic motion, lead ball rounds fly through broken glass before striking Alexandria in the chest and neck. As the other rounds fly into the tavern hall, Wilfred cannot move as he watches his daughter's lifeless body collapse to the ground.

"Alexandria!" The old man groans in agony.

"Fuck!" Adahy shouts, ducking down and getting low to the ground.

More lead ball rounds shatter the glass-paned windows, rocketing into wood slabs and splintering into the air.

Snap, *Snap*, *Snap*,

A round travels through another window, impacting a patron in the side of his head, quickly splitting it apart and killing him instantly.

As the tears run down his cheeks, Wilfred turns to the windows, removing the two flintlocks on his waist and fully cocking them in one smooth motion,

"Ahhhhh! You bloody cowards!"

As the words leave his mouth, he fires. Three rounds enter the chaos, and he is cut down as they impact his chest and neck.

Snap, *Snap*, *Snap*,

More rounds impact other patrons as they sit entirely blindsided by the incoming waves of Brown Bess rounds from outside. Their screams blend with the constant stream of lead.

Snap, *Snap*, *Snap*,

James flips the table over, taking cover behind it. Elias and Ester follow.

"I was looking forward to that roast!"

James and Ester look at Elias, stunned, and shake their heads.

"Let's get out of here," James shouts.

Elias and Ester nod.

Low to the ground, Adahy tries to look around and assess the chaos unfolding. Noticing the others behind the table, he crawls to them.

Snap, *Snap*, *Snap*,

"James, we need to get out of here now," Adahy shouts.

With a stale look, James responds, "Ya, you think?"

BOOM,

With a force Adahy hasn't felt in a long time, he is thrown backward and rolls into broken chairs. Everything goes black.

Moments pass. *Fuck that hurt*, he thought as he tried to open his eyes. Everything is muted, and dust consumes the air. A few small fires began taking hold in pockets of the tavern.

"Was that a fucking cannon shot?" Adahy shouts into the chaos and looks up.

His eyes meet Ester's as she's holding her stomach with her right hand, which is covered in blood. He looks left and sees Elias knocked out behind a large support beam, and James Robinson is squatting, taking cover against the thick front wall and pulling out his two flintlocks.

Ester, he thinks and crawls to the older woman.

James rises from his squat and fully cocks both pistols. Adahy arrives at Ester. There is a small pool of blood, and she smiles at him.

"God dammit, Ester, this isn't good!" Adahy shouts.

Snap, *Snap*, *Snap*, *Snap*, *Snap*, *Snap*, *Snap*, *Snap*, *Snap*, *Snap*, *Snap*, *Snap*, *Snap*, *Snap*, *Snap*,

The shots intensify, and the destruction matches the chaos. Each patron who tried to stand up and return fire with their personal weapon was slaughtered upon standing. The immediate destruction of the tavern was incredible in scope.

Each window is busted out of its wooden frames, and a blend of glass, wooden splinters, and lead ball rounds ferociously consumed the air, whipping in all directions.

"We need to get out of here now!" Shakespeare shouted from behind the thick wooden beam.

"We need to get Ester out of here, now! Where is the door?!" Adahy shouts.

"In the back!" James Robinson shouts over the loud chaos, pointing to the rear door.

The crackling of the newly burning fires takes the place of the erupting muskets upon their silence outside. Broken pieces of glass fall off the shelves, and the raging flames eat the burning wood.

"They are shuffling their troops outside," James says to the others as he peers out the broken window. As the musket smoke clears, he sees him, "Fuck, you'll never believe this…"

A familiar voice cracks into the outside air,

"I kept my word. I told you we would be seeing each other soon," the Major-General shouts before speaking in a regular tone to his men, "Torch it."

Two British foot soldiers walk with torches and toss them on the ends of the tavern. The flames spread quickly over the roof, and the fire begins meeting and melding with the inside fire. Quickly, the flames spread, burning toward the walls of the well-built wooden tavern.

"Wheel up the Grasshopper!" The Major-General's command echoes through the night air.

A squad of 4 artillery soldiers roll up the light three-pound cannon and begin prepping to fire. The British foot soldiers surrounding the tavern begin converging toward the front, ensuring their safety from the soon-to-be multiple cannon fire.

"Ready, Sir," the lead artillery soldier shouts sternly.

"Fire," Commander Ivey replies smoothly to the man. The cannon outside the tavern erupts,

BOOM

It shakes the ground. The three-pound iron ball destroys anything it encounters, making its way through the building.

Emerging from after the shot, Adahy looks at the bar top, *Ah, time to get out here,* he thinks and begins formulating an idea.

"Elias, I need pieces of cloth, multiples of them," Adahy requests as he moves quickly and carefully to avoid fire patches. He arrives at the bar and starts taking down whatever non-broken bottles he can find. After he collects a handful, he cautiously makes his way to his previous location.

"Stick one piece of cloth into the bottle and get it wet with the rum. Then, on my mark, use the flames to light the exposed end of the cloth," Adahy says to Elias quickly.

James Robinson stands up during the lull and rapidly examines the enemy forces. He raises and fires off his two flintlocks out one the broken front windows. The two shots explode from the pistols, impacting their desired targets. The two British Sentry Rangers fall to the ground, clutching their throats, gurgling their blood, trying to pass air through their newly ruptured windpipes as they quickly bleed out. Following the release of the rounds, the large man ducked back under the wall.

"There's about 30 of them. Ester, you, okay?" James Robinson asks, concerned, looking over at the wounded woman.

"I'm good, but there is just a minor discrepancy," she replies, smiling through the pain. They all know it's a rough injury. Acceptance of pain washes over their faces as they continue to fight.

"Take this," Adahy says to James Robinson, handing him a liquor bottle with a cloth. "We use the flames to our advantage. Hide behind them and on my mark; we throw these at the clusters of redcoats, then fire as many shots as possible at the others," Adahy says to the others.

Commander Ivey takes everything in. He notices the dead men, and he recognizes that no one has tried to exit the tavern. The two soldiers on the ground were dying, so there was no need to attempt any aid. *'These fucking rebels,'* he thought as he waited impatiently for the grasshopper to be reloaded.

"Is the cannon reloaded?!" He asks with fire in his voice.

"Yes, Sir," the lead artillery soldier replies.

"Fucking Fire!"

The flames begin enveloping the tavern, making it hard for the Sentry Rangers to make a closer approach. Black smoke rose out of each of the gaps like a demented chimney.

BOOM

The cannon fires, echoing into the night sky, informing all near of the destruction ensuing and death profiting.

"Now!" Adahy shouts as the cannonball flies across the opposite end of the tavern, finding its way through the wall and exiting through its rear, destroying everything it connects with.

The three men light the ends of the rags and find openings to launch their alcohol bombs. The first three bottles find perfectly grouped soldiers too closely arranged and impact the ground, breaking apart and catching the British foot soldiers on fire near the explosion. The fire latching onto every drop of alcohol grabs ahold of the British soldier's wool coats. The 12 men on fire scream uncontrollably from their melting clothing, and fire seeps onto their flesh, boiling and cooking through. The British foot soldiers ablaze are terrifyingly running in circles from the inescapable flames.

"God dammit! The rest of you on me!" The Major-General shouts, dismounting his horse. The chaos fuels his motives as he unsheathes his sword and removes one of his flintlocks. His grip tightens over his weapons of death as he prepares for the face-to-face encounter with the King's Bane.

The rest of the British foot soldiers scurry and rally behind their commander. The fierce Major-General moves toward the tavern. Out of the bellowing smoke came three bottles aflame. Noticing them at the last second, he jumps out of the way.

"Take cover!" Commander Ivey shouts to his men, but it is useless.

The three liquor bottles explode, catching several soldiers behind him on fire. The remaining few men around him close in on the burning compound. The men on fire are agonizingly crying out and falling to the ground, slowly succumbing to their burn wounds.

Once they released their liquor bombs, the three men turned to Ester.

"We need to go now," James said frantically. He grabbed her with her pain in mind. Easing her out the back door, doing his best to avoid the fire. With his arms under hers, he drags her away from the burning tavern through the snow, far away from the chaos.

With panic in his eyes, "What are we to do? Ester, this isn't good," Elias says as he looks at his friend in pain. Her abdomen carries a piece of the wooden beam the size of his arm. *God dammit*, he laments.

As they all get to the tree line, James rests and drops to the ground with Ester in between his legs, and she rests up against him.

"This fucking Agador Ivey! He needs to die," Adahy says fiercely.

"Aye, that he does… he came with the intention to ensure we do not survive this," Ester says weakly.

"No! We will get through this," James replies passionately.

Within Ester's wrinkled face, she smiles, "James, my dear… look at me," with a look of acceptance, her smokey-gray eyes look to her abdomen and the protruding tavern beam and then back to him, "You three go to Philadelphia…" Her eyes begin to roll, and she loses consciousness.

"Ugh, Ester!" James shouts.

From the corner of his eye, Adahy notices four men moving around the burning tavern. Angrily, he stands and removes his tomahawk and medium blade.

"Adahy, wait!" Elias tries to shout as Adahy makes his way into the falling snow and billowing smoke.

In his right hand, Adahy chokes up on the handle of his tomahawk and quickly releases it toward the nearest redcoat. The tumbling weapon slams into the face of the soldier. As his lifeless body drops to its knees, Adahy removes the tomahawk from his face. Warm blood follows.

The three other redcoats can't believe their eyes and try to aim and shoot him. Adahy moves like a cat and, with his left hand, glides his blade across the nearest redcoat's neck, slicing every artery and tendon. In the same stance, he brings the tomahawk in his right hand and uppercuts the blade into the next redcoat's chin.

The fourth redcoat fires his Brown Bess and misses. Frustrated, he throws his musket toward the ground and tackles Adahy in the chest. Both men tumble on the cold, snow-filled ground. As they roll, Adahy gathers himself. Recognizing he's carrying his knife in his left hand, he begins stabbing the man in the back as they roll. Coming to a stop and the man's blood flowing out of every wound, Adahy throws the corpse off his body and stands.

A familiar voice comes from the front side of the burning tavern, "Come out, come out, you cowards!"

Brushing off the snow, Adahy moves toward the front by way of the horse stable adjacent to the burning building.

Where are you? He questions as he crunches through the snow.

Embers from the tavern fire swirl around the air, blending with black smoke and exterior snowfall. Almost immediately after rounding the stable corner, he notices a few crimson figures reloading their muskets.

Being too far for a clear hit, he places his tomahawk back into the waistband of his chest rig. With his newly freed-up hand, he removes his sea-service pistol, fully cocks it in one motion, and fires. The lead ball round flies between the falling snow and through the face of the closest Sentry Ranger. His skull cracks and rips apart as the shot kills him instantly. The other three soldiers see their companion fall and go on the offensive, attacking Adahy with their muskets-like swords.

Adahy flips his pistol, using the hand grip to block their incoming thrusts. He skillfully removes a blade in his left hand and parries their attacks with his knife. All four men reset their stances and commit to the fight ahead.

"Come on, ya bastards," he smiles as he scans the three redcoats intensely. His grip tightens on his weapons as anticipation builds. Blending with the dancing flames, one of the redcoats thrusts his bayonet. Adahy shifts his body, nearly getting stabbed. Quickly, he spins along the length of the musket, moving closer to the soldier, and in one swift rotation, he slams his pistol's handgrip into the man's temple. Within the motion, Adahy can feel the man's skull collapse upon impact.

As the redcoat falls to the ground, Adahy scoops his Brown Bess from his lifeless arms. Quickly situating his weapons within his hands to enable him to hold the musket, he fully cocks the weapon and fires point blank into the face of the next nearest redcoat. The man's skull erupts in all directions, scattering into the snow

The third and final Sentry Ranger held a face of pure horror, looking at his friend, "Fuckin' hell?!"

As the man's eyes return to the native, he stands nose-to-nose with him. Adahy tilts his head slightly, and the redcoat looks down at the blade protruding from his chest. Looking back up, he sees snowfall in Adahy's green eyes,

"The earth will repurpose your soul. Be at peace."

He sharply removes the blade and upward thrusts the sharp steel into the man's neck, slicing into his skull. Adahy removes the blade with a warm outflow of blood following. Gently, he pushes the dead man, and his body falls backward into the cold, hard ground and thuds upon impact.

"Where are you?" He mutters to himself, searching the open area around Mug Tavern.

Without thinking, he begins the process of reloading his pistol. Keeping his eyes alert for movement, he grabs a cartridge and bites it open. Quickly, he dumps a small bit of powder into his barrel, followed by the charge and lead ball. As he drops the ball down the barrel, he removes the ramrod and packs it smoothly. Next is his powder horn, which he uses to fill up the flash pan before closing it. With one last movement, he fully cocks the weapon.

"Time to die," he whispers to himself.

The bodies of slowly dying and wounded British foot soldiers littered the cold, snowy area, and Adahy finally could see the devastation the liquor bombs had caused. As the snow fell, it began to blanket the lifeless redcoats he and the others killed. Now standing in front of the tavern on the main road that leads to Boston, the Major General is nowhere to be found.

"Ester, James, & Elias!" Fear consumes his actions as Adahy begins sprinting to the rear of the building.

Irrespective
Snowfall

Situated securely within his hand, covered with gray fingerless gloves, is his 1729 Sea Service Pistol, and Adahy quickly rounds the burning tavern corner with the barrel leading.

As he sprints to the rear of the property, the snow crunches underneath his steps, blending with the crackling and burning wood. Some redcoats still groan and gurgle their last breaths in the cold night air. Within two more steps, he stops. Like a signal lantern on the rough seas, a crimson phantom emerges in the distance through the falling white snow.

At the feet of the British officer sat James Robinson, attentively holding Ester in his lap and Elias on a knee beside them. Adahy doesn't recognize the looks on their faces.... It was fear. The youthful King's Guard Commander's voice traveled easily through the air,

"So, you mutinous filth are the King's Bane? Pathetic."

As the word leaves his lips, the officer's blade slides into Ester's chest, robbing her of the remaining life she carried.

"NO!" The three men cry out in unison.

Adahy holsters his pistol, his legs pick up, and he sprints at the redcoat officer. Elias's blue eyes meet Adahy's emerald eyes,

"Kill this basta—"

As he speaks, the ruthless officer pulls the trigger of his fully cocked flintlock that was pointed directly at Elias's plucky face.

The blast from the pistol erupts, displacing the man's face. His bones and flesh spray onto James and the surrounding snow with ferocity. As his lifeless body falls backward to the cold ground, Adahy's rage erupts.

"Ahhhh!!" he shouts in anger as he moves as fast as he can toward the man.

As the Major-General removes his sword from Ester's chest, James, with love, rolls her off him and spear-tackles the British officer.

The two men become entangled and begin rolling toward Adahy. Ever stronger than most men, James Robinson gains the advantage through strength and gets his hands around the Major-General's neck. Slowly, he begins to cut off his air supply. The British officer maneuvers his free hand on his second flintlock, managing to pull the hammer back. He fires into the large man on top of him.

James Robinson's face goes from revenge and hatred to confusion and pain. Within a few moments, the large man is unconscious and slumps onto the Major General. Hearing the shot as he arrives at the two men on the ground, Adahy doesn't know who shot who but quickly learns the outcome. The Commander's black hair moves in the snow, and He quickly rolls James off. As he tries to stand and grab his sword, Adahy ends his sprint and spear-tackles the Major General back to the cold ground.

The two men struggle against each other, "You fuck!" Adahy's voice cracks in agony from watching his best friends be murdered.

Adahy gets on top of the Major-General and connects with the officer's face with a tight fist.

Commander Ivey tries to position his forearms up, beginning to block the fierce punches, and uses his hips to toss Adahy off and over his head.

Winded and rolling over to stand up, "You think you will win, you feral red skin?"

As Adahy is tossed off and rolls, he stands up, recovering from the toss almost immediately. Shock fills the Major General as his cold blue eyes analyze his opponent. Adahy does the same, watching the well-groomed British Major General reaffirm his stance and grip on his sword. In one motion, Adahy removes a blade from his chest rig and lunges at the shorter British officer.

The Major-General wipes off the blood on his face and expertly lunges backward, parrying the incoming blade. He smiles,

"You may know violence, but you do not carry a sword."

"I carry my hands," Adahy replies, lunging at the man again with ferocity.

With a strong downward parry, the Major General connects his blade with Adahy's, thrusting him downward. Adahy leads his blade into the ground, and the black-haired Commander's hardened fist slams into Adahy's high-sitting cheekbone. He folds and tumbles into the snow-covered ground.

"Your hands?" He chuckles and walks to Adahy, looking down at him.

Adahy notices the Major General's eyes shift away, and he acts. Taking his right hand, carrying his knife, he slams the eight-inch blade into the Major General's foot.

"ARGHH!"

He stumbles backward, and Adahy uses the moment to stand up and reset his stance. Seeing an opportunity, Adahy sprints, lowering his shoulder, and tackles the man. He carries the Major General a few steps with all his might, and together, they slam into the ice-cold ground.

Floating embers mingle with the incoming snowfall as the two men try to catch their breath. Wood creaks and crackles under the contagious flames next to them as the tavern slowly falls in on itself. Adahy's green eyes reflect the dancing inferno echoing in Agador's ice-blue eyes as they rise and confront one another. Standing in cold snowfall with the flames eating up the dense wooden compound near them, the two men, for the first time, see the true nature of the other.

"So, you're the blonde-haired native?" the Major General remarks.

Adahy smiles, "I am." Raising his left hand, he motions for the British commander to attack.

The sharp sword disrupts the falling snow as Agador Ivey slashes it swiftly toward Adahy's face. Raising his tomahawk to block the blade, he deflects the blow to the floor. Orange and red flames dance aimlessly by the two fighting men. Each struggling for a foothold in the fight. The black smoke thickens each second, and exhaustion consumes them with each swing and block.

With another expert parry with his tomahawk, Adahy sidestepped to the left of the Major-General. He withdraws his sea-service pistol from the chest rig with his free hand. He rapidly fires at the pale, newly shaven face in one seamless motion.

With expert awareness, the seasoned Major-General notices the glimmer of the barrel and moves. Adahy's index finger smoothly eases up off the trigger, and through the quickly dissipating barrel smoke, he notices he missed.

"You will die here by my sword, bringing me enjoyment beyond understanding!" Commander Ivey smiles as he turns, looking back at the native.

Enraged, Adahy flips his pistol and catches the barrel, holding the pistol like a small wooden club. In his left hand is his tomahawk, and in his right, his pistol,

"You don't even know who I am."

"It matters not. Your death equals mission completion, and I do not fail my missions."

In his crimson coat, he lunges forward with his sword expertly.

Adahy barely parries the attack with his tomahawk and pistol. He steps forward as Agador steps back. Under their feet, each step is a crunch in the snow-covered ground. Now, both men nearly eye-to-eye.

"I will not stop..." the stocky Major General struggles but gains control of the fight, "Until you die!"

In one strong movement, Agador thrusts Adahy backward. In anticipation, Adahy reads every movement and looks for opportunities to shift himself off his back foot.

"My family has been hunted and killed like wild game by your King since before my time. I know not the reasons he sent you to kill me or us, but I know this... you killed the people who are closest to me. You will die."

Agador's face carries rage,

"AHH!"

Upon shouting, he lunges forward and inhales a black ball of smoke. Smoothly, Adahy sidesteps, dodging the redcoat officer. Flames grow as the tavern continues falling in on itself next to the two men in the open, snow-blanketed area.

Maneuvering away from the officer's attack, Adahy once again readies his stance for defense.

"You fail to see…." *Cough, cough,*

"The killing of the King's son and mistress pushed me here." *cough, cough*

With his right hand, he moves the sweat-filled hair out of his face, "You think you're right with your attacks on the King's shipments, disrupting trade, and murdering soldiers of the crown?!"

"Fuck the King."

Rage consumes Major-General Ivey's face as the words penetrate his ears, and he tightens his grip on his sword,

"Before I kill you, you will know true pain."

"Pain is a dear friend," Adahy replies coldly, breathing in a bit of smoke before lunging at the Major-General with his tomahawk and flipped pistol.

Agador moves swiftly, expertly avoiding the tomahawk blade, blocking the incoming assault from the violent man. Adahy, with his pistol, is slamming it into the man. Agador tries blocking each attack. The two men fiercely attack the other, blow for blow under the cold night sky. The smoke affects the men's breathing and stamina as they gruelingly defend and attack each other.

Agador's sharp steel cuts the air swiftly, meeting Adahy's right shoulder and slicing the skin upon impact.

"Argh!" Adahy growls in pain, wincing.

As if in syncretic rhythm, the remainder of the tavern roof collapses. Embers and fire blow into the night sky upon the crash. Flames begin crawling like gripping hands over the soil, eating away at every piece of unscorched wood it can find. Adahy opens his eyes and looks down at his new wound.

Agador moulinets with his sword, slicing the air and snow before pointing the tip of his blade at the Adahy.

Exhausted and near delirium, he smiles, "Time to die, redskin."

He lunges his steel blade toward Adahy's chest. Gracefully, the young man drops to the ground, barely escaping the steel. He springs forward and upward under the officer's blade. In pain, Adahy's wounded shoulder sharply impacts Agador's chest, and the two men tumble to the ground.

The tavern, now a burn pit, keeps producing dangerous flames. The men struggle on snow-covered ground. Their exhaustive groans battle as their bodies match the sounds. Each breath is a pocket of black smoke. Debilitating each fighter as they struggle for a defeating blow on the other. Adrenaline and hate fuel their movements. They each try to gain the upper hand on the other with a violent volley of fists.

They struggle and roll into pieces of the fire. Slowly, the flames spread to their clothing, and Adahy is atop the officer. In the gray fingerless gloves, his hands make their way to Agador's throat; he adjusts his grip from the man's sweat and can feel his pulse pumping as he tightens his fingers.

Hatred mirrors the flames in Adahy's emerald eyes as he focuses on killing. Unaware, his gold talisman slips out from behind the tightly secured leather chest rig, revealing itself. Glimmering light in all directions from the reflective bright flames of the broken golden shard as it dangled from his neck.

As Adahy's hands tighten, Agador's eyes catch a piece of the light glinting off the native's necklace. Within moments of death, his mind goes back to his childhood and the moment before King George II and the hunters… he's attracted to it. A force pulls him. He knows the truth. He focuses on the distinctly shaped gold shard wrapped in the wire. His ice-blue eyes widen as he sees it. And with barely any room for the air to squeeze out of his throat,

"The…"

Adahy can't think. Action and killing are all.

"...Aureum... Pentagonum."

The British man's raspy words break Adahy's focused hatred.

What did he say?

Knowing the words he shared with his uncle, his mind shifts, if only for a second. Noticing the lull, the Major-General breaks Adahy's grasp with bursting energy and throws the blonde-haired man off him.

Commander Ivey crawls away, trying to catch his breath, but the cold air and residual black smoke in his lungs make it tough. Adahy does the same as he is thrown backward and tumbles into the clearing. Each man struggles to catch a clean patch of air but clings only to black smoke. Agador pulls himself away from the heated flames of the burning building until he can stand. Noticing a dead Ranger's flintlock pistol, he leans over and picks it up.

As the ice-cold air enters Adahy's lungs, he wheezes harder and enters the open clearing.

Cough, cough

Crawling on his knees, stumbling away, trying to stay alert, he attempts to catch his breath.

"Oh, shit!" he mutters, noticing a small fire on his greatcoat before patting it out and standing.

A strong, cold gust of wind came through the rustling, chilled tree branches. The frozen air cuts at the exposed patches of his skin.

Fuck, it's cold, he thinks as his new wounds sting and his body shivers. Even the thick orange flames were no match for the cutting ice-cold air.

"Is that why you let your friends die?!" Anger rushes over Major-General Ivey as he screams manically into the night sky, knowing he and Adahy are the only ones alive to hear it.

The heat radiating from the collapsed tavern burns and fights with the cold night air for dominance over the dominion of the moment. Out of the cold, deep darkness came the shrill, haunting cry of a large white owl—

"Keeek!" Its screech reverberated off the silence spread throughout the trees and snowfall shrouding the icy ground.

Both men's eyes dart to the large white bird as it circles above them before landing on a high-perched branch.

Adahy's green, bloodshot eyes follow from the bird to the opening in the clearing. He looks over and sees the black-haired Major General standing across the clearing,

"Clearly, you've failed to realize…"

Cough, cough

"What it is you carry around your neck!" The Major-General shouts, coughing, trying to catch his breath.

The wounded King's Guard Commander points his sword at Adahy, and the fire illuminates along the side of the sharp steel. Flickering flames light in all directions, revealing new shadows mimicking the light. The flames burn the thick wood in the heap, spewing unimaginable heat and being met with the cold, snow-filled weather of the night.

"You'll die before it sees your hands!" Adahy stands up straight, trying to hide his pain.

"We shall see," the Major-General replies coldly before one last exhaustive sprint at Adahy with his sword, ready to attack.

Adahy does not move until the man is a few feet from him. Smoothly, his hand reaches for his medium-sized blade on his leather waistband. Feeling the hilt, he secures it and flings it expertly. The seven-inch blade slices through the night air and snowfall, sticking into the Major-General's lower right abdomen. The sound of the blade tearing through the bloodred overcoat and into his flesh rivaled the loud, fiery blaze.

"Argg…," he lets out a low, painful groan before slowly coming to a stop.

Adahy begins to dry heave, no doubt his body trying to remove the black smoke. For moments, he dry-heaved and tried to catch his breath. The black smoke had consumed his lungs; he could feel that with each pull for air.

Slowly wheezing, each man struggles for more, cleaner air.

Through his bloodied eyes, Adahy watches as the redcoat officer struggles to reconcile the protruding blade in his side.

Wheezing and covered in pain, Agador struggles. He grabs the blade's hilt, grips it as tight as possible, and removes it.

"Ugrh," a warm outflow of blood follows the blade, spilling into the cold snow, steaming as it connects to the chilly ground.

Wheezily exhaling, Agador looks disappointedly into the night sky mixed with thick gray clouds. The stars blanket the blackness, melding and seemingly dropping the snow from each scattered white dot. A sense of failure sweeps over his bloodied, broken, and bruised body, followed by a wave of rage. With his left hand, he looks down at the pistol he grabbed from his dead soldier; he moves it from half-cocked to fully cocked with the palm of his right hand.

Watching the Major General ready his pistol, Adahy copies his movements. With his right hand, he removes his sea service pistol. Upon aiming up, the two men have the other in their sights.

The men wheeze with each breath. Agador's low voice cracks into the night air softly,

"Irrespective Snowfall sheaths the gentiles in their blasphemous ways."

Adahy's emerald eyes pick up movement in the Major General's finger as he pulls the trigger, and he does the same. Their motions mimic one another.

Their hammers release simultaneously, slamming their flintlocks, sparking the powder in the pans. Each of their lead balls erupts from the barrels. Passing the other in midair, slicing through the falling snow, the rounds slam into their shoulders.

Each man winces as the rounds destroy their clavicles, and they begin to collapse. Major General Agador Ivey, leaking blood, falls first and goes unconscious as he hits the snow-covered ground.

"Raven…" the whimper follows Adahy's breath into the cold night air, and he feels himself falling forward. The mare's beautiful long face flashes in his mind. Everything goes black as his bloodied eyes shut, and Adahy fades from consciousness.

Within the softly falling snow, circling above the fallen men, a large white owl… High above the littered bodies and the crackling ruble of the burned-down tavern, the bird flaps and pulls itself higher, deeper into the dark nighttime clouds. Falling ever so gently, the thick snow begins to layer over the two unconscious men, blanketing them to the frozen ground.

Epilogue

528 A.D.
Athens, Greece

Warm air, dancing with the salty breeze, drifts off the coast, between the rolling hills, and into the city. Streams of sunlight drape through the library openings, making pillars of light throughout. Moving swiftly through the corridor, he avoids all contact, looking for one specific text in the library. The clatters of his steps echo throughout the large building, acknowledging the thick silence layering open spaces. He slows his steps, and the sound reflecting off the books and walls becomes muted.

"It has to be here," he mutters under his breath.

Grime begins collecting under his index finger as it slowly runs along the spines of the elder literature.

"Ah, here it is," unraveling the scroll, dust swirls out as the elder man opens it.

Squinting, and through his dark golden eyes, the old man begins scanning the scroll.

Nox Tinibrus eft Allacritus Lux
Vnus eodem, astris gleba caligine tectus
Veniunt in odium et amorem

sic et nos
Allacritus Lux et Nox Tinibrus omnia simul et omnia
aedificant

Within the vast expanse of nothing,
Nox Tinibrus moved with deliberate purpose,
 the silence of depth wrapping itself upon the darkness.
In contrast sat Allacritus Lux,
a radiant burst of vitality,
effervescent with eternal expansion.
Together, these entities wove existence within a paradox of
harmony and contrast.
Shaping and forming galaxies for eternities,
worlds gathered under their watchful presence and purposeful
reasoning.
Symphonies of life spawned across the expanse.
Surrounded by the deepened shadows where Nox Tinibrus
existed,
Allacritus Lux imbued clarification and light.
Universes are seeded by the eternal interplay of the two.
The expanse that once was void of all swelled with life. Creation
begins as whispers in the darkness,
touched and nurtured but the light.
The two amalgamated entities existed not as rulers but as forces,
the origins,
the sustainers of all.
Interwoven cosmoses were birthed from the void teeming with
sentience yet blocked from outright influence or connection from Lux and
Nox.
Though there was creation, removed was connection.

"Elmir. Pleasant seeing you in the library this morning," the shorter, pudgy man says happily, clearly not minding interrupting.

Snapping back to the present, the old man looks to his right,

"What do you want with me today?"

"Merely giving acknowledgment to your presence as I stroll through the halls. Time has a way of covering the past. These scrolls hold many stories... I enjoy the silence they provide on my walks."

"Ironic, you're disturbing my silence right now."

With a stank look of bewilderment,

"Hmm," he exhales sharply out his nose and walks away.

"Now, where was I?" He murmurs to himself as he returns his focus.

Points within time,
One of recorded memory and history
Nox Tinibrus attempted transformation
On Earth
Lucid dreaming, by way of,
Nero,
Legionnaire in sword and spear
Held the essence of Nox
Death followed as sentience carries two truths
Birth followed by Death
The Golden Five, the Aureum Pentagonum,

He inhaled suddenly, simultaneously dropping the scroll. The worried words crawl from his lips, marrying the stale, warm air,

"The Aureum Pentagonum..."

His mind began to race as if a thousand dying souls suddenly burdened his shoulders, and he collapsed to the ground.

The dreams…. May not be dreams… his mind swirls.

Tears welted within his dark golden eyes before streaming down his face. Collapsing, he folded into himself on the ground with his arms wrapped around his knees.

"The Golden Five… entered an ancient blood oath…" The words fell out from his old lips, blending with the falling tears, barely heard, muffled into his knees.

What if…. He wonders as an intriguing thought enters his mind.

The library corridor became silent. Lifting his head next to him, he notices the scroll. Slowly, he extends and picks it up with his left hand,

"Could it be?… Is the Aureum Pentagonum the key to escape?"

His mind expands with the possibilities the scroll possesses within its text. Reading the lines a couple more times, he closes it and places it into his robe pocket.

"Time, indeed, does have a way of covering the past*,*" he whispers.

Stepping off, he moves with intentionality, staying as muted as possible,

"A hidden past shall stay hidden, never spilling over… I will ensure it," the words quietly and gently leave his mouth as he makes for the exit.

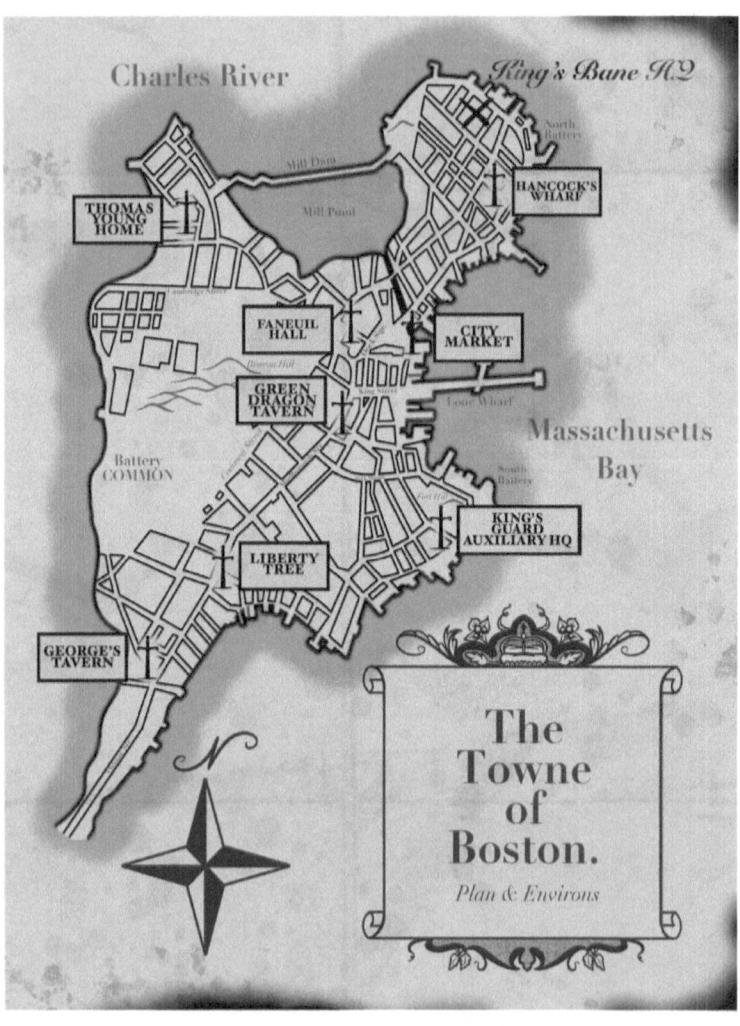

Adahy will return
in
ADAHY AND THE
AUREUM PENTAGONUM

pressure plate
publishing house
u n c o v e r i n g   e x p l o s i v e   s t o r y t e l l e r s

since
2023

Pressure Plate Publishing House LLC.
West Palm Beach, FL 33405

"Uncovering Explosive Storytellers"

www.ppph.us
www.justineggen.com
@pressureplatepublishinghouse

For "Storyteller Submissions," please email:
Info@pressureplatepublishinghouse.com

Justin Eggen was born in Florida, USA, in 1989. He is best known for his award-winning *'War Poetry,'* written from his experiences in the Marine Corps in searching for Improvised Explosive Devices (IEDs), and the gritty short story *'Teufelhunden:1918.'* He is a Father, 2x National Award-Winning poet, Political Science scholar, and Marine Corps Veteran.

Justin Eggen served in active-duty Marine Corps from 2008 to 2012 as a combat engineer attached to the 2nd Combat Engineer Battalion, 2nd Marine Division, serving in Marjah 2010 & Sangin 2011. He holds a B.A. & M.A. in Political Science and is a current Ph.D. student at Florida Atlantic University

Follow on Social Media:

IG & YT: @justinthomaseggen
TW: @eggenjustin
www.justineggen.com